The Second Daughter

J. Jeffrey

Top Press
Penthouse Suite
16245 Park Avenue
New York, NY 10031

ISBN: 1480043214
ISBN-13: 978-1480043213

Cover painting by Heather Ogston

This is a work of fiction. Any resemblances to any person or event are entirely coincidental.

"The things we do for love."—10cc

"The things we do for dessert."—Theodore Gale

"What they said."—J. Jeffrey

DEDICATION

She knows who she is.

CONTENTS

Part I The End

Part II The Beginning

Inconclusive Unscientific Postscript by the Author

Part I
The End

CHAPTER ONE
CHANGE OF SCENERY

1

Almost everything was gray.

The warm rain dropping from overcast skies, the dirty wet pavement, the faded sidewalks; the apartment buildings in their long depressing dark rows. It was an old city street scene from black-and-white television, complete with the rounded windshield-wiping vehicles streaming by, the businessmen in their dull hats and raincoats pushing through the lunch-hour crowd, and the unmistakable sense that everything everywhere was about to change.

And there, at the corner of Seventeenth and Waterhouse, at one of the payphones, was a delicate woman in a shiny pink rain jacket with matching pink boots and umbrella. She was cradling the phone against her slender neck while holding a cigarette in her left hand and her little pink umbrella in her right. She was laughing, displaying a nearly perfect smile as she did so between short breaks for sharp puffs.

The payphone next to hers was empty.

Her back turned, she was telling her friend Jacqueline something she had just learned about their old geezer of a gynecologist way back in high school, Dr. Monroe. Suddenly something caught violently on her umbrella and knocked it from her hand.

"Tchiao!"

The enormous teddy bear of a man who'd uttered this strange sound was standing in the rain at the payphone next to hers and laughing loudly, his oversized black umbrella tangled with her little pink one in the large puddle between them.

"Mister!" she exclaimed.

"Sorry, sorry!" he said, still laughing. He bent over, picked up her umbrella. "I suppose this is yours?"

1

There was a long rip across it.

"That was a gift from my mother," she said.

"Well, she has great taste," the man said quickly. He then got a good look at her face. "Whoa! And apparently some pretty good DNA."

"May I have my umbrella back, please?"

"Of course, of course."

They looked at each other in the rain.

"Hey," he said, gazing at her. "No fair taking my breath away."

"No fair attacking from behind, I would say."

He smiled. "Right-o. Sorry about that. Hey, listen," he pointed at the rip in her umbrella, "you're getting wet."

"You have a keen eye for the obvious, Mister."

"One of my many strengths!" He winked as he raised his umbrella over both their heads. "Please, let me make it up to you. Let me take you to coffee. Right now and not a minute later. I know a terrific place around the corner. They import their beans."

"I'm sorry?" She looked at him. He was actually quite goodlooking beneath that unruly hair and that thick dark beard; and his intelligent blue eyes, behind those thick-rimmed glasses, were warm and inviting. He was a little large for her taste perhaps, but large in a gentle way, an almost cuddly way. She sort of wanted to press his belly.

"Seriously, it's the latest thing. They come from Central or South America somewhere, they make a fine beverage—none of the local dishwater brew, if you know what I mean. And the owner is a friend of mine. My treat, of course. How about it?"

How about it, indeed, she thought. Picking up random men on the street was not exactly her style; but then again her life lately had seemed awfully quiet, and here was some noise suddenly blowing into it.

"I prefer tea," she said softly.

"They import their tea leaves too!"

"Also I have to go back to work."

"Ah, work—I've heard of that!" he laughed. "So let me take you to dinner tonight instead. I know another place, really nice. How about it ..." he peered at her through his thick glasses, "whatever your name is, pretty lady in pink?"

There was a brief pause.

"Helen," she said quietly, extending her hand.

"Theodore." He took her hand firmly yet shook it delicately. "I am *very* pleased to meet you."

They arranged to meet for an early supper at Cozzen's Café, a trendy new spot that had just that weekend received a rave review in *The Citizen Inquirer*. When Helen suddenly remembered she was still holding the phone with Jacqueline on the line Theodore bowed his head, winked at her, and took his leave, withdrawing himself and his massive umbrella—without, Helen only realized much later, making the phone call he was presumably intending to make at the adjacent payphone.

Jacqueline, who had heard the whole thing, was beside herself with excitement.

"What did he look like?" she demanded.

"I don't know," Helen said.

"You don't know?"

"Hm. Think 'bear.' With glasses."

"That doesn't sound very attractive."

"And yet he is."

"Oh," Jacqueline said. "And how old is he?"

"I also don't know. Our age? Maybe younger. Or older."

"That's very illuminating."

"I suppose," Helen said, "we are done talking about Dr. Monroe?"

"Helen," Jacqueline said, "call me as soon as you get back from the date tonight. And please tell me things that would make Dr. Monroe turn over in his grave."

2

"The last man I was … with," Helen was saying slowly, "told me that I am damaged goods. Or something to that effect."

Theodore shook his head. "That is very rude."

"The truth, sometimes," Helen said, "can be."

How unlike her, she was thinking as she heard herself saying this, to speak so openly to a man she had just met; to anyone, really. But then again it was unlike her to be out in such a lovely restaurant on a work night, to be bathed in such soft candlelight, to be sitting before a second glass of the smoky Pinot Noir she had selected from the wine list. Not to mention to have waited beyond her ordinary ten-minute grace period for her date's late arrival.

"Let me tell you what I think of that," Theodore was saying

from across the table.

Maybe it was the rain, or just her mood of late, but the day had gotten off to that kind of start, from the moment she'd awoken and begun dressing for work. Her best friend Jacqueline had been married several years already and was now both very pregnant and very thrilled to leave her nursing "career" behind for baby-making. Her next closest friend Melvin, sweet Melvin, was also married and seemed to be happy with Michelle even if, during their own dinners together, she caught him gazing at her in that glassy-eyed way of his again. Helen herself, meanwhile, was once more on her own, not dating anybody, taking a break (as she liked to say) from taking a break from her singleness. She stood before the bathroom mirror applying her makeup. She really was pretty attractive, for a twenty-seven-year-old spinster already. Her eyes still sparkled with hazelness, as Eddie Love had once said, surprising her at the time that he knew the word "hazel." She puckered her delicate lips, imagining a kiss as she contemplated her choice of lipstick, her thoughts lingering on Eddie Love.

This, she thought, would be a good day for some bright pink, and plenty of it.

It was just her third week on her new job, at a small imported goods company conveniently located a few blocks away, but her mind today was elsewhere. Outside her office window the rain was coming down as she counted the minutes until her lunch hour. She couldn't wait to tell Jacqueline about the old letter from Dr. Monroe she had found at her mother's the night before, communicating the results of his examination of her daughter. "Your daughter's maidenhood," the old man had written, "is indeed intact, so you may rest assured that your concerns are unnecessary. Whatever she may have been doing with that young man, her virtue has been preserved."

The letter was dated in the early fall of her senior year, after her summer with Eddie Love.

Her first instinct was anger at her mother's invasiveness. But that quickly transformed into the not unpleasant realization that the old girl, back then, had not been so wrapped up in her ongoing grief over her husband as to overlook her attractive teenaged daughter's running around with the greasiest greaser in town. She had been sure that Edna had had no idea of what she was up to then; but apparently she had, enough so as to realize that Helen's virginity was at risk.

With a heavy sigh Helen had folded the yellowed letter into her handbag.

And now here she was, one umbrella collision and long afternoon at work later, sitting in Cozzen's Café, relaxing to the strains of a lovely viola concerto (was it Telemann?), hearing herself order a second glass of wine on a work night, opening up to this gentle giant of a man, this man with the deep tender eyes who spoke so beautifully with what seemed to be a trace of a British accent. Opening up to him, perhaps, because he was himself being so open with her.

"My mother is really not … well," he had told her, those blue eyes welling slightly as he added that his mother had just been institutionalized. "And it pains me to admit this but my father, bless his heart, is both irritatingly simple and maddeningly obtuse."

"Oh, is that all?" Helen said tentatively, unsure whether he was being entirely serious.

"No, he's also embarrassingly slow. When you meet him, I'll remind you to speak slowly and use small words. But here's the truly beautiful thing about him."

"Yes?"

"He's just a good man through and through. Pure good will. He really thinks we could end the Cold War if everybody would just sit down over some ice cream together. And he'd be happy to provide the ice cream."

"That is sweet."

"It is, quite. He's as sweet as his ice cream, my mother used to say, at least before she stopped speaking intelligibly altogether. And he'll just fall in love with you the moment we walk into his store, I promise. In fact he'll probably name a flavor after you, once he stops weeping from joy." Theodore paused. "He's a good man."

Helen smiled, gazing at him through the candlelight. Warmed equally by the wine and by the suggestion that she would meet his parents, she found herself wanting to remove his glasses to have a better look at those eyes.

But this thought was interrupted by the arrival of their supper. For her it was a modest Veal Cutlet; for him a Beef Wellington, which she tried not to notice was the most expensive thing on the menu. Theodore apparently knew how to choose a restaurant, for their meals were excellent. He was clearly interested in food, or at least interested in her, because he listened so intently to her reviews of their dishes, her analysis of the recipes, her discussion of possible variations. He was such a good listener that she soon found herself talking not just about the food but about herself, and about her mother who was such a splendid cook, and even a bit about her father who had so loved that cooking. It all just came pouring out so spontaneously that she barely had time to become self-conscious about it, and somehow failed to notice that Theodore's hand had rested itself upon hers on the table between them.

"The last man I was … with," Helen was saying, just now feeling the comforting weight of his masculine hand, "told me that I am damaged goods. Or something to that effect."

"Let me tell you what I think of that," Theodore said, squeezing her hand.

He stood up and walked around the table, then kissed her almost imperceptibly on her lips and touched her dark hair so gently that he barely disturbed its perfect bouffant. Then he returned to his seat and just looked at her.

"No fair," Helen said, "taking my breath away."

"No fair attacking head on," Theodore said, "I would say."

There was a long moment with just the candles and the silence between them.

"Who taught you that?" Helen asked.

"What?"

"How to be such a sweet talker."

Theodore smiled as his hand took hers again. "Listen, my pretty lady in pink. Everything is about to change. Tomorrow night, and not one night later. I promise you that."

Maybe that's what was so attractive about this man, that could draw Helen out of herself, that could almost turn him into the spiller of her secrets, into her unraveller: his self-confidence, his extreme, irresistible self-confidence.

Indeed you had to be confident of yourself to offer to cook for Helen Faire, which is what Theodore Gale proposed, the next night, to do.

3

For Helen Faire had been trained in the kitchen by Edna Faire and nobody, but nobody, cooked like the late Mayor Alden Faire's wife

Edna. From the stovetop to the oven, from Monday morning's marmalade toast to the secret recipe banana cream pie the first Sunday of every month, it was all there, in the lilac-covered notebook Edna had given to Helen a half-dozen years before upon her daughter's twenty-first birthday. True, in light of Helen's current spinsterhood, nobody but nobody was appreciating Helen's cooking except for herself and occasionally her mother. But that, along with everything (if Theodore made good on his promise), was about to change.

Helen arrived at his apartment building at precisely 5:45 PM, directly from work. She looked sharp in her light raspberry blouse and matching paneled skirt and handbag. She had also opted for some new shoes, the open-sided, lacquered-heel pumps she had acquired over the weekend.

She took a deep breath and pressed the intercom.

It buzzed back immediately.

When she arrived at his floor she found him standing at his open apartment door, wearing a warm smile and a rumpled chef's apron with the slogan *Make Supper, Not War* hand-painted on it. Scattered on the kitchen counter behind him, Helen could see as she approached, were various food products in various stages of preparation. A multiplicity of smells worked their way out of the apartment into the hall, not all of them appealing.

He just gazed at her, beaming.

"Aren't you going to invite me in?" Helen asked.

"As soon as my heart resumes beating," Theodore replied. "Ah, there. And now, my beautiful lady, please enter my humble abode, such as it is."

"Humble" was perhaps too humble a word for the apartment. It was small, stuffed with books and papers along with numerous unidentifiable items perhaps intended as art, and not exactly the paradigm of cleanliness, from Helen's perspective anyway. Barely any of the early evening light was filtering in through its one streaked window, which, she thought to herself, forcing herself not to stare at an impressive dark stain on the rug as she entered, was probably for the best.

"My place will be more appealing," Theodore was saying, "as soon as I finish my dissertation, or we finish this bottle of wine. My experts tell me this is an especially fine vintage."

Theodore had produced a bottle of the same Pinot Noir they'd had at Cozzen's Café the night before. In one smooth motion he opened it, poured two glasses, and ushered her onto the large old sofa taking up more than its share of the room.

"Thank you," Helen said with a cautious smile.

"Now you make yourself comfortable. I'm running a few minutes behind here. Let me just put on some music while I get the salad ready."

He put the new Beatles album on the record player next to the sofa and then stepped into the kitchen, roughly seven steps away. Helen sipped her wine, listened to the music, actually found herself enjoying it despite her preference for classical music.

"Sorry about this," Theodore said from the kitchen, chopping something. "The time got away from me somehow."

"Maybe that is the problem?" Helen nodded toward the clock on the wall that was either seven-and-three-quarters-hours fast or four-and-a-quarter-hours slow.

"Been meaning to fix that," Theodore smiled. "That got away from me too."

Helen laughed. "May I help somehow?"

"Only by continuing to drink, please. I'm basically done. This other thing just needs a few minutes longer in the oven and we'll be ready to eat."

The next hour went by quickly. They sat on the sofa drinking their wine as she answered his questions about her new job at A World Away. The work consisted of the same mind-numbing menial tasks as always, filing and typing mostly, but her new boss seemed to like her and, more importantly, she loved the employee discount on the home goods in which the firm specialized. She was going to be modest in her acquisitions, however. She had almost saved enough to start planning her "long journey," as she called it, to the place she liked to call "the promised land," so she would have to balance her immediate pleasure in being surrounded by beautiful things with her deeper desire to be elsewhere, to be, in particular, *there*.

"And what's so special," Theodore asked, "about *there*?"

Helen looked at him a moment but then shook her head. "Some other time."

Theodore nodded, then moved closer to her on the sofa as he refilled their glasses and started telling her about his own work. Though only a few years into his graduate program he was well along on his dissertation research, on some important if obscure early modern figure, and he had already published several significant articles. But he wasn't merely cloistered in the university, he didn't believe in that, so he'd also been writing for the local media, had published some op-eds in *The Citizen Inquirer*, was even doing community theater when time allowed. Not that it allowed for much of that, what with his regular visits to his sick mother, and to his father, out in the "old country"—as he liked to call his old neighborhood—not to mention the hours he spent volunteering at the animal shelter. And not to mention, too, that being a people person he felt that a rich social life was important, so he also had some terrific friends, such as his fellow graduate student Chuck and Chuck's wife Maxine to whom he couldn't wait to introduce her.

Helen was wondering how it would feel to run her fingers through the thick tufts of chest hair sticking out of his shirt when he suddenly jumped up from the sofa and announced that whatever time it was exactly, the thing in the oven was probably ready.

Along the way a second bottle of wine had been opened. This was now standing in front of her on the checkered-tablecloth-covered table somehow squeezed into the space between the kitchen and the living room. With a dramatic flair Theodore delivered a plate from the counter and placed it before her.

"*Voilà! Poulet a là Theodore!*" he exclaimed.

"And he speaks French, too," Helen smiled, feeling just tipsy enough to be unable to focus clearly on whatever it was that was on her plate.

"But of course. Now *mangia, mangia!*"

She carved off a piece of the meat to which Theodore had referred, for some reason, with the French word for chicken. She placed a small portion in her mouth and delicately set her teeth to work upon it.

"And? And?" Theodore asked eagerly.

He was still standing beside her, not having moved since serving her, and still wearing the chef's apron even though their date was over an hour old.

"It is … amazing," Helen answered tactfully, in fact referring to the unique combination of culinary ineptitude and personal self-confidence that this man was demonstrating.

9

"Thanks. It's an old family recipe." Theodore proudly slipped into the seat opposite her and served himself a generous portion.

"Oh. There is actually a recipe similar to this in this month's *Ladies Home Journal.*"

"I didn't say it was *my* family recipe," he winked.

"Except that one called for chicken."

"This isn't chicken?"

"Not where I come from."

Theodore reddened, then recovered quickly. "I'm kidding. Of course it isn't chicken. I was just exercising a little creativity in the kitchen."

"I will tell you what," Helen said, almost surprising herself. "Next time let me cook for you."

Theodore smiled broadly. "It's a deal."

That old dog Maxey was a genius. His "botch the cooking job and she'll propose the next date" scheme had worked beautifully. And Theodore couldn't wait to tell him about his using the wrong type of meat; that had been pure spontaneous genius of his own at the butcher's that afternoon. And the reddening of his cheeks— more genius, of which his acting coach would be most proud.

"Have another glass of wine, my ravishing lady in red," he said, gazing at her.

4

It wasn't just in the kitchen. You had to be confident of yourself to offer Helen Faire, of impeccable taste in every sense, *anything* purporting to be tasty.

For each of their dates Theodore brought her not just flowers but candies, chocolates, pastries. She was always gracious but Theodore, under his friend Maxey's guidance, was a master of people's "tells": he could see in the slight tremor of her eyebrow, the subtle coloration of her creamy cheek, whether he had done well. She liked candies, he learned, but only some: sour and spicy or hot was good (the Charms Sour Pops, the Atomic Fireballs), but the gummy chewy things (the Jujubes, the Wax Lips, the Teaberry Gum) were not. She liked pastries, but only those from the better bakeries downtown. And as for chocolate, well, had Theodore not been a quick study this relationship would have foundered long before it even began.

For Theodore, for example, bliss was a Milky Bar or a Dairy

Crunch bar and double bliss was both—and so on their fifth date, a picnic the first Saturday afternoon of September out at East Rock, he brought her one of each.

"Some sweet chocolate for my sweet lady," he said, laying out the two bars on the blanket with the rest of their spread and commencing the kissing of her long golden fingernails.

"Thank you, Theodore," Helen said, her nearly perfect smile marred only by the smallest quiver of her lip.

"What's wrong? Wouldn't you like to munch a little Dairy Crunch?" he cheerfully echoed the television jingle. "Doesn't everybody love chocolate?"

"No, and yes, respectively," Helen answered with continued graciousness, though slightly taken aback that Theodore was still kissing her fingers. "Chocolate, yes. But 'Dairy Crunch' is more of a candy than a chocolate, don't you think?"

"What's the difference?"

"As soon as you stop mauling my hand and light me a cigarette," she smiled, "I will be happy to explain."

And she would have been, too, had Theodore stopped his seduction of her hand, which he did not: this date marked the real beginning of their physical relationship. It took until this fifth date before anything beyond a brush on the lips occurred, as Helen's body language made it clear—she had this way of tensing up at key moments—that she was not comfortable with more. This struck Theodore as unusual, since if love had not yet become free in this era it certainly had begun its drastic decline in value. And then when things did begin, now, they began slowly, with Theodore only making oral love to each of the lovely long fingers on Helen's right hand in turn. The next date Theodore did the same to her left hand, the next he attended to her forearms, and then after that she allowed him to run his hands over both her elbows, through the sleeves of her bright teal blouse of course. He didn't think it possible but this woman had incredibly sexy elbows. After returning to his apartment that evening he treated himself to erotic thoughts of her triceps.

The slow pace, her discomfort—a little odd, but hey, Theodore reported back to Maxey, he almost didn't mind the delays even if his desire was bursting. For the relationship was going so well overall: they were seeing each other several times a week, spending the weekends together, having a wonderful time. The verbal sparks between them were particularly exhilarating. Theodore liked nothing more than banter and debate and found himself excited by Helen's ability to keep pace with him here. For though her nature was more reserved than his she was possessed of a sharp tongue and she loved to use it—at least verbally, Theodore noted one night, two months in.

"Maybe she's just not into, you know, men," Maxey replied. They were at one of Maxey's apartments on the west side of the city, and he had just poured Theodore a tall glass of dark beer from his private stock. "That's really in these days."

"You think?"

Maxey manually blinked his otherwise unblinking left eye, a consequence of some nerve damage he'd suffered under undisclosed past circumstances. "It's one possibility. The other is that she's just not into *you*."

Theodore laughed as he gestured toward his barrel chest. "Not possible, my friend. I mean, we're talking about me here."

"Well, then I suppose you'll have to just keep working on it, big guy."

"Yeah," Theodore said thoughtfully. "I suppose I will."

Maxey would have smiled were his nerve to have permitted it, since he had just begun accepting bets from his customers on when Theodore would manage to sleep with this woman and was hoping the affair would go on for a while.

Meanwhile Theodore was experiencing an unusual new sensation. It wasn't merely the sex he wanted but the actual woman herself. She was so sharp, so classy, all the things he had always wanted to associate himself with, as far removed from the musty world of his old country parents as you could get. She didn't merely pretend to enjoy violin records, for example, she *actually* enjoyed them; and when her eyes had closed during the symphony she had taken him to recently—the night before his mother Dottie was diagnosed with the uterine cancer she immediately claimed the doctors had implanted in her—it was because she was appreciating the music, not sleeping through it. Theodore found himself enjoying the symphony too, despite his preference for the British Invasion that was all the rage those days. Maybe it was because while Helen's eyes were closed he could simply gaze at her lovely face, at her tender lips pursed just ever so tautly, as long as he wanted.

And then there was her skill, her *artistry*, in the kitchen.

Prior to meeting Helen his own culinary standards—or so he had joked upon arriving for their third date, just a few minutes late, at her bright and immaculate apartment—were perhaps not *quite* as demanding as hers: as long as the thing could be reasonably classified as food he was guaranteed to like it.

"Well then that is about to change," she had replied drily. "Tonight, and not one night later."

Not even an hour later, it turned out, for by that time Theodore had already interrupted her surprisingly penetrating questions about his dissertation to inquire just what delectable thing it was, exactly, that they were eating?

"It's called Chicken Divan," Helen answered.

"You must mean Chicken Divine."

"Thank you," she smiled. "It's my mother's recipe."

"What's her secret?"

"The main thing is to use chicken."

Theodore nodded gracefully. "*Touché.*"

"Not to mention a touch of cayenne."

"Ah, so that would explain my elevated body temperature?"

Helen smiled again. "Perhaps you should see a doctor."

"Oh I'll be all right," Theodore winked. "After another glass of wine."

He was indeed all right after the wine, and even more so after the dessert. When it was over he pushed his empty plate away and announced, "You realize, Helen Faire, that you're going to have a hard time shaking me now that I've tasted your apricot thing here?"

"I am duly warned," Helen said as he lit her after-dinner cigarette. "But may I remind you that I do have older brothers, at least three of whom would protect me if ever necessary. At least with some advance notice." She had told Theodore that one of her brothers was in prison for some offense she would not specify, and the other three were dispersed across the country.

"Well then perhaps I should advise you to notify them now."

"I actually did before inviting you to dinner. I was hoping at least one would be here before I brought out the tart."

"It's just as well. I've always preferred my tarts unescorted, you know."

Helen laughed. "Just wait. Stick around until next month and you can have an unescorted piece of my mother's banana cream pie too."

"It's that good, huh?"

"You," Helen said, taking a puff, "have no idea."

And so, from all of this, from the perfect package which was Helen Faire, Theodore found himself experiencing yet another new sensation: the realization that he was willing to be *patient*. No, he couldn't quite understand why, with all the verbal electricity between them, there weren't a few more physical sparks as well. But he was willing to wait; to the point even where he put away his main instrument for meeting women, his oversized black umbrella. Not permanently, mind you, just in the coat closet in his apartment. But it was now out of sight, no longer next to the front door, no longer ready at hand for every rainy trip out.

That she wasn't a lesbian, he thought, was clear. As their relationship approached the three-month mark they were fooling around plenty for sure, and it wasn't only *his* hands that were roaming over the other's body. Helen definitely felt desire. He could feel her desire, feel the way she snuggled into him, the way she touched him. She, he thought, was fascinated by him, by his large masculine body, by his sheer physicality. They spent long suppers, cooked exclusively by Helen now, in sparkling conversation followed by long evenings, usually on the sofa but lately in the bedroom, of physical exploration. But then—suddenly—she would tense up, become uncomfortable, stop. The first few times she begged off because it was late, because she had to get up for work in the morning, because she had a headache from too much wine.

But last night she hadn't even offered an excuse.

"I need to stop now," she said, rolling away from him. She was wearing only her white lace panties. As he watched her turn her perfectly shaped small breasts away from him his throbbing penis nearly exploded on the spot.

"But Helen Faire, I want you," he exhaled, still breathing heavily from the heavy petting which had just broken off. "All of you. Every last bit of you. I want to eat you up."

"Do you, now?" she said, looking back at him.

"Yes, I do now. Now, and not a moment later."

"Good," she said, looking away again.

No, he didn't quite get it. She had dated other men, she was not inexperienced; and she couldn't possibly be a virgin at twenty-seven years old in these burgeoning days of sexual liberation. So why was she holding out on him? Was there some terrible dark secret from her past, something keeping her from doing what other women had done so readily—namely yield to the awesome manliness that went by the name of Theodore Gale?

Whatever it was, he imagined himself telling his one-day future biographer, he was going to find out.

And then he was going to liberate her.

5

Maxey suggested a change of scenery.

Laws and rules only apply within specified jurisdictions, he pointed out, a fact he had often exploited to his own advantage; so sometimes, he observed one night over beers at another of his apartments on the west side, when you take the woman outside the usual geography she, and the rules she follows, might relax.

"Take her on a little camping trip or something. A weekend away might move things along."

"You mean, like—in the woods?" The closest Theodore liked to get to "nature" was in taking his showers *au naturel*. His idea of roughing it was to order only one dessert at a restaurant rather than his customary two.

"Take it easy, big guy. You can use my cabin."

"The one with that Jacuzzi bath pump?"

"Nah, Tabitha's crashing there now. I'm talking about the cabin in Hoxsie County. The mountains."

"I thought you broke up with Tabitha."

"Different Tabitha." Maxey fixed his unblinking eye on Theodore. "You'll take the Barracuda, too. Get her there quick. Are you in?"

It was autumn, Theodore thought. At least there won't be so many bugs.

And so Theodore proposed a weekend camping trip in the late fall, just past the three-month mark of their relationship. It would be a small get-away, he assured Helen. Just a two-hour drive in this fancy car his friend was lending him, out to this nice cabin in the mountains the friend was also lending him, and this friend liked cutting-edge technology and comfort, by the way, the cabin was probably a luxury hideaway; come on my lovely lady, he said, it will be *fun*.

Now Helen Faire wouldn't ordinarily want to go camping either. She was the sort of person whose greatest pleasure was a clean, well-ordered apartment; whose second greatest pleasure was stylish clothing, in particular shoes, of which she had an impressive collection; and whose third greatest pleasure was cleaning and then ordering her impressive shoe collection. But then again this was the same Helen Faire who was feeling the physical presence of this man in a way she'd never felt any man's presence before, who found herself wanting to stop being herself for a while, to leave behind all her sorrows and injuries and voids; who even found herself fantasizing about finally shedding that albatross of a virginity to this bear of a man on a bear rug in bear country, and who swore to herself that she would *not* bring her prized Hoover to vacuum the rug both before and after, and possibly during, the act in question.

So she said yes.

It was cold; it was the end of November. They got a late start since Theodore had trouble tracking down Maxey to get the keys to the cabin and Barracuda, and then when he did track him down Maxey had forgotten the keys so they had to go back to one of Maxey's places and had then gotten distracted by the beer in one of Maxey's fridges. (It didn't expedite matters that Maxey kept disappearing into the other room, to answer the phone for last-minute wagers on whether this was going to be Theodore's Big Night.) Then Theodore had gotten lost on the way up to the mountains. Very little caused Helen more anxiety than getting lost, except maybe getting lost with Theodore at the wheel. Like most males Theodore wouldn't admit he didn't know where he was; but unlike most males he actually didn't *realize* he didn't know where he was and so would confidently drive as if he did know. Helen had the map open on her knees and was trying to read it, in the early darkness of the season, with the little flashlight her mother had wisely insisted she bring along after giving up trying to convince her against going in the first place.

"I think that may have been the turn we wanted, Theodore," Helen said delicately as they whizzed past one of the few clearly marked roads in Hoxsie County—if this *was* Hoxsie County.

"No, it's this way, sweetness," Theodore said, with exactly the same confidence with which he had insisted ten minutes earlier that it was the opposite way before Helen had convinced him to turn around.

Was that snow hitting the windshield? Helen wondered twenty minutes later when they had turned around yet again. No, thankfully not; just a passing flake or two. Fortunately that had stopped by the time they made it to the cabin around 8:00 PM. Helen sat in the car with the heat running while Theodore got out to open the cabin and get the heating unit started inside. She was exhausted from both the length and stress of the drive, and closed her eyes for a minute while she waited.

Theodore suddenly opened the driver's door and slid in beside her. "Good news, my baby! The place looks spectacular, the heating unit looks brand new, and just like I told you, there's an enormous bear rug in front of the fireplace!"

"And the bad news?" she joked.

"I saw all that through the cabin window."

"What?"

"I left the keys at Maxey's place."

"Oh Jesus, Theodore."

"Listen, Helen," Theodore said with sudden seriousness. He touched her cheek and turned her face toward him. "I admit, from one perspective, this appears off to a bad start."

"That is definitely one perspective."

"But there's another perspective. Trust me. If we survive this ordeal—"

"Theodore!"

"Kidding! But seriously, look at it this way. It's totally out of our control at this point but that, I submit to you, can be utterly thrilling. It's an adventure. Let go, my baby. Just feel the thrill." Somehow he had slipped one of his hands inside her orange cashmere sweater and was now caressing her breast. He squeezed a finger into her bra and gently manipulated her swelling nipple.

"I'm sorry?" she said, involuntarily leaning back in her seat and spreading her legs slightly as his other hand moved toward her groin.

"I was saying something about the thrill," he whispered in her ear, his beard gently scratching the side of her face as he nuzzled her. A hand was now groping her other breast.

"How do you do that?" she whispered back, leaning into him.

"What?"

"All those hands."

"Trade secret," he whispered as one of his many fingers slipped into her panties.

That's about when the Barracuda ran out of gas. Theodore's hands stopped doing what they were doing while he got out of the car, checked the trunk, and then slid back in beside her.

"Well, the good news is that we definitely have no gas."

"That's the good news?"

"Yeah. The other news is that it's snowing."

Helen moaned softly, in distress, in pleasure, or some combination of the two as Theodore resumed where he'd left off and the thick wet flakes began accumulating on the windshield. It felt almost as if they were hibernating, an indefinite amount of winter passing outside while Theodore kept her warm in his embrace within. Maybe it was an hour passed, or maybe two, or maybe just a few minutes when Helen found herself almost letting go, managing, inside the dark vehicle, under the warm large blanket of this man, to stop thinking, to stop remembering. She said something, she whispered it, maybe she just thought it, but then they were in the back seat and Theodore was moving, shifting, attempting to maneuver despite the cramped quarters of the coupe's rear compartment, his ample size, the articles of clothing tangled around their limbs. But that small delay was just enough. For Helen now heard herself saying something else, whispering it, maybe just thinking it, apologizing, beginning to cry, and this man, this tender and sensitive man, resting his bearded cheek against her own soft and smooth, was stroking her hair and whispering in her ear don't cry, don't cry, it's all right. Maybe it was another hour passed, or just a few minutes, and he was saying, "Just tell me, my baby, let me help you," and she wanted to, to tell someone, to tell *him*, out here, somewhere in the woods, somewhere under the snow, but she couldn't. The windows were now completely covered. She was starting to feel cold, she had no idea what time in the night it now was, and Theodore was speaking quietly but quickly.

"We're orphans, you and I," he was saying.

"No," Helen whispered.

"No, really. I'm the only child of two only children. My mother is as good as gone, now. My father has never understood me, appreciated me, has no idea what I am about. I have no one."

Helen squeezed his arm.

"And you," Theodore added.

"I have my mother. And my brothers."

"Your brothers?" Theodore said gently.

"All right, then. My mother. And cousins, and uncles."

"You've barely seen them since your father ... passed."

"My mother."

Theodore was silent a moment. "I wonder if you," he said, "are more for her than she is for you."

Helen wished she could see his eyes, if only it weren't so damn dark. "Theodore," she finally asked, "what are you saying?"

"Helen. We should be together."

"We are together."

"I mean *together*."

"This isn't *together*?" Helen managed to pull an arm free and gesture, somehow, to the tangled bundle of their arms and legs packed into the rear portion of the vehicle.

"I'm serious."

"Theodore—"

"Just say yes."

"To what?"

"To getting married. Obviously."

"To getting married?"

"Obviously."

There was a silence.

"Theodore," Helen whispered.

"Is that a yes?"

"I think—"

"Don't."

"What?"

"Think. Just say yes."

"But Theodore. We do not have much money. I just have my salary, and you are still—in school."

"Now, maybe, Helen. But we have futures. Your boss loves you. I'll be finished in a year or two. And my advisor already thinks my dissertation will be a book. He has big plans for me."

"We have never discussed—family. I—am not sure—"

"We'll work it out."

"But," she whispered, "we barely—know each other."

"We know enough, Helen."

"You do not know *me*, Theodore."

"But I do," he insisted gently. "And I want to be the one who saves you."

"I'm sorry?"

"It's very, very simple."

She shook her head. "But Theodore—it *isn't*."

His warm breath was on her neck as he whispered in her ear, "I love you, Helen Faire, secrets and all. It couldn't be more simple."

"But Theodore," she whispered back after a long time, or maybe just thought. But she did not continue and Theodore did not answer, he just held her, held her, all through what remained of that dark and long cold night.

CHAPTER TWO
STARLAC'S POWDERED MILK

1

Despite being overwhelmed by caring for his institutionalized wife, Theodore's father, Benny, had adored Helen from the start and wept copiously upon the news of their engagement. Helen's mother Edna also wept, at least after her failed attempt to convince her daughter to hold off on such a big decision.

"You're only twenty-seven," she urged.

"I am twenty-eight next week, Mummy," Helen said, lighting a cigarette, more than a little irritated by her mother lately. "And anyway, he is smart, and handsome, and thoughtful, and—fun."

"Fun?"

Helen shrugged. Edna resumed weeping.

Her friends at least were more supportive. Jacqueline, moments away from giving birth, admitted that she didn't really understand Theodore's graduate school thing—"If he is such a genius as you say, then why doesn't he get a real job?" she said when Helen tried to explain Theodore's dissertation—but she agreed that the man had the animal magnetism to compensate for his lack of income, and anyway she just loved weddings. And Melvin, sweet Melvin, after the color returned to his face, asked quietly, "Do you love him, Helen?"

"I do, Melvin. He is just so good to me."

"Well if you love him, Helen," Melvin said after a long pause, "then I love him." He gazed at her a moment before asking her permission to hug her in congratulation.

For the venue the newly engaged couple settled on a restored mansion in Moswanicut Park downtown called The Casino, which Theodore particularly favored because (he joked) marriage was the biggest gamble most people took with their lives and which Helen initially resisted for the same reason. Edna, now resigned, helped Helen choose the floral arrangements, and expressed surprise when

Helen opted for hibiscus, lotus, and blood-red orchids rather than her cherished purple pansies. "Just because, Mummy, that is why," Helen explained, refusing to explain. Theodore, in charge of the music, worked through Maxey to obtain an A-list local band whose sexually charged lyrics (in those early days of raunchy rock'n'roll) were aimed to offend everyone over the age of thirty. And finally the couple was to spend the night of the wedding in the absurdly priced Monarch Hotel Bridal Suite, about which even Helen was excited despite recognizing that it alone would set her long journey to her "promised land" back by at least half a year. After all, she was determined that this was finally going to be *the* night, and she might as well do it right.

There was only one small wrinkle on the way to the wedding.

Three months before the date they went to obtain the marriage license. While at the City Clerk's office Helen just happened to notice that the name Theodore entered on the form was not his own.

"Who," she asked, confused, "is 'Enoch—Pnkl'?"

Theodore's face reddened behind his facial hair. "A technicality," he said, and explained why—for reasons which ought to be obvious—he had chosen to drop the name his old country parents had originally inflicted upon him, adding that he'd not yet gotten around to changing it legally.

Helen—for reasons which also ought to be obvious—was feeling some distress about the revelation. "What else don't I know about you, Professor Missing-Some-Vowels?"

"Nothing else. I swear to you."

She peered more closely at the form. "I thought you were twenty-eight."

"I will be," he said slowly. "Just two-and-a-half more years. But that's it. There's *nothing* else. My baby."

Helen did not know what to think about him, literally. "How am I supposed to be able to trust you, 'Enoch'? Is that even how you pronounce it?"

"I swear to you, my fair Miss Faire," he said earnestly, "I will *never* lie to you again."

She looked at him and tried to turn off her mother's voice inside her head. A technicality, she thought, or perhaps answered her mother, and then signed the form.

But this moment really *was* but a glitch, one easily

counterbalanced by the passion between them, by Theodore's love for her, by the way he took care of her. Helen couldn't be thinking about her wedding, for example, without also thinking about the absence of her father. The late Mayor Alden Faire had been loved by all, beginning each day by exclaiming "'Morning, morning!" and then spreading that cheer wherever he went, to the many customers at his flower shop to his many constituents in their modest suburban town. But then a brain aneurysm had taken him from this life when Helen was but a girl, his darling "girlie," of ten. His departure devastated not only his wife and children but the whole extended family, which disintegrated over assorted squabbles in the year following his death. Although Helen just would not talk about him it was clear to Theodore how deeply she missed him. "Who," she would whisper to Theodore, breaking into tears in his arms, "is going to give me away?" Yet Theodore not only understood what a minefield this issue was for her, and for them, but also possessed the empathy to navigate it.

There was a quick foray through practical solutions: one of her brothers perhaps, though obviously not *that* one, the imprisoned one, who must have done something awful to her for her to despise him so. Or her mother, maybe; or maybe Benny, who already loved her as his own daughter. But Theodore soon saw that practical solutions were not what Helen needed, at least not most of the time. So he would simply stroke her hair or hold her while she wept. He would ask her questions about this marvelous person who had been her father, listen attentively to her often evasive responses, desist when he sensed he was approaching forbidden territory; and all the while falling more deeply in love with her for her concern about his own mother's deteriorating condition even while she was so busy dealing with *her* own sadness and loss.

"Maybe, my beautiful wife-to-be," he might say while caressing her, basking in the scent of her green tea perfume, "we should think of the wedding as about the future, about our future. What matters is less where we came from than where we are going. Less who shall give us away than who shall receive us. Together we shall leave this place and make that journey to your promised land."

And somehow when these words had been uttered the practical solution itself became clear. Theodore's father would accompany Helen down one aisle at The Casino while Helen's mother would accompany Theodore down the opposite aisle, to join up at the intersection for the ceremony, for the future, itself.

The wedding didn't work out the way they'd planned.

In fact it turned out way better, at least once Theodore showed up.

"So sorry, my baby," he said, his cheeks reddening as he rushed into The Casino twenty minutes late. That awful crazy-eyed Maxey was a few steps behind him. "We lost track of the time."

"Theodore, are you—inebriated?" Helen whispered anxiously, yet with the grace appropriate to a woman wearing a Jacques Heim white chiffon wedding dress and gorgeous white Ferragamo shoes.

He grimaced. "Lost track of that too. But listen."

Helen arched her eyebrow and listened.

"I think," Theodore said, tilting his head, "your mother is happy to see me too."

Helen looked where he'd indicated and saw that her mother had begun weeping upon Theodore's entrance. Despite herself, she smiled. "Now come, my lovely lady," Theodore was whispering, "let's get hitched."

It was a wonderful evening.

The flowers weren't merely beautiful but stunning; and their utter sensuousness seemed to put nearly everyone in a subtle state of arousal. Maybe that was why the raunchy band ended up not only *not* offending those people over thirty but instead got them out of their seats and dancing to the music all the young people were listening to these days. In fact at one point every single guest along with half of The Casino staff were on the dance floor bumping and grinding, at least if their rheumatoid joints allowed it. Theodore's friend Chuck and noticeably pregnant wife Maxine were doing things that expectant couples probably shouldn't be doing, and even Benny stopped weeping from the ceremony long enough to grab the First Widow Edna and take her for her first spin in the many years since the Mayor had bequeathed that sad status upon her.

As for the newlyweds themselves, well, after their whirlwind romance and long-delayed gratification, and with that beckoning goal just within their reach, they simply couldn't make it to that expensive hotel suite. Instead at Theodore's urging they crawled out the window of The Casino's Bridal Room during the frenzy on the dance floor and found themselves a soft spot on which to lay their blanket in the small wooded area behind the building. And then just as Benny and Edna were returning to their separate seats to resume their respective weeping inside, Helen was closing her eyes and turning off her thoughts and forcing herself to do nothing but just feel this man, to feel him feeling her, touching her, moving her. She inhaled, she held her breath, she didn't let it go as *she* let go, and she let him hold her and feel her and move her; and then at last she felt him taking her, *taking* her, across, across at long last, to the other side.

Shhhh, Theodore whispered, caressing her, while she sobbed.

And when it was over, when Helen had resumed breathing and had smoothed down her Jacques Heim dress and let herself be spooned back into Theodore's arms, warming herself from the September night chill, Theodore whispered in her ear, "So how does it feel being knocked up, my wonderful woman in white?"

"Rather," she whispered back, leaning into him, "like being knocked down, I would say."

"It's probably twins, you know. I'm a *very* manly guy."

"I'd have thought at least triplets," she half-smiled. She gazed at the canopy of pine trees above them and the few stars poking through, then added quietly, "So, was it worth the wait, Professor?"

"Is heaven worth the wait?"

"You don't believe in heaven."

"I do now."

"I bet you say that to all the girls."

"I do. And it works every time. But more importantly," he tickled her under her arm, "was it worth the wait for *you*, my baby?"

"The jury," she said, slowly, "is still out."

"How about some more evidence?"

"I thought you put that away!"

"It popped back out. I told you I'm manly."

"Please, Theodore," Helen suddenly said, pulling away. "Maybe we should go back in. They are going to start looking for us any minute."

Theodore sighed. "All right, my magnificent new wife. But I must tell you that, years from now, we will through the fuzzy haze of recollection gaze back upon this moment and regret, only, that we did not linger longer upon it."

"Since when do you know poetry?"

"I don't. That's by the great Theodore whatever his last name is exactly. But Helen, wait," Theodore pulled her in close to him once more and said gently, "before we go back in, will you please tell me now? Finally? Why did you hold out like that? Why did you make us wait so long?"

"Trade secret," she answered softly.

"But what trade, exactly?"

"Darkness," she whispered. "Deep. Packed. All the way down." She was not smiling as she pulled away and smoothed down her dress again. "Now can we *please* go back inside?"

The next couple of days were busy. There was Theodore's mother's unexpected funeral to attend, and Theodore's move into Helen's apartment to attend to. A honeymoon would have to wait of course, since all the money had been spent on the wedding.

2

"I … am … King of the … *Beasts!*"

Theodore pounded his hair-covered barrel of a chest. Three-and-a-half weeks after the wedding he had just been informed that there were things occurring inside his new wife's body that neither his ever appreciative eye nor his many hands, despite now being familiar with more of its nooks and crannies than even she was, could yet detect. "I *told* you I was manly!"

Helen squeezed back into his arms, cozy on this late September morning in what was now their bedroom, in what was formerly just Helen's apartment. "How can you be sure it was the wedding night? After all the last three weeks we—"

"Please. It's me. I'm sure."

"And are you sure we are ready for a child?"

"What's to be ready? We'll just do it."

"All right, then," Helen said contentedly enough, closing her eyes. "You're the boss."

"Damn right I'm the boss. Now prepare for some dictation, young lady!" As Theodore said this he dexterously peeled off her lavender panties for some quick morning intimacy before she got ready for work.

"But wait," Helen objected, "are you sure we should do this if I am pregnant?"

"Think less. Act more," Theodore answered, the point moot since he was already acting.

Theodore loved the idea of his new wife being pregnant. He loved fantasizing about the brains and brawn and future batting ability of Theodore Jr., in between fantasizing about all the things Helen was now allowing him to do with, to, and in the general vicinity of her perfect little female body. And he simply loved loving *her*, this elegant woman, bringing her the gourmet chocolates that she liked, the purple flowers she favored, the books of crossword puzzles she enjoyed in the evenings, even if she was in effect providing him the money for these luxuries from her own salary—which was measurably more than his graduate student stipend even supplemented by his freelance writing.

And Helen, too, was happier than she had ever been. All those years of pent-up sexual energy pouring forth as from a burst dam. The still-lingering high from the wedding, which had actually met her aesthetic standards. Even her career: her boss clearly appreciated her, and recognized her taste and talents, and had recently mentioned the idea of promoting her to a Buyer for the company. And most of all the oversized bundle of spontaneity which was her new husband engaged and stimulated her in ways she had never before experienced. She found herself as aroused by his masculine body as by the brilliant chapters he'd written on that thinker with the strange name of Ignoratio P. Elenchi; and she was moved by his not merely insisting she read those chapters but by his then taking her comments on them so seriously as to actually revise them.

"Professor Madame Gale," he would whisper during foreplay, "I'm here for your office hour."

And Helen loved being pregnant.

Of course this pregnancy was easy to love: it was smooth, uneventful, painless. For most of it she barely was even aware of it, only starting to feel it really when her tummy became suddenly big in the final months. Or big for Helen Gale anyway. Somehow she maintained almost to the end what many other women would covetously have considered a svelte figure even had it not been pregnant. The only qualification here were her breasts, which became very plump. Theodore found this appealing but he had already learned—from Maxey—not to say anything, for it was precarious territory. If he acknowledged that the larger breasts were attractive then what would that imply about their normal size? But if he expressed a preference for the normal size then wouldn't that mean that he now found her less attractive?

"Easily solved," Maxey advised him one night. "Just hump her so much that she never thinks to ask your opinion of her rack." (Maxey was now accepting bets on the date of the new child's arrival and its sex.)

"I can do that," Theodore said.

It turned out that Theodore *couldn't* do that—not because he was not capable of making love to her frequently (he was) but because it was mathematically impossible for Helen not to query him, as the pregnancy entered its latter stages, about the changing state of her body.

"What do you think, Theodore?" Helen asked as she undressed for bed a mere twenty minutes after Theodore returned home from receiving Maxey's advice. Helen was standing before the bedroom mirror, her hands cupping her ample round breasts over her swollen belly, studying Theodore's expression in the mirror.

"Let's make love," Theodore said, grabbing his belt buckle.

"Yes, but what do you think? Do you like them like this?" Helen turned to face him and was manipulating her thickened left nipple with her thumb. Her areolas—or areolae, as she would say—were also larger and darker than normal.

"I *said* let's make love," Theodore stammered. A line of sweat had broken out upon his forehead in that small space between his hairline and thick eyebrows.

"What's the matter with your—?"

Normally Theodore would have been working toward his second climax by now. Instead his limp member was drooping, half-obscured by his unruly thicket of pubic hair.

"Give it a minute. How was work today?"

"Theodore, do you find me unattractive this way?"

"Tchiao!" Theodore exclaimed when his anatomy suddenly did the thing that evolution had trained it to do. "Now less yak, more sack!"

The battle, that evening at least, went to him, although the war was ultimately, as with most couples in this situation, to go to her.

3

Theodore was wonderful during these months.

The chocolates and flowers continued apace. He was immediately obliging whenever Helen requested a hot water bottle to soothe a spot of nausea or some aching muscle. He was always happy to give her foot massages, leg massages, back massages, and didn't mind that these only sometimes eventuated in his own orgasms; and he barely argued when she insisted that pregnant women did not require regular vaginal massages.

"Make way, that's my wife!" he would say, clearing a berth through the crowded sidewalks before her.

"Yield your seat to a pregnant lady, buddy?" he might say, picking some poor sap up by the collar on the crowded bus to Wickenden's, the main department store downtown, en route to buying maternity clothing and baby supplies.

And when she was sad—when thinking about her father never meeting his grandchild, for example—Theodore was right there beside her, comforting her, embracing her, and often refraining from attempting to massage her vagina.

No, it could not have gone more smoothly.

Everything was in place. The baby's room was decorated and furnished. Her boss was giving her a four-month maternity leave at half pay, an act so unprecedented in its generosity in those days that Theodore was prompted to comment, to Helen's discomfort, that the man must be in love with her or something. Helen's mother was expressing enthusiasm about caring for her grandchild after Helen returned to work. The bag was packed for the hospital and the phone number for the taxi was posted on the Frigidaire.

"Theodore," Helen whispered in the middle of one warm night in the second week in June. "Theodore!" she repeated, more urgently.

"Elenchi," he mumbled, or snored.

"Theodore, I think my water just broke."

There was no response. The legendarily deep sleeper had already fallen back asleep.

With difficulty in her now bloated condition Helen pulled herself up in bed and headed into the kitchen to call the taxi.

4

Several hours later Theodore found the note Helen had left for him on the kitchen table. Arriving at the hospital he found her stalled in labor.

"My baby!" he exclaimed as he swooped through the heavy metal door of the room and kissed her sweaty forehead, scratching his straggly beard along her nose. She was sitting up in the bed, looking through a fashion magazine the nurse had brought her.

"Why didn't you wake me?"

"I assume that is a rhetorical question?"

"I don't think you try very hard."

She had poked him, pushed him, yelled at him, and slapped him twice, hard. After the second slap he had opened his mouth as if in silent protest, then closed it and rolled over. "Come a little closer, my darling, and I will show you how I tried."

"Right-o." Theodore winked and stepped back. "So how's Theo Jr. coming along?"

"I assume," Helen groaned as a contraction began, "*that* is a rhetorical question."

Theodore smiled and stroked her hair as the contraction receded. "Tell me what you need, my baby. Some tea, maybe? With a drop of milk, like you like it?"

"A cigarette would be nice."

"They allow that in here?"

"No."

He smiled. "Tea it is."

His beard had scratched her nose again and departed before Helen could remind him that they didn't allow caffeinated beverages during labor either. Not that it mattered much, for no sooner had the door slammed shut behind him than another long contraction began.

Forty-five minutes later a nurse retrieved Theodore from the cafeteria, where he was busily engaged with another expectant husband in a smattering of fisticuffs somehow triggered by the final episode of *The Dick Van Dyke Show*. Theodore swooped through the door again, and after regaining the consciousness briefly lost from his glimpse of the bloodied sheets he jumped to his exhausted wife's bedside.

"My baby!" he exclaimed, stroking her damp tousled hair.

Weakly she pointed to the bassinet on the other side of the bed.

"My baby!" he exclaimed again, choking out a loud sob as he was introduced to the product of his very manly sperm.

Oh how he loved this infant at that moment and not a moment later! After immediately taking three rolls of pictures with their new color Polaroid camera he took a good look at the baby. "Little Theo," he pronounced, "looks just like me! Don't you just *love* him? Helen?"

Theodore turned to look at his wife.

There was an anxious expression on her face.

With the exception of her friend Maxine (who was something of the hippie-dippie type popping up those days), none of her friends nursed their babies. After all, these were the days when women were being liberated not merely from their bras but from their breasts, when baby formula was being touted as the greatest invention since sliced bread, and anyway, speaking of bread, didn't Helen have her career to think about, her soon-to-be career as a Buyer, especially since she was going to be the primary winner of the bread until Theodore finished his dissertation a year or two away?

Yet Helen, watching her husband cradle the infant in his arms, her husband so comfortably oblivious to the whirrs and creaks of the machinery in the room, to the medical personnel wandering in and about, and to little details like the family budget, experienced in herself the realization that she was actually—*afraid* to love this little creature—and that she was going to have to work at it. And so she decided right there, with a spontaneity far more characteristic of her husband than of herself, that she was going to nurse this child to create the maternal feelings she knew she was supposed to be feeling.

"Theodore," Helen said softly from the bed. "Do you think I could feed her now?"

"Her?" Theodore asked, entering that awkward first moment of restructuring his worldview to include a daughter rather than a smaller version of himself.

Helen brought baby Regina slowly, tentatively, to her breast.

And Regina, beautiful Regina, latched on easily and immediately, and began suckling while her ecstatic father looked on.

"You did it, my baby," Theodore said, stroking Helen's forehead.

"We did it," Helen answered, gazing down at her newborn.

She was going to love this baby.

5

Theodore enjoyed sports of all varieties. He enjoyed participating in them, especially football where his size was an advantage. He enjoyed watching them. And sometimes he might bet on them, at least when he had some extra cash on hand at Maxey's. And so it was not surprising that the metaphors which first came to his mind with respect to Theodore, Jr.—Regina—were athletic ones.

"We," he boasted to Maxey and the men milling about Maxey's largest north side apartment, the one overlooking Howland Square, "have hit a grand slam here. Have a cigar, mac!" He distributed the Cubans which Maxey had somehow acquired for him despite the recent embargo.

"She's a slam dunk, Benny!" he exclaimed to his father during one of his rare visits out to the old country, offering the old man a thick Cuban. The confused expression on Benny's face caused by the phrase "slam dunk" quickly shifted to a different confused expression caused by the proffered cigar, since Benny had never smoked.

"She's a perfect hat touch trickdown," he babbled to himself late one night, stumbling drunkenly down the middle of Elgin Street after some departmental event he already could not clearly recall, except that Chuck was there, there were plenty of Rusty Nail cocktails, and there may have been one or two attractive young women as well.

And to be sure, Regina entered their lives as smoothly as a perfectly executed handoff to a speedy running back behind an outstanding offensive line. There was barely a pause, a hiccup, as they adjusted to their new lives. She was a perfect little baby and they were the perfect parents. She slept beautifully, ate beautifully, barely ever even cried. Everybody loved her, her toothy smile, her guffaw of a baby laugh, you almost didn't notice her occasional tendency to bite and to pinch and to scratch, and if you did notice you almost didn't mind—it was just all so cute!

Edna loved her, Grandma Edna who was thrilled to have a new little person to love, who was overjoyed to take on the childcare responsibilities when Helen returned to work.

Grandpa Benny loved her, or at least you had to assume he did given his inability to refrain, every time he saw the baby, from bawling like one. If you measured Benny's feelings by his tissues then Benny loved Regina about two cases of Kleenex's worth per visit. To get a sense of the scale, an excited child simply walking into his incorrectly named "Iced Cream" ice cream store was good for one hanky's worth, maybe two hankies tops.

And oh how Theodore loved her.

He loved bringing her to his office, strolling her around,

showing her to everybody. He loved bringing her to whatever class he was teaching, lecturing grandiloquently while carrying her in a sort of sling he had designed for that purpose. He loved bouncing her on his knee, on his belly, always striving to get that baby guffaw. He would spend a week's grocery money on Polaroid film which he would use up in an hour: here's Regina sitting, here she is sitting in a slightly different position, here she is crawling, and here she is gnawing on his finger (no big deal! just a Band-Aid!)—she was so cute! Oh and here's Theodore changing a diaper—a rare occurrence, especially in an era when few husbands could even tell you where the diapers were stored—but Theodore was all smiles giving Helen instructions about the angle from which to shoot, not having noticed that Regina was busy peeing on the change table. But heck she was so cute it didn't matter. So cute, he didn't mind when Helen confiscated the fun but expensive Polaroid and insisted they get one of the new less expensive Instamatics. So cute, it was almost no sacrifice to have converted the apartment's second bedroom from "Theodore's mess" to the nursery, and almost no bother that baby gear was crammed everywhere in the apartment.

And so the firstborn daughter had a splendid first year.

All that love, all that attention; what's not to like? Who wouldn't be happy having your loving grandmother take care of you, your loving grandfather burst into joyous tears every time he sees you, and most of all having two loving parents in love both with each other and with you? Regina needed merely to reach and she was picked up; to open her mouth and she was fed; to poop and she was changed. It was lovely, it was wonderful, and it was all so easy that first year. The hardest part, Helen once or twice observed, was organizing the several thousand Instamatic snapshots that Theodore managed to produce instead of working on his dissertation.

A good hundred-and-forty of these documented Regina's first birthday party, including the shots of Regina's first taste of the famous secret recipe banana cream pie. "Give her some more!" Theodore exclaimed. "I need some close-ups!" More of the pie ended up on her face and on the floor than in her mouth, naturally, but the crowd just ate up her not eating it up. The party was such a smash that it even got written up on the Society page of *The Citizen Inquirer.* (Of course Theodore had already begun writing his amusing parenting columns for the paper, so the publicity was easy to come by.)

Almost everything was perfect.

Helen quit smoking. All right, not entirely: the habit begun in Eddie Love's convertible thirteen summers before would not be abandoned so easily, but with this beautiful little girl to take care of Helen simply didn't feel the same burning need to smoke. At the high point (or was it low?) she was down to two or three cigarettes a day, and only barely feeling the withdrawal.

True, there was the "soulmate" episode with Chuck and Maxine, a few months after Regina's birth, but its ramifications were not really to be felt for several years to come. And then Chuck finished his dissertation, got a terrific job at a first-rate university far away, and vanished along with Maxine and their little girl Donna; that was a rough spot for the Gales, but even the gloominess of the midsummer day on which they moved away was offset by the fact that Helen's boss had told her that morning that by the beginning of the following year he was planning again, after the pregnancy delay, to promote her to Buyer.

So Mr. and Mrs. Theodore Gale were feeling good. They were a family, Helen found herself thinking often, when they were out with Regina at the parks and playgrounds, when they were all three cozied into bed together. For the first time in a long time she felt part of a family.

They were complete.

And since their second wedding anniversary was approaching it was obvious they should do something special to celebrate it.

"The island," Theodore blurted to Helen one August weekend morning, in bed with fourteen-month-old Regina asleep between them. "Let's do it—just me and you—a long weekend."

"And the baby?" Helen asked.

"Your mom."

"For a whole weekend?"

"She'll manage." Theodore smiled and made the gesture of tipping a wine glass to his lips.

"Theodore, please."

"Right-o, beautiful, sorry. Benny, then."

"You know I love him almost as my own father, Theodore, but he would be so busy weeping he would forget to feed her."

"Helen." Theodore reached over to massage Helen's vagina through her tangerine nightie.

"Theodore!" Helen pushed his hand away.

"What? She's asleep."

"Please."

"All right. But Helen. Me and you—three days—alone. The island wants us that way. That is its whole purpose in existing. To be there for us. Us and this gorgeous love thing we have going on. Let's do it for the island. My baby. Let's make it happen."

And so make it they did.

Edna was actually thrilled to have Regina for a whole long weekend. Theodore and Helen more or less stayed in, on the island, the whole time—and indeed, as Theodore pointed out, he too more or less stayed in the whole time, in Helen. Or at least he did once Helen had given the old shack her parents had built on the speck of land decades before the usual once-over with her prized Hoover and twice-over with the disinfectants. On the night before their second anniversary Theodore proved once again that, despite being two years older and a little bit hairier and heavier, he was still pretty much the King of the Beasts.

Not triplets this time either, though, nor even twins.

Just one.

6

The second pregnancy was different from the first.

Much nausea, muscle ache, back pain, and correspondingly many hot water bottles, generally to little avail. Plenty of difficulty sleeping, even beyond that caused by her husband's production of deep-throated snores not unlike the mating calls of extremely horny grizzly bears. Hormone-induced mood swings presenting great emotional challenges for someone limiting herself to just a few cigarettes a day. This time she grew large quickly and was continuously aware of how unattractive she was, despite her husband's constantly suggesting they make love. Worst of all she developed gestational diabetes toward the end, which meant the suspension, at least, both of chocolates and of dessert. She even stopped making the banana cream pie in the final months. Combining all that with having to care for a toddler, with working full-time almost to the end, and did we mention the deficiency of nicotine, and Helen was having herself a pretty miserable time.

It didn't help much either that the toddler had taken lately to smacking her belly all the time.

Nor was it possible to conceal the pregnancy very long. Since she obviously couldn't do the necessary traveling while in the family way Helen had reluctantly informed her boss, by December, by her thirty-first birthday, that the promotion to Buyer would have to be delayed again until after the second baby arrived.

"Well, Helen," her boss said after a moment, standing quite tall and absolutely still in his crisply pressed Valentino suit. They were in his sunny office, surrounded by lamps and paintings and glass shelves lined with glossy craftwork from a world away. "Congratulations on the happy news. You must be overjoyed."

"We are," Helen said, not quite returning his gaze.

"Though I must admit I am sorry, for our sake, to hear of it."

"I admit I am sorry, for my sake, to say it."

He hesitated again, then smiled. "Well, you won't object this time, will you, if I acknowledge the happy news with another four months leave at half pay?"

Helen returned the smile and nodded, and appreciated the generosity of the offer; although she couldn't help noticing that this time he didn't offer to hold the Buyer position for her.

So it was a long and hard pregnancy, permeated with the disappointment of having to delay again the desired promotion. As the weather finally began to warm it was all Helen could do not to reach for the cigarettes stashed in the bedside table.

And then.

7

Artists and political leaders were being shot, violence was erupting on streets and campuses, and Helen's water broke—again—in the middle of a warm night in the second week in June.

Theodore was so deeply asleep—again—that she couldn't wake him. So she got out of bed and called the taxi, placed the pre-assembled bag of toddler food and snacks and diapers by the door, and got dressed. She then grabbed a grumpy Regina from her crib and together they set off from the apartment into the muggy early morning of the little girl's second birthday. Helen would have to remember to cancel the birthday party they'd planned for later that day.

When Theodore arrived at the hospital his wife was—again, again—stalled in labor. This time in the cafeteria he struck up a conversation with two other men who were first-timers and very nervous. He regaled them with the story of Regina's birth two years previously, which by now he'd nicely polished for his one-day future biographer: how he had rushed Helen to the hospital, spent hours by her side during her labor, wiped her forehead, gotten her water, assisted in the delivery, and then accepted the scissors and cut the umbilical cord.

This time there was no violence, at least.

Theodore returned to Helen's room some time later, bearing two paper cups of hot tea with milk. His arrival, thankfully, preceded the newborn's.

"My baby!" he exclaimed, kissing her forehead as he placed the cups on the shelf behind her and dropped into the chair next to her bed.

"Let me guess," Helen smiled weakly, looking up from the magazine the nurse had brought her, "you either made some friends or adopted some abandoned animal."

"Even better, I did both, my baby. I'm picking up the dog next week and we're sailing with the Wilsons as soon as you're back on your feet."

One of the men in the cafeteria had been the director of the local animal shelter and was much relieved to find a home for the poor animal with the cardiac condition. The other man had invited Theodore out to the marina for an excursion on the bay, and then, when Theodore mentioned his lifelong desire to learn to sail—formulated pretty much at that moment—he pulled out a business card and said, "Perfect! My wife's kid sister is working her way through college giving sailing lessons. Call her any time."

Helen put down the magazine. "Theodore."

"What?"

"You have a good heart."

"I know. Isn't it fantastic?"

"But we *are* about to have our second child. I am not sure that bringing home a—dog—right now is such a good idea."

"Of course it's a good idea. Kids love dogs."

"They are a lot of work. And money."

"But Hel," Theodore said earnestly, taking her hand. "The mutt has a *bad* heart, apparently. For which he needs a good home. Our home."

"Our small apartment, you mean."

"It's big enough, my baby. We'll make it work."

"And sailing? With a toddler and a baby?"

"We'll make that work too. Your mother can watch them. If we're brave enough." Theodore pretended to tip a wine glass to his lips and winked. He ignored Helen's disapproving sigh. "Speaking of whom, I assume she's got the older one?"

Helen sighed again and nodded as the nurse entered the room to check on her progress, or lack thereof. She knew that the best strategy was simply to wait: Theodore's admirable enthusiasm would likely wane before any concrete steps were taken toward actually acquiring the animal, much less arranging to go sailing.

They remained silent while the nurse took care of her business, but when it appeared she was going to be a while Theodore tentatively resumed.

"Listen, my beautiful wife. What's your sense of the timeline here? You know, how long till, um, Theodore Jr. makes his appearance?"

"A while, apparently. I am still barely dilated. Why, are you in a hurry?"

"Well, no, but Maxey and I—"

The nurse, overhearing, scowled at Theodore.

He glared back at her then looked back at Helen.

Helen took a deep breath as she felt the initial stages of another contraction. "No good," she said softly, "will come of that man."

"Maxey isn't that bad," Theodore protested.

"I was talking about you."

The nurse stifled a laugh.

"Do you mind?" Theodore said harshly.

"Press the button if you need anything, honey." The nurse left the room, though not before directing another backward scowl toward Theodore.

Theodore and Helen looked at each other.

Theodore looked closely at her delicate lips, the perspiration glistening just above them. If that wasn't a grimace of pain it just might have been the hint of a smile.

"You know, my baby," he continued cautiously, "with Regina you were in labor forever. Maybe that's your thing. You could be doing this all day. And it's not like I'm contributing anything to the process here anyway."

"True. Your contribution lasted about ten seconds, nine months ago."

38

No, Theodore realized, it was definitely *not* a smile.

"All right, I hear you," he said, winking, then standing up. He leaned over and kissed her forehead again. "I just need to make a quick phone call. Do you need another tea, or anything?"

Helen looked at him. He had made it to Regina's birth, two years ago to the day—the children were going to have the same birthday!—or at least he was on the premises at the crucial moment, and that wasn't bad for a man who needed periodically to be reminded where he was lest he wander off in search of the very spot where he already was standing. She'd had a dozen hours of labor with Regina, and every indication was that this one was going for the long haul as well.

But still.

"Nothing, thank you," she said softly.

"All right, then. And by the way," he added perfectly pleasantly from the door, "it's not the quantity of the contribution but its quality. I'll be right back." He winked again and stepped out.

Helen sighed heavily, looking at the closed door, not sure that its quality had been any more impressive than its quantity.

Her husband of almost three years already could be maddening, for sure. But you know, that could be all right; it *was* all right. He was everything she was not, but that wasn't *always* a criticism. Maybe he was too spontaneous for her taste sometimes, but his spontaneity was also one of his attractions. Maybe he was too inclined to favor a good time over the responsibilities of a spouse and a parent, but then again she, she knew, was too little so inclined. And maybe he wasn't always as attentive to grooming and hygiene as she might prefer; but then again she was the sort who washed the dishes before putting them into the brand-new electric dishwasher Benny had given them for their second anniversary and then rinsed them again upon taking them out—which even she realized might be a little excessive.

"If opposites attract," Theodore sometimes said in that occasional British accent of his, "then we, my lovely lady, are simply *smashing.*"

The intensifying contraction interrupted Helen's reverie.

8

And so off Theodore went.

But not to make a phone call.

Helen had entered labor at a most inconvenient time. He and Maxey had had tickets for months to that afternoon's important game. What made the game important was that it marked the debut of Maxey's latest innovation, where his customers could now place bets not merely on the game's outcome but on the precise totals of runs, hits, and errors. In those days before computers this sort of bookmaking required elaborate systems of bookkeeping, which Theodore had helped Maxey develop. Theodore had assured Maxey that Helen's love for him was so strong at this point that she would have no problem with his popping out to the game, despite the circumstances. The stadium was just twenty minutes from the hospital after all, and he could call in from a payphone every inning. Maxey had wagered him that Theodore wouldn't even have the guts to mention the game to her.

There was a reason Maxey was so successful.

Maxey was sitting in the general waiting area of the hospital. He had brought a small cooler of beers imported from one of the few remaining nations where human slavery was still legal, and had reserved several seats in front of the large black-and-white television so they could spread out. Theodore asked the receptionist to notify him if the delivery got underway and sat down beside Maxey as the game was starting.

"I can only stay a few minutes," he said, forking over several bills from his wallet.

"So you say, big guy."

"Just one quick beer," Theodore said.

Maxey twisted open a bottle and handed it over. This was in the days, incidentally, before twist-off bottle caps.

Theodore spent the first three innings trying to convince Maxey how terrific family and fatherhood were, how much he loved his wife and his daughter and couldn't wait for Theodore Jr. to join them. He already had big plans for teaching the boy about sports, about chasing girls, and especially about the sport *of* chasing girls. Maxey, who knew better than to complicate the good thing he had going on—his life—with women, or at least semi-permanent women, resisted Theodore's arguments. There were plenty of guys to play sports with after all, and few were better at chasing girls than he; having a kid could only hamper his own successes at scoring, both in sports and with females.

Theodore would not give in.

"You just can't imagine," he said, grabbing another beer at the start of the fourth inning, "how amazing it is having this little creature to whom you mean absolutely everything in the world. Those little eyes look up at you, worshipping you. And you just think: 'I made this thing. It's mine, and it worships me.'"

"Yeah," Maxey said, "that's pretty much the way chicks look at me when I'm balling them." For emphasis he turned and directed his unblinking eye at Theodore.

"No, seriously."

"What you seem to want, Teddy boy, is to be a god. Me, I'm happy being just a sex god."

"I'm not disparaging sex godhood, Max. But it's transient. It fades. While fatherhood, my friend, that's permanent, it's good for your whole goddamn life."

"Well, it works all right for me," Maxey said, becoming distracted as the visiting team scored a run: if they could hold precisely that lead he stood to make a fortune.

The receptionist was heading their way.

9

"So?" Theodore rushed into the delivery room.

There were people everywhere, doctors, nurses, others. Machines were whirring and creaking, fizzling tubes connecting to fizzling tubes, everyone talking at once. Theodore saw Helen in bed with her face as white as the pre-birth sheets, utterly exhausted, having just pulled through a difficult breech delivery with dangerously heavy bleeding. She would have to remain in the hospital, she would soon learn, for more than ten days after the delivery. But she had at last made it and was now just managing to cradle the screaming newborn swaddled in her arms.

"My babies!" Theodore exclaimed toward mother and child, pushing through, averting his gaze from the soiled sheets.

"Theodore," Helen whispered weakly.

"Let me see him! Is he as handsome as his dad?"

"No," Helen answered almost inaudibly beneath the roar of the room. "Only as hairy. Do you think," she could barely lift those soft hazel eyes toward her husband, "you could take her please?"

"Her?"

Little furry Debra was not enthusiastic about entering this world. After resisting delivery feet first she promptly commenced an hours-long crying jag that the medical staff was still talking about months later. Hers was a soul-piercing scream, an agonizing howl that even penetrated the low-blood-pressure-induced nearly comatose state into which Helen was just falling, and certainly threatened emotional harm to the medical personnel still working in the room. Helen remained just alert enough to look at her hirsute new baby and wonder how she would nurse the little thing if she were to pass out, which she almost did.

Theodore approached for his first look at his screaming new daughter, without taking her from his wife's arms.

"Well, *that's* a generous nose," he finally said, "if it *is* a nose." True, little Debra had gotten a bit mushed up on the way out, and with all that screaming as a distraction it wasn't so easy to identify all her features.

"Theodore," Helen whispered.

"My baby," Theodore said, looking at her.

It only occurred to Helen later that Theodore never took the Instamatic out of the bag she had packed for the hospital.

10

If little Debra was unhappy about arriving then Regina, her elder sister by exactly two years, was not any better pleased.

As an adult Regina would sometimes brandish a certain intense expression in which she pursed her lips, arched an eyebrow, flared a nostril, and glared. When she directed it toward you it made you long for an icy arrow through your heart, since that would be less unpleasant. Whatever you were doing, you had to do something different. If you were approaching, you'd immediately retreat; if you were retreating, you'd accelerate; if you were cheerful you became depressed; if depressed you became suicidal. This expression made its debut when Regina, accompanied by her Grandma Edna, entered the hospital room and saw baby Debra for the first time. The toddler had had no *real* idea of what was coming, of course. She'd noticed her mother's growing belly, had sort of understood that she had a sibling on the way even if you couldn't quite be sure that her repeated blows to her mother's belly had anything to do with that sibling. She also knew that something important was happening when her mother woke her in the night and took her to the hospital, from where her grandmother had then whisked her away for a couple of days; and she vaguely grasped that her birthday party had been canceled; yet she had never fully pieced it all together. But that moment when she entered the room, saw her mother in bed, saw her holding—that *thing*—she suddenly understood and she was none too pleased.

The toddler froze on the spot and unleashed the expression.

"I don't think," Edna observed, "that Regina is very happy to meet her sister."

"Of course she is," Helen insisted, as optimistically as she could given her complete lack of sleep in the forty-eight hours since Debra's arrival. "Regina, can you say hello to your new little sister? Can you say, 'Hi, Deb'?"

Regina glared.

Slowly her lips unpursed, a little.

"Dub," she said grumpily.

"That's so cute," Helen whispered. "Don't you think so, Dad?"

Benny was sitting in the corner of the room, weeping. Baby Debra—little Dub—was oblivious to Regina's glare and merely continued screaming. Theodore, who had just finished another year of graduate school, was over at the university distributing Maxey's Cubans instead of figuring out how, as he had been assigned, to squeeze the second crib into Regina's small room at their apartment.

He never did get around to the shelter to pick up that dog.

11

As if the screaming and mushed features were not enough, Debra's acceptance into this new world was made even less smooth by the fact that she was born with a seriously unattractive case of eczema. Only Helen could even tolerate Deb in those first few days, but by the end of the first week of all that screaming even she was an absolute wreck, alternatively contemplating infanticide, suicide, and mass homicide. Her doctor insisted she see a psychoanalyst, whom she somehow squeezed into those hectic weeks after the arrival of a new baby, especially a second baby, especially one that was being so ridiculously impossible to breastfeed. The analyst, an arrogant bastard fresh from his fourth or fifth graduate degree, immediately proclaimed that her murderous desires were not due to her having just gone through a long stressful pregnancy and life-threatening delivery but to her whole preceding lifetime of harboring painful secrets that only he could expose and expunge.

"Four or five days of analysis a week," he pronounced as he peered at her through his tiny round glasses, "four or five years tops, and you'll be a new woman—guaranteed."

This diagnosis and prognosis did wonders for Helen's mood, as you can imagine.

Meanwhile Theodore could not bring himself to touch the new baby.

At the beginning he was subtle about it, merely disappearing at diaper-changing times and bedtimes. Helen didn't realize what was going on since she was too busy thinking about what weapons to acquire to care about other people's motivations. But after a couple of days Theodore became less subtle, and finally he just said: "My baby, this kills me to say this, but I just find that skin thing sort of—repulsive. Honestly, Hel, I feel terrible. But I swear to you, I'll pull my weight around here once the doctors get it cleared up."

And throughout those first couple of weeks, while the doctors were dealing with the eczema and Theodore was invisible and Helen was doing everything just to hold things together, the toddler Regina could invariably be found in the background glaring at the new, ugly, loud addition to the family.

And oh, the travails with the nursing of this new baby, this little why-must-you-be-so-difficult Dub! Who knew that something so natural could be so terribly unnatural?

The sleeplessness; the screaming, hungry infant gumming at her sore swollen nipples every two or three hours; the painful recovery from labor and delivery, her aching swollen genitals, the healing stitches, the hemorrhoids from pushing so hard; the long frustrating wait for the milk to come in; the painful engorgement as the milk finally began to dribble into her breasts, then dribble out, and then flow copiously in but still only dribble out for some reason; the difficulty in getting this baby to latch properly onto the areolae and not merely to gum, hard, her oversensitive and now cracking nipples; the mastitis which developed when the milk got backed up which felt like a thousand burning hot needles piercing every ounce of flesh in her breasts; and did we mention the sleeplessness, the swollen genitals, and the hemorrhoids?

Edna was there, ostensibly to help—and she *was* doing most of the cooking and cleaning during those first weeks back home—but still Edna came from the generation where nursing was straightforward and had had no trouble with all five of her own babies, so she just couldn't understand what the problem was, especially since everything had gone smoothly with Regina. Nor was it helpful that Benny visited constantly during these weeks, despite all his fresh ice cream, since Helen was not exactly comfortable whipping her breasts out in his presence and so felt extremely inhibited in this difficult project of trying to love her new baby. Thank goodness that Jacqueline was too busy with her own two little girls, and Melvin with his two boys, to be offering any additional "help."

And Theodore—well, Theodore was all right, despite his inability to touch little Dub.

He brought in the chocolates, which Helen could now begin consuming again. He kept the pansies fresh around the apartment. And he was supportive in just the right ways throughout the breastfeeding ordeal. Early on, when it became clear that it was not going to be easy, he had first said, tenderly, "My baby, listen to me. These days women are being liberated not merely from their bras but from their breasts. And baby formula is being touted as the greatest invention since sliced bread. And anyway, speaking of bread, don't you have your career to think about? The promotion? Do you really want to be shackled by feeding a baby instead?"

"Theodore," Helen said gratefully. "I appreciate those points. I really do. But this is something I need to do. At least through the maternity leave."

"Right-o," Theodore said without hesitating. "Then we shall do it." (He later included this exchange in his article on the politics of breastfeeding in *The Citizen Inquirer*.)

Theodore's support was essential those first weeks. And thus one would so dearly like to say—and Theodore did imagine himself saying to his one-day future biographer—that by means of his heroic support they were able to reach that happy ending; that after the trials and tribulations the new baby was finally to figure out what to do with her mother's breasts, that those breasts were finally to figure out what to do with the new baby, and that they were all to start building their new life as a truly complete family of four auspiciously approaching the Age of Aquarius.

Alas, that was not to be.

After a few weeks little Dub finally stopped screaming *quite* so much. Around the same time the doctors managed to get her eczema under control until even Theodore was willing to pick her up. By this time Helen's murderous rage had become more modest in scope and intensity, focused now on the psychoanalyst himself, toward whom she found herself with feelings both of deep love and of violent murder. Regina too stopped glaring so continuously, slowly realizing that her glare alone would not rid the house of this abomination and that she'd have to wait until she was older, bigger, and stronger before taking matters into her own hands.

And along the way, maybe four weeks in, Helen woke up one morning after another awful night with this sleepless baby, just blurted out the words "Fuck this!", filled up a bottle with the Starlac's Powdered Milk that Theodore had thoughtfully stashed next to the bed and stuck it, perhaps a little too forcefully, in the baby's mouth. With some maneuvering with her other hand she managed to withdraw a cigarette from the bedside table too, light it, and stick it, perhaps a little too forcefully, in her own mouth.

Theodore, on hearing the news later in the day, tried to stroke his wife's hair.

"Please don't," she said, and turned away.

Maxey, meanwhile, just smiled. He had made a killing on the wagers he'd been taking on the date on which the nursing project would be abandoned.

The business of childhood got underway.

CHAPTER THREE
SEPARATE BUT EQUAL

1

History is filled with game-changing events. The inventions of written language, the wheel; the birth of Christ; that sort of thing. It would obviously be an exaggeration to suggest that Debra's arrival was to the three-member Gale family as any of these events was to the subsequent course of the world.

But maybe not by much.

"Theodore," Helen had said in bed after almost two-year-old Regina had gone down to sleep, a few weeks before little Dub debuted. "Have you thought about childcare after the baby comes?"

Theodore was reading beside her while she knitted a new cover for the hot water bottle. Their bedroom was crammed with the toddler and baby gear that had no place else to go in the apartment, including the crib Jacqueline had given them—with each of her own babies Jacqueline upgraded to the latest models—still waiting to be assembled. The subtle scent of Helen's green tea perfume was just detectable, if you concentrated.

"No," Theodore said without looking up from his book.

"Well since your offspring is almost here, Professor, would you consider giving it some thought now?"

He put down his book and thought for a moment. "Done."

"And?"

"Your mother."

"What about my mother?"

"Can't we just carry on as we have?"

"I don't think so, Theodore. Two children is not the same as one. And—" She pushed his hand away from her thigh. "Stop that! This is important!"

"So is this, my baby."

She half-smiled. "Please, Theodore."

"All right," he harrumphed, withdrawing his hand. "So what's the problem? Regina's easy. She naps half the day, according to Edna. And the baby will just lie there. Why can't the old lady take care of them?"

"Because that old lady is getting older," Helen said gently enough, "and because, as I was saying, two small children is at least one more than one."

"All right, then, what's your proposal?"

"Well, how would you feel about taking a break from your program?"

"No, seriously, what's your proposal?"

There was a long and heavy silence.

Both were now sitting straight up in bed.

"Consider the facts objectively, Theodore," Helen continued cautiously. "We cannot afford both children in a commercial daycare. My mother cannot take care of both children, at least not full-time. So one of us will have to contribute."

Theodore remained silent.

"And there is the financial aspect. I make more money than you do at the moment, and will continue to until you finish your program, especially with my promotion after the maternity leave. If I stop working we simply cannot get by with two children on your stipend. But if you take a break from your program then between you and my mother we can get both the children and our bills covered. Unless …"

"What?"

"Do you want to ask your father for help?"

"I am not asking Benny for help. Not for this."

"Then the conclusion is inescapable, I think."

"No conclusion is inescapable, my baby," Theodore answered, having finally concluded that this conversation was inescapable. "Listen."

"Yes?"

"I can't stop the program, Helen, not now. My articles are getting some attention now. I'm already probably the world's leading expert on Ignoratio P. Elenchi and once I finish my dissertation the world is going to know that—and that is our ticket out of here. I'm talking big—a big job, a big salary. Once I'm finished I'll get you to your promised land without even cracking open your long journey box to get there. It would be a *tremendous*

48

mistake for me to stop now."

"But you have been in the program—seven years already, Theodore."

"That's what it takes, my baby, to do groundbreaking work. Just a year or two more now. I promise."

"And what are we to do when this baby comes?"

"There are other options for making money."

"You are *not* going to mention those 'Make Supper, Not War' aprons again."

Theodore cleared his throat. "I suppose not."

"Or those pamphlets on how to promote hair loss."

"Hey! We live in hairy times. It was reasonable to assume other men share my condition."

"Next."

"Fine, fine." Theodore licked his lips. "How about this, you beautiful, gorgeous, red-hot mama. Maybe *you* could go part-time at work."

"I'm sorry?"

"Hear me out. You go part-time at work while I finish my degree. You'll still earn more than me, and with that income and my stipend, and between you and your mother, maybe we can get both the kids and our bills covered, as you put it. That way you get to work, I get to finish my program, and everyone is taken care of. And then once I'm finished I'll be making much better money, the kids will soon be in school, and you can go back to full-time, if you want."

"Our finances would be very tight."

"For a while. But we'll make it work. I'll make it work."

Helen paused. "I do not believe I could become a Buyer working part-time."

"Talk to your boss, my baby. He loves you."

"I *know* that I could not be a Buyer working part-time."

"I'll talk to him."

"You will do no such thing."

"Listen. My baby," Theodore said. "I'll help out with the childcare too. Maybe some afternoons here or there. I promise. We can make this work. There's just too much at stake with my work for me to abandon it now. And we could hold off on your promotion for a while. Long run, we get everything we want. The promised land too, maybe. Think about it?"

"Stop that!" She sharply pushed his hand from her thigh.

And so, after several more conversations and some serious soul searching, Helen resigned herself to delaying her promotion to Buyer yet again. When her generous maternity leave was finished she returned half-time to her regular mind-numbing job, working afternoons while devoting mornings to the much harder job of being a Mummy. She would get to be with her babies, she thought to herself, trying to overcome the disappointment.

And anyway it would just be for a year or two, until Theodore finished.

2

Theodore meant to live up to his promises. But life with two small children can get pretty overwhelming, and Theodore was never one to flourish, exactly, when things got overwhelming.

Their screaming bundle of eczema was brought home to their suddenly *very* small apartment ten days after its appearance, after Helen's health had been cleared from the delivery. The first change in the household, after the new decibel level, was that Regina promptly stopped napping. The running theory was that she did so to keep her eye—her glare—fixed on this thing which had not only taken away her second birthday party but was now making moves on the splendid Regina-centered world she had spent two glorious years cultivating.

The next change was that Helen's mother seemed suddenly to decline. Before Debra's birth Edna had been a spry sixty-one-year-old, enlivened by her role as the primary caregiver for the world's most perfect toddler. Deb's arrival—and Edna hated to admit this—felt like an intrusion into this private domain. Almost overnight Regina seemed more wary, her eyes no longer on her doting Grandmother but tracking, always tracking, the new baby. And whereas Edna's days with Regina used to leave her energized she now found herself feeling more run-down, and in need of more, and earlier, glasses of wine. She particularly dreaded the afternoons, when she was alone with both little girls at once.

The next change was that Theodore began to fear for his safety within his own home.

Sure, the baby Regina had left marks on him, but somehow it was always adorable when she pinched or bit or scratched. But new baby Debra had a *serious* tendency to pinch and to scratch, and as her teeth came in also to chew, and somehow it was never adorable when *she* did these things. Theodore could only hope it was no portent that one of the first things she did once he began to hold her, after the eczema cleared up, was to slap his face repeatedly with her little hand, which she did with startling vehemence. And when he learned to hold her facing outward to avoid the slapping she promptly learned the reverse head butt, thrusting her head back hard into his chest, throat, and/or nose. Remarkably this never seemed to faze her, even when everyone present clearly heard the loud smack of skull against Theodore's bones.

No, it was *not* adorable, Theodore thought one evening, fingering a large bruise in that thin sliver of red skin between his beard line and his right eye; but at least some good came of it, as his classic column in *The Citizen Inquirer* ("The Hidden Dangers Of Childhood—For The Parents") enjoyed some acclaim.

But again, he really tried to make it work. For those first few months he continued bringing home chocolates and flowers even though Helen seemed more irritated than pleased. He'd bring home some fresh pansies, for example, and she would comment, "I suppose we can do without the grocery money this week"; or he surprised her by picking up the new LP of Schubert's Trout Quintet she'd been talking about and she only commented that he was late to dinner. But he persisted. When Edna needed to leave early one afternoon to get some medical tests done he offered to watch the girls in her place.

"I'm sorry?" Helen asked.

"I'll do it," he repeated.

"Are you sure?"

"It's only for an hour. You'll be back by 5:15, right?"

"Definitely, if you are watching the children."

He laughed. The teasing was refreshing; there hadn't been much of that recently.

"Look, just leave some instructions, some phone numbers, plenty of diapers. How hard could it be?"

"Thank you, Theodore," Helen said gratefully, though it did cross her mind that something felt off about thanking your spouse for watching your jointly produced children. "Why don't I just show you now where I keep the formula?"

The day arrived.

Theodore, who'd spent the morning at his office doing

something or other, returned to the apartment just ten minutes late, at 4:25 PM, to relieve Edna. Edna was relieved to be relieved; thin and pale, she was exhausted by the task of keeping Regina away from the baby all afternoon long. She donned her thick coat against the early autumn chill, got into the taxi Helen had ordered, and headed off to find out exactly what was wrong with her lately. Theodore looked at the clock—4:29 PM—looked at baby Debra kicking quietly on her back in the bassinet, and then looked at Regina standing in the corner, staring at the bassinet and clearly trying to calculate whether she could get there before being intercepted.

"Aw, you're so cute," Theodore said, somehow mistaking her expression for one of affection for her sister. "Now what should we do for the next—oh Jesus, forty-six minutes?"

Helen managed to leave work early and not a minute too soon. She walked in the door at 5:01 PM, just thirty-two minutes after Edna had walked out, to find the apartment in disarray, baby Debra screaming naked on her back in her bassinet, Regina screaming in her playpen restrained by the toddler harness that Theodore had wound through the playpen bars, and Theodore also screaming, flat on his own back on the living room floor, while a small fire burned for some reason in the kitchen trash can.

"What's that stench?" Helen shouted, wisely running to extinguish the fire first.

"Poop everywhere," Theodore moaned.

"You couldn't get them changed?"

"I'm talking about myself."

"Jesus! What happened here?"

"It's all just a terrible blur," Theodore moaned.

Helen had picked up Debra, who finally stopped screaming, and was now trying to free Regina from the playpen.

"What is this?" she demanded.

"European Death Knot," Theodore answered from the floor. Maxey had taught him this one for one of their recent endeavors. "Sounds worse than it is."

"Jesus," she said, setting Regina down on the floor, who promptly began trying to reach up to pinch the baby.

"Helen," Theodore said quietly.

"You will wait," she said, "until I am smoking."

Theodore knew better than to interrupt. Helen fumbled

through her purse, holding Deb just out of Regina's reach, found herself a cigarette, lit up, and inhaled deeply.

"This is not," Theodore finished, his eyes still closed, "for me."

It wasn't exactly for Edna, either. After learning that this, that, and the other in her bloodstream were not all they were supposed to be, it became clear that she couldn't maintain all the childcare they had counted on her to do. To pick up the slack Helen dropped down to just ten hours a week at her job. Well, she would get to spend even more time with her babies, she consoled herself, about as convincingly as that sounded.

Theodore, meanwhile, continued to progress on his dissertation at exactly the same pace—whatever that was.

3

Though Theodore and Jacqueline agreed on little, they did agree on this.

"You're ridiculous," Theodore also said when Helen confronted him about the soulmate question, three-and-a-half years after the fact.

Let's briefly step back those several years. Snipers were gunning down students and cultures were revolving when Theodore and Helen were celebrating their first wedding anniversary on that sunny but cool Labor Day afternoon. Chuck and Maxine were over at the apartment with their eight-month-old Donna, enjoying drinks and cigarettes and departmental gossip. While three-month-old Regina napped in her crib and Helen was busy in the kitchen mixing more Rusty Nails, Theodore had, in honor of their anniversary, just told the story of his umbrella's fateful engagement with Helen's at the payphones at Seventeenth and Waterhouse.

"Far out!" Chuck exclaimed.

"That, Theo," Maxine added, holding Donna at her breast, "is the world's sweetest story."

"And how did *you* two meet?" Helen asked, returning to the room with the fresh drinks on an exquisite ivory serving tray.

Just as sweetly, it turned out. A restaurant hostess had mixed up their separate blind dates, leading Chuck to Maxine's table instead of the man Maxine's girlfriend was actually trying to fix her up with. Ten minutes later the embarrassed young woman brought the intended man over, a smug business type in a fancy suit who loudly began demanding that Chuck leave. "So Chuck glances at him,"

Maxine's eyes twinkled, "and says, 'I'll thank you not to speak that way in front of my soulmate, pal.' He then stands up. And he was of course maybe twice the guy's size."

"Now *that*," Helen said, "is the world's sweetest story."

"Yeah," Maxine smiled. "That guy now runs one of the biggest electronics companies in the world. And I'm stuck with a graduate student."

"Hey, baby," Chuck laughed, "it's not my fault if *your* soulmate is a graduate student."

"Theodore," Helen suddenly said, moved both by the alcohol and by the romantic story. "Am I *your* soulmate?"

Jacqueline told her she was overreacting.

"He said *yes*, Helen, for crying out loud!" Jacqueline said the next morning over the telephone. "What more do you want?"

"There was something about the *way* he said it," Helen answered, smoking as she watched Regina in the living room trying to turn onto her tummy on the new Couristan rug. "He *hesitated*."

"Helen. Maybe he just had to inhale before speaking."

"No, there was definitely a pause. As if he had to think about it."

"You're totally ridiculous, and I'm hanging up now." Jacqueline hung up to resume watching television while her babysitter was out strolling with almost two-year-old Caroline, and also to let the sperm inside her finish making her next daughter.

No, Theodore and Jacqueline never did get along well. Jacqueline, unlike Maxine, thought that the only husband worth having was one who not only wore expensive clothes but more importantly bought expensive clothes for his wife. Despite making some effort she was simply unable to suppress how little she thought of people who spent their whole lives in school. The fact that she never exactly understood the difference between college and graduate school only increased the friction. Jacqueline, maybe attempting to be nice, might ask Theodore how college was going, or what he was majoring in, much to his irritation.

Anyway Theodore and Jacqueline did agree on this.

"You're ridiculous," Theodore also said, about three-and-a-half years later, smoking one evening with Helen in that same small living room with the no-longer-so-new Couristan rug.

This was now almost two years after Deb's birth. In contrast to her older sister Deb was a difficult baby—colicky, a bad sleeper, impossible to nurse—and that of course only raised the level of tension in the house. By the unfortunate order of her birth as well it was Deb who often shouldered blame for the family's increasingly tight finances, which in turn sparked any number of unpleasant conversations. This particular quarrel was triggered by Theodore's arriving home after the girls were in bed and announcing that, despite his still not having completed his dissertation a full nine years into his program and Helen's promotion having been delayed again by Debra's arrival, he had on a whim purchased a small sailboat.

Helen—exhausted by her parental responsibilities, her sleep deprivation, her job, and the fact that it was her responsibility to make family ends meet—responded as any normal person would. We needn't determine here how the sailboat discussion led back to the soulmate controversy; suffice to say that, as these things tend to go, this one did.

"How is that ridiculous?" she demanded.

"For more reasons than I can list," Theodore continued, firmly putting out his cigarette in the crystal ashtray on the tea table. "First, I doubt that I did hesitate. Second, even if I did, it meant nothing. Third, most of all," he was getting even redder than usual, "that was over three years ago and here you are mentioning it like it occurred yesterday!"

"So?"

"Have you been simmering over this for the past three years?"

"Not continuously."

"Helen, please. You can't hold me responsible for ancient history."

"Three years is hardly ancient history."

"The key word is 'history.' It's done, over, past. I don't even remember what you're talking about, so how could I possibly defend or explain it? I sincerely doubt it even occurred, frankly. You were probably just overthinking, overanalyzing. Like you always do."

"Maybe. Or maybe not."

"Helen. Listen. You are my gorgeous wife, and the mother of my gorgeous daughters, and I love you and you are my soulmate. I said all that as quickly as I could."

"Yes, almost as quickly as you bought that dinghy."

Theodore sighed. "It's a sailboat, Helen. And this was going to be a surprise, but I've also started sailing lessons. I just thought about how much fun we could have this summer. Drop the girls with your mother, maybe with Benny, go sailing on the bay, just the two of us. It will be a blast. Fun, you know? Don't you think?"

Well, maybe she *was* being too hard on him, she thought as she looked into his deep blue eyes. She could imagine him looking handsome in a sailor's outfit, that barrel chest of his stretching the white fabric. And maybe in a couple of years, when the girls were older, they could all go sailing as a family. That would be—fun.

"All right," she finally said, gently extinguishing her own cigarette next to his. "I suppose we shall figure out how to pay for it."

"Exactly!" Theodore said, now hopefully. "I'll see if the chair can get me an extra course to teach in the fall or something. So, are we good—soulmate?"

They were good, for the time being anyway. And they did have a great adventure sailing on the bay some weeks later, thanks to an unexpected storm and their exciting Coast Guard rescue.

Much less great was how that day worked out for their babysitter.

For poor Edna Faire, whose life in every meaningful sense other than biological stopped when her husband's biological one prematurely did, whose beloved boys had scattered in pursuit of careers or marriages or long prison sentences, it would be pretty much downhill from this day, literally. For at about the same moment that Theodore and Helen were culminating their sailing adventure back home with some energetic lovemaking on their Couristan rug, Mayer Alden's widow was rushing up the steep staircase to the third floor of her home to retrieve her younger granddaughter, who had just scampered up there screaming.

"Debra!" she shouted up, pausing to catch her breath a half-dozen steps below. "You come back down this instant!"

The toddler was too busy screaming, or maybe just too busy being almost two years old, to pay her any attention, and continued climbing.

Grandma Edna gently moved the older granddaughter out of her way and resumed her pursuit. Whether she slipped or tripped is not clear; but in any case what resulted was a significant stumble down that was definitely inadvisable for an already declining woman in her early sixties. Just as she came to a rest at the bottom of the stairs she felt a small twinge in her hip. The injury itself was a minor hairline fracture. But the fracture wasn't treated properly, and led to an infection which was not diagnosed in a timely way; which then required a surgery, resulting in a complication, and in turn an extended hospital stay. And as almost any competent doctor can tell you the hospital is about the last place you want to be if you want to stay healthy. They never were able to diagnose just which bacterium was ultimately responsible. Five months after the fall down the stairs, Edna was not entirely unhappily reunited with her dear husband.

Helen was alone with her mother when she passed.

She just stared silently for the longest time when the breathing stopped.

This chain of events naturally meant the end of the Gale family sailboat. Theodore's interest in sailing had diminished by the summer at any rate, a few weeks after the adorable sailing instructor graduated from college and moved on to other pursuits, roughly a year before they were able to sell the boat, at a loss, to an underfunded public summer camp, and long before they ever got around to going sailing together as a family.

4

What if Debra hadn't been born.

Then Theodore wouldn't have met that guy in the hospital cafeteria, and that guy wouldn't have given Theodore his wife's sister's card, and Theodore wouldn't have called the sailing instructor and bought the sailboat, and he and Helen wouldn't have dropped the girls at Edna's to go sailing, and Edna wouldn't have died (or at least not then). But Debra *was* born and all that happened, and six months after Theodore finally earned his doctoral degree the Gales moved all their things from their cramped downtown apartment along with most of Edna's old furniture from storage into the new old house that Grandpa Benny bought for them out on Riverbend Road.

By this point young Debra no longer screamed *all* the time. This was possibly because in that alternative reality of small children she believed that her older sister was simply the most wonderful thing in the world. The four-year-old younger sister adored Regina and continued to adore Regina, long after the empirical evidence suggested she might do otherwise. During her several-year-long screaming phase in fact nobody could calm her down the way Regina could, who merely needed to enter the room for Deb's screams soon to turn to snorts, then whimpers, then giggles. Not that Regina was always aiming for this effect. Sometimes she'd cast her most intense glares at her sister and the stupid little girl would be giggling before she knew it. This annoyed Regina terribly, almost as much as when she would wake up in the morning to find Deb on the floor in her room next to her bed gazing at her, waiting for her to get up so they could play.

"Get out of my room," the older sister grumbled the first time this occurred.

"Let's have a tea party!" the younger sister exclaimed.

By the time Helen intervened, maybe two minutes later, Regina had screaming Deb in the headlock that Theodore had taught her, having learned it himself from Maxey's recent reminder of a small past-due IOU. Oddly, though, Deb didn't learn the lesson, and there she was the next morning on the floor next to Regina's bed, waiting for Regina to get up so they could play.

And play they did on that next day, at least for a few minutes, before Helen had to intervene. This was during the early years, before Helen learned to stop intervening altogether, for at some point you realize that your efforts are doomed to fail—and who knows what frustration Helen might have been spared had she learned what Theodore learned so quickly, that the conflict between the two sisters was just slightly less resolvable than the Middle Eastern one all over the news those days and just slightly more likely to result in violence?

As they got older the competition between them became ruthless. If one received three pancakes for breakfast then the other had to have four, which meant the first required another helping. If one got a new bike the other had to have a new bike, of the same color at least. Back-to-school shopping had to be done on the same day lest one have something even a day before the other. (This was the one advantage of their sharing a birthday: they received their presents simultaneously.) And when Regina began piano lessons at the age of seven Deb had to begin them on the same day at the age of five; it was all Helen could do to work out who would have the first lesson, and at what time on that day. Her initial proposal was to get them separate teachers so they could start at the same hour but both girls objected, worrying that the other's teacher was the better teacher. The obvious response here was to switch the teachers but each girl objected again, worrying that maybe she'd been wrong about who was the better teacher.

It was around then that Theodore wandered in. Instead of taking a break from his dissertation he was now taking a break from the book he was producing from his dissertation.

"What's with all the accounting gear?" he asked Helen. She had some yellow legal pads before her scribbled with notes and was pressing buttons on the adding machine she used to pay their bills. She was even sporting the little green plastic visor she'd acquired during one of Wickenden's terrific sales.

"I am trying to implement your suggestion that the girls take piano lessons."

"What's the problem?"

"What *isn't* the problem? First there is the piano. Then there are the lessons. And then," Helen reached over to separate the girls, who were pulling each others' hair, "there are the girls. And did I mention the money? Or lack thereof?"

"Well, my baby, I am here to solve your problems. First, the money: we'll make it work. Second, the piano: the university sells off its old pianos every fall, which just happens to be next week. Third, the lessons," he'd glanced at Helen's notes and gleaned the basic issue, "they'll just take lessons together, at the same time with the same teacher."

"And the girls?"

Regina and Deb were at opposite ends of the table glaring at each other.

"Sorry, got a meeting," Theodore said on his way out the door.

The money? Helen made it work, this time by cutting back on their contributions to the long journey box for their eventual trip to the promised land. The piano: the solution was to rent one, since they couldn't afford even the used ones from the university. The lessons: the first two teachers quit before the first hour was up, unable to tolerate the constant bickering between their pupils. Finally Helen simply flipped a coin to determine that Regina would get one teacher and Deb another, and declared that if one teacher happened to be available for the first lesson before the other, then so be it. The girls surprisingly acquiesced with only minor grumbling. Or maybe not so surprisingly: Helen had calmly put out her cigarette before declaring and even they knew enough to behave when their mother appeared outwardly calm when not smoking.

In this case at least their competitiveness had one benefit, for they were competitive quitters too. When Regina announced after about six weeks that she had had enough Deb immediately quit as well, afraid that Regina had found something more fun to do and not wanting to risk being left out.

Helen, as relieved at the end of their fighting over practice time on the piano as she was annoyed that they'd already paid the minimum three-month rental, sighed and lit another cigarette.

5

Of course Helen couldn't dwell on the piano problem since there were plenty of other things to get upset about. Clothes, jewelry, food, toys, personal space: everything was a source of friction if one girl had more of it or less of it than the other. Deb learned to count, Theodore wrote in one of his parenting columns, only to make sure her portions were equal to Regina's. Not that he knew this firsthand: he was often so busy writing these columns that he had to rely on Helen for material.

You might think that the solution was just to ensure their portions were always equal. Then again you'd merely have to drop by for a few minutes during these years to understand why peace was more likely in the aforementioned Middle East than in the house on Riverbend Road.

Start with this typical breakfast scene.

Regina had asked for Frosted Alpha-Bits; or more accurately demanded them despite Helen's efforts to get her to sprinkle an occasional please and thank you into her speech. But before Helen could even retrieve the bowl Deb began to cry and refused to stop until she got her own Frosted Alpha-Bits for breakfast.

"You shall have them, just be patient a moment," Helen said, retrieving two cereal bowls from the cabinet.

"Mine first!" Regina demanded. "I asked first."

"You shall get them at the same time."

"I want the purple bowl!" Deb objected as Helen slid that bowl in front of Regina.

"No, I get the purple bowl! I asked first."

"You asked for the cereal first, not for the purple bowl!"

"If I get the cereal first, you retard, I get the bowl it comes in."

"Mummy!" Deb wailed.

"Debra," Helen inhaled deeply, "it does not matter what color your bowl is. And Regina, why are you not eating?"

"I don't like Dummo Dubbo always copying me. I don't want her eating the same cereal as me."

"Mummy!"

Helen ignored Debra's wail. "But what difference could it make to you if Debra has her own bowl?"

Regina didn't reply, too busy spelling out the words "I HATE DUB" in her bowl. The girl was stubborn. Helen puffed frantically on her cigarette, waiting for Regina to eat the cereal as the minutes before departure for school and work ticked off. She finally gave in, quickly making Regina a bagel for breakfast instead. But the respite was both illusory and brief. No sooner did Deb see the bagel on Regina's plate than she began screaming for a bagel too, and on the purple plate.

Maybe all this would have been tolerable had it been all Helen had to deal with on a school day. But breakfast occurred after getting dressed had occurred, and getting dressed occurred after waking up. And neither of those were walks in the park either.

By this period Deb was taking after her father in her ability to sleep through thunderstorms, earthquakes, and small nuclear holocausts. Waking her up in time to get her through her dawdling approach to dressing in order to get her to breakfast and out the door on time generally required the use of at least two cattle prods, on Helen, to subdue her rage at continually failing to be punctual. It was actually a tough call for Helen, pitting an ethical principle against an important one of etiquette: allow Regina to slap her sister awake every day, bruises and all, or allow them all to be late for school and work?

"I want my red Davy today," Regina demanded.

"I do not respond to such language," Helen replied.

Regina rolled her eyes. "Please."

Helen was reaching into Regina's closet for the red Davy Jones T-shirt when Deb wandered into Regina's room, a fresh welt under her left eye, and immediately began crying. "*I* want to wear my red Davy today!"

"And you shall." Helen wearily pulled the T-shirt over the older sister's head. "Just be patient a moment, will you please? There is no need to cry."

"Why does she always have to copy me?" Regina complained.

"Because she loves you."

Debra resumed wailing.

"Debra, what is it now?" Helen sighed.

"I don't know," the younger sister murmured through tears.

Regina had removed her red Davy.

"Regina, what are you doing?" Helen exclaimed. "You need to get dressed. You need to eat breakfast. We are running late!"

"I'm not wearing my red Davy if *she* wears hers. I'm going to wear my yellow Davy."

"*I* want to wear my yellow Davy!" Debra wailed.

Helen just stared at them. Without another word she removed a cigarette from her pink bathrobe pocket and lit it. She would have to ask Theodore about that European Death Knot he was so keen about; maybe to the dresser here, maybe leave them both here until they'd worked it out—it being everything—themselves. How long would that take, really? One year, two years tops?

Theodore, meanwhile, was sleeping late in the master bedroom, a deep calm sleep not even rippled by the commotion next door.

6

Helen settled on a general solution to the girls: separate but equal, or divide and conquer, she referred to it depending on her mood. Of course it wasn't really a solution; nor did she manage to conquer anybody; nor was the dividing particularly equal, usually ending up with Deb as the younger and more irritating getting shorter shrift. But at least with a system in place the situation could be handled, at least sometimes.

The basic idea was that each girl was assigned her own domain from which the other girl was excluded unless negotiations leading to explicit permissions were to occur. Their bedrooms were each girl's own "sovereign territory," as Theodore called it, while the common areas—the hallways, the bathrooms, the rest of their grandmother's old dining table beyond their assigned seats, etc.—were in "international waters."

But then the idea was applied as widely as possible.

With respect to colors for example, Helen awarded Regina the reds, pinks, oranges, and yellows, while Deb was assigned the teals, blues, indigos, and violets; greens were in international waters. Thus when clothes were purchased Helen would buy the girls identical outfits except for the colors; on rainy days they'd wear identical rain slickers except that Regina's was pink and Deb's was purple.

Similarly for foods. When Helen's sumptuous suppers were served Regina got the soup and Deb got the salad, Regina got the drumsticks and Deb got the wings, and Regina got Grandpa Benny's chocolate ice cream while Deb got the vanilla; the banana cream pie was obviously in international waters. On pasta nights Helen would serve both the Regina Special (a tomato sauce) and the Debra Special (a butter sauce), while at breakfast the Frosted Alpha-Bits became Regina's (who was better at spelling) and the Crispy Critters became Deb's (who so loved animals). If on some evening Deb's hand might inadvertently stray across the imaginary border Helen would gently intercept it with the reminder, "But Debra, sweetheart, you don't eat drumsticks."

And so it was that Regina got the board games while Deb got the card games; that Regina got the Dana Girls while Deb got the Nancy Drews; that as they got older Regina's afterschool activities were sports and home economics (though she was talentless at both) while Deb, to bolster her always faltering academics, got the Mathletes and the Model United Nations Club (though *she* was talentless at both). And so it was, too, that the girls were separated into more abstract categories: Regina was the smart one while Deb was the distracted one, Regina was the physical one while Deb was the emotional, Regina was quiet and quick and Deb was loud and lingering, Regina was tidy and Deb was not—and so on.

It didn't matter that Regina was actually better at burning pasta than at tossing a softball while Debra's mathematical abilities were limited to comparing the number of drumsticks on Regina's plate with the number of wings on her own; nor that Regina's own impressive aptitude in math was perhaps to be equaled by Deb's eventually earning her own Ph.D.; nor did it matter that Regina might occasionally enjoy a good sob as might Deb some good quiet brooding. The physical and conceptual separation kept the girls as far apart, physically and metaphorically, as possible. The classifications were neither particularly accurate nor even fair—why did Regina usually get first choice? why were Regina's assignments often similar to Helen's own preferences?—but they, at least sometimes, helped keep the peace.

And then there were the dolls.

Barbie dolls.

7

Or Barbie dolls plus every conceivable piece of Barbie paraphernalia, to be precise.

The two sisters got along best when playing with Barbies. They'd play all sorts of games, acting out every kind of scene. One might play a waitress, the other a customer; or a teacher and student; or a mother and father bickering over money; and they especially loved their Barbie-themed tea parties. These affairs could go on for hours, the girls finding it endlessly entertaining, somehow, to pretend to order and deliver imaginary imported teas and cookies and cakes. Sometimes Helen would listen in and breathe the deepest sighs of satisfaction and relief as she heard her daughters chatting and giggling.

But then there were the *other* play sessions.

Regina might allow Deb to complete her turn (or her Barbie's turn) at waitress: she'd let Deb take her order, run down to the kitchen for (real) cookies and milk, then serve Regina (and Regina's Barbie) at their little Barbie table. But when it was time to switch roles Regina would stand up and say, "Oh, I completely forgot! I'm supposed to play with Kimberly today," and disappear out the door, leaving Deb in mid-fantasy and starting to cry.

Or if she were in a particularly dark mood Regina might say, "Oh yes, let me take your order. What will it be today, missies?"

"Yes," Deb would happily say, "I'll have the brownies, and Beverly will have the pudding. And two cups of tea with milk, please."

"Right-o," Regina would say, and wink, then disappear to the kitchen and walk out the front door to go see if Kimberly was home.

Or else when Deb had placed her order Regina might say, "What was that?"

"I'll have the brownies and Beverly will have the pudding, please."

"Huh?"

"Brownies and pudding, please."

"What did you say?"

"Regina! Brownies and pudding!"

"Sorry, again?" she'd reply as Deb burst into tears.

Or Regina's favorite ploy of all: in a nearly flawless imitation of their mother she would start reprimanding Deb for her table manners, or for leaving drawers and cabinets and refrigerators open, or for leaving lights on and toothpaste caps off, or for failing her room and closet inspections, or for always leaving her shoes everywhere except where they belonged.

"And I am just sorry," Regina would conclude as Deb burst into tears, "but the Barbie Restaurant cannot serve such untidy people!"

Once in a while, though, Regina might realize she had gone too far. Something about the particular tone of her little sister's sobs; or maybe the suffocating way the little girl was squeezing whatever pet was in the house, or one of her innumerable stuffed animals, to console herself.

"Dubs," Regina might then softly say, the *other* Regina, "do you want to play with my Barbie Bakery?"

The younger sister, never entirely sure just which Regina was making the offer, would slowly stop crying as she reached out for the little plastic rolling pins.

8

The dolls were where the territorial issues were murkiest.

Early on Helen tried to buy everything in duplicate—clothes, school items, toys—to minimize the girls' fighting. But this strategy couldn't accommodate the Barbies long. These were the girls' favorite toys and they each demanded for their shared birthdays every item in the Barbie line, which was as expensive as it was extensive. The "two of everything" policy soon became a serious strain in a household already strained by Theodore's slow progress on his book, his impulsive acquisitions of animals and sailboats, and Helen's not quite voluntary decision to postpone her promotion at work.

Once during this period Theodore, in one of their conversations about money—which were increasing in frequency as their conversations about parenting were decreasing—tried to bring the two subjects together by suggesting that Helen cut down on her smoking.

He was met with a silent stare.

"Even by half, Hel," he continued, bravely. "If you could get back to your pre-Deb levels that would put some change in our pockets. And maybe a few cents into your long journey box. We could continue buying two of every doll, maybe placate those two insane little girls. Maybe keep the peace around here a little?"

More silence and staring.

"Right-o, I've got a meeting," he said on his way out the door.

For a while Helen attempted a "separate but equal" policy for the Barbie stuff too: each girl owned her own Barbie things. The thought was that they would learn to cooperate out of self-interest, since the only way to gain access to your sister's stuff was to offer access to your own. This was a lovely thought, about as closely related to reality as thoughts about unicorns, Santa Claus, and Theodore's actually obtaining the tenure-track teaching job he kept saying was imminent.

Consider just one example. On their shared eighth and sixth birthday Regina received the three-story Barbie dollhouse complete with elevator and backyard patio set while Deb got the three brand-new Barbie convertibles along with a three-car Barbie parking garage set. The gifts were opened at the same moment on that early summer Saturday morning. One moment later each girl was eyeing the other girl's present. Theodore popped into the room, saw the looks the girls were giving each other, and popped right back out.

"You ... playing ... with that?" Regina said tentatively.

"Um...." Deb had no idea what was a safe response to make.

"I'll let you play with my dollhouse later if you let me play with your cars right now."

"Mummy?" Deb asked, seeking guidance.

"Regina, let Debra play with your dollhouse now," Helen answered tensely, "if you want her cars right now."

"But two of the cars are my colors!" Regina grabbed for the red and the yellow vehicles.

This grab allowed Debra to slip in and start furiously pressing the button moving the dollhouse elevator up and down.

"Get your hands off my dollhouse!" Regina exclaimed, trying simultaneously to grab the third Barbie automobile, her dollhouse, and Deb's closest pigtail all in one motion.

Negotiations over sharing only degenerated from there.

Within about three minutes Helen had threatened to throw away both presents, a threat which briefly opened up some new diplomatic pathways between the girls; the pursuit of these, combined with Helen's smoking of two beautiful cigarettes in rapid succession, increased the amount of time the girls owned these items by a good twenty-five percent.

But by lunchtime it was over.

In a scene burned into Deb's memory, Helen removed both the dollhouse and the parking garage set, furniture and automobiles trapped within, and before the girls' very eyes dropped them into the trash bin in the garage. They screamed, they wept, they tore their hair—each their own for a change—but Helen would not yield.

They also screamed, wept, and tore hair the next morning when she woke them up early to make them watch the garbage man empty the bin into his truck. Even Regina, who had a memory like a sieve, claimed years later to remember the precise tone of Helen's maniacal cackle as the garbage truck drove away.

The girls were stunned.

This wasn't just some article of clothing or regular toy or maybe even a record (Regina was already getting into Motown albums then, despite her young age).

This was … *Barbie.*

You would like to say that the girls learned their lesson from this, that maybe they learned to cooperate and share. Then again you would also like to say that Santa Claus was real and that Theodore did not spend more time imagining his one-day future biographer's interview questions than actually doing anything to inspire someone to write his biography.

It *was* right around this period, though—the Barbie fights becoming only more vicious after that birthday, and Helen being in that strange long funk manifesting itself in being especially hard on poor little Deb—that Theodore published his classic column, "The Second Child." Ostensibly it explored theories about how best to introduce another child into an already perfect single-child family; but in fact it came across more as a manifesto against ever ruining a good thing by having more children. Second and third children everywhere wrote *The Citizen Inquirer* to complain, not that Theodore minded: relishing the excitement generated by the column sure beat working on that so-called book of his.

Debra never knew about that column, fortunately; Debra never knew about a lot of things, apparently, in her family history. Many years later she discovered a beautiful pomegranate-patterned case of her mother's she didn't recognize, and on opening it found it packed with their old Barbie gear. She was surprised to find these things. Her mother was never sentimental about her daughters' childhoods, speaking of them more in military terms than nostalgic ones. But even more surprising to Deb, who had a memory like a trap, was how little of the stuff she recognized. She went through it slowly, examining every piece. The familiar things moved her deeply. She remembered all the pieces perfectly and the specific games and fantasies she and Regina used to play or play out with them. But the unfamiliar ones: a total blank. It suddenly dawned on her that Regina must have had her own secret Barbie stash. How like her, and their mother, that would have been! And then it also dawned on her that, after all these years, when Barbies no longer meant anything to her, it still really hurt to realize that Regina had had that stash back then and that their mother had been in on it.

Slowly digging a bit further in the case Deb then discovered the Barbie dollhouse and the parking garage, the furniture and convertibles still stuffed within. Helen must have retrieved them from the trash bin after the girls had gone to sleep that night. That morning scene, making them watch the garbage man take them away, had just been a bit of theater. Probably her mother had held onto them waiting for some moment when things would improve, when the two sisters would get along, when maybe she could return the toys to them.

Deb gazed at them a moment and closed the case.

CHAPTER FOUR
SORRY OL' BUDDY OL' CHUM

1

"It wasn't your fault," Dr. J., her de facto therapist, would tell Deb years later, while she sat weeping in the comfy chair opposite him. The doc was actually a physician she'd originally met at the Emergency Room, a warm and compassionate man who later became a close friend and to whom she referred as "Dr. J." when they were in that conversational mode. "You never had a chance."

"But how do you know that?" Deb dabbed her eyes with a tissue.

"I hear these stories. It's not hard to see."

"But you only hear them from me. You only get my perspective. How do you know I'm not lying?"

"You're obviously not lying."

"How do you know I'm not—crazy? Maybe I've just misunderstood, misperceived. Maybe I've just been making it all up. There's no record, no confirmation, of anything. I'm the only witness. Maybe I even deserved it. Maybe I'm the one who was always provoking *her*?"

The doc gazed at her. "Debra, listen to me. Nobody can *prove* anything about their past. But you have this nearly perfect memory, this amazing ability to recall details. There's always room for interpretation but I hear the facts, the objective facts."

"So it's an objective fact that my sister hated me?"

He smiled and touched her arm in that gentle way of his. "It may not be as black and white as you sometimes suggest, Debra. But it's clear enough that you provoked her back then simply by existing. You can't be blamed for that."

Speaking of the objective, there was indeed a period when Regina's primary one clearly *was* to drive Deb from the family. This period began roughly with Deb's birth and, possibly, had not yet

69

entirely ended. Deb's biggest mistake during this period would be to show any sort of attachment to or affection toward some object. That would be Regina's cue for losing, harming, or just disrespecting that object. For a long time, for example, Deb's favorite toys after the Barbies were two miniature dolls she named Thumbkin and Thumbelina. These were given to her by her kindergarten teacher, Mrs. Glenellen; the sweet old woman, seeing how much love the little girl had to shower on things, rightly thought these would be a good vessel for that love. From that moment on they were almost never out of Deb's presence. Even when Deb was busy with Barbies her little "babies" were nearby, looking on. When she wasn't busy with Barbies Deb loved to dress and undress and redress her babies in any of their many outfits, to match the mini shoes with the mini clothes, and, because they were so small, to take them with her everywhere.

Mrs. Glenellen might as well have given them to Regina, they were such a gold mine for her.

"How are your little dolls doing?" Regina might ask Deb.

"Don't call them dolls! They're my *babies*."

"Love those dolls!"

"*Babies*!"

"You should ask Mummy and Daddy for a dollhouse for your dolls."

"Shut up!"

"Dolls dolls dolls!"

"*Mummy*!"

For their ninth and seventh birthdays the girls received the new child-model Polaroid cameras, Regina's being orange while Deb's of course was purple. Theodore was especially keen on these gifts, still resentful that Helen had banned him from the grown-up Polaroid after Regina's birth; in fact when Helen had complained a few years back that they barely had any baby photos of Deb he had blamed the Instamatic, which by requiring film to be developed delayed gratification to the point that all the fun was gone.

The new birthday present didn't delay Regina's gratification, however, for she put it immediately to use.

"Hey Dub," she said after opening the package that summer morning in their Riverbend living room. "Want to take a picture of you with your dolls?"

Deb glared at her, about to object when she realized that she *would* like such a picture, Regina's "doll" slander notwithstanding.

"Good," Regina said. "Go get them dressed."

"They are dressed." Deb had brought them to the living room for the opening of the presents.

"That is not how one dresses for a portrait." Regina sounded just like their mother. "Do they not have something nicer?"

Deb went off to her room and changed the dolls into their fanciest outfits. Given how tiny they were this was a painstaking process. She finally returned to the living room.

"Ready?" Regina said. "Say cheese!"

Regina took the Polaroid. Eagerly Deb grabbed it from her.

"Oh, darn," Regina said. "I messed up."

There was Deb and the two dolls' faces, but the dolls' bodies and their fancy outfits were cut off entirely.

"You did that on purpose!"

"I did not."

"Did so!"

"Look, we can try again. Come on, Dub!" Regina ushered Deb and the dolls into a pose. "Now smile for the camera!"

Eagerly Deb grabbed the film from her. This time the outfits came out beautifully. Only their heads were missing.

"Now how did that happen?" Regina wondered aloud.

"You definitely did that on purpose!"

"Did not!"

"Did so!"

"Hey, let's try it again. But maybe you should wear something else. You and your *babies* probably should match if you're going to be in the same picture. Wouldn't that be lovely? And you must have a nicer pair of shoes in that untidy closet of yours?"

Deb was suspicious, but her eagerness for the portrait overrode the suspicion. So she trudged off to her room and changed into a light teal outfit matching the shade of the babies' outfits. Regina then took another shot, an intimate close-up of Deb's generous nose with not a trace of either doll. Deb began screaming in a way reminiscent of her infamous post-partum crying jag, to the point even where Regina briefly became the other Regina and attempted to comfort her. Helen, busy scrubbing the oven in preparation for her Sunday baking and thinking about how peaceful it was with her head in there, reluctantly removed herself to go render a verdict. As she entered the living room Deb was hyperventilating while Regina was watching TV.

Helen calmed Deb down enough to hear out her complaint.

"She wouldn't take the picture! She kept taking the picture but then cutting out my babies' heads. She did it on purpose!"

"Sweetheart," Helen said gently, never quite sure what to do besides offering some awkward strokes of her younger daughter's hair. "Please stop crying."

But Regina's best fun was in hiding the little things, especially before family trips.

Their summer weekend trips out to the island (for example) included many pleasurable traditions—from the mosquitoes' odd tendency to attack only Theodore to the two days of methodical packing Helen inflicted upon them prior to departure—but none more pleasurable than Deb's reliable last-minute realization that Thumbkin and Thumbelina were missing. So precious was that moment—the Plymouth packed and running, even Daddy ready to go, Mummy standing by the front door scowling at her Ladies Timex and calling for Deb to come down—when Deb realized that she couldn't find her babies. Such a scene! Deb screaming, Mummy reproaching her for always being late, Regina innocently strapped into the car, flaring her nostril at her sister; a thing of beauty.

Eventually the dolls were found wherever Regina had tucked them, hidden just well enough that it took some time to find them but not so well as to be implausible that Deb had misplaced them herself. Deb would complain that Regina had stolen them. Regina would blame Deb for not keeping track of her dolls. Deb would scream "*babies!*" Helen would light another cigarette and scream at everyone to stop screaming. Theodore would merely sit at the wheel of the car, trying to listen to the radio, wondering in the midst of the screaming why nobody had yet invented a competent mosquito repellent.

2

Living with two children constantly at war would take its toll on anyone.

It didn't help that money was always an issue. Helen's opportunity to become a Buyer was now gone, as her boss, unable to wait for her, had hired someone else. Theodore was now earning more than that measly graduate student stipend but not much: several years after his doctorate he still couldn't find a full-time teaching position and was making do with part-time adjunct gigs at the university. Contributions to the long journey box during the first few Riverbend years were minimal; simply keeping the family afloat on the long journey between paychecks was hard enough.

Theodore attempted to assuage Helen with assurances that things would get better once he landed a real job. But of course this meant that he needed to produce his book as soon as possible, which meant that he needed to be at his office a lot—for he couldn't do his deep thinking in an environment where one minute one girl was chasing the other screaming through the room and the next minute the other girl was chasing the first girl screaming back.

Unless Helen had any better ideas about how to control the girls?

"What are the rules these days?" he asked her after both girls had been sent to their rooms yet again without some delicious supper that Helen had prepared. (This time it was a Fluffy Mackerel Casserole adapted from one of Jacqueline's Weight Watchers recipes, since Helen had noticed that Theodore had recently been putting on some weight.) "Are we allowed to hit them?"

Here the parenting columnist was researching his next column, by interviewing an actual parent.

"No," Helen said evenly, smoking.

"Right-o, no hitting. Then I've got another idea. A sure way to make some money until I'm done with my book. Do you want to hear it?"

"No."

"'Air Unfreshener': When You Need a Few Moments Alone."

Helen looked at him blankly and exhaled.

"For people like us," Theodore explained. "Stressed parents who need a few minutes break from the fighting kids, the dishes in the sink, all that sort. You go into the bathroom and clear your head, meditate, whatever you need to do. When you're ready for reality again you just spray a little unfreshener to smell up the place, step on out, and nobody will know the difference."

"Theodore, is there something wrong with you?"

"What? You don't like it?"

"I won't even dignify that with a response."

"Jesus, Hel, how about a little support here? You shoot down every idea I have to improve our lot, but it's not like you're bringing anything to the table."

Helen just stared at him.

"Fine," he said. "I'll get the book done. But that means I've got to get out of here. If you need me, generally speaking, I'll be at the office." He stood up but then sat down, realizing it was the first Sunday of the month. "I'll leave after the pie."

Meanwhile poor Helen slowly began to—well, not do so well.

There was so much to be upset about. The conflict, the screaming, the occasional physical violence between the girls; the professional stagnation; the stress about money; the effectively single parenting, since her husband, as even he admitted, was more a theoretician of parenting than a practitioner.

And worst of all was the way these things intersected, in the way that all parties other than herself treated their home.

Helen was not materialistic. Her parents had been comfortable but not wealthy and she was not impressed by expensive things. But her parents had had taste and she liked nice things, clean things, beautiful things. The Gales did not have the most expensive fabrics but Helen's curtains and linens and tablecloths were always attractive. They couldn't afford the fanciest dishes or the best clothes but what they did have was *nice*. And of course Helen had the things she inherited from her parents, the old furniture, her mother's miniature tea service collection, some of her father's favorite artworks, the old-fashioned family radio. Some of these were in the curio cabinet in the Riverbend dining room and it gave Helen great comfort to see them daily. The rest was packed carefully in boxes in the basement, and it gave her equal comfort to go down there to dust and clean. Even just occasionally handling her mother's broken toaster and rusty iron was soothing.

Theodore was messy, for sure. The various pets that streamed through their lives were messy and destructive. But nothing took quite the toll on the Riverbend house as the two little girls.

Scuffs on the floors, dirt streaks on the walls. One of the girls—each accused the other—had scraped a long section of paint off the deck in the back. There were rips in the furniture, in her parents' old sofa, in the lounge chair; gashes in the girls' furniture; broken lamps which otherwise would have been valuable antiques; a long magic marker stripe across the queen mattress in the master bedroom. Could one of her daughters have done that deliberately? And those lovely curtains in the living room—well they *were* lovely now that Helen had replaced the ones which Deb, playing "let's clean house," had doused with a bleach spray bottle. (Deb was too hysterical before the irate Helen to communicate the fact that it was Regina who had suggested the game and given her the bottle.)

And then there was the time that someone practiced her scissor skills on the chapter of Theodore's dissertation that Helen had just spent three hours typing. Or left the refrigerator open overnight spoiling the food *again*. Or dragged home some strange animal and gave it a bath, leaving the bathtub drain clogged with some matted *thing* that neither the plumber nor the veterinary lab could identify. Or the times that someone spilled milk or juice or coca-cola on the furniture, the floor, the back seat of the car, the mattress on the bottom-bunk bed on the island, or on the chapter of Theodore's dissertation that Helen had just spent three hours *re*-typing.

You try maintaining your cool when order matters to you and you live with Theodore, various wild animals, and those two girls.

And especially the littler girl.

You know, the one who wasn't so good with scissors, who left refrigerator doors open, who loved every animal she saw so much that she had to bring it home, and who was never much one for keeping her drinking vessels upright.

Maybe it was the girls' different personalities. Regina was more like Helen, even from infancy: quieter, reserved, maybe even brooding a little. As she got older she remained like her mother, fastidious and neat and clean. Right from the start Helen felt bonded with her older daughter, everything was so easy with her. That was it: it was *easier* with Regina, who in contrast to Deb not only didn't challenge Helen's sense of order but actually promoted it. Most of the time Regina wanted to be just like Helen: to dress like her (so smartly!), to talk like her (so elegantly!), later to smoke like her (so gracefully!). Regina so identified with her mother that whenever Helen was angry at Deb, so was Regina. And in fact nothing upset Deb more than, when Helen was angry at her, she'd see Regina standing behind Helen also glaring at her with her arms crossed and her nostril flared.

Even the very young Deb was aware of that bond between her mother and her sister.

"Everything was separate," Deb told the good Dr. J., years later. "Foods, colors, toys, you name it. Regina got the drumsticks, I got the wings. For most of my childhood I never ate a drumstick, I swear to you. But the thing is, what Regina got was also what my mother liked. *They* ate drumsticks while I ate wings. I would sometimes try to take one and my mother would smack my hand. 'You don't eat drumsticks, Debra,' she'd snap at me. Which basically meant, 'you're not one of us, little girl.'" Deb hesitated. "You know, I didn't even like drumsticks. I just didn't like being the one who couldn't eat them."

"Nobody would," the doc said gently.

"And the matching outfits—Regina got the reds and yellows and pinks, which just happened to be my mother's favorite clothing colors. We'd go out and Regina would be dressed like my mother while I just tagged along, an outsider.

"And worst of all, they were always whispering. Especially late at night, especially when Theodore was away, which seemed like always as the years went on. I had to go to bed before Regina, and I'd fall asleep with my door open listening to them whispering downstairs at the kitchen table. I'd wake up later and hear louder whispering, and peer out of my room, and realize they were in my parents' bedroom down the hall. That room was off-limits to us— their sovereign territory, Theodore would say—but Regina was *in there* with my mother. More than once I crept down that dark hallway and came to the door and pushed it open. Regina would be lying in bed with my mother engrossed in some intimate conversation. When they'd notice me at the door, standing there in my purple pajamas, squeezing my stuffed animals in each arm, my mother would say angrily, 'Debra, go back to bed.' And Regina would lie there beside her, giving me that ice glare of hers. I'd go back to my room and cry myself to sleep."

The doc squeezed her arm.

"You know, the worst part of it all," Deb was speaking quickly, "is that I even started to believe that this was how things should be. Once things started to deteriorate my mother's favorite pastime was to complain about Theodore and her second-favorite pastime was to compare me to him. Even the good things about Theodore were bad: he would rather have fun than do what needed doing, he never met a good time he could decline even when some bad time was more important, at least by my mother's standards. Bad times like cleaning the house, for example, which she did constantly, in a kind of vicious cycle—the more distant Theodore became from her the more crazily she cleaned, driving him further away because of her weird obsession with cleanliness. But of course I was just like Theodore: shirking responsibilities, goofing around, always late, and always so emotional. She was constantly telling me to keep my feelings to myself. Like I was encroaching on her in some way by crying, or by loving our pets too much. The same way I was always encroaching on her with my shoes everywhere, and by being so untidy. Even as a toddler my sister's favorite game was, like, stacking things and putting them away in drawers and cabinets, whereas I was—I was—"

"Normal?" the doctor said softly.

"Yes," Deb whispered, starting at last to weep. "I was normal, doc. I liked pulling Tupperware *out* of the cabinets and spreading it around the floor. I was maybe three years old. My mother would light up a cigarette and just stare at me like she wished I had never been born."

"Debra," Dr. J. said softly after a few moments, handing her a tissue and then squeezing her hand.

"Mmm."

"Do you remember when you had the mumps? You were maybe six or seven?"

Deb nodded, dabbing her eyes.

"You told me that your mother stayed home with you for a week—feeding you mashed bananas and homemade chicken broth, refilling hot water bottles for your upset stomach and wiping your feverish forehead all day with a cool cloth."

She nodded again, gazing at him through moist eyes.

"The two of you watched reruns of *Gilligan's Island* and *Get Smart* all day, cracking up together, at least when you felt well enough."

The good doctor paused, meeting her soft gaze.

"Debra, remember. That is the same woman."

She resumed weeping.

3

"There," Helen said with a sigh.

"Where?" Deb asked, trying not to cry.

"Right before your eyes, sweetheart. Just look more carefully."

"Where?" Too late. The tears were now coming.

Mother and six-year-old daughter were kneeling, leaning low over the shag-carpeted bedroom floor by the dresser. Helen guided

77

Deb's hand with its index finger extended to the back wall under the dresser, the dresser which had once been Helen's mother's and then Helen's, just next to the rear leg. Deb's finger was now pointing at a small dustball. There was always something to point at: a dirty sock next to the hamper, a shoe not put away, linens imperfectly folded, a dresser drawer slightly ajar.

"Sweetheart," Helen was saying, "you are old enough now to keep a tidy room. You are old enough to put your shoes away and close your dresser drawers."

"Yes, Mummy."

"All right, then. Please finish under the dresser. Then you may come downstairs for some ice cream."

Helen looked at her daughter a moment with a furrowed brow. As she left the room even little Deb got the sense that Helen was upset by something more than just this week's particular violation.

Regina was standing in the doorway. "Hey, Dub," she said—it was the other Regina today—"how'd your room inspection go?"

Theodore was away, some performances out of town with his theater troupe, he said. Grandpa Benny had gone home a while earlier, having babysat overnight while Helen was out late at the party her boss had thrown her for her tenth anniversary on the job. The house on Riverbend was mostly quiet now except for the sounds of Helen downstairs furiously washing, disinfecting, and vacuuming, pausing only to light cigarette after cigarette. (For some reason she was to spend much of the week to come staying home, in a particularly frenzied bout of cleaning, from the job which had just fêted her.)

Deb ignored her sister, concentrating on stopping crying as she dropped the dustball in her trash can.

"Failed again, huh?" Regina asked softly.

"Leave me alone."

"I'm just trying to be nice."

"Get out of my room!"

"I'm not in your room. I'm in international waters." Regina pointed to her toes just outside the threshold. "By the way, Mummy said she was proud of my room today. As usual."

"So?"

"So maybe I could help you on your inspections, you retard."

Deb stared at her suspiciously but didn't answer.

"So?" Regina asked.

"So? Sew your buttons."

"Come on, Dub—"

"Go away."

"You can't tell me to go away. I can stand right here if I want to."

"Go away!"

"No you go away, loser," Regina scoffed. "Loser who always fails her room inspections."

"Shut up!"

"No you shut up! Loser!"

"Mummy!" Deb pushed out of the room crying past her sister.

There was no response from downstairs.

Helen was taking long drags on her cigarette as she started in again dusting the curio cabinet in the dining room.

4

"Sweetheart," Helen said some other Saturday afternoon with some other heavy sigh, standing just inside the doorway of Deb's room.

Deb hesitated, recognizing the tone of voice. She was playing in her room with her frog Fritz. Fritz didn't do a lot. Playing with him consisted of dropping some food in his tank and gazing at him, in love with him. But that was all right. He just let you love him. Deb pulled herself away from him saying, "You be good, little Fritz," and followed her mother to the bedroom closet. Deb felt the first pangs of another upset tummy.

"What is that doing on the floor?" Helen suddenly asked, pointing at Fritz's tank in the middle of the room.

"I was playing with him."

"Please, Debra, you know the tank must remain on the dresser. Otherwise you will almost certainly knock it over. And what is that?"

Deb followed Helen's gaze to her dresser. Next to the plastic mat whose purpose was to protect the dresser's finish was a water stain exactly the shape of Fritz's bowl.

"Debra, sweetheart," Helen was saying through taut lips, "that dresser was your grandmother's when she was a little girl. It survived her childhood, and my own childhood, and has survived several moves. It is a valuable piece of furniture. You need to take better care of your things. Please." Helen took a deep breath. "But perhaps this is my fault. I should not have allowed your father to give you that frog."

"I'll be more careful, Mummy," Deb answered, her eyes down.

"All right," Helen said quietly.

They turned back toward Deb's closed closet door.

The night before Theodore had shared a new parenting theory with Helen, about how to approach the inspections if she absolutely insisted on continuing with them; and although she didn't like to admit it, it was perhaps worth a try.

"You are old enough now, Debra," Helen continued tentatively, "to be responsible for your belongings. You are old enough, now, that I am willing to try trusting you. If you tell me that your closet is in order, then we shall consider the inspection passed."

Fully occupied with loving Fritz that morning Deb had completely forgotten about the weekly closet inspection. During the week, with school, homework, and her other chores, she could barely keep most of the mess out of her room by tossing it into the closet. Organizing her closet was more or less impossible for her. Regina somehow didn't have this problem. Regina had just as much school, homework, and other chores but her room was always neat and her closet even neater. Then again Regina didn't have the same shoe situation to deal with as Deb. For despite being like Helen in most things Regina was unlike Helen in this most important of things, and simply didn't care about shoes. Deb to the contrary was as in love with shoes as she was currently with Fritz, but, alas, unlike her mother, was incapable of maintaining them in order. At the moment Deb's shoes were in a large pile in her closet, with no individual near its partner and several individuals simply MIA.

But at least the shoe disaster wouldn't be noticed immediately, should the closet door be opened, since the shoes themselves were buried beneath a week's worth of Deb's dirty rumpled clothes. Deb knew that if her mother looked inside the closet there would be penalties; that Deb would fall even lower in her mother's esteem; that Regina would, as usual, be the princess of the house.

She would have to lie, clearly.

"It's not," Deb said softly, her tummy as unsettled as her closet, "in order."

So much for the deceit.

In that long moment between Deb's reply and Helen's

assignment of penalties Deb was sure that her mother was thinking, why couldn't Debra be more like Regina? The usual Regina, that is, who was standing just outside Deb's doorway with her arms crossed, her eyebrow arched, and her nostril so grotesquely flared?

5

When poor frazzled Helen was being particularly hard on Deb there could sometimes be a consolation prize: Theodore might be extra nice to her, at least when he was around. Maybe he'd take her on a secret ice cream run out to Grandpa Benny's store on a Saturday afternoon; maybe they would load up on Jujubes and Wax Lips at the movies, which tasted all the sweeter knowing that Helen would disapprove of these selections. Or if Deb's penalties for her lousy chore work involved doing extra chores Theodore might even come help her a little, as long as it could be done discreetly. He might do some scrubbing in the kitchen for her, or carry the heavy laundry hampers down to the basement; once or twice he even helped her through some intimidating piles of folding.

"Keep this between you and me, Dubs," he'd say and wink as they worked together in the basement or kitchen. "If your mother knew I was helping she'd probably double the penalties."

These were nice moments, for Deb. She sometimes wondered whether they made it worth it to violate Helen's rules. Or at least she wondered this *during* these moments, for during the moments she was actually failing her inspections *nothing* could make them worthwhile.

But then again there were the animals.

There were the Saturday afternoons Theodore would spend with her in pet stores and animal shelters, when she could shower all the little critters with love for hours at a stretch. Theodore might have often been a distracted parent but even he treasured these afternoons. What bliss, to play with a cute little puppy all day, without having to think about taking care of it!

And when things got *really* tough on Deb, who could blame him for bringing home a pet or two to comfort his poor little daughter? Well not for *her* exactly. The sibling dynamics made it impossible to bring home something for one sister and not the other. So either he brought two of the thing—gerbils, fish—or made a show of the one thing being for both girls. But however it was presented it always worked out the same. Regina didn't actually like animals any more than her mother, and for the same reasons—they were dirty, smelly, and created more housework—so she would briefly express enthusiasm about the new arrival but then would soon relinquish responsibility (and love) for the pet in question to Deb.

The trickiest part for Theodore here was dealing with Helen, which he did as with most issues: dive right in, sort it out later.

"Please tell me you did not," Helen might say when Theodore walked in the door carrying some sort of beast in some sort of carrier.

"Of course I did," he'd reply, depositing the new member of the family where Deb could most quickly begin petting it, squeezing it, and loving it, then immediately exiting the house to give his wife time to smoke her way back down to sub-mariticidal levels.

And so Deb's childhood contained a series of animals, including fish, gerbils, a bird, a ferret (briefly), a frog, more gerbils, another bird, a cat, a dog, and later another cat. She didn't have much luck with most of these animals though, despite loving them desperately and caring for them carefully: most reached unfortunate ends before their natural times. The fish, for example, just kept eating each other. Theodore would bring home some gorgeous tropical fish, add it to Deb's tank, and the next morning they'd find that the newcomer either had gobbled up, or been gobbled up by, one of the tank's previous residents.

"It's a fish-eat-fish world, little Dub," Theodore would murmur reflectively, stroking his bushy beard, Deb sobbing beside him.

When the last fish died in an allergic reaction to having eaten the penultimate fish Theodore, ignoring Helen's latest moratorium on household pets, brought the girls (i.e. Deb) another pair of gerbils, which soon became a family of gerbils and then an extended family of gerbils. They gave away as many as they could, but even so they couldn't keep up with the fertile rodents. Before long the gerbils were doing what they always do when grossly overcrowded: like the fish they were eating each other. When Helen discovered the mass carnage going on she put her foot down yet again and insisted Theodore get rid of the survivors.

"You tell her," Theodore replied to Helen that evening after the girls had gone to bed. He attempted a subtle sniff to see if she were wearing her green tea perfume but came up with nothing.

"Why must I always assume the unpleasant tasks?"

"You're the one who wants to get rid of them."

"But surely you recognize that they have become unmanageable."

"So, they're a little crowded in there. What's the big deal?"

"Theodore, you cannot be serious. They are eating each other. It is disgusting."

"It's natural. It's nature."

"Nature? You *cannot* be serious."

"Why not?"

"Your idea of a nature walk is a stroll through the produce section of the grocery store. Since when do you approve of nature?"

"I don't mind it when it's contained in a tank."

"The nature contained in that tank is disgusting."

Theodore sighed heavily. "But she loves them, Helen."

"Theodore," Helen said. "Even Debra—the child in this scenario—understands that they have become unmanageable."

"Fine, fine. I'll tell her you want her to get rid of them."

"Theodore." Helen's eyes narrowed as she withdrew a cigarette. "You always leave me to do the dirty work. You waltz in with the animals and then you disappear when the mess begins." She paused to light up. "You will tell Deb that *we* think it best to dispose of the gerbils. And then you will either bring them back where you got them or you will release them into that *nature* of which you are so enamored."

Theodore knew when to quit in these arguments, which was basically the moment Helen began speaking. Two days later he surprised Deb by picking her up early from school. She enjoyed the excitement of having the principal come get her from her second-grade classroom and bring her to her father, waiting in the office. Theodore had concocted for the principal some story about a sick relative who needed an immediate visit for some reason.

"Got a surprise for you, kiddo," he said as he and Deb walked to the car.

"What is it? What is it!"

"Wait and see."

"*What is it?*"

"Just wait," Theodore said, searching for his car key among the many, mostly unidentifiable, keys on his key ring. "Good things come to little kiddos who are patient. Ah, got it."

"What is it?!" Deb cried, rushing into the car.

In the back seat of the Plymouth there were two cages. In one was a parakeet, in the other a cat.

"I couldn't decide which one to get," Theodore explained.

"*I love them so much!*" Deb exclaimed, peering into first one cage then the other, then back to the first, then bursting into tears. "Eenie!" she pointed at the bird; "Meenie!" at the cat. "But wait," she added, despite being the child in this scenario, "Mummy doesn't like cats."

"She doesn't like me much anymore either, Dubs," Theodore answered, starting the car. "But she's learned to live with me."

On the way home they swung by the old country for some ice cream at Iced Cream. Benny too burst into tears at the unexpected visit, though he did cast Theodore a strange look when Deb told him about her new pets. Sitting on the bench outside the store, licking their cones, Theodore casually mentioned to his daughter that with the new pets there might not be room to keep the gerbils. Deb—who loved the gerbils dearly but who was, after all, a young child—didn't seem to mind this information. Anyway she already was as deeply in love with Eenie and Meenie as she was with the chocolate ice cream she was licking. (Theodore did not always respect Helen's rules about which girl got which flavor, incidentally.)

By the time Helen got home from work that evening the gerbils were gone. But Eenie had also escaped from his cage in Deb's room and was flapping around her ceiling pooping on everything, Meenie had peed on Helen's parents' vintage carpet in the entrance hall and thrown up all over the kitchen floor, and Theodore had left a note saying he had a late meeting and would probably just stay that night on the cot he'd recently installed in his office.

The situation was not, obviously, a stable one.

It also wasn't a very long-lasting one.

During the following week Helen did not speak to Theodore, Theodore paid no attention either to Helen's silence or to the new pets, Regina complained every day that Deb had gotten to name the pets, Deb decided that when she grew up she would have a big house which she would fill with animals to love which she would name without any hassle from her sister, Eenie developed the habit of squawking loudly between 2:00 AM and 5:00 AM every night, and Meenie threw up on Helen's favorite throw pillow, the mocha silk one stuffed with Canadian goose down, twice.

Oh, and Meenie also scratched Deb rather badly after the little girl had hugged him a little too intensely. Helen, so frustrated, was unable to muster up much compassion as she tended to her daughter's wound, and merely said, "That's what happens when you smother things as you do, sweetheart. They lash out."

Helen still did not speak to Theodore. Every evening during dinner she would sit at the table smoking, glaring at him, at least when he was home. On the other evenings she just glared at his empty chair.

The next day Meenie ate Eenie.

Maybe Deb had let the cooped-up bird out of his coop. Maybe Regina had slid Deb's door open so the cat could get in. Maybe Theodore was responsible since he was, in Helen's eyes lately, responsible for everything.

However it happened, it happened quick: three or four bites and the deed was done. His belly full, Meenie crawled off to find someplace quiet to sleep. That quiet place was the drum of the industrial strength dryer in the basement. The Gales had industrial strength appliances because every week Helen washed everything in the house that could physically be removed from its place and fit into a washing machine. The dryer was a top-loader with a very heavy lid. Normally this would be closed when not in use because nothing irritated Helen more than open drawers, cabinets, and dryer lids. Someone must have inadvertently left the lid open on this day—unless someone had acted advertently? For it seems inconceivable that Meenie could have poked his nose under the lid and lifted it enough to squeeze himself in.

But in he went, and because his little feline mind was woozy from his recent feast, or maybe just not very bright, not much thought was given about getting out. Nor did he give much thought when someone—okay, Theodore—started some laundry in the adjacent industrial strength washing machine. Theodore had been spending his evenings avoiding Helen out with Maxey avoiding the law, and had some soiled clothing that needed immediate laundering. If Meenie was awake at all he was probably lulled back to sleep by the repetitive throbbing of the washing machine. Probably the first concern crossed his mind when a load of heavy wet clothes came tumbling in upon his head, just a moment before that heavy lid closed above him. "Meow?" he might have mewled, but whatever precise thought he was expressing would have been quickly replaced by the next thought—the one concerning the fact that everything was beginning to spin and it was starting to get awfully hot.

It was Meenie's bad luck to have ensconced himself in there on a Saturday afternoon after Helen's regularly scheduled laundry; and it was his extremely bad luck to have chosen the rare occasion when Theodore was even near the basement appliances. At some point later that day the chaos began upstairs. Deb walked into her room and discovered the open birdcage and the scattered feathers and began screaming. Regina, standing just outside Deb's room, was doubled over in laughter. Helen, smoking as furiously as she was furious with everyone, set them all in search of the missing cat. Nobody thought to look inside the dryer. Why should they, when Theodore had just been down there doing his laundry anyway? The industrially strong drum of the dryer must have drowned out his yowls. It could not have been very pleasant for him in there.

Helen found his body the following Wednesday evening after the girls had gone to bed, when she was doing the regularly scheduled linens.

It was not very pleasant for her either.

6

Deb came home from school with Regina the next afternoon. Helen was sitting at the kitchen table smoking, home early from work.

Regina bounced in with the note of praise she'd brought home from her teacher for her latest academic achievement. She received a nice kiss from her mother before disappearing upstairs to play with her secret Barbies in her bedroom.

Deb, who at least this day didn't have a note of dispraise for her latest academic disappointment, wanted to get a snack from the Frigidaire. But seeing her mother's face she began heading toward the door instead, to resume her daily neighborhood search for her cat.

"Debra," Helen said quietly. "Sit down."

Deb reluctantly returned to the table.

"I am afraid you do not need to go looking for your cat this afternoon."

"But yes I do. He's out there somewhere. He's probably hungry—"

"Sweetheart, listen to me. Your cat is in the garage. In a—bag. Your father is going to dispose of him this evening. At least if he comes home."

Deb's stomach turned.

"But—"

"No buts. No maybes. I am sorry, sweetheart. The cat is dead."

The little girl began sobbing. "Mummy—"

"Debra," Helen said, wanting to comfort her daughter but simply unable to, unable to stop herself from speaking this way. "Please stop crying. Enough with your crying all the time. With the screaming and the fighting with your sister. It is just too much. I cannot take it anymore."

This was about as effective in ending the little girl's tears as you would imagine.

"No more animals in this house," Helen continued despite herself. "I have had enough. You and your father have to stop bringing them home. You are not capable of caring for them. Loving something is not the same as taking care of it. And moreover—"

At this point Deb ran from the kitchen and upstairs. Her bedroom door slammed. Helen, trying to control herself, began puffing relentlessly. If only things had gone on this way, with Helen smoking in the kitchen for a while, eventually calming down enough to make some supper; with Deb upstairs sobbing for a while, eventually calming down enough to realize she was hungry for supper; with Regina in her room listening to her sister's wailing next door and eventually feeling really bad for her, almost to the point of crying herself. If only Theodore hadn't decided to come home right at that moment and not a moment later; if only he had not come home for supper (as was his habit of late) then maybe, just maybe, what did occur next might not have occurred.

But there he was, this red-faced bear of a man barreling in the door almost as if, well, as if he lived there.

"What's for supper, Hel?" Theodore said cheerfully, feeling good today and assuming that everyone shared his mood, oblivious to the situation into which he was walking and for which he was indeed largely responsible.

"*I hate when you call me that.*" Helen was so angry she extinguished her cigarette in the ashtray in order to enjoy the calming effect of immediately lighting up another one.

"Right-o, sorry." He noticed her expression. "What? What'd I do this time?"

"What *didn't* you do? The goddamn animals, Theodore. Enough. Stop bringing them home. Stop killing them. I cannot tolerate this any longer."

"What are you talking about?"

"I cannot maintain this house in these circumstances. You destroy it and disappear. You leave me with these girls who cannot stop bickering for one instant. You spend all our money and never seem to earn any. The house is falling apart. Have you seen the basement lately? That wiring down there looks very tenuous to me."

"Helen, calm down." Theodore realized this was serious. Usually Helen's complaints came one at a time but now she was going through them all at once.

"Who are you to tell me to calm down? You are the reason I am not calm. You do not *dare* tell me to calm down."

"Listen, Hel, we can handle this. Whatever this is. We'll just break it down."

"*We* can handle this?" Helen burned her gaze into him. "Where are you all the time, Theodore? You're barely here anymore."

"I'm working on the book, Helen, you know that. As we decided. *We.*"

"I've called your office."

"I'm often in the library. I've told you." Theodore looked at her. "But look, I'm here now. Let's talk about this. What if—"

"What if," Helen snapped back, "you lived up to your responsibilities, for a change? What if you came home when you said you would? And what if you fixed the things you say you will? The broken banister? Those moldy shingles on the roof?" She glared at him. "Those basement wires?"

"Helen—"

"And while we're what-iffing, Theodore, what if I had left Cozzen's Café after ten minutes, instead of giving you fifteen? And what if I had never agreed to marry you? If I had married Eddie Love, for example, instead of you?"

"Jesus, Helen, don't get all metaphysical here! Whatever this is about, we'll fix it. *I'll* fix it. Just tell me what it is already, for

Christ's sake!"

"All right, then," Helen said, moving from anger toward reflection now, poised, she thought afterward, on the fine line between perfect clarity and perfect insanity. "Less metaphysical. What if you had just worn a condom?"

"Helen, come on," Theodore said.

"I am just thinking aloud. Things were good, Theodore. Just us. And Regina. I was about to become a Buyer, you were making such a good start in graduate school. Even the promised land did not seem so far away. Do you remember our anniversary trip to the island? We were happy. And then we had to ruin it. If you had just worn a condom, as I begged you—"

"My baby," Theodore said almost gently, "you can't blame Deb for our problems. That's totally unfair."

"It is not so hard to see, Theodore. When it was just the three of us everything was—perfect. But then. We stopped sleeping. The money became tight. The girls started fighting. Regina, that lovely toddler, has become a mean and mean-spirited little girl. There is constant tension in this house. You are never around. I cannot take it anymore."

"Helen, please stop."

"There is filth everywhere and the house is falling apart."

"Helen."

"I have given up my career. You have stagnated in yours." Helen added softly, "My mother passed away."

"You're not blaming Deb for that!"

"She hurt herself chasing that child up the stairs, Theodore."

"Helen, that's not fair."

"And you," Helen said, softly.

"What?"

Helen extinguished her cigarette. She was perfectly calm now. "All I am wondering is how things might have been if only we hadn't—had Debra."

This conversation was occurring at the kitchen table. Just around the corner was the stairway leading up to the second floor, with its broken banister. During the course of the conversation the girls had finished wailing and listening to the wailing respectively and, hearing the spirited voices downstairs, come partway down the stairs to listen to their parents fight. This was a treat since usually their parents saved their fights for the evenings in the living room, when the loud TV would obscure most of what they were saying.

But not on this day.

The two girls were sitting side by side, their bodies pressed against each other, about halfway up the staircase. It's unclear exactly when they had begun listening, exactly how much they had heard.

But Regina's eyes were open as wide as they could be.

"Wow," she said softly. "I'm really sorry, ol' buddy ol' chum." The knuckle dead-arm she applied to her sister with this remark was genuinely affectionate in its half-heartedness.

Her eight-year-old sister's eyes were shut tight.

CHAPTER FIVE
YEAR OF THE DOG

1

Along the way—several years earlier—something remarkable had happened: Theodore finally earned his Ph.D. It took eleven years, all told. But as he liked to say, it went by quickly: it barely felt like ten.

There were many reasons it took this long, including legitimate ones.

The topic was difficult, the details complex, the research extensive: Ignoratio P. Elenchi was so obscure that no extant texts were unambiguously attributable to his authorship, and his magnum opus, *Erucarium Ortus*, was entirely lost to history. Nor did you have to take Theodore's word on the difficulty, you could also (he would insist) make a long-distance call to his advisor. (The advisor had moved to Oxford University, where Theodore's sometimes British accent would have been right at home.) And of course Theodore's personal life was busy during those years, including his mother's institutionalization and death, his own engagement and marriage, the births of two daughters, the injury and death of his mother-in-law, and the increasing complexity of his schemes to wring some cash from his father out of the unexpected wealth his crazy mother had left behind. (Theodore would never forgive Dottie for having composed, some time before her mind degenerated, a one-sentence will stating simply, "Enoch gets **nothing**.") Theodore was a busy man during those years, and anyway *you* try writing a dissertation if you think it's so easy.

And on top of all these distractions there were always other things to write: op-eds, articles on parenting, pamphlets promoting hair loss. There were always other things to do: learn to sail, take acting classes, adopt animals, go to sporting events with Maxey. There were always other ways to make some money, products to invent. How could Theodore focus on his thesis when there was so much else going on?

But he prevailed.

After a successful dissertation defense (absent his overseas advisor) Theodore announced one late spring day that he was now officially a "doctor." There was an improving atmosphere in the Gale's apartment at the time. The pall cast by Edna's death a year-and-a-half before was clearing, Helen was at last about to return full-time to A World Away, and now with his degree Theodore could finally apply for tenure-track teaching positions. They were all looking forward to the summer: the girls, almost six and four, were starting at a day camp, Theodore was gung-ho about the job search, and Helen was thinking that maybe, just maybe, they could soon buy a house.

Sharing the news of Theodore's doctorate with Benny one evening she was glowing.

"Your son," she said, serving him some warmed-up lasagna, "is a doctor!"

They were seated at Benny's dimly lit dinner table, at his apartment out in the old country. Since her mother's passing Helen had taken to calling him twice a week and driving out to visit every Tuesday, bearing groceries and leftovers, leaving the girls at home with Theodore for his weekly parenting practice.

Through the soft dusk at the table Benny looked confused.

"Not a medical doctor," she explained again slowly. "It is a degree. It means he is ready to become a professor."

"I would have been happy with a son," Benny answered without much emotion. In this moment, at least, his disappointment with his son was mitigated by the relief that Enoch had finally finished whatever it was he'd spent the last decade doing. Or maybe just by the fact that this was a Helen night, and the meal was as spectacular as always. (Tonight's Lasagna Bolognese was made with her new green peppercorn béchamel, not that Benny could describe it as such.)

Helen sighed. "Dad, I have been thinking. Perhaps we can use this as a turning point."

"To turn what, my darling daughter?"

"Theodore has been trying really hard lately. He not only finished but he seems to be taking his responsibilities more seriously. He has been writing to every university within two hours to find a position. He is already turning his dissertation into a book. And he has been spending more time with the girls." She paused. "I think now might be a good time for you and he to have a conversation."

"Helen, my darling girl. I would *like* a conversation with my son. I would ask him why he doesn't call his father on his birthday. I would ask him why he never visits his mother's grave. I would ask him why he never visits *me*."

Helen squeezed his arm. "I know. But let's try to look forward, Dad. Theodore is in a really good place at the moment. And you are not getting any younger."

"For you I would do anything, my girl. For my beautiful granddaughters, anything." A few tears arose in Benny's eyes, as always happened when his granddaughters were mentioned. "But what can I do for Enoch? I have raised him, I have paid for his education, and I have even helped him with his crazy ideas. I can forgive he never thanks me. I can forgive he never pays me back, even though he promises to. I am not so sure I can forgive he never calls or visits." Benny gazed at her. "And I can never forgive how he treated his mother."

"I know, Dad, I know. But your Enoch is, well, our Theodore. He has never been one for," she sought the right word here, there were so many, "paying attention. But maybe think of it this way. What he has given you are two beautiful granddaughters and a devoted daughter-in-law. He may never be exactly the kind of son you would like, but at least he has given you that."

"But what can I do? Beyond what I have done?"

"He needs to feel appreciated, Dad. All the time. You know this, I know this. But he does not feel fully appreciated by you. Rightly or wrongly, that is how he feels."

"But I have raised him, I have—"

"I know. But he is not one for," she added with a smile, "paying attention."

"So what can I do now?"

"Let us celebrate his doctorate. Really celebrate it. Throw him a party. Invite everyone. Print up the invitations. Make sure his name is in big letters. Bring every flavor in the store. Invent some new flavors. Name them after him. And of course we shall tell him that this is all your idea."

"You know how I feel about ice cream," Benny answered more

93

brightly, "but you think it can even help *this*?"

Helen smiled again. "That, and the name 'Dr. Gale' in very large print on the invitations."

And so that summer began with an ice cream party to end all ice cream parties.

We can pass over most of the details. The setting, at Moswanicut Park downtown, the site of their wedding seven years earlier; Helen's boss, in a crisply pressed button-down shirt above equally crisp Bermuda shorts, oddly arriving both with flowers and without his wife, apparently thinking the celebration was for Helen; Maxey's dramatic entrance, emerging from his new fire-engine red Buick Riviera with two inappropriately clad (and inappropriately young) women; Regina's and Deb's consumption of three or four large servings of ice cream, inserting so much sugar and cream in their systems that they spent the entire afternoon playing peacefully together, one that both would remember fondly long afterward.

What matters is that Helen was right: the ice cream, the warm summer weather, or maybe the large print on the invitations did a good job softening Theodore's heart toward his father. But an even better job was done when Benny spontaneously burst into tears and announced that he wanted to buy his beautiful daughter-in-law and granddaughters, and perhaps also his son, a house to call their own.

"Dad!" Helen exclaimed.

"Benny!" Theodore exclaimed.

"We want more ice cream!" Regina and Deb demanded and whined respectively.

For the rest of that summer Theodore behaved wonderfully toward his father. He called, he visited with the girls, all the way through the months of househunting, the signing of the contract for the roomy if worn-down three-bedroom colonial on Riverbend Road, and the mid-winter move both of their belongings from the apartment and of Helen's parents' old furniture from storage. Of course over the next few years the relationship would need some booster shots, which usually occurred when Benny released more dollars from Dottie's surprise stash. These were typically starter funds for Theodore's latest money-making project, but Benny was grateful for his son's attention despite thinking it unlikely that anyone would ever want their own "personal computer."

Following Helen's advice Benny indeed "appreciated" Enoch as often as possible even if he never really understood what sort of doctor Enoch was or why he always seemed to need money. He attempted to be supportive of his son, to help out by babysitting the girls, taking them overnight every week or two, taking care of that sick dog of theirs for a few weekends when Helen took the girls out to their island and Enoch was away at conferences or at performances with his theater group. Benny even paid for the family to take a week's vacation on the peninsula at one point, as we'll see. He hoped, for Helen's sake, that this would boost their marriage in the way such offers were boosters for his own relationship with his son.

Wonderful Benny, as sweet as his ice cream, as simple as vanilla.

2

"You slept through that?" Helen said when Theodore finally emerged from the bedroom and came downstairs.

"Through what?"

The sisters were seated in their little plastic princess chairs on opposite sides of the Riverbend living room, each silently facing her respective wall and scowling.

"Never mind. Theodore," Helen arched her eyebrow, "what are you wearing?"

"Slick, isn't it?" he puffed proudly.

He had just begun his jumpsuit phase.

"Are you serious?" Helen asked.

"What? It's alive, and it's in. It's *me*, my baby. But in bright blue."

"More like neon aqua, I would say," Helen said with a sigh. "Could you at least zip it?"

Its single body-long zipper down the middle was undone to just below the level that would be appropriate for a family-oriented outing. Theodore was indeed a hairy man.

"The people should see this," he explained, pointing to his chest fur.

"Theodore."

"Fine," he harrumphed, and zipped. He then withdrew an enormous pair of sunglasses from one of his many zippered pockets, exchanged them with his own glasses, and turned to address his scowling daughters. "I'm ready, girls. Let's blow this popsicle stand!"

Admittedly Theodore had not been well equipped to deal with small children. Nor was he any better equipped than Helen to deal with the girls' relentless fighting. But he was at least equipped for having fun, and he couldn't wait to recount to his one-day future biographer the great effort he was making to get involved in the family, at least when he was around. His best work here was in the year after that awful conversation with Helen we recently overheard, when even he realized that his wife was starting to crack. One glance at her murderous glare when he suggested finding that shrink she'd seen after Debra's birth told him everything he needed to know. And so with a nod to his harried spouse he would lead his daughters to the long journey box to make a small contribution, and then off the three of them would go on the weekends to do something fun while Helen maintained her sanity by immersing herself in her housework.

Typically they would spend the day doing as many things that Helen disapproved of as they could. They'd eat fast food, greasy hamburgers and milkshakes and french fries, and do so *with their fingers*. They would put elbows on the table and point with forks. They would talk with mouths full, *even while chewing*. Then when Theodore was feeling particularly adventurous he would say, "Girls, are you feeling particularly adventurous?"

Yes, yes! they squealed.

"Okay, first, we check for Mummy's spies." They cast furtive glances around the decrepit old-fashioned diner. "Coast clear, ladies?"

Yes, yes! they squealed.

"Then here goes nothing!"

Theodore belched, openly, loudly, *not even covering his mouth*. The girls squealed again as the customers in nearby booths looked around for the offender. When they caught Theodore's eye he'd wink at them at them with his big beardy grin.

Often too on these weekend days they went bowling, or to a movie. Theodore liked going to movies with the girls because then he could see the movies he enjoyed, the comedies, mysteries, *Star Wars*, a nice respite from his regular mind-cracking intellectual work. Helen to the contrary preferred to clean the house listening to Liszt rather than waste her time on low-brow entertainment. Theodore pointed out how well they complemented each other. "Together, Hel," he would say, "we can accomplish both our housecleaning and our consumption of low-brow entertainment!" Helen had to acknowledge both that she enjoyed housecleaning and that she preferred her quarreling daughters' and husband's absence to their presence, so there was little she could prefer to cleaning the house *in* their absence.

"Go lower your unibrow," she'd tease him and off he'd go, grabbing the girls while she grabbed a duster, a cloth, or a mop.

Wherever Theodore went with the girls they loved to play "The Russians Are Coming!" This involved pretending they saw Russian aircraft coming in, or Russian soldiers on the streets, then taking evasive action by driving crazily: ducking as if to hide beneath the dashboard or seats, Theodore frantically swerving the car, pulling it under trees for cover then darting out again, turning on the windshield wipers and squirting the washer fluid while screaming, "Duck! Duck! The Russians are coming!" The girls knew that it was just a game of course, yet the fear and adrenaline would rush as Theodore drove madly down the streets, breaking only for short breathers beneath the trees until someone yelled out "The Russians are coming!" again and Theodore took off once more.

Helen was no fan of this game, naturally. They knew enough not to arrive home all sweaty from ducking Russians because she would know immediately and begin distributing penalties. So to cool down they would first go out for ice cream before heading home and pretending to be hungry for whatever scrumptious supper Helen had prepared. Theodore was on such nice terms with Benny those days that they often went all the way out to the old country to get their ice cream at Iced Cream. These unauthorized visits Benny cherished so much that he agreed to keep them secret from his darling daughter-in-law. Unlike the only other secret he had from her, as we shall see, this one he actually maintained.

You had to admit it: Theodore was a pretty fun dad, when he was around. For a good year or so in particular after that earlier awful conversation Theodore tried hard to make everything work, with Benny, with Helen, with the girls.

It was a good year, or so.

And then.

3

He finally came home with a dog.

Officially the animal was a birthday present for both girls, having been brought home to Riverbend on the afternoon of their eleventh and ninth birthdays. Less officially the canine came home because the male Gale spontaneously decided he needed a dog, and needed one immediately, and so headed straight for the pound to snare whichever sorry beast was next scheduled for the electric chair. Never mind the moratorium on pets that Helen had established the year before, after that cat's demise in the dryer. He was done with that.

It was pouring rain that day when man and dog blew through the door and shook themselves dry onto Helen's clean floor. Helen was out with Deb shoe shopping (as was becoming their birthday tradition) while Regina was off with friends somewhere, all to meet up at home for supper and birthday banana cream pie. Theodore loved the new creature immensely for about an hour-and-a-half, an interval comprised of about ninety seconds during which it consumed the leftover Veal Cordon Bleu from the Frigidaire and then about ninety minutes during which it slept on the threadbare sofa, snoring moistly, while Theodore napped in the adjacent ragged but still pretty comfy chair.

The two animals were still deep in REM when all three female Gales happened to return home simultaneously. Laden with packages, Helen and Debra were just walking up the wet driveway from the bus stop as Regina was being dropped off. "Happy birthday!" they all three said together, cheerfully enough, though Debra's greeting was perhaps more enthusiastic than Regina's, who was busy casting ironic glances at their packages.

The two girls preceded their mother inside and discovered their father and new pet snoring in concert.

"He's so fat!" Regina exclaimed, presumably referring to the dog.

"I … I *love him!*" Deb cried, presumably also referring to the dog, and started to cry.

"Happy birthdays, ladies!" Theodore exclaimed as he jolted awake.

"Theodore," Helen asked, restraining herself from mentioning either the pet moratorium or the wet mess in the front hallway, "is there something wrong with its rump?" The dog had an open sore on its rear, one which had left a small reddish-yellow mark on the sofa cushion where it was sitting, panting happily, enjoying the attention of its new family.

"It's no big deal, Hel," Theodore answered, "they said it's just a rash. Remember when Dubs here was born? We still loved her like crazy!" He winked at Deb, apparently not recalling his inability to touch her for her first few weeks of life. "Now, ladies, what shall we name him?"

"Marvin!" Regina answered, that being the name of the pop singer with whom she was currently infatuated.

"*I* want to name him Marvin!" Deb instantly complained.

"Then Marvin it shall be," Theodore pronounced.

"Whose Marvin?" Regina demanded.

"What?" Theodore asked.

"She's asking," Helen called out from the kitchen where she was now calming herself—about both the moratorium and the mess—with a smoke before making supper, "whether his name is the one she gave the dog or Debra gave the dog."

"But it's the same name."

"Ha!" Helen laughed, puffing.

Theodore sighed. "Fine. We'll name him Marvin Marvin. And now," he gestured toward the panting pooch and back to the girls, "let's take this chunky puppy for a walk!"

Out they went, the girls fighting over who would hold the leash while Helen went looking for the leftover veal she'd planned to serve for supper.

4

Marvin Marvin was a wonderful dog.

He had one goal in life: to be near you. When you were away he slept; but when you came home he was so happy to see you that he would almost explode. If he could talk he would just say your name, over and over. You'd look at him on the sofa and swear he was gazing at you dreamily, that sloppy tongue dripping out of his love-struck smiling snout. You almost didn't mind that the sore or rash on his rump was growing so rapidly.

But it was going to be a rough year.

Plane crashes were killing rock stars and video games were eroding young minds just as the early autumn was turning cold and gray. Theodore was at last hired to a tenure-track line at the university, but while this was good news the accompanying pay raise was too modest to make any real impact on their finances. Meanwhile the poor dog's skin disease was slowly spreading over his body, which itself was becoming even larger despite Helen's attempt to manage his food intake. Regina often entertained herself through the late fall comparing the mutt's growing ugliness with Deb's. Helen was worried about their inability to afford a visit to the vet, not to mention about the reddish-yellow pus stains accumulating each evening on the new floral bedspread she carefully made each morning.

Deb just felt terribly sorry for the poor beast.

Marvin Marvin himself maintained his sunny disposition—happy to see you!—through what must have been a painful condition. "Dogs aren't like people, you know," Theodore pointed out, perhaps to console his daughter. "Whatever their ailments may be they don't wallow in self-pity, which is really what hurts most complainers."

"Dogs *aren't* like people," Helen answered in a rare moment of agreement with her husband. "People generally don't leave pus stains all over." She followed this remark by delegating to the girls responsibility for stain control in different domains. Regina was assigned the front hallway, dining room, and her bedroom, while Deb got the living room, upstairs hallway, and her own room. The kitchen and master bedroom Helen reserved for herself.

Regina soon pressed the arrangement to her advantage.

When she noticed a sore opening she would wipe Marvin Marvin's rear on a living room cushion, which both decreased her labor in the other rooms and increased Deb's. Marvin Marvin was perfectly amenable to this, loving the relief from the itching. Regina also learned to time the deed for immediately before Helen's return from work, which not only gave Deb more cleaning to do but also got her in trouble for not doing the cleaning she was supposed to have done. Helen would remind Deb about keeping up with her responsibilities while Regina silently exulted.

The cold and gray late autumn merged seamlessly into a cold and gray early winter.

The price of heating fuel rose; the morale in the house declined, and with it, to Helen's further concern, the grades on Debra's report cards. Around the same time Marvin Marvin's breath soured, taking a turn for the worse one especially cold crisp morning.

Regina noticed it first.

"Hey sis," she called upstairs to Deb, whom Helen was helping to dress for school. "Come here and smell yourself!"

"Mummy!" Deb complained to Helen.

"Sweetheart, please get your top on," Helen merely sighed.

When they made it downstairs, Deb coming first with Helen coming down right behind her prodding her, Helen went over to the coat closet to get the girls' coats and promptly tripped over one of Deb's shoes.

"Debra," she said tensely, "*please* put your shoes away."

Deb looked down at the floor. Regina beamed, pleased that the planted shoe had worked just as she'd planned. Just then Marvin Marvin—who was gazing at them all lovingly—yawned loudly. They all received a whiff of his breath.

Even Helen couldn't help herself. "Oh, dear!" she muttered.

"It's Deb's fault," Regina volunteered. "She's always feeding him leftovers."

"Shut up!" Deb shouted.

"Girls, please!" Helen, running out of energy, dying for a cigarette, turned to her younger daughter. "Debra, please tell me this is not true?"

Deb face was red.

"Sweetheart, how am I to manage this poor dog's weight if you keep feeding him?"

"But he's hungry, Mummy."

"He is also terribly fat."

"Don't forget his stinky breath!" Regina added.

"Shut up!" Deb shouted.

"Girls will you *stop*!" Helen exclaimed.

Deb's punishment for illicitly feeding the dog was to assume the linens-folding duties for two weeks. This was no mere slap on the wrist. The family of five—including the oozing dog and Theodore, whose ability to leave dirty wet towels in heaps around the house was widely known—dirtied a lot of linens.

5

March was tax preparation time and thus especially stressful for Helen, who was in charge of the finances. Now Helen was an extremely good cook, managing to provide nutritious and tasty meals within their limited budget. She had excellent domestic skills and could keep clothes wearable long after their fashion expiration dates. All in all she did a remarkable job keeping the family above water.

But she was not a miracle worker.

"Theodore," she said one night after the girls had gone to bed.

They were sitting in the living room. Theodore was reading, Helen was smoking. The television was on because its sounds filled up the room with something, at least, when they weren't quarreling, and helped mask their quarreling when they were.

"Yeah," Theodore said, not lifting his eyes from his book.

"There is an exposed wire in the basement," Helen said, suppressing the urge to correct his *yeah* to a *yes*.

"I'm on it," he said, still reading.

"Theodore."

"That's my name. Don't wear it out."

"I am serious."

"All right, all right. I'll seriously take care of it."

"It's dangerous. The girls could touch it. It could start a fire."

"I'll take care of it."

"You said that a week ago."

"'I'll take care of it'; future tense. When I do take care of it, soon, what I said will be true."

"By the time you take care of it, the house will have burned down; future perfect tense."

Theodore put down his book. "Helen, please. I promise, this week."

"I would like to call an electrician."

"It's just a wire. I can tape it. Or replace it. I'll fix it."

"You said that about the dishwasher. Now the girls wash the dishes by hand."

Theodore took off his glasses and rubbed his eyes. "Fine. Call an electrician." He put his glasses back on and picked up his book.

"Theodore," Helen said.

He sighed again. "Yeah?"

She suppressed again. "There is no money for an electrician."

"Why is there no money for an electrician?"

"Perhaps you can tell me. You said your salary was going to increase with the tenure-track job."

"Helen, you know I don't pay attention to details. Maybe it's a probationary period. Maybe the salary increase kicks in next year. Maybe it's a mistake." He recognized the look in her eye. "I'll find out. This week."

"That is not the point. I want *you* to fix the wire."

"All right," he said, exasperated. "I'll fix the wire. Like I said."

Helen gazed at him. Twelve years married to him already. How was this possible? Although gazing at him as he sat there, back to reading, that broad, built man, his wild hair, his dark-rimmed glasses, his blue eyes, she had to admit: he was handsome. Not at the peak of his handsomeness lately, especially with the weight gain, but still handsome. She thought briefly of Eddie Love, back in high school. He was handsome too, and a lot of good that did her.

"Theodore," she said.

"Helen," he said, softly, putting down his book again for what he knew would be the duration of the conversation. "What is it?"

"You must have noticed that the dog is not doing well."

"All of Riverbend Road has noticed. We're starting to get cease and desist letters from the homeowners' association."

"Very amusing. But this is serious. His rash is spreading. He has become increasingly obese despite the diet I have him on. One of his eyes is clouding over."

"So?"

"Deb asked me today why we haven't taken him to the vet."

"And why haven't we?"

"You'd have heard her ask if you'd been home this afternoon, as you were supposed to be."

"Was I?" Theodore answered quickly. "I had a meeting."

"You had a meeting Tuesday."

"I'm a professor. Meeting is two-thirds of our job description."

"Perhaps being a member of this family should be two-thirds of *your* job description."

Theodore looked at her silently.

"Between your meetings and your book and whatever else you are up to," Helen added, "you are not exactly home much lately."

"Hel," Theodore said, very softly. "What is your point exactly?"

She looked at him. "I hate when you call me that."

"Helen, then," he answered, averting his gaze.

"The point is, I have made an appointment with the vet."

"I thought you said there was no money for a vet."

"I said there is no money for an electrician. There is money for a vet. I am taking it out of the long journey box."

There was a *long* silence.

"Have you anything to say?" Helen was demanding.

He didn't, really. But for some reason that didn't stop him.

"I don't know," Theodore answered sharply. "Maybe you should go to work on Benny instead. He likes you. For you he might loosen that little fist of his a little."

Helen frowned. "That is an awful way to speak of your father, Theodore—especially since he has been more than generous toward us already." She made a broad gesture indicating the house as a whole.

"All right, then, Helen. If money is the issue here, then how about you sell some of your parents' furniture?" He made the same broad gesture. "Maybe it's worth something. And anyway this place is like a museum. Or a mausoleum. I'm tired of living surrounded by all this old—"

"I'm sorry?" Helen glared.

He looked at her. "All I'm saying is that people pay good money for stuff like this, old things, antiques. Someone would probably even pay for your mother's old ironing board in the basement. Me, I like new things. Out with the old, in with the new, all that sort. It's an option, that's all, if money is the problem."

"It is not an option. And money is not the problem."

"Jesus, Helen, you're impossible! Then what *is* the problem?"

But the conversation was over. Helen had lit another cigarette and was now staring at the black-and-white television they had inherited from her mother.

6

The vet prescribed some skin treatments along with a special diet to manage the animal's obesity. Deb and her mother jointly did everything the vet recommended, including the nightly baths with the medicated shampoo. These were the only times Marvin Marvin failed to be giddy with happiness, being giddy instead with absolute ecstasy. Helen and Deb would be on hands and knees next to each other leaning over the tub, both scrubbing, while Marvin Marvin lay there in bliss. Helen would say, "Deb, rub like this," and Deb would rub just like that, and Helen, well, seemed actually pleased with Deb's work. Sometimes Deb might splash water on the floor and Helen wouldn't even make her clean it up immediately. Once, even, during a fit of giggles triggered by the happy mutt's underwater flatulence, Deb gently leaned into her mother and lingered ever so briefly and her mother barely even tensed up from the physical contact. Deb found herself feeling almost as giddy as the happy puppy in the tub.

Regina was not at all pleased with this turn of events.

It was time for the shoes.

It was almost too easy to add a shoe or two, in some provocative location, to the shoes of her sister's already scattered around the house. Nothing irritated Helen more than Deb's shoes being where they didn't belong, and even the generally unflappable Theodore could be counted on to bellow at Deb whenever he tripped on her footwear. No wait, there *was* one thing which irritated Helen more than finding Deb's shoes around the house: finding her *own* shoes around the house. When things were *really* grim Regina would sneak into Helen's closet, approach the main shoe rack and, nervously, choose some pair to be planted somewhere. Since it was Deb who shared Helen's love of shoes, especially of *Helen's* shoes, it was always Deb who was blamed when they were discovered either to be missing or somewhere where they shouldn't be.

"It wasn't me!" Deb would wail, to no avail. For everyone knew that Deb was the untidy one while Regina was neat. That Deb was irresponsible while Regina's chores were done on time. That Deb was always distracted while Regina's head was on straight. And most of all that Deb was in love with shoes, with her mother's shoes. Everyone knew the facts, Deb's denials notwithstanding, and so poor little Deb was simply not to be believed. (In fact Deb herself was so poor at keeping track of her things that she didn't always believe her own denials, either.)

And yet these episodes were just minor setbacks for the younger sister. Marvin Marvin was getting better, her mother was being nicer to her lately, and even Theodore, the last few weeks anyway, seemed to be in a particularly pleasant mood, at least when he was around.

"Of course he's in a good mood, sweetheart," Helen replied to Deb one evening when the almost-ten-year-old had remarked upon her father's disposition. Helen was having her cigarette with her daughters at the kitchen table, where Regina was helping her younger sister with some remedial math homework. "He barely works throughout the school year, and now that the term is ending he's looking forward to not working at all."

Things, for the moment, were looking up.

7

One evening when Theodore was home for dinner he made an announcement. "Girls, Lady," he said, tapping his glass with his fork, "and Mutt: what say you to a week at the beach?"

Helen interrupted the girls' excited squeals. "Theodore?"

"Hel, it'll be great. We'll celebrate the end of the semester with a week on the peninsula. I got a great deal on a house. Pre-Memorial Day rate. Two bedrooms, a porch, indoor plumbing, two toilets, the whole package! We can even bring the mutt, if you want."

"*Pre*-Memorial Day?"

"Yeah, it's next week. I had to act fast to get the deal."

"Next *week*? But I have got to work. The girls are still in school."

"We'll take them out for a week, it won't kill them. You'll get the time off, that boss of yours worships you. Remember that extra week he gave you, a few years ago? Why not another?"

Helen cringed at the reference. "But—"

"Some sun and fun on *the peninsula*, baby!"

"But it is not even warm on the peninsula before Memorial Day. And—Debra has not been doing well in school. And the girls would have to share a room. They have not been able to go fifteen minutes without fighting lately. And—the dog," she said, "is practically blind now. Bringing him to a new place would disorient him." She was speaking rapidly now. "Did you give this any thought at all?"

"We won't fight!" Regina proclaimed.

"We promise!" Deb exclaimed.

"You think too much, my baby," Theodore said. "A week at the beach. An incredible deal on a house. You can spend the whole week smoking on the porch if you like. And—indoor plumbing, Hel, indoor plumbing!"

"But what is wrong with the island? We go every summer. Whenever we want. And it does not cost anything."

"The island is a lonely shack on a rock with a lot of mosquitoes. I'm talking about a week at the beach, the whole town a few minutes' walk away. And anyway," he added, "I've already paid."

"Theodore," Helen said after a pause, "perhaps we should

discuss this later."

Theodore sighed. "Once you would have jumped at the chance for indoor plumbing at the beach, Hel. Life as a fat cat has really spoiled you." He winked, but not at anyone in particular.

"Theodore," Helen said evenly.

"All right, all right." Theodore looked over to Deb and mouthed the words, "indoor plumbing," before returning his attention to his wife's outstanding Parmesan Cheese Soufflé.

They did discuss the proposal later, with the television turned up. Helen castigated Theodore for being irresponsible, for committing to a beach house when funds were so tight, for not being home enough, for still not having fixed that exposed wire in the basement. While she was at it she registered her perennial complaint that he was too easy on the girls, always having fun with them but never sharing in the discipline, and as she got fully worked up she threw in the observation that he was letting himself go lately, gaining weight, neglecting his personal hygiene, and most of all doing nothing about the fact that he seemed to be the only man in history to suffer not from a receding hairline but from an actively advancing one.

"That," Theodore said with a start, "is cold, woman."

"The truth, sometimes," Helen replied, "can be."

Yet Theodore was conciliatory.

He could do some summer teaching to help pay for the vacation. Over the summer, too, he wouldn't have so many meetings and could be home more. He'd be happy to punish the girls once in a while too; Helen would just have to guide him as to when that was appropriate. As for letting himself go, well a week at the beach would be just the thing to jump-start an exercise program. And as for his hair situation, well, he said, perhaps they should all just learn to live with it. "I am, after all," he noted, "just as God made me."

"You do not believe in God."

"Evolution, then?" Theodore winked. "And by the way that wire," he added sincerely, "I swear to you it has moved to the top of my list."

"You also do not have a list."

"Okay, second on the list, right after 'make a list.'"

Helen smiled despite herself.

"I'll fix it before we leave," Theodore added, realizing that his charm offensive had for once been heavier on the charm than on the offensive. "I promise."

So they worked it out.

Maybe a few days away would be good for them, Helen thought to herself a few nights later, smoking in bed after Theodore had fallen asleep beside her. She thought a bit about the early days of their courtship. For their first date at Cozzen's Café he had shown up fifteen-and-a-half minutes late. She had just left but he'd chased her down the block and sweet-talked her into carrying on with the date, and she, choosing to think less and live more, had allowed herself to be moved by his persistence and charmed by his intelligence and wit, and had accepted his claim that being fifteen minutes late was irregular for him. It wasn't until late in their first year of marriage that she appreciated that fifteen minutes late *was* irregular for him: irregularly *early*.

Still, before that had become clear she had enjoyed his spontaneity, had enjoyed the sense with him that ordinary rules didn't always matter. This trip to the beach almost felt the same way. Almost decadent, really. Like they used to be, at least a little. Theodore used to look so handsome in his bathing trunks, his rainbow sunglasses dangling on his broad tanned hairy chest. Or at least he did before the years had started to take their toll. Before that long haul through graduate school. Before the professional disappointments, the inability to get a permanent position, the financial stress and humiliation of relying on his wife to support the family with her own meager salary. Before the emotional stress of having two little girls constantly at war. Before having to live up to the impossibly demanding standards of a wife who thought too much and maybe really did live too little.

Helen glanced over at the case of cleaning supplies she had already packed for the peninsula and smiled. Decadence had its appeal but there were limits.

"Theodore," she whispered to him in bed. He was breathing quietly, regularly, deeply. "Theodore," she repeated.

He did not stir.

8

The weather was pleasantly warm when they arrived at the peninsula. The next morning, the first of their vacation, Helen actually slept late.

She was dreaming about Theodore's sailboat. At the time he had somehow convinced her, apprehensive as she was about large bodies of water, to come sailing on the bay with him. The convincing was effected mostly by his self-confidence, his at that time athletic build, and the fact that the sailing lessons (he claimed) were going beautifully. They dropped the girls at Helen's mother's and drove down to the marina. The first twenty minutes were splendid, namely the part where they packed the boat and pushed off into the bay under sunny skies. Things started to degenerate when the sail got stuck halfway up the mast, leaving the craft unsteerable. Then it began to rain. The Coast Guard rescued them two hours later as they were drifting toward the open ocean. Helen's most significant memory from the event was that during its last hour or so even Theodore seemed afraid.

"Breakfast! Pancakes! French toast! Eggs!"

Helen was startled awake by the chorus of voices, discovering the entire family in bed with her, barking dog and all. A quick glance assured her that Marvin Marvin was not soiling the blanket. Relaxing, pleasantly surprised, recovering from her dream she said, "That would be lovely."

"Yes it would!" Theodore poked her playfully. "I'll have the Blueberry Pancakes, the girls will have the Maple French Toast, and I'm sure Stinky McNickles here would love one of your Three-Cheese Omelettes. And would it kill you to put on some coffee?"

He winked at her. Helen's instinct was to glare. For a moment she felt herself still on the uncontrollable sailboat in the bay, the wind picking up, the rain pouring down. But then she looked at her two beautiful not-so-little girls in bed with her, still in pajamas, Regina, almost twelve, starting to develop into a young woman, Deb, almost ten, as innocent as could be, and she looked at Theodore, all smiles, enjoying his sense of humor, enjoying their daughters. They were on vacation, she thought, they were at the beach, they were a family. She remembered that after their rescue she and Theodore had returned to their apartment where they'd showered, warmed up next to the portable space heater wearing only some thick violet towels, and then made love on the rug. That feeling, almost, returned to her here in bed, with Theodore, with their daughters, and suddenly she found Theodore's joke, even if at her expense, almost as amusing as they all did.

They were on vacation, she thought; they were a family.

"One Deb special, one Regina special, and one Theodore," she said, smiling as she climbed out of bed, "not so special, coming right up."

"Don't forget Marvin Marvin, Mummy," Deb said.

"I suppose a break from his diet," Helen agreed, "won't kill him."

9

It was a wonderful week.

Or it was until the day before their departure.

The day was overcast, cool, not very beach-friendly. They'd run low on provisions and nobody felt like going out so Helen and the girls breakfasted only on some toast and marmalade. Theodore didn't get up till late morning. The girls spent the morning watching videos, at least during the moments when they weren't fighting over which ones to watch, in what order, when to fast-forward, etc. Helen constantly had to interrupt her cleaning to make peace, at least temporarily, between them. When Theodore finally did wake up he was grumpy and annoyed to discover nothing interesting to eat. He ate his toast in sullen silence, watched videos with the girls for a while, but then couldn't deal with the bickering anymore and went back to sleep. Helen knew it wasn't worth trying to convince him to walk into town for supplies for their last day, and so figured it would have to be her. The only question was whether the girls could be left on their own without harming each other.

"I'll go," Regina announced, after Helen had paused the video and explained that she was going out and if there were any bruises on anybody when she returned there would be hell to pay.

"I'm sorry?" Helen said.

"I'll do it," Regina repeated, getting up from the couch. "I'm sick of sitting around this place with Miss Ugly here, anyway. I'll take the dog, too. God knows he could use the airing out."

Deb began to protest (Marvin Marvin was her dog to walk, after all) but then stopped herself. Despite her love for the beast she also relished this rare opportunity to watch videos without her sister around.

Helen was skeptical—pre-teen Regina actually volunteering for something?—but it would make things easier if Regina went. Helen could get some cleaning done and not be so pressured before tomorrow's departure, and maybe she could even convince Deb to finish up the schoolwork she'd been assigned for the week.

"All right then. Thank you, sweetheart. And don't forget your sweatshirt. It's cold out there."

"Back in a jif," Regina said, leashing the mutt. She stepped over to her sister, sitting on the couch. "See you later, ol' buddy ol' chum," she added, knuckling Deb with a rock-hard dead-arm.

The older sister returned about ninety minutes later. She was carrying a small bag of groceries, another bag with a carton of cigarettes for her mother—adolescents could still buy cigarettes for their parents in those days, at least in beach towns—and her face was flushed from the chilly air, her hair wet from the drizzle. A storm was coming in.

Marvin Marvin was not with her.

10

Helen could barely hear anything above her younger daughter's wailing.

"What do you mean, you lost him?" she demanded of Regina.

"I lost him," Regina repeated, flushed, still holding the groceries.

"How could you lose him?"

"He lost me. He ran away."

"He ran away?"

"He ran away."

"He was half-lame and more or less blind. How could he run away?"

"I don't know. He crawled away. He's gone."

"How could he be gone?"

"Mummy," Regina said. "He's gone."

Deb wailed so loudly that Theodore, asleep in another room, almost stirred.

"Tell me," Helen said evenly, "exactly what happened."

"I went to the store," Regina said, tears forming in her eyes. "I tied him up outside. When I came back out, he was gone."

"Gone? Just like that?"

"Gone."

"Did somebody take him?"

"I don't know! And why would anybody take *him*?"

Helen ignored this. "Did you look for him?"

111

"Of course I looked for him. That's what took me so long."

"Jesus," Helen said. She fumbled with the new carton, pulled out a pack, and withdrew a cigarette. Outside it was just miserable, the cold rain picking up.

"Mummy," Deb wailed. "We have to go find him."

"I know, I know," Helen said, biting her lip. "Regina, you go wake your father. We'll deal with you later. Debra, come, let's get your raingear on."

Out they went, the army of four, in search of their missing canine. Helen paired with Deb and Theodore with Regina; it was clearly impossible for Deb and Regina to be together, Deb already having screamed that she would hate Regina forever and Regina replying that that would suit her just fine forever. Theodore, eyeing the weather, first suggested that they just wait and see if anybody reported finding a dog, but when met with Deb's angry glare he joined the search.

Their searches were cold, wet, and fruitless.

Collectively they combed the streets of the small town, the nearby beaches, peered into yards, climbed up dunes, but nothing. The rain picked up and the temperature went down as they wandered back and forth and sideways, asking the few people outside in this weather if they'd seen a jolly corpulent mutt with cloudy eyes and diseased skin. Time was running out. They would have to vacate the house, and the peninsula, the next morning. By late in the day they had reconvened at the house to discuss strategy. It was out of the question that the girls would continue searching at night, and in this weather. They would stay at home and prepare missing-dog flyers to be posted everywhere, the next morning before departure, should that prove necessary.

It thus fell upon Theodore to continue the search that evening after supper.

"Fine," he said with a deep sigh as he re-donned his raingear and disappeared into the darkness.

It was a long night for the female Gales, sitting at home, listening to the rain splattering on the roof. It was a long night for Deb, whimpering, thinking of her poor dog out there somewhere in this tempest alone, hungry, and shivering. It was a long night for Regina, the other Regina, the one who herself began to cry as she listened to her sister's pained whimpers. And it was a long night for Helen trying to console her younger daughter, trying not to believe that her older daughter could possibly have been so cruel as to deliberately lose that unfortunate beast, and wondering precisely what was taking her husband so long. For surely *Theodore* of all people wouldn't spend the entire night out there in the rain looking for that dog?

11

Early the next morning the sun was shining, the temperature was warm, and a bleary-eyed Marvin Marvin straggled home beside a blearier-eyed Theodore Gale. Though the beast was much the worse for wear, he still mustered some of his characteristic happiness to see them—if at this stage he was seeing much at all.

It was, to be sure, quite the coup for Theodore with Deb. "Daddy!" she squealed with delight, alternating enormous hugs for both the man and the animal before dragging the dog away to lather him with love. Theodore turned toward Helen expecting the hero's welcome and was annoyed by her strangely mixed reaction. Meanwhile the regular Regina—who had also returned by morning, though in a mildly attenuated form—merely muttered, "It's just a *dog*," and returned to packing her suitcase. She'd had quite enough of this peninsula and couldn't get out of there soon enough.

But out they got, just by their noon deadline, and headed home to begin that decisive summer in their family story.

12

They were welcomed home by the first ninety-degree days of early summer. These might not have been so dreadful had they not also revealed the fact that their air conditioning had succumbed to the extended lack of proper maintenance. Nobody was much in a good mood when the heat wave hit, and held on.

Theodore was gone more often than ever, having perhaps followed up on his pledge to do some summer teaching or more likely just taking advantage of the university's air conditioning. The girls were attending a day camp, where Helen dropped them on her way to work and picked them up on the way home. That meant that Marvin Marvin spent a lot of time alone in the overheated house, deteriorating. So much so, in fact, that even Theodore, coming home so seldom for supper these days that Helen requested he knock before entering the house, noticed.

"Hey," he said one Sunday evening, twirling long strands of

capellini on his fork and splashing a drop of its puttanesca sauce on the embroidered placemat Helen had inherited from her mother. "Old Marvy over there," he nodded toward the listless dog, "isn't looking very marvy. Have they given up on him?"

"The vet doesn't think there is much to be done," Helen replied softly. She was determined to make this a pleasant meal. The girls were at Benny's and so she and her husband were having one of their rare opportunities to be alone. "That night really did something to the skin."

"Yeah," Theodore said, now chewing. "He really smells lately."

"It's terribly sad. It's awful."

"Yeah. If we lived in the Arctic the Eskimos would ask us to leave the continent."

"He cannot help it, you know."

"It's just a shame to see him suffer like that."

"He still seems—happy."

"You think? He looks pretty miserable to me."

Helen put down her fork. "What are you saying, Theodore?"

"What do you mean?"

"Are you suggesting we—get rid of him?"

"Who said that? And who *would* say that?"

"You, and you."

"Why would I suggest that? Just because he smells awful? Because he needs to be walked five times a day? And taken to the vet three times a week? Who," he pointed his capellini-entwirled fork toward the dog, "would want to get rid of *that?*"

"It is rude to point with your fork."

"Right-o." Theodore put it down.

"In any case, you are not the one taking care of him. You are not the one cleaning the house. For all practical purposes you do not even pay the bills. What is it to *you* what condition he's in?"

"I live here, that's all."

"Hardly!"

"Look, Helen," Theodore answered. "All I said was that he smells. You don't need to turn this into a harangue. You've got to stop over-interpreting everything I say. Everything I say, everything I do, I feel like I'm just—*stepping* in it with you. In fact—"

"Forgive me for resisting, Theodore, when you wander in here every other blue moon and start expressing opinions."

Theodore stared at her. "The only opinion I now care to

express," he said sharply, getting up from the table, "is that one of us needs a large serving of dessert." He left the table in search of something rich and sweet and preferably creamy. This quest took him through the kitchen, past the Frigidaire with the fresh banana cream pie inside, and directly out the back door of the house without another word; and he drove off, not to return that night.

Or for the next several, for that matter. Spent, he later claimed, in the air-conditioned comfort of his office, on the cot installed there for just that purpose.

13

That's about when the animal started chewing on things.

He started out modestly, on dirty socks of Theodore's that belonged in the trash anyway. But by late June he had destroyed some of Regina's things, including some of the jewelry she had lately begun wearing. Regina could not stop complaining about him, which naturally caused Deb to start demanding she stop, which led to several instances where the girls, arming themselves with the cooking utensils Helen had recently given them, had to be physically separated.

But then the poor fellow chewed through the portrait of Helen's parents that her father had commissioned for her mother right after he—or as he would say, they—won their first mayoral election. Helen discovered the damage one Saturday morning while doing her regular top-to-bottom dusting of the house. She took a deep breath and looked at the dog. Then she stopped dusting and went outside to sit on the front porch for a smoke in the hot morning air.

It was just a painting, she thought to herself.

That's when he found her shoes.

How he found his way into her high-security walk-in closet no one could say. How he had the energy in that summer-long heat wave to make his way upstairs into that closet and chew a half-dozen different shoes—all from different pairs—was hard to explain. The animal had been unlucky enough in life to have been abandoned at the pound, to have been abandoned overnight in the storm, to have been inflicted with inexplicable medical problems. To these he now added the misfortune of coming between one wits'-ended Mrs. Helen Gale and her shoes.

It was straight to the basement for him.

"I am sorry, sweetheart, but that," Helen explained to Deb, over the girl's wails as she tried to stop Helen from dragging him downstairs, "is where he must now reside."

"Good riddance," Regina chipped in from the kitchen. She was enjoying a second cold glass of lemonade not because she was thirsty but because she wanted to ensure that none was left for her sister.

"Mummy!" Deb cried. "Please don't put him there!"

"I am afraid that this door must remain closed," Helen said, closing it behind the animal.

"He'll die of loneliness down there!"

"I already *said* good riddance," Regina added cheerfully.

"Shut up!"

"Debra," Helen said as she slid the lock across the basement door. "Please stop crying. He will be fine."

"He'll die," Deb sobbed.

"Sweetheart," Helen said, taking Deb by the shoulders. "You must learn to control yourself. You are ten years old now. This is no way for a big girl to behave." She knew she should probably caress her daughter's hair or something but didn't quite know how. "He will be fine."

But he was not fine.

It was Deb who found him two hours later, when Helen unlocked the door so Deb could get him for a walk. The not-so-big girl ran downstairs and discovered her beloved companion lying on the floor seizing, his eyelids flickering, his body quivering, his mouth open and drooling. In that open mouth was the exposed and very much live wire which her father had never gotten around to fixing. Helen heard her daughter scream and went running down the stairs to find the little girl hugging the animal and sobbing.

"Oh my Lord," Helen exclaimed.

She slowly extricated Deb from the dog and then the dog from the wire. Then, somehow calmly, she managed to get both girls and the dog, no longer seizing but now unconscious and weighing at least sixty pounds, into the car and on the way to the animal hospital.

Nobody knew where Theodore was.

14

Marvin Marvin survived.

Theodore turned out to be out of town. At a conference, he said, sorry he'd forgotten to mention it. Helen filled him in curtly, trying to quell her ever increasing suspicions about his behavior in order to devote full attention to the needs both of the dog and her younger daughter.

"He's got some burns, but these can be treated," she told Theodore on the phone when he'd called in from wherever he was. "And the vet doesn't expect any permanent damage from the wire. She said he was already alert this morning, seemed to be smiling at her."

"Wow," Theodore said, thoughtfully. "I should have fixed that wire."

Helen paused. "When were you planning to be back, exactly?"

"Probably tomorrow."

"Probably?"

"Right-o. Tomorrow."

"All right then. The vet wants to keep him another day for observation. Do you think you could pick him up tomorrow afternoon on your way home?"

"You got it."

"And please do not forget to bring home whatever medications they prescribe. We will need to take care of the burns right away."

"Aye-aye, Captain," Theodore said. He was probably winking on the other end of the line. "Over and out!"

Theodore did come home the next day, as promised. It was early July, exactly thirteen months from the day when Theodore had first brought Marvin Marvin home.

Except on this day, as Debra saw immediately from her anxious perch on the porch, he came home without the dog.

Her tummy sank.

15

"You did what?" Helen said over Deb's wails.

"Everybody hated him," Theodore said.

"Wow," both Reginas said simultaneously.

"I do not understand how this is possible," Helen said, wondering, hopelessly, how to comfort her younger daughter.

"Your shoes, Helen," Theodore explained. "I know how much those mean to you. And Regina here has been trying to get rid of the thing ever since she ditched him on the peninsula!"

"I did not!" Regina protested.

"You did too, you big liar!"

"Don't you call *me* a liar, you liar!"

"I will not be spoken to this way by a—thirteen-year-old!"

"She's twelve, Theodore," Helen said, not knowing where to begin. "And never mind us. Her ten-year-old sister loved that dog."

"She complained about him too."

"I did not!" Deb exclaimed.

"I complain about *you*, Theodore," Helen objected sharply. "But that does not mean I have you murdered."

Deb recommenced wailing.

"Listen," Theodore said, rapidly fluctuating between feeling flustered, irritated, and outraged. The little bits of skin on his face that weren't obscured by hair or glasses were bright red and he was sweating furiously, even beyond that warranted by the eighty-five-degree temperature inside the house. "I thought this was what you wanted."

"How could you possibly think that?" Helen asked.

"The dog was chewing everything. He was obviously suffering. What else should I have thought?"

"I kinda liked him," Regina offered, happily lying in order to increase Theodore's own suffering.

"But he wasn't suffering," Helen said. "The vet said he was still happy."

"Look. The hospital bill was huge. The medicines the vet mentioned were ridiculously expensive. You're the one always complaining about the budget. I did it for you. There was no other way."

"I'm sorry?" Helen said.

"They said they'd forgive the hospital bill if we donated his body to research."

There was absolute silence, except for the whirring of the fans everywhere throughout the overheating house.

The three females just stared at him.

"He was a very special dog," Theodore added. "Medically speaking, anyway."

Nothing was said. Not a word.

Just staring.

"It was for science?" Theodore said softly.

But what he was thinking was, *what the fuck do you people want from me?*

They just stared at him, these three females, and it was these stares and this silence which would confront him repeatedly, in various manifestations, over the next several years; it was with these stares and this silence that the year of the dog came whimpering to its quiet close.

CHAPTER SIX
THE VERY BUSY DAY

1

The peninsula. The dog.

Theodore slogging through the rain, cursing the rain, cursing the dog, cursing Benny for sending them on this trip in the first place. He walked into the town—a few shops, a couple of restaurants, a pub—but he was not going to spend any more time outside looking for that mutt so he headed straight for the pub. It was warm and dark and most of all dry inside as Theodore removed his rain slicker and shook himself off. Since it was not yet high season and the weather was awful the place was nearly empty, as he could see through the dim tavern lighting. A few couples or threesomes scattered around the tables. Someone throwing darts along the wall. A few people at the bar. Among them was a very tall woman, sipping a martini. She had long dark hair and was by herself.

Theodore loved tall, dark-haired women who were by themselves at bars.

He shook himself off once more and deposited himself on the stool beside her. He promptly noticed she wasn't wearing a ring. Theodore had stopped wearing his own wedding band a while back: at some point during his weight gain it had stopped fitting comfortably and he was afraid of its getting stuck.

"My wife doesn't appreciate me," he said, going for the direct approach.

"I can see why," the woman answered without looking up.

"Tchiao!" Theodore said for lack of anything else to say while he quickly worked out a new approach. "Listen," he said to her, signaling the bartender. "You haven't seen a dog around here, by any chance? A mangy mutt, big as a hippo, with some kind of skin disease?"

The woman looked Theodore up and down, noting that he

himself roughly fit that same description. His full facial hair precluded her from determining precisely the state of his skin, though from what showed, around his eyes, all red and puffy, all signs pointed to yes. She'd also noticed—who could have not?—the way he'd shaken himself dry upon entering the pub.

"As a matter of fact I have," she said. And, as a matter of fact, she had.

"My name's Theodore," he extended his large hand, "and I am *very* pleased to meet you."

Jane Nepean had just left her most recent husband two weeks before. After giving her legal team instructions about the assets of his she intended to acquire through the divorce, she'd come to the peninsula to relax for a few days in the summer house she intended to keep for herself. Late that afternoon she had discovered a mangy mutt, big as a hippo and with some kind of skin disease, whimpering on her porch taking shelter from the rain. Feeling pity for the creature—perhaps inspired by the way he seemed to smile at her despite obviously being so miserable—she had fed him, though she didn't have quite enough pity to actually take him inside her house. She'd then headed to the pub for supper, leaving him waiting for her on her porch.

As Deb would often say to Dr. J. later, Theodore Gale was consistently lucky in inverse proportion to what he deserved, and never more so than now. Jane Nepean, it turned out, loved sex and food, and preferably in combination with each other. Sex before and/or after food or food before and/or after sex; sex using food or eating food during sex; it was all good. She maintained her rail-thin figure mostly by sexing off all that food she consumed. After two or three husbands, too, she was in no mood for any immediate commitments either. She just wanted to enjoy all the goodies her lawyers had extracted from her various exes.

Theodore was so damn lucky.

Jane Nepean looked at him in the soft light and thought to herself, that will do. She placed her long-fingered hand inside his. Half an hour later she had taken him back to her summer house and was doing very un-Helen-like things to his body, not caring in the slightest whether he had a wife, much less one who appreciated him; and then she was perfectly content to send him home the next morning, bleary-eyed but satisfied, with a bedraggled mutt named Marvin Marvin trotting along and her phone number scribbled on a scrap of paper in his rain slicker pocket.

Oh, and she also happened to have just moved into a comfortable three-bedroom condo with some delicious air conditioning not twenty minutes from Theodore's office at the university. It was here that Theodore cooled off after many hot days that summer by getting sweaty with Jane on her enormous round bed. It was from here, too, from this bed, that Theodore would call home from his many "conferences" that summer and beyond. And so it was from this bed that Theodore called home to learn that the dog he had once boasted of rescuing from the electric chair had nearly been fried by the exposed wire he had once boasted of being about to repair.

Deb, just ten at the time, never forgave him about that dog. The episode also marked a shift in the balance of power between him and his older daughter: Regina could now invoke it whenever it was useful, not least by referring to Theodore as the Kanine Killer, the Mutt Murderer, or just Homo Homicidus. (She had just learned the Linnean system in school and, being just the right age, loved the idea of a "homo" category.) "Don't annoy him," she would warn Deb in front of him, to annoy him, "or he'll just have you killed." As for Helen, well the dog episode was just one more piece of the increasingly disturbing puzzle which was Theodore, though admittedly a generous one.

Not that Theodore cared much in the several years to follow what the female Gales were thinking or even doing, exactly.

2

Actually Theodore did care what they were thinking and doing over those years, for that's what justified what *he* was thinking and doing.

His wife did *not* appreciate him. He had big plans and ambitions; she was small-minded and limited in imagination. He wanted to make an impact, to write that groundbreaking book on Elenchi; she wanted only to make sure the pansies were watered and the pie was in the oven on Sunday morning. He wanted to do things, to travel, to experience, to have fun; her idea of having fun was doing her Saturday housecleaning early so she could travel to the musty basement and experience the joy of dusting her parents' junk down there. He wanted to be spontaneous, unpredictable, let his bushy locks down a little; her idea of being wild was to venture into a travel agency once a year and ask about the cost of airplane tickets to the promised land, only to come back home and sadly announce that the long journey box did not contain enough to go this year.

The only thing they had in common anymore, in fact, was that they both liked to smoke cigarettes after sex. But even here Theodore was an occasional smoker who wanted to have sex continuously, while Helen was a continuous smoker who consented to have sex only occasionally—if she ever truly consented at all.

And his daughters. Well they used to be good for some fun, at least before Helen got her hooks into them. It was becoming clear that she was brainwashing them, forming them into a little cabal against him. Regina had always been allied with Helen of course, and always been insolent, but there had been an unmistakable increase in her hostility to him after the episode with the mutt. She couldn't care less about that dog, he knew that, but then suddenly she was pretending it had been the nearest thing to her heart. But now even his little Dub, whom he'd tried to shelter from Helen's unfair demands, whom he'd tried to, well, *love*, while Helen was blaming her for everything wrong in their lives—even she was lately turning into a Regina, developing a snottiness as oversized as the breasts which, at thirteen, she was generously sporting.

"That girl's got a triple-D attitude," Theodore had said to Jane Nepean one recent night at their condo. It was "their" condo now, according to Jane. No, his name was not on the papers but he had more or less moved in over the past year and she was insisting he contribute to the monthly maintenance fees.

"Get her an attitude bra, then," Jane said wearily. Her project to diminish his complaining about his family was still very much a work in progress.

"It's not just the younger one," he continued, "it's all of them. So damn ungrateful after everything I've done for them over the years. Like all the time I've spent playing with those girls. The things I've gotten for them. The pets I've brought home. Putting up with that dog, going out in the pouring rain to look for him. And all that cost money, you know, not to mention the hard work to earn that money. Do you have any idea how hard I've worked?"

"I do," Jane said, "but listen, Theodore: you can't let them treat you this way. You need to grow some—what is the medical term—'balls'?" She gazed at him. "Now why don't you freshen up our cocktails and tell me again how hard you've worked?"

How hard had he worked? Theodore continued, pouring the Captain Morgan's Spiced Rum (his with a couple of rocks, hers straight up). Toiling for years through graduate school, finally earning the tenure-track position, working long hours on that book so as to ensure he would receive tenure in the coming academic year—that is what he had done for his family. And in response all he got when he was home were cold silences and shoulders, sullenness beyond even that expected of teenagers, and a wife who had long stopped setting a place for him at the supper table. No wonder he was spending most of his time at Jane Nepean's, he would tell his one-day future biographer. The female Gales had driven him there.

"Jane," Theodore had said the night before, yet again, "my family doesn't appreciate me."

This time Jane attempted a different tack.

"That's easy to fix," she answered from inside the bedroom closet. She was rummaging for the mask and snorkel she had put away after their underwater intercourse in the bay the week before. (They'd roped themselves to the small yacht her lawyers had acquired from her first ex-husband and gone at it like a swarm of jellyfish.)

Her remark was followed by a muffled reply.

"Sorry?" Theodore said, sitting on the edge of the round bed.

Jane removed the tube end of the snorkel from her mouth, making a loud "pop" sound as it escaped her powerful lips. "Time for a new family, I said."

Theodore stared at her.

She reached out and began rubbing his scrotum through his pants.

"Give me some babies, baby," she said, now rubbing upward.

"Suddenly you want children?" The only discussions about children they'd had so far, in their three-and-a-half-year affair, had been one-sided: Theodore ranting about his.

"It'd be a hoot."

If there was one sticky spot in their relationship—prior to the topic of kids, which was clearly about to become the second—it was her use of expressions such as "hoot."

"A hoot?!" He was having difficulty concentrating as she began rubbing the shaft of his penis directly. "Hootness is not a reason to have kids. And besides, you swore you didn't want children."

"I swear a lot of things. Hey, how does this feel?"

"Jane," Theodore was struggling to focus, "do you have any idea how much children cost?"

"Don't talk about money when I'm about to fellate you," she answered, opening his zipper. "It makes me feel like a whore."

"Wait, do or don't?" Theodore gasped.

Jane might have been smiling though it was hard at this point to tell. Anyway Theodore couldn't trouble himself with that question, aware as he was, alternately, of the sensations imposed upon him by Jane's firm tongue and the anxieties imposed upon him by her firm powers of persuasion. Theodore couldn't think of anything more pleasurable than what she was doing to him or anything less pleasurable than having more children. He was forty-two years old and could not afford his share of the maintenance on their condo and his share of the bills at Helen's house—and without that strangely lax credit limit on his charge card, Benny's occasional boosters, and the couple of times he had ventured to borrow money from Maxey recently he would have had to forfeit at least one of these abodes. On the other hand Jane could be very convincing, and whether it was all that red meat in her diet, her biological clock now that she'd turned thirty-five, or her love of hoots, her high-suction lips were being very persuasive.

3

Benny Pnkl, in the meanwhile, had had a good run.

His life had contained its hardships and sorrows, to be sure, and its share of hard work. Most of all there was the heartache which was Enoch himself, the son who didn't want to be their son, who didn't want the family business or even the family name, who pretended his past had never existed.

But all in all he'd had a good run. And he had his girls, his Helen, his Regina, his Deb, little Deb who having just turned fourteen wasn't so little anymore. And through it all he'd always had his health. He'd never missed a day's work in the store due to illness, or not his own anyway.

But now on the morning of his sixty-eighth birthday this late September, something wasn't right. True to his nature he didn't even notice it himself at first.

"Dad," Helen said. She had made the long detour to Iced

Cream on her way to work, bearing a small bouquet of flowers and conveying big birthday hugs from the girls, who were at school.

"Yes, my darling daughter?"

"I have made an appointment with Dr. Kanata for you."

"Dr. who now?"

"I am worried about you the last few weeks."

"But I'm fine, my sweet daughter. I've never felt better. At least since your hot water bottle."

"I am glad it helps, Dad. But just to be sure, I have scheduled you for a check-up. *I* will feel better when Dr. Kanata confirms that you are fine."

Benny frowned. "I'm sorry, dear girl, but I just don't have time to see your doctor. I'm at the store every day."

"Regina will cover for you after school next Tuesday." Helen didn't mention that Regina had insisted on being paid for doing so.

"A young girl should be out having fun after school."

"One day of work will not kill her. It will be good for her, in fact."

"I'm fine, Helen. I don't need your old quack to tell me so."

"Would you prefer some other old quack?"

Benny laughed. "All right, my beautiful daughter. For you, I will visit your doctor. Meanwhile," here Benny became serious, "how is my son?"

"He sends birthday wishes," Helen lied quickly. "He said he will call you later." Helen planned to spend her lunch hour tracking Theodore down and pressuring him to call his father. Benny had no idea how infrequently Theodore was around the house these days, having moved semi-permanently into his office (or so he'd claimed). "Now let me go find something for these flowers."

Helen did not succeed in locating Theodore that day, or the next. Theodore did not call his father to wish him a happy sixty-eighth birthday. But then again Theodore hadn't called for his sixty-seventh or his sixty-sixth birthdays either. When Benny would occasionally berate him on this subject Enoch would deflect the charges by saying that the telephone simply wasn't his thing. That might have satisfied Benny had Enoch ever bothered visiting in person. His darling daughter, Benny thought sadly, had no idea how infrequently his son dropped by the store these days.

Still, hope springs eternal; Benny found himself hoping that the phone would ring that day. But springing equally eternally is the pain inflicted when hope remains unfulfilled. The phone did ring a few times in the store, but only for ice cream matters. And though the bell above the door tinkled a few times too—a slow day, it being already late September—it was only from customers and then, after school, when Deb and Regina came by with more birthday hugs. Regina left after her hug, to find her friends; Deb hung around till closing time and Helen returned from work to take them out for supper. Benny loved every minute of that afternoon with his granddaughter, and of his birthday supper. But every ring of the phone and tinkle of the door was another wound in his heart.

His heart which, it turned out, was not merely metaphorically wounded.

Dr. Kanata called Helen a few days later. There would be further tests, medications, dietary changes. Helen took this all in stride, ready to dedicate herself to her father-in-law's welfare. Even Benny—who had *not*, he realized, been feeling fully well—was willing to go along for the sake of Helen and the girls. Regina actually offered to help, and didn't even demand compensation for the afternoons Helen assigned her to work at the store. Deb, on hearing the news, begged to help at the store too. Helen declined, citing both Deb's younger age and her needing the afterschool hours for extra tutoring.

Just then Theodore happened to drop by the house one day to pick up some tools. It was mid-October. One of the sinks was leaking at the condo and he had promised Jane he would repair it. Of course he had also promised Helen months earlier that he would repair the dripping washing machine pipe in the basement at Riverbend. That basement pipe had by now been leaking so long that Helen stopped complaining about it. She merely trudged regularly downstairs to empty the bucket beneath it and only barely noticed the increasing frequency of needing to do so. In any case Theodore was down in the basement, admiring his plumber's tool belt, when he heard Deb come into the kitchen upstairs. She was supposed to be at school; he didn't know that she had been skipping school a lot lately. When he heard her crying upstairs he found himself at least curious, and maybe even a little empathetic.

"Dubs?" he said softly, emerging from the basement.

His appearance startled her—he hadn't been home in many days—so she just gazed at him through her teary eyes and didn't respond when he asked why she was crying. She hadn't realized he'd become so heavy. And there were streaks of gray through his bushy hair and beard, and through the tufts popping out at the top of his shirt. And why was he wearing that ridiculously small plumber's belt with the "I'm the Man" logo across the waist?

"Excuse me," Theodore was now saying sharply. These girls' non-responsiveness was just so damn offensive. "But where I come from it's rude to ignore a grown-up who has spoken to you."

"If it's so great there, then maybe you should go back," is what Helen or Regina might have said, both of whom were better at the snappy retort than Deb. Instead Deb merely said quietly, "Grandpa is sick."

Theodore's eyes opened wide. "Something serious?"

Deb just stared at him. Theodore's expression was somewhere between concern and hopeful optimism. But then Deb looked closer and saw it was only the latter.

"Go to hell," she said.

"Young lady, where I come from ..." Theodore began to lecture, only to realize that his daughter had already stormed out of the room.

But it didn't matter. A phone call to Helen the next day got him some additional details, details Helen was eager to provide, hoping that this information might get Theodore to give his father a call. But then again Helen could sometimes be unreasonably optimistic—as she was, for example, in smoking two packs a day even while the news was daily declaring that cigarettes were not so good for your health.

Yet Theodore did call Benny a few days later, and even wished him a belated happy birthday between all his excuses for not calling sooner or more frequently or ever, really. To make it up to him Theodore insisted on taking his father out to dinner that very evening and not an evening later. Benny resisted—it was a Tuesday, a Helen night, his favorite night—but Enoch was insistent, and Benny was aware that this might be a fleeting opportunity, so he relented.

And so father and son, late October, had a date for dinner.

4

Theodore selected a restaurant called Orleans Park Manor in the best neighborhood in the city. He picked up Benny early and made him go back inside to put on his one suit—the embarrassment Theodore would feel at Benny's being underdressed being just greater than that he would feel at Benny's wearing a suit three decades out of style.

For Benny it was all a blur. Going out in the evening, dressing up, driving through strange dark neighborhoods, it was all unfamiliar and confusing. Equally confusing was how comfortable Enoch was in this environment, leaving the car with the valet, waltzing through the door, being greeted familiarly by the man at the desk, by the waiters. Since when did Enoch patronize establishments like this? Where did the money for all this come from, if Enoch was always asking for money from *him*? And by the way when did Enoch and Helen get that fancy big car Enoch had picked him up in?

Once they were seated the waiter handed them small printed cards.

"What's this?" Benny squinted in the dim light.

"Tonight's hors-d'oeuvres, Monsieur," the waiter confirmed stiffly.

"Eh?"

"We'll have the Matignon Mushrooms and the Braised Scallops," Theodore said quickly.

"Eh?" Benny asked, never good at deciphering Theodore's strange accent.

"Very good, Monsieur Gale. And may I start the gentlemen with something to drink?"

"Water," Benny said gruffly.

"Iced water, with lime, for my father," Theodore corrected. "And your best Cabernet for me, toot-sweet."

"I can't read this," Benny complained after the waiter had replaced the hors-d'oeuvres card with the equally small entrées card. But of course even had he been able to make out the font he wouldn't have understood the words; and even had he understood the words his new dietary restrictions would have precluded him from ordering almost anything.

Theodore ordered for both of them.

"Benny," Theodore said seriously, meaningfully, holding up his wine glass. "Happy birthday, old man."

They clinked, wine glass to iced-water-with-lime glass. Helen, preparing Benny for the dinner, had reminded him that Dr. Kanata ruled out alcohol.

"This water's too cold," Benny complained.

"Benny, please," Theodore said distractedly, eager to set upon the mushrooms which had just arrived. "Try not complaining for a minute. This is a fancy place. Important people eat here. Enjoy yourself for a change."

"Since when," Benny was suspiciously eyeing the strange-looking other things which had also just arrived, "do you eat food like this?"

"Since I became an important person."

"Eh?"

"You don't appreciate this, Benny, but I'm a professor at the university. I expect to be tenured shortly. I'm involved in the community. My inventions change people's lives. People know who I am."

"Eh."

"Your son is a doctor, and all you can do is say 'eh'?"

"Who asked for a doctor? I only wanted a son."

"Well other people think that being a doctor is pretty damn impressive. Important people. Would it kill you to say a nice word about it?"

"I am proud of you, Enoch. I gave you a party when you finished college." Benny, like Helen's friend Jacqueline, was never fully clear on the difference between college and graduate school. "I am happy that you are a 'doctor.' But would it kill *you*," he said, pleased with himself for the retort, "to also be a son?"

"Why can't you just appreciate what I've accomplished, Benny?"

This was said so softly, so apparently sincerely—and were those tears behind Enoch's glasses, reflecting in the candlelight?—that Benny answered even more slowly than usual.

"What I *would* appreciate," he replied equally softly, and sincerely, and with perhaps some tears in his own eyes, "is a phone call from my son, now and again."

Theodore was silent a moment. "All right," he said. "I admit, I forgot to call on your birthday. I'm sorry. I'm just so busy these days. Important things. But that's why we're here. That's why I'm taking you out to the fanciest place in the city. To make it up to you."

"I don't need a fancy restaurant, Enoch."

"Everyone needs a fancy restaurant, Benny."

"No, Enoch. Just a phone call."

Theodore took a deep breath. "Okay. All right."

There was some silence as Theodore began his assault on the thick red steak now before him, or at least silence with respect to conversation if not with respect to the chewing and swallowing. Benny picked at whatever it was on his plate, occasionally sipping his freezing cold lime water. He thought briefly of Dottie, who would never have touched foods such as these. But then again by the end she was afraid to touch anything other than Iced Cream's own ice cream.

"Monsieur Gale," an elegant tuxedo'd man appeared beside their table, "everything is satisfactory?"

"May-whee," Theodore wheezed, entering that trancelike state now that the impressive slab of meat was in his impressive belly.

"And how is the always lovely Madame Gale?"

"Oh, Helen never mentioned this place," Benny said innocently. "Enoch, are you all right?"

Theodore had reddened even beyond his post-meal norm.

"Allow me, Monsieur," said the maître d', quicker with the hanky than he was in realizing his faux pas. He was rapidly dabbing Theodore, whose sweat was suddenly pouring out all over. The maître d' snapped his fingers toward the rear of the dining room, signaling for more hankies.

"I'm good, I'm good," Theodore replied hastily. "I just ate too fast." Turning to the maître d' he said in the best French he could muster something roughly equivalent to "ix-nay on the adame-May, see voo play."

"What was that?" Benny asked as the tuxedo'd man vanished from their table.

"Just ordered dessert," Theodore said. This was true; even during what may have been the first of the coronary episodes he was eventually to suffer he had managed to order the renowned Crème Brûlée for himself and some vanilla ice cream for the old man. "Listen, Benny," he continued, redirecting as he always taught in his parenting articles, "I have this idea I want to tell you about."

Benny was not a complicated man and he was not prone to complicated thoughts. Theodore, to the contrary, preferred the complex to the simple and the opaque to the clear. Benny had thus long learned not to try to the follow the details of his son's pitches.

Instead his strategy was to nod along as long as he could, hoping to extract a phrase or two from Enoch's strangely British-accented monologues that would give him some vague idea of what his son was proposing. Inevitably, invariably, he would acquiesce despite not seeing the use of whatever the man was proposing, saying to himself, as he wrote the check, that this was for his darling daughter, and his girls.

But he was pretty sure that whatever Enoch was proposing this time, he wasn't going to fund it. In fact he almost immediately stopped listening to the word salad his son was tossing his direction. Instead he was thinking that they had been here an hour already and Enoch hadn't asked after his declining health. That Enoch somehow believed that taking Benny to frivolous places like this compensated for not behaving as a proper son. That Enoch was asking for money again even as he was driving a new car, wearing new clothes, and eating large quantities of unpronounceable foods.

Benny, a simple man with simple thoughts, was also thinking that Helen would have mentioned something if Enoch had ever taken her to this strange place. He was so absorbed in this thought that he didn't notice that Enoch had, after eating his own brown pudding dessert, set to work on the dish of vanilla ice cream that had at some point appeared before Benny.

5

The three weeks leading up to the end—to one *very* busy day, as we shall see—were difficult for everyone.

Jane Nepean was miserable as her desire for a child became overwhelming. There was something about passing over the hump of that thirty-fifth birthday that was making her crazy. She who had for years been more than satisfied with excessive amounts of food, sex, and expensive things suddenly felt an emptiness in her heart as large as the emptiness in her womb. And if there was one thing she had learned from Theodore in their now four-plus years together it was impatience. She wanted that child now and not a moment later, and she wanted Theodore to do whatever was necessary to allow it to happen.

Theodore was also miserable. The pressure from Jane for a child was directly proportional to the vigor of the sexual gymnastics she was both bestowing and imposing upon him, and it was all he could do to withdraw himself in time every night since he would neither trust her to use protection nor deign to strap anything on himself. The financial pressures were mounting too. The dual life in two households required cash which Theodore, even as a professor hopefully just days away from tenure, simply didn't have. Not to mention the general demand to Keep Jane Happy, itself key to Keeping Jane period. Her previous marriages had left her most wealthy, and if Theodore was to father her child—and maybe become the next in the line of spouses—he would have to contribute to her stash. At this point he was deeply in debt, most pressingly to Maxey, and Theodore understood well that remaining long in debt to Maxey was not consistent with remaining long of sound body.

And on top of it all he was shocked that Benny had refused his newest project. It was a sure winner, an incredible investment opportunity: Theodore and his sponsor would get rich quick by his writing a book on how to get rich quick. Theodore was perfectly positioned to author such a tome, with his endless stream of ideas and his invaluable experience. All he needed was seed money for research, maybe get some leave from the university to give him time to write. But Benny hadn't even listened to him, had just nodded absently, and then when Theodore had asked, "So how about it, Benjamin?" had simply said "no" and refused to elaborate. What was that about? Maybe the old man's illness was rattling his brain.

But then again, maybe that illness would provide what that expensive dinner at Orleans Park Manor had failed to, namely access to that pot of money wasting away all these years; and in so doing finally provide him the life he so richly deserved, and had been unjustly deprived of, by being born as Enoch Pnkl, son of Benjamin and Dorothy Pnkl. The old man could not hold on forever.

And that old man, too, was miserable.

Benny's health was definitely declining. He was closing the store early, struggling to make it up the stairs to his apartment. But more than that he knew now that his relationship with Enoch—he would not say "son"—was finished. He would not, could not, forgive that man for carrying on with another woman, for that was the only possible interpretation of what had occurred at the restaurant. With some subtle questions to Helen it had become clear that she had never been to that restaurant, and indeed that she hadn't been seeing much of her husband for some time. And so now Benny could see what was, in hindsight, so clearly to be seen. And what he had seen he could not forgive.

His poor, poor daughter, he thought to himself, sitting alone at his kitchen table early one chilly November evening. To have been treated that way by his—by that man. And his poor, poor darling girls, to have that man for their father. There wasn't anything Benny could do to prevent the harm coming their way when they, too, learned the truth. But he had decided, alone all those evenings with just the memories of his Dottie and the anticipations of his girls' next visits to keep him company, that there was one thing he could and must do anyway.

Benny sat down that chilly evening alone at his table to write a letter to that man to inform him of his decision. The next morning, bundled against the late fall weather, he made an appointment with a lawyer for the following week to draw up the papers.

Benny's granddaughters, too, were miserable but mostly just because they were teenagers. Okay so they had an absent jerk for a father but since he was such a jerk it was actually good that he was absent. And in fact teaming up against him brought them closer than they'd ever been, even despite Regina's still occasionally exclaiming that she wished Deb had never been born. Theodore's extreme jerkhood had even overcome their natural teenaged tendency to distance themselves from their mother, for in this period all three female Gales spent many an evening around their ancient dining table smoking cigarettes and bashing their common enemy.

In fact being the aggrieved spouse suited Helen, in a way. She rather liked being a martyr. She liked the sympathetic attention she received from her friends. She loved Jacqueline's outrage at Theodore's latest offense, and that Jacqueline had enlisted her own three nasty teenaged daughters in the "We Hate Dr. Humongous Club." She loved hearing sweet Melvin whisper on the phone, "If you hate him, Helen, then I hate him." And despite the misery, Helen enjoyed the intimacy with her daughters during their nearly nightly "rap sessions" (as the girls called them) about The Large One. Lately these had consisted mostly of strategy debates about how to track down the owner of the phone number they'd found in one of Theodore's pockets.

He was no longer sleeping at the house, overnighting permanently, he said, on the cot in his office. The female Gales were not so naïve as to believe this but neither were they anxious to disconfirm it. They were especially suspicious because Theodore would frequently call home simply to ask, "Were you trying to reach me? Did you call? I just stepped out for a bite to eat"—just in case they had tried to check his story. But again it's one thing to have suspicions and another to prove them true. Theodore had stopped by for some more of his clothes and inadvertently left behind his old rain slicker. Regina, rummaging through it in search of any forgotten coins, found in one of the inner pockets the slightly yellowed scrap of paper with a phone number on it.

She showed it first to Deb.

"Call it," Deb said promptly. Regina did, only to discover it was disconnected.

"We should get an old phone book," Helen suggested that evening after work when the girls shared their discovery.

That took a few days, but after several calls to the telephone company they were supplied with thick phone books dating back five years. The books made a daunting pile on the dining table.

"It's not like we have anything better to do," Regina said, reflecting their regular complaints about how hard it was to find a half-decent boyfriend or husband.

"We should start with the oldest and work forward," Helen said, lighting a cigarette and passing the matches to Debra.

They each ripped out a few pages and spent a half-hour or so a day working down the columns of their pages looking for the number. They didn't fool themselves into thinking this would be quick and easy, but then again they *didn't* have anything better to do. For a while, at least, the excitement of the detective work even meant that it could be fun. And the huge potential payoff—maybe cutting His Enormousness down to ordinary human size—would make it worth the effort.

And anyway, Deb at least thought to herself as she worked down column after column, it sure beat doing the schoolwork which, had she been bothering to go to school much, she was probably being assigned.

6

Gasoline tankers were exploding, the forgotten war was being remembered, and a spectacular late November sunset welcomed in the eve of The Very Busy Day. It was two days before Thanksgiving of that year, sixteen-and-a-half years after Regina's birth, fourteen-and-a-half years after Deb's birth, four-and-a-quarter years after the sad demise of Marvin Marvin, four years before the return of Eddie Love to our story, twelve-and-a-half years after Theodore's affair with the adorable sailing instructor, eight-plus years after his affair with the actress from his troupe during an out-of-town run, and six-and-a-half years before the very beautiful thing which maybe, just maybe, would make all of it worthwhile.

The sun was setting as Helen assembled the cooler to bring to Benny's. She had made his favorite dish to cheer him up, a Sauerbraten Pot Roast, or at least it was his favorite before she'd doctored it as the doctors ordered for his strict diet. He hadn't been feeling at all well this past week and was depressed about it. Moreover there was clearly something on his mind. He seemed anxious, morose, and his eyes had been welling up even more than usual on her past few visits with the girls.

Deb was at the kitchen table, keeping Helen company as she packed the cooler. While they chatted she was also working through some phone book columns in search of the mystery number. For whatever reason her determination to find the number only increased as the days of searching added up. Or maybe the search itself just gave her the latest reason to skip school, one of the additional advantages of which being that Deb was home to intercept the threatening letters the school had been sending.

Regina was upstairs in her room listening to awful music and smoking the cigarettes she'd stolen from Helen's purse. She didn't come down to say goodbye when Helen set off for Benny's.

On her way out Helen hesitated awkwardly—as the anti-Theodore bond forming between her and her daughters had passed a certain critical point she found herself feeling she should kiss her daughters goodbye—then told Debra not to bother with the dishes, she would do them herself when she got home. This was not like Helen, to leave the kitchen cluttered with pots and pans. But then again nothing was much like it used to be.

Regina finally came down about forty minutes later, to join Deb for dinner and in the search for the number. The two girls were at the dining table amidst their dirty plates, smoking, when Regina looked up with her face suddenly white.

"Dub," she breathed.

"What?"

"*I found it.*"

"Oh my God! Let me see!"

Regina pointed to the line on the page matching the number scribbled on the paper.

"J. Nepean," Deb said. "You think that's her?"

"Of course it's her. Who else would it be?"

"It could be a man."

"Jesus, I've got a retard for a sister. Men put their whole names in the phone book. Women only put their first initials."

"Oh my God!" Deb exclaimed again. "Should we call Mummy?"

"Are you crazy? At Benny's?" Somehow Regina's use of her grandfather's first name was a mark of affection while her use of her father's first name—she had stopped calling him "Dad" years ago, and had called him "Theodore" even as recently as the past year, when she had begun the weight-themed name-calling just mentioned above—had only been a mark of scorn. "Poor old guy would drop dead on the spot."

"So what do we do?"

"We call *her*." Regina pointed at the sheet.

"Oh my God," Deb said, turning white herself.

Regina removed the current phone book from the kitchen drawer and put it on the table. Sure enough there was the name J. Nepean, only with a different phone number next to it.

"You do it," Regina commanded, pushing the book to Deb.

"No way! You do it."

Regina grunted, or maybe snorted. "Fine, I have to do everything around here," she said, even though in fact she barely did anything around there other than barricade herself in her room smoking cigarettes and listening to unpleasantly loud music.

She removed the phone from its cradle on the wall and pulled it, with its long cord, to the kitchen table. Acting as cool as she could she stuck her fingers into the appropriate holes and dialed the number.

Certain memories are famously burned into people's brains, such as where they were when presidents were assassinated or when men landed on the moon. Regina, who as an adult could never accurately recall facts or dates, would be able to relate every detail about the kitchen that day, about the phone, about what she and her sister were wearing. Deb, who as an adult *would* be known for her incredible recall, would later tell Dr. J. that this moment was so deeply burned into her mind that she was almost sure it was she herself who was on the line, dialing the number, and hearing the voice which in fact must only have been heard by Regina.

"Hello," said that fake-accented, all-too-familiar baritone, a hello uttered in the middle of chewing some piece of meat. You could visualize the thick stubby fingers glistening with grease as they held the phone on the other end.

"*You fucking pig,*" Regina hissed into the phone, and hung up.

7

Helen was seated at the table with Benny. The warmed-up faux-Sauerbraten was only slowly disappearing from their plates.

There wasn't much conversation.

Benny had a lot on his mind. He was not feeling well but he was not going to burden Helen with that information. Nor could he stop thinking about the letter he had posted yesterday to Enoch. Benny did not come from a time or place where men were expected to have feelings, much less share them, and here he was having done both. Not that he had any illusions about the outcome. Enoch would shrug off the complaints Benny made about his son's treatment of him. And he would explain away Benny's accusation of an affair. Benny hardly had proof, true, yet there wasn't the slightest doubt in his mind. But that was why the best strategy was to tell Enoch in a letter that he *knew*, because had he told him in person then Enoch would just have started speaking quickly with long words, and he would have ended up convincing Benny that it was all some big mistake.

What Enoch *would* genuinely respond to was the news that Benny had made the appointment, for tomorrow, to revise his will. Everything—the apartment, the store, the money left by Dottie—would go to Helen and the girls, for the latter placed in a trust until they came of age. As Dottie had done before him so now Benny did as well: dictate that that man was to get **nothing**.

But how exactly that man would respond, that wasn't clear to Benny, nor to Helen. Benny was holding the copy of the letter he'd made for her in his hand.

"Enoch is to get nothing," Benny said quietly. "He has finally crossed—the line."

"The line?" Helen asked softly back.

What to do, Benny brooded unhappily. He did not want to burden her with the awful news of the affair, even though he understood that at some point soon she would have to know. But was it for him to inform her? And was this that point?

There was a long silence, the "Sauerbraten" as suspended on their plates as the conversation.

"Have another piece," Helen finally said, not waiting for an answer before serving him. Benny also didn't want to burden her with the awful news that, though this was his favorite dish, he could tell that Helen had had to remove almost everything that made it so.

"My darling daughter," Benny began gently.

"Dad, I know," Helen interrupted.

There was another silence.

"How long ..."

"A long time. It has been perfectly obvious. The girls know, too. Not that we ever acknowledge it explicitly. At least not until recently."

"I am so sorry, my beautiful daughter." Benny reached out and touched her hand. Helen realized it had been a long time now since anyone had touched her hands.

"And I, for you," she said softly.

There was another silence.

Benny was gazing at her with tears in his eyes. Having been married to a woman who for years communicated primarily by facial expression he was now studying hers.

"My sweet, sweet daughter," he said ever so softly, "it isn't your fault." For a man from a time and place where men didn't do such things, Benny was doing them beautifully.

"Dad," Helen said, tears in her own eyes. "I need to tell you something. About eight years ago maybe I—"

"Helen, *I* know."

"You know?"

"I know. I was awake when you came home in the morning."

Helen was white. "I am so sorry that I let you—"

"Ssshh," Benny was saying, stroking her hand. "It's all right, my girl. My girl."

Maybe it was the heavy air in the house, the rapid transitions between present and past, or just a trace of his own genuinely old country accent, but somehow what Helen heard was *my girlie, my girlie.*

Benny held her the whole long while that she wept.

"While we are in confession mode," Helen finally said some time later, collecting herself, pulling away, "I have something even worse to tell you. About the pot roast."

"I know that too, my daughter," Benny almost smiled.

"You do?"

"I do. But it's still delicious."

"Thank you for saying that. And especially for actually eating it. That is better than you have been doing with your medicines."

"Yes, but Kanata is a quack. While you, in the kitchen, are a miracle worker."

"But you need the medicines to save your life."

"And your cooking to make it worth saving."

"You, Mr. Benjamin Pnkl," Helen said affectionately, "are really something. But you have not yet seen what I've had to do to my banana cream pie."

"You don't mean…?"

"Sadly, I do," Helen answered, and then uttered the two most horrible words to utter to a man who has made his life, his living, in ice cream. "Low fat."

"Ohhh," Benny groaned, clutching his chest. "Get me the quack, quick!"

The mood now somewhat lightened, they removed to the living room. Helen sat on the sofa while Benny sat in the comfy chair he'd spent almost every evening in for the past forty-some years, both quietly enjoying their low-fat dessert except for the part about enjoying. After a little while they fell back into silence, Benny thinking about Enoch and Helen, Helen thinking about Theodore and Benny. Benny was terribly worried about how Helen and the girls would cope with everything coming their way; Helen was terribly worried about how Benny really was not looking well, and had now after their moments of levity at the table returned to that almost deathly pallor.

That's where they were when Benny suddenly turned dark red and seemed to freeze in the chair which, as suddenly, was not so comfy.

"Dad, what is it?" Helen asked anxiously.

Benny, sweating, stood up, and pointed in deep shame at the front of his pants, where a dark stain was growing.

"I'm sick, Helen," he said, beginning to cry. "I'm sick."

8

Helen returned home to Riverbend around 11:00 PM. The first floor was quiet. The girls had cleaned up the kitchen; that was unusual. They had left on all the lights; that was usual. Helen closed up and went upstairs.

There was a light on in Regina's room. Helen tapped lightly on the door and opened it. Both girls were in the room, Regina lying on her bed, Deb sitting on the floor leaning back against the bed. Both had clearly been crying.

But then again, so had Helen.

"Mummy," Deb sobbed, standing up.

The three female Gales spent the night together, all fully clothed in Helen's still somehow lonely bed. Downstairs, down two flights, in the basement, that leaking washing machine pipe was also finally succumbing to the pressure which had been building up for a long time now.

Regina discovered the flood in the morning.

It was she who had done the fatal load the afternoon before, putting her underthings into the washing machine after school and then forgetting to transfer them, during all last night's drama, to the dryer. She thought of them immediately upon waking up in Helen's bed and rushed downstairs to transfer them so she could wear her favorite bra to school. She flew down the basement stairs and stepped into about three inches of cold dark water.

"Jesus Christ!" she exclaimed.

"Jesus Christ!" Helen also exclaimed when Regina dragged her down a few minutes later. Deb didn't say anything. She just stood on the basement stairs and resumed crying where she had left off in the middle of the night before.

"What am I going to do about my laundry?" Regina muttered, standing halfway down the stairs, three steps above Helen. "Is it even safe to use the dryer?"

"I don't know," Helen said, reaching for her cigarettes. They were crumpled from her having slept in her clothes but otherwise fine.

"Goddamn Theodore," Regina muttered. "It's his fault."

"Of course it's his fault," Helen said.

"What are we going to do, Mummy?" Deb cried.

"We," Helen said, "are going to go to school. Girls, get dressed. I will go in late to work and deal with this."

"Well then I'm using the dryer," Regina said. "If it electrocutes me, then fuck it." She plunged right in and transferred her things to the dryer without incident, though with a stern glance from Helen for the profanity.

The girls packed off to school, the plumber called—he couldn't come pump the water and repair the pipe till later that morning, so Helen would leave the house unlocked for him when she left for work—Helen, wearing her old pink rain boots, headed back down to survey the damage. She wasn't too worried since her family had experienced smaller basement floods before and she had long learned not to keep anything valuable on the floor. And indeed she kept her basement as orderly as her house, dusting and vacuuming monthly the things on the shelving units down there. Her concern now was only whether she could stop the flow of water, and if not, to see whether anything on the bottom shelves, about five inches off the floor, might need raising.

She hadn't actually been down here since the last time she'd cleaned almost a month earlier; the girls were now doing all the laundry and much of the cooking (Deb in particular was starting to get the hang of the kitchen), so there wasn't much need for Helen to come downstairs lately. So down she went, almost pleasantly distracted from last night's revelations—the seriousness of Benny's illness, Theodore's disinheritance, the confirmation finally of his infidelity—to do only some basic maintenance before the plumber's visit.

The phone began ringing as she descended, but she let it ring.

Helen hadn't been down there lately but, she now saw, Theodore had.

In one of his surreptitious daytime visits to the house he had apparently decided to live up to that ancient promise to fix the washing machine pipe. Things had been moved, space had been made, maybe even a wrench had been turned once or twice. Who could say now just what had transpired. Whatever he was up to, he had, in the course of being up to it, moved some things around—

Helen's things—and she discovered to her horror that several of her boxes were on the floor.

Or rather just above the floor, floating, gently bobbing, in the dark icy water.

Unlike her boxes her stomach sank.

Three boxes, only three, she tried to console herself as she approached them. It could have been worse. But if it had to be three boxes it couldn't have been three worse boxes. The first box was labeled "Girls." The second box was labeled "Mummy."

The third was labeled "A. Faire, Florist."

The phone finally stopped ringing upstairs as Helen gingerly lifted each of the soggy boxes onto the raised platform at the bottom of the stairs, an inch-and-a-half above the water line. Slowly she opened the third box. On top was the Faire family calendar, the one that was adorning their Frigidaire when the Mayor so suddenly passed away. Its days were filled with the bits and pieces that constitute a vibrant life in a lively household of active parents and five rambunctious children, or at least they were before the date of the Mayor's passing, being almost entirely blank thereafter. Not that anyone could tell what those bits and pieces were before that date, since the scribbled pencil marks were now waterlogged and illegible.

Helen, barely breathing, lifted the soggy stack of papers from the box and placed them on the platform next to the box.

She immediately wished she hadn't.

For directly underneath the calendar was the last photograph ever taken of Mayor Alden Faire with his not-yet-ten-year-old daughter Helen. It was the one that won him his final re-election, some said, featuring him and the sweet young girl sipping tea with milk at the flower shop counter as they gazed out at one of the shop window's legendary autumn sunsets. Looking at it you could almost hear the Mayor whispering to his little girl, telling her all about the promised land, about how they belonged over there, they were not at home here, they would return there one day, some day. Looking at it you could almost hear the winning campaign slogan, the Mayor looking to the future, ready to lead his family and his daughter and all his constituents on The Long Journey to the Promised Land. Looking at it you could know instantly that this little girl was not merely her father's girl, but his girlie.

Not that you could look at it right now and know all this. For what was left of it was only some washed out, streaked lines, for some reason faintly colored despite the black-and-white photograph, rather like the diffracted setting sunlight as seen through the flower shop's autumn window. Maybe if you squinted you could make out something resembling her father's shape.

But Helen wasn't squinting. She was just staring.

She did not open the other boxes.

The phone started ringing again upstairs.

9

An hour later Deb doubled back from school.

She had taken the bus with Regina that morning, carrying her backpack, the lunch Helen quickly packed, her cigarettes stashed away. She had intended to go to school, thinking it would do her good to be distracted from, well, everything. But no sooner had the bus arrived at school than she realized that it wasn't going to happen.

Regina just nodded at Deb when she saw her sister going the opposite direction.

She walked straight home, a vigorous twenty-minute walk in the cold air. The mail was already in the box next to the front door. She saw a familiar envelope from the Principal's Office, picked that one out, left the rest there, and, finding the door unlocked—the plumber had not yet come—went inside. There was no sign of Helen. The basement door was open but Deb wasn't interested. Indifferently she opened the envelope, saw that it was her "Final Warning" about failing this term of ninth grade, and just as indifferently pulled out her BiC lighter and burned the letter in the sink, then scooped the ashes into the trash. She grabbed Helen's cigarettes from her backpack along with her lunchbag, and headed up to her room to go be a fourteen-year-old for a while. Since such adolescents didn't bother answering ringing phones that weren't for them she let the phone, which had just started ringing, go on doing its thing.

That's where she was—lying on her bed, smoking, staring at the ceiling—when she heard a car pull up outside. She figured it was the plumber and ignored it. But then she heard a key jiggling in the front door, directly beneath her bedroom window.

"Goddamn it," Theodore's voice carried up to her.

His efforts to turn the key had in fact been locking the door. He hadn't slept much the night before, having spent half the night ranting to Jane about what the hell to do now that the cat was out of the bag, nor had this morning gotten off to any better a start, with the mail having brought the news of Benny's legal appointment for later today. Over his years of community theater Theodore had developed a real talent for playing cool, but he wasn't particularly good at actually *being* cool.

Finally he got inside the house, looking back at the door and muttering "Fuck you!" to it. The instant he walked in he smelled the dampness. Following his nose—his expertise as a gourmand had developed his sniffer well—he made his way to the basement stairs. He flipped on the light, headed down the stairs, and saw what he had most recently wreaked upon this family.

"Jesus Christ," he muttered halfway down the stairs, feeling something resembling empathy for a brief moment. It never crossed his mind that he had anything at all to do with this.

"Jesus Christ!" he muttered more forcefully down a couple more stairs, now noticing Helen's waterlogged boxes on the platform at the bottom. He had no idea what that watery pastel-streaked thing was on top of one of the boxes but he was pretty sure it wasn't a good thing, at least for Helen.

"JESUS CHRIST!" he exclaimed on making it all the way down to the platform.

In the middle of the basement were two large suitcases. *His* two suitcases, designer luggage he had spent a fortune on some years ago instead of fixing the Plymouth's recurring transmission "problem," including having them personalized with his initials. As an important person, after all, he traveled often on academic and theater and entrepreneurial business and it was important that he travel in style. It was these two suitcases that he had come this morning finally to retrieve, after filling them with whatever remained of his possessions in the Riverbend house. Lazy as he was he would in other circumstances have been pleased to discover that Helen and the girls had spent the previous night packing the cases for him. In other circumstances he would have exclaimed "Tchiao!," perhaps pumped his fist, then dragged the suitcases and himself out of the clutches of the female Gales forever.

But these were not other circumstances. In these circumstances the two suitcases were lying open, half-submerged, in four inches of water, the initials "TG" invisible below the water line.

It had taken Helen twenty minutes that morning to drag those heavy suckers downstairs and position them in the deepest part of the basement. But it was worth it. Her sole regret was that she wouldn't be around to see the look on that man's face.

The only person around was Deb, who heard Theodore cursing in the basement and didn't care enough to come see what it was all about. In fact she didn't care enough to see what Theodore was doing in the kitchen a few minutes later, when she heard cabinets slamming and the Frigidaire being opened and shut. Indeed had she been down in the kitchen she would probably have just sat there smoking cigarettes indifferently watching him pack foodstuffs into the shopping bags he had removed from the cabinet. She certainly didn't care enough to answer the telephone, which had begun ringing yet again. And she felt only the smallest of pangs as she peeked out through the blinds of her bedroom window and watched her father drag both his ruined suitcases and the stuffed shopping bags out to what appeared to be a rather cool new car, throw them into the trunk muttering a few more profanities, and then drive, she was thinking—it turned out wrongly—out of her life forever.

On his way out Theodore nearly smashed into the plumber's truck as it pulled into the driveway.

Debra continued staring out the window as she lit another cigarette.

10

If Helen had arrived to work late that day, she also left early. There was an ill father-in-law to check on, a flooded basement to deal with, and she still had her Thanksgiving cooking to do for tomorrow. This was hardly the most thankful of times for her small clan but she was determined to preserve at least the semblance of a holiday spirit. She left her desk at 2:00 PM, wished and was wished a happy holiday to and from her boss and officemates, picked up the fresh turkey she had ordered from the butcher, and headed home just as a cold slushy rain began to fall.

The front door was locked; good, the plumber must have come. She dropped the turkey on the kitchen table and peeked downstairs to confirm both that the basement had been pumped and that the suitcases were gone.

"I guess it's just the three of us now," she said softly, to no one.

She lingered a moment, then opened the Frigidaire to put the turkey away only to discover it almost empty.

"Jesus," she muttered yet one more time on this most "Jesus"-provoking of days.

That bastard. He would probably steal the medicine from his dying father's medicine cabinet and then find some way to justify it to himself. Thank goodness she had long ago transformed the long journey box into a savings account in her name or he'd have emptied that out too. The loss of her holiday groceries was indeed another blow—but, she reminded herself, small in the greater scheme of things. She'd now have to run out before the stores closed to replenish their supplies. And she wouldn't have time now to cook everything she had planned.

She went to get her coat back out from the hallway closet, and her umbrella. She thought she smelled cigarette smoke coming from upstairs. The girls weren't due home from school for another half-hour; hmm. Well she didn't have time to investigate now. She was just on her way out the front door when the phone began to ring.

This time she answered it.

11

As Deb would say later to Dr. J., Theodore Gale was consistently lucky in inverse proportion to what he deserved.

He was lucky in love, having found in Jane Nepean perhaps the only woman who could be satisfied by him, at least insofar as he shared her commitment to a life full of sex, food, and money. That he weighed upward of two-hundred-and-fifty pounds by this point only increased her attraction to him.

He was to be lucky in life, or at least in living, managing eventually to survive several heart episodes as well as one pancreatitis- and two diabetes-induced comas which each could have brought down a horse.

He was lucky in his career, in the end. No, he had not yet finished that book on Ignoratio P. Elenchi and he had only published a few academic articles but somehow, in a decision that surprised almost everyone except for him, the university tenure committee had voted to reward him with tenure. The chair of that committee had been calling him all day at the Riverbend phone number but no one had been picking up. It was not until a few days after the Thanksgiving Break that someone finally tracked Theodore down in his office with the good news.

But it was not this ringing phone which Helen picked up on her way out the door to the grocery store. For Theodore was also lucky in other people's lives, or rather living—or rather not living.

Early that miserable afternoon Mr. Benjamin Pnkl dressed slowly, carefully, in his one suit, looking at his unfashionable self in the mirror as he knotted his only tie. He put on his nice shoes, his nice overcoat, and remembered to take an umbrella since the weather report was calling for cold slushy rain. That rain was just starting to fall a few minutes later when the bus arrived. He moved to the rear of the bus where it was less crowded and found a nice seat to himself by the window for the long trip downtown. It was warm in the bus, and with the monotonous rhythm of the windshield wipers and the slushy drops dripping down the window beside him he found himself getting sleepy. He hadn't felt well that morning; and while there was some relief in having shared his burden with Helen the night before, that didn't mask the fact that he simply lacked the vigor that he'd had even a few weeks ago. It really was warm in the bus. It was rather a lengthy ride to the attorney's office, surely there was no harm in just closing his eyes for a moment. Outside it was already starting to get dark. He felt in his pocket for the piece of paper on which Helen, last night, had written out her and the girls' social security numbers. He could hear the monotonous rhythm of the windshield wipers.

He'd had a good run, all in all. He'd worked hard, had loved a good woman, had nurtured a beautiful daughter-in-law and two beautiful granddaughters, and had done what he ought to have done, just as he was now on his way to doing what he had to do.

Benny Pnkl allowed himself to close his eyes for a moment.

He was sixty-eight years old.

Part II
The Beginning

CHAPTER SEVEN
ENEMY OF THE ENEMY

1

You fucking pig.

The same thought was in the minds of all three female Gales.

In sixteen-year-old Regina's mind it was an inner hiss, just like the outer hiss with which she had said those words over the telephone five days earlier. In fourteen-year-old Deb's mind it was obscured by her sobs. And it was even there in the normally proper mind of Helen Gale, articulated most elegantly.

The occasion was Benny's funeral.

Because it was Thanksgiving weekend, or maybe because the Pnkl family was now extinct, only a few people were present. Among them was the fucking pig himself, who at least had been half-decent enough not to bring his whore—Regina's word—to the ceremony. (Actually it was the whore who had had that half-decency and refused to come, since Theodore, furious about Helen's flooding of his suitcases, wanted to rub her face in it.)

From the corner of his eye Theodore glanced across the aisle at the members of his family, at least legally speaking, at least for now. None of them was looking at him, and poor Dubs was taking Benny's death hard. Wait, did he just think "poor Dubs"? In the end she had treated him no better than the other two, and he would not allow himself to feel sympathy for her. He fingered the letter in his jacket pocket, the letter he'd received from Benny the very day the miraculous event itself had occurred. What a stroke of luck, the old man's stroke that is, occurring before he could get to the lawyer's and do the dastardly deed. The letter had now been in Theodore's pocket for several days and indeed he was to keep it there for good luck for many months to come.

The man running the thing was now calling him.

Theodore lumbered up to the dais, fiddling with his thick eyeglasses. It was freezing outside but the room was overheated and he was sweating profusely.

"My father," he began.

He glanced around the room. The female Gales were all looking down. He cleared his throat in the way his theater coach had taught him would suggest he was fighting back tears.

"My father was quite the man," he said, for lack of anything better to say. "He came from the old country, and, in a way, never really left." Theodore had no idea what that meant, but thought it sounded good. "He was a dedicated father"—who had died on the way to disinherit his only child—"a loving husband"—who had committed his wife to a mental institution—"a successful businessman"—if a run-down ice cream store in a run-down outskirt of town is a success—"and I," here Theodore dabbed his eye with the hanky he had brought for this moment, "shall miss him terribly."

Theodore paused dramatically. It seemed like he was waiting for applause, rather like the way he did after each of his university lectures. Realizing that none was forthcoming he threw in another eye-dab and removed himself from the podium.

No eye contact was made with the female Gales.

Outside at the graveside, the bitter November wind chilling everyone to the bone, Theodore looked deep into his soul (as his coach had taught him to do) and drew out some sobbing sounds as he tossed in the first shovelfuls of dirt. He then handed the shovel over to the man earning the minimum wage to finish the job and made an impressive show of leaving the grave, the grief-stricken son. Was he hesitating again, there, still hoping for applause? With a last glance back at the grave he turned and departed, his hand in his pocket still fingering the letter.

2

"Let's destroy him," Regina urged.

It was almost three weeks after the funeral.

Things had been quiet after that Very Busy Day. Neither Regina nor Deb had gone to school much in that time, nor had Helen gone to work much, still reeling from all the drama and fortunately having some vacation days still due her. Her boss also was sympathetic about the loss of her father-in-law and offered some bereavement days as well. The three females spent a lot of time at home eating ice cream. They had no choice, really, about the ice cream: it was just going to go bad sitting in Benny's closed-up store.

But the quiet was unnerving.

"He is up to something," Regina said.

"I hate him so much," Deb said.

"Let's destroy him," Regina said.

Helen had made the mistake of telling her daughters about Benny's letter to Theodore. She had seen Regina angry plenty of times—that flared nostril—but never as much as when the teenager learned how lucky Theodore had been and how unlucky they in consequence now were. Their Riverbend house was falling apart. The heating system still hadn't been fully repaired from the flood damage several weeks before. And now all that money from Benny's estate, from Dottie, was going to Theodore instead of to them.

"It will work out," Helen insisted.

"Yeah right," Deb said.

"Yes it will," Regina said. "When we destroy him."

It had taken a couple of weeks for Benny's will to be read. Iced Cream was to be liquidated, so to speak, but given the store's condition and location it wouldn't fetch much. Dottie's fund, however, amounted to a Very Tidy Sum—that being Theodore's expression for it as he salivated over the numbers when he first saw the statements. This Very Tidy Sum would do a Very Tidy Number on his quality of life. It would terminate Jane's complaints about his encroachments on her own Very Tidy Sum, itself due to her numerous ex-husbands. He wouldn't have to bother working on his book on how to get rich quickly since he had now already gotten rich quickly. And it would help his quantity of life as well, since he could retire his overdue debt to Maxey.

Theodore would eventually get the divorce from Helen of course, but right now there wasn't much rush. Things were fine with Jane, who was not interested in remarrying despite her sudden longing for babies. There was the one asset from the marriage he wouldn't mind getting his hands on, though: the Riverbend house had appreciated decently despite its condition and despite his having taken out, a while back, the second mortgage, needing to placate both the charge card lawyers and those large men Maxey had sent around. He smiled thinking about his coup in getting that mortgage without Helen's knowledge. Anyway, with the Very Tidy

Sum on its way he was about to embark upon a Very Tidy Life—especially if he could resist Jane's baby demand—so why mess with a Perfectly Tidy Thing?

But this was not a tidy life for the female Gales, for it was they who were living in the old house with the limited income, and it was they who had been screwed over by *him*. Helen had come downstairs this Friday morning in her pink bathrobe wanting, before breakfast, to get some cigarettes from the kitchen. It being early she was surprised to see that both her teenaged daughters were already puffing away at the table. The three weeks of silence from Theodore was getting to all of them.

"Let's make him bleed," Regina urged between puffs.

"Mummy," Deb added between her own, "let's."

That morning they drafted a letter to Theodore. Obviously there would be a divorce, which they would prefer to undertake sooner rather than later. Obviously they would split the assets, most importantly the house—perhaps sell it and divide the proceeds while the females moved somewhere more affordable—but, and here was the important point, perhaps Theodore would be amenable to some fair deal concerning the inheritance from his father. After all they had proof that Benny did not want Theodore to get that money—any of it—and rather than drag something out in the courts it might be best to find some accommodation and settle it. And they were ready to be more than fair: they would not seek the entire sum despite Benny's clearly stated wish, but would settle for half. Helen enclosed a Xerox of Benny's letter to Theodore (or rather, of the copy Benny had given her), then Deb and Regina spat on the seal and rode their bikes through the wintry air to the post office to send it on its way.

3

"Sounds about right to me," Jane Nepean said when Theodore showed her the letter the next afternoon.

His face was red, he was sweating, and his glasses were steaming up. "I don't think so."

"But fifty-fifty on everything makes sense. And that's pretty fair. You're dumping *them*. They didn't even think to ask for child support. And let's face it, you're lucky to get that. Had your pop not popped for another twenty minutes, you'd have nothing."

"I don't think so."

"What do you mean, you don't think so?"

"I just don't think so."

"I mean *why* don't you think so?"

Theodore harrumphed. "How could you, of all people, ask me that?"

"I haven't a goddamn idea what you're talking about."

"You, of all people, know what those witches put me through. You, of all people, know that they don't deserve a penny of this money."

"I, of all people, think you have a warped sense of reality."

"That's a wonderful thing to say to a man whose babies you want." Theodore was breathing heavily now. Of course he was often breathing heavily these days, as the weight he'd been accumulating demanded that much more oxygen.

"I didn't say that was a bad thing, big man." She squeezed in next to him on their leather sofa. "Only a man with a warped sense of reality would let me do the things to him that you let me do. Now," here she made a move with her hand that's best left undescribed, "why don't you tell me again how terribly those witches have treated you?"

The usual grievances, but Theodore enjoyed going through them so. He had worked so hard for that family, had spent years working on his degree so he could support them, had sacrificed his personal needs to make them happy. Serving as husband and father had meant limiting his passions, the sailing, the writing, and all that time he had spent with his daughters—especially Dub—had meant less time for himself. And how ungrateful they were! Every time he did something nice for Helen she'd just complain. He would bring home chocolates, the fancy stuff, and she'd complain that he was late for supper. He once brought home a cat as a surprise and all she'd done was complain that she didn't like cats! And then when he brought home that dog instead she'd lamented about the mess. And forget the attempts to go out, do fun things, to loosen up. He suggested sailing that time and she said she couldn't swim. He suggested camping that other time and she said what, outside? He'd propose going out for dinner, or drinks, or dancing, and she'd say why pay four times the price for what I can cook better at home, you know you become a boor when you drink, and the last time we went dancing you broke two bones in my left foot, respectively.

What a sourpuss, after all he did for her.

And those girls. Her little coven.

After how much he'd sacrificed to bring them into the world, to take care of them, after how much fun he had tried to have with them—even now the memories of The Russians Are Coming could almost bring a smile—and all he got for it was their sullenness, rudeness, disrespect. It was like they had devoted themselves the past couple of years to torturing him. The goddamn shoes all over the house, for example, intentionally placed to trip him up. And what was worse, the obnoxious way they spoke to him or the silent treatment they inflicted upon him? At least with the latter he didn't have to endure their deliberately detailed discussions of their menstrual cycles. But then again when they were in silent mode they would do things like clatter pots and pans outside the bedroom door when he was trying to sleep and then just stare at him silently when he emerged enraged.

But no, on further thought: the speaking was worse.

Snotty, snide, insulting. Whispering around him, behind his back, in front of his face. Some time back they had stopped calling him "Dad" and instead would call him "Theo," with a rude emphasis on the first syllable, like a foghorn: "*Thee*-o." This irritated him no end, and finally he had said to them—they were sitting at the broken dining room table that Helen refused to get rid of, smoking Helen's cigarettes—"I am your father, and you will refer to me as such. 'Dad,' 'Pop,' 'Father,' I don't care which you choose but you will not refer to me by my given name."

"Given name?" Regina snickered and both girls burst into laughter. Helen had recently told them about Theodore's name change, much to their amusement. "You mean, *Eeeee*-noch?"

"You know what I mean," Theodore said trying to contain his anger.

"Theodore," Regina said, that nostril beginning to swell, "I don't think I can call you 'Daddy.' You know, the whole, um, not really being a father thing."

"Very well, then you will refer to me the way people your age are expected to refer to me. You may call me 'Dr. Gale.'"

"What's up, doc?" Regina said.

Deb blew a smoke ring in his direction.

Theodore stormed out, aware of his tactical error. Sure enough he had opened himself up to even worse abuse as the girls would say things like, "Oh, how good it is to see you, Dr. Gale—that is, if you *are* a doctor"—referring to the rumor which Helen was lately fueling that he had never really completed his Ph.D. (It was unusual to "defend" a dissertation without the advisor present, Helen noted, and she had never actually seen any documentary evidence of his degree.) Or worse, Regina would say, "Dr. Gale, I have a cold, what should I do? Oh right, you're not a *real* doctor ..." It was almost a relief when they finally gave up that whole trope and just began referring to him as *him*.

Maybe not "they"; Regina was the worse offender. Deb just went along for the ride, sometimes blowing smoke rings for emphasis but not really the aggressor. He still held out some hope for her. From early on Helen had grabbed Regina for herself while his younger daughter had more in common with him, and he and she had had their share of moments, especially when Helen was being so hard on the poor girl. But still, right now—recently—Deb too had gone over to the other side.

And finally, the combination of all of them together, unbearable. Just the conflict over the years between Helen and Deb alone would drive an ordinary man crazy. Deb the hyper-messy, Helen the hyper-neat, all day long Deb disordering the house with Helen right behind her trying to reorder it, always reproaching her to pay more attention and do her chores and be more tidy.

It would drive anyone crazy.

Who could blame him for getting out?

"I earned that money," Theodore droned on. "I put up with Benny all those years, I was nice to him, I took him out to expensive dinners. And you know he wasn't all there in the end. Those witches took advantage of a senile old man and brainwashed him against me, that's what it was. I earned that money, I deserve it, and I am not parting with a single penny of it. And another thing—"

He looked down beside him, not having noticed that at some point Jane had stopped doing that thing she was doing to him. She was fast asleep, and had been for a good long while.

"And another thing ..." Theodore continued.

4

At least they didn't have to wait long for Theodore's reply.

The mail came early afternoon, that New Year's Eve.

Deb retrieved it from the box next to the front door, flipped through it, and saw the business envelope which clearly meant business: thick, heavy, an in-your-face return address, lying there like it was offended it was mixed in with the regular mail. She called her mother at work, who told her to put it aside and they would read it together when she got home. Regina, who had been upstairs in her room listening to awful music, came down as Deb was hanging up.

"Mummy said we should wait," Deb told her.

"Yeah right." Regina tore it open.

"What does it say?" Deb asked eagerly.

"That fucking pig," Regina muttered.

Helen, arriving home later, concurred.

The copulating swine had lawyered up. But not just with any lawyer: a fucking pig of a lawyer named Stephen Bilker, most famous for having converted the city's only facility for disabled children into a recreation center for lawyers. Helen, being naïve, hadn't been thinking about lawyers. She hadn't been thinking at all, actually, if she thought Theodore would respond to her reasonable proposal in a reasonable way. And she certainly hadn't been thinking about Bilker, having no idea that Theodore was connected to that scoundrel. But then again there was much about Theodore that Helen had no idea about, including his multiple affairs, the fact that he had been living with another woman, and more or less any scheme he was involved in with that crazy-eyed Maxey. And it was indeed through Maxey that Theodore had retained Bilker, since Bilker had gotten Maxey out of almost as many legal jams as women Theodore had attempted to bed over the years.

Theodore's response—or Bilker's—to Helen's proposal was not accommodating.

No mention was made of Benny's money. Instead the letter informed Helen that they were moving immediately to divorce on the grounds of spousal abuse (Helen almost tore that thick letterhead as she read that phrase), that they demanded the immediate sale of the Riverbend house and the removal therefrom of the entire coven (it didn't use those exact words), and that they were claiming the entire remaining value of the house, once the two mortgages were paid off, on the grounds that Mr. Benjamin Pnkl had bought the house and that Dr. Theodore Gale, as his sole heir, was entitled to it.

"Two mortgages?" Helen wondered aloud.

"What are we going to do, Mummy?" Deb asked.

"We destroy him," Regina said.

"That fucking pig," Helen muttered.

Both girls gasped.

"What?" Helen said.

"Just not used to that from you," Regina explained.

"*That fucking pig that fucking pig!*" Helen exclaimed.

The girls almost laughed.

"So what do we do now, Mummy?" Deb asked again as they settled down.

"This is what we do. We smoke this pack of cigarettes. We enjoy our New Year's Eve. And then tomorrow morning we call Melvin."

"Him?" Regina asked. "He's such a loser."

"He is a lawyer."

"A loser's lawyer."

"Perhaps." Helen withdrew three cigarettes and distributed two to her daughters. "But we work with what we've got. Now which one of you stole my lighter?"

5

Melvin was now a partner at a major law firm downtown, specializing in tax law and other boring subjects. Little about him had changed over the years. He was still not exactly a man's man and was still the regular victim of merciless teasing, not only by the other partners of the firm but even by the newly hired interns. Nearly twenty years adequately happily married to his mousy wife Michelle, he was also adequately satisfied with his three small children: two boys and a girl, ages eighteen, seventeen, and fifteen respectively, but none over 5'3" tall. He was still in love with Helen Faire—in his heart he never had recognized the marriage to Theodore—though he had long learned not to reveal that love explicitly anymore. And he was still prone, when Michelle and the children were out, to trying on a little makeup now and again.

"Perhaps," Melvin said to Helen.

It was the next afternoon. They were seated on the ratty old sofa at the Riverbend house, cups of tea on the tea table before them. Melvin had come to the house since he knew he would be providing his services *pro bono* and it would be easier not to bill Helen if they didn't meet at the office. Out of courtesy to Melvin,

Helen was refraining from smoking despite the army of red ants crawling through her bloodstream.

"What do you mean, 'perhaps'?" Helen was already annoyed with her legal representation, or maybe just having trouble with the ants. She had just shared with Melvin the fornicating slop-eater description of Theodore which she and the girls had been muttering repeatedly for the last twenty-four hours.

"Well, you did use to love him once," Melvin said nervously. The last time he had simply concurred with one of Helen's negative remarks about Theodore she had chastised him for always agreeing with her.

"That was before she knew he was a fucking pig!" Regina shouted from the stairs, where she and Deb were eavesdropping.

"Girls, please, back to your rooms!" Helen shouted back.

"Fine," Regina grunted. The sisters trudged up a few steps and settled into their new perch.

"Melvin," Helen said, "just what are our options here?"

"Well, you know, divorce law is not my area. I'll have to do some research."

"Melvin I know that, but just speculate with me. We have no idea even how to begin thinking about this."

"Well ..." Melvin began, and then commenced breaking down the available options, doing so with such apparent confidence that even Regina, despite her usual skepticism, began to think maybe there was a reason Melvin had made partner in one of the biggest firms in town despite being such a *loser*.

It was unlikely, Melvin thought, that Theodore would get the entire proceeds of the house given the amount of time they had lived in it together. But it was also unclear how much weight the court would give Benny's disinheritance letter, since it was so riddled with spelling mistakes and incoherent ramblings that one could question the state of the old man's mind. In Melvin's opinion the best thing to do would be to be aggressive: any sign of weakness would be pounced on by Bilker, so their best strategy was to keep him on the defensive.

"And how shall we do that?" Helen asked.

"Go after Theodore's pension."

"His pension?"

"Exactly. As a professor a percentage of his salary is matched by the university, put into a tax-deferred fund for his retirement.

He's been teaching there how long now?"

"A dozen or so years. If you include the time before the doctorate."

"And did I hear that he just received tenure, too?"

"Yes, apparently. It happened right in the middle of everything."

"Even better. That increases the university's percentage. We can get the figures, but he probably already has a nice amount put away there, and the future looks better. So we go after it. Or at least half of it."

"I do not understand. Why would the courts think I am entitled to his pension? He's the one who," Helen almost choked on the words, "earned it."

"Helen," Melvin said, boldly taking her hands. Just the touch of those delicate fingers made his heart pound. "*You* have earned that pension. Or at least half of it. You supported him through graduate school. For what, a decade? You gave up your career to raise *his* children. You settled for a job with a fraction of the salary so he could meander through his program. You even typed his dissertation for him," Melvin was speaking as rapidly as his heart was beating, from the image of her blazing fast fingers on the typewriter, "and then as the girls got older you returned full-time to your second-choice job since he couldn't even get a permanent teaching position. You kept earning most of the family income even as he squandered it with his schemes. It now turns out that he secretly took out a second mortgage on the house, and has done God knows what with that money—we shall find out, I assure you. And so it seems to me, my dearest Helen," Melvin stole a squeeze of those magnificent hands, "that it was your work that made it possible for him to do what he's done. If he has now got some money aside in his name, you are clearly entitled to it."

It was a lovely moment. Melvin, losing himself, went for another squeeze. Helen pulled her hands from his.

"So we go for the pension," she said.

"That's right." Melvin jotted some notes on his pad to give his hands something to do. "We go for everything. We settle for half."

"We go on the offensive."

"We cut his balls. He's a fucking pig. That's what he deserves."

There was a loud guffaw from the stairs.

"Girls!" Helen shouted. "To your rooms!"

But even Helen had to admit that this was a side of Melvin she hadn't seen before. Despite the passage of roughly three decades she still tended to visualize him in a curly wig and with deep purple lip gloss. This little bit of—manliness—was actually rather attractive.

"This isn't going to be easy, Helen," Melvin was saying. "But I will be with you all the way."

"Melvin," Helen asked gently, squeezing *his* hands, "would you mind if I smoked now?"

6

Melvin should have stuck to tax law.

The tax code with which Melvin spent his working hours was onerous but at least it couldn't directly hurt you. In this way it was unlike Stephen Bilker, Esq., who ate little lawyers like Melvin not for breakfast (too unsatisfying) but as an appetizer *before* breakfast. Maxey had told Theodore of their frequent hunting trips together and how Bilker preferred to forgo the weapon and instead kill his prey—baby deer particularly—with his hands and teeth.

Well, Melvin, to Bilker, looked like one juicy plump baby deer, blinking at him in the headlights.

Melvin's castration strategy began with a polite letter declining Bilker's proposal and suggesting an alternative. Mrs. Gale was willing to sell the marital home, but felt strongly entitled to at least half of those proceeds in light of Dr. Gale's having already withdrawn much of the value through the secret second mortgage. Moreover Mrs. Gale felt that Mr. Benjamin Pnkl's bequest should be resolved in some fair and judicious manner, particularly in light of Mr. Pnkl's explicit desire, as reflected in the letter copy enclosed herein, to leave the money to Mrs. Gale and the Gale daughters; and in light of that desire the fair and just resolution would be to award all that money to the female Gales. In addition and consequently, in light of Mrs. Gale's extensive spiritual and physical and financial contribution to Dr. Gale's own career, and pursuant to the professional sacrifices she made on his behalf, there was the matter of Dr. Gale's pension, a matter which could be resolved efficiently were all parties to agree, as surely was fair, to awarding Mrs. Gale half the current value of that fund. Very sorry to trouble you, looking forward to working with you, etc., Melvin.

"What the hell does he want?" Bilker barked at his assistant, a beautiful law student just starting her second week of spring break internship with his firm. Her first week had been spent mostly fending off Bilker's attempts at her pants.

Melvin's letter had been sitting unopened for several weeks since Theodore's case was not high priority to Bilker. In fact Bilker was extremely busy taking over the stubborn senior center at the corner of Ninth and Hull in order to replace it with a much needed *larger* recreation center for lawyers. (With some competition-sized squash courts, for crying out loud!) That case was requiring his finest wrangling and he was annoyed to have to take on a two-bit divorce case with the bloated professor. Indeed had Maxey not been such a profitable client for him he would never have bothered with the case.

"Split the house, split the pension, take all the bequest," the intern answered quickly, inching just out of Bilker's reach.

"Yeah, I don't think so." Bilker was staring at her, unclear whether he was referring to Melvin's proposal or her own efforts to keep his hands off her body. "Take a memo."

Team Bilker was not playing nicely, was how Melvin summarized Bilker's memo.

"Tell me," Helen trembled.

The many-weeks delay in the response had done a number on her nerves. Even Regina had been losing her bluster. Oddly it had been Deb whose resolve had been steeling while the other two were losing steam.

"Tell *us*," Deb corrected.

"Well," Melvin said, "they have ignored the inheritance again."

"All right," Helen said. "And?"

"They are willing to split the house now."

"Well, that is progress."

"There are some conditions. They will split the proceeds only *after* the second mortgage is debited, not before."

"That's bullshit," Regina said.

"Regina," Helen said sternly.

"I'm sorry, it is," Regina replied.

"What else?" Helen returned to Melvin.

"They demand the house be put on the market immediately. They want you out."

"More bullshit," Regina said.

"All right," Helen said softly. "And?"

Deb remained silent, looking down.

"Just one more thing," Melvin continued. "The pension."

Helen and Regina looked at him, waiting.

"They'll grant you half his pension."

Helen's eyebrow arched. "But that is good, no?"

"There's a condition."

"Oh for Christ's sake Melvin, just out with it already!"

He took a deep breath. "They will grant you half of Theodore's pension, but they are also notifying you that the division of marital assets must include the home on the island."

There was a stunned silence.

"That is complete and total bullshit," Regina said.

"Melvin," Helen began, but she couldn't speak.

"Have a cigarette, Helen." Melvin was a little slow, though, since Regina had already begun distributing smokes to her mother and sister.

After two long drags Helen continued. "Melvin, that isn't a home, it's a cabin, at most. A shack, really."

"I know, and they know. But you must also know that it has appreciated considerably in the years since you inherited it. Not just the home, but the land itself, the island."

"What does that mean?"

Melvin scribbled a figure on a pad. For a lawyer who dealt with the tax code all day long he was uncomfortable discussing money, and all the more so with the female Gales. Also he needed something to do with his hands since he was yearning to clasp Helen's. "I had it assessed. 'Shack' plus island. That's what it's worth."

"Wow," Regina said.

"We're rich?" Deb asked, not sure if this was good news or bad.

"Melvin, how is that possible?" Helen asked.

"The real estate market has been booming, Helen. Particularly—"

"I am not an idiot, Melvin! I am not talking about the appreciation. I am asking how it is possible to suggest that *he* is entitled to that house."

"Well, have you lived there—"

"No one has ever lived there. It is just a cabin. Especially Theodore, he never wanted to go, even for the weekend. He didn't like sharing a bathroom with the girls. He complained about the mosquitoes, even though the rest of us barely noticed any. He hasn't even been there in maybe five years."

"You acquired it after the marriage, isn't that right?"

"Of course. When my mother passed away."

"Then that would be their argument."

"Melvin, my mother explicitly left the property to me. There was a clause in her will that said something like 'Under no circumstances will *he* have a stake in this property.'"

"That," Melvin said, "is cold."

"Yeah," Regina added between puffs, "*he* has a habit of getting cut out of wills."

"Nevertheless—"

"Nevertheless, nothing," Helen said. "My parents bought it. My mother left it to me. That place has been in my family for decades, long before *he* entered the picture. He has not even stepped foot on it for years. Melvin?"

"I'm sorry, Helen."

"No, Melvin, listen. That is my house. That is my security. I am forty-six years old. I do not have my own pension. That house is for me. For my daughters. Ours."

"Nevertheless," Melvin said, his heart breaking to see the color, briefly risen to Helen's face, beginning to fade, "they are going for it. If you go for the pension, they go for the island."

"Jesus Christ," Helen said softly.

"Fucking pig," Regina muttered.

"Mummy," Deb said sharply. "Don't let him do this. Don't give in."

"He's such a fucking pig," Regina muttered again.

Helen didn't say anything.

7

That's where things stood in the spring of Regina's junior year of high school, of Deb's freshman year, and during the female Gales' final months living on Riverbend Road. That was also how things would still stand about five years later.

Of course a thing or two happened along the way.

The two sides exchanged many unpleasant letters in a fruitless effort to move the negotiations forward. Or at least Bilker's weren't pleasant. Melvin couldn't keep himself, despite Helen's reproaches, from such phrases as "my esteemed colleague" and "warmest regards." Meanwhile the female Gales moved on with the sale of the Riverbend house despite the irresolution. The good news was that the booming market allowed them to sell it for a good price; the less good news was that those proceeds were decreased once the two mortgages were paid off; and the bad news was that what remained was then placed into escrow pending a final property settlement and divorce decree. The silver lining here, though, was that the money bequeathed by Benny also got tied up, so although the female Gales didn't get it that also meant that *he* couldn't get it, and squander it, either. So if Helen's dream of one day getting to the promised land had to remain on hold, at least she could continue dreaming.

It was a bittersweet day in early June, just before the girls' seventeenth and fifteenth birthdays, when the move from Riverbend occurred. Human artifacts were leaving the solar system and iron ladies were returning to office as the three females sat smoking in the beat-up old Plymouth, at the curb, watching the movers carry boxes from the house. "Almost eleven years," Helen said reflectively, after a puff. "A lot of memories associated with this house."

"Yeah, bad memories," Regina snorted with her own puff.

"But *our* bad memories," Deb said from the back seat, restraining her tears.

"Hey what's that one?" Regina asked. The movers were carrying an unfamiliar pomegranate-patterned case from the house.

"Will you give me back my lighter, please?" Helen ignored her.

"I can't believe this is happening," Deb whimpered from the back seat.

"Can't you go ten minutes without crying?" Regina snorted again.

"Regina, my lighter," Helen said sternly. "And please stop making that sound."

Regina harrumphed, or maybe snorted once more; it was hard to distinguish. But at least she complied, and restrained herself for nearly another hour.

"What is she *doing* in there?" she finally complained. Deb had disappeared into the house forty-five minutes earlier as the movers were finishing up. "Saying goodbye to every room?"

Indeed she was. At that moment the almost-fifteen-year-old was gazing into her abandoned bedroom, from just over the sill of international waters. She was remembering both the many room inspections she had failed in this space and the many nights she had snuggled under her blanket with poor Marvin Marvin, when it seemed that she and her dog were loved by nobody other than each other; she was sobbing equally nostalgically, oddly, about both.

"Probably," Helen answered Regina between cigarettes out in the car, wavering between her own melancholy memories of the Riverbend years and her anxiety about the approaching Teagarden years. They had found a two-bedroom apartment, on the third floor of Tower One at the nearby Teagarden Towers; and while the modest space was a step down, it at least kept them in the same school district and was near several bus lines so the girls could get the hell out as teenagers are wont to do. It was also far more affordable than Riverbend, an important consideration given their unclear financial future.

Or maybe one should say that it was *two* steps down.

For the decreased space meant, first, that Helen could no longer surround herself with her parents' things, or at least those that survived the Riverbend flood. The movers had picked up the old furniture, the old radio, the box containing her father's yellowed undershirts and antiquated shaving kit, the box with her mother's doilies and placemats and scraps of the old kitchen wallpaper, on the same day as they picked up everything else. But instead of moving them into Teagarden they diverted them to a climate-controlled storage facility three-quarters of a mile away, in a warehouse on Dedham Road where Helen could visit them regularly.

And second, the decreased space meant that Regina and Deb were to share a bedroom.

Or at least they were until one of them either moved out or was murdered by the other. "Could you get your stupid shoes out of the way?" Helen overheard Regina say to Deb as they retired to bed the first night in the new apartment.

And yet with their life as a whole suspended in escrow, the sisters' mutual antagonism seemed to get suspended as well. The girls were as astonished as Helen when the first week had gone by and Helen had called neither the superintendent, the local authorities, nor the FBI. No, you could not say there was real warmth between the sisters but there was perhaps the next best thing: an alliance, one which had formed in the months leading up to The Very Busy Day and during this first phase of The Divorce. The enemy of my enemy is my friend, you might say, except for the friend part. Or as Dr. J. would put it years later, the sisters approached actual friendship in their lives about as closely as Halley's Comet approaches the sun, and about as frequently. Not exactly making contact, in other words, but compared to all that time sailing alone through cold dark empty space, it almost felt—to Deb anyway—like a warm embrace.

8

Speaking of the extraterrestrial, space shuttles were launching one late August afternoon, fourteen months after the move into Teagarden, just as an airport lounge was hosting airport scenes: people waiting, people saying hello, and people, Gale people, saying goodbye.

These were the days before security lines, before anyone cared how old you were before selling you alcohol. The lounge was conveniently located beside the departure gate. It was busy with travelers, those saying hello and goodbye to travelers, and a few people who simply liked drinking in airport lounges. Very much the sort of place where Theodore might have enjoyed a rendezvous or two during the years of the marriage. In any case here, in one small corner, the three female Gales were nursing their drinks and smoking their cigarettes and not speaking much.

There wasn't much left to say.

As she was finishing high school a few months back Regina had announced that she had won a mathematics scholarship to some impressive college far away. Helen, preoccupied with the protracted divorce-related matters and with melancholy murmurings over the state of her life, had barely noticed that Regina was completing high school much less plotting her escape. She'd offered a weak objection—"Must you go so far away?"—to which Regina had offered a strong reply: "Yeah."

And now the day had arrived.

Helen looked terrific, she herself would admit, for a woman in her late fifties. The fact that she was only forty-seven was best not to mention. And hey, as Regina would put it, what forty-seven-year-old lifelong smoker who'd just gone through phase one of The World's Most Unpleasant Divorce from The World's Most

Unpleasant Person would look even half as good as Helen? Not that Regina looked so great herself, for that matter. From that sweet baby with the infectious guffaw and warm gap-toothed grin she had become a morose eighteen-year-old with an infectious scowl and a gap-toothed sneer. Recently she had cut off almost all her hair, stopped trimming her fingernails, ceased wearing untattered clothing, and stopped speaking altogether unless you counted the occasional grunt as a form of speech. But then again, from Deb's perspective, all that was actually an upgrade in Regina's personality.

"Regina, please," Helen said wearily.

Regina sullenly removed her cigarette from the gap in her front teeth.

The airport sounds around them were almost comforting. Conversations, pouring liquids, loudspeaker announcements, the screech of a luggage cart. Indeed they were so lulled by the ambient noise that they almost missed the relevant announcement.

"Regina," Deb said.

"Yeah," Regina said.

"Yes," Helen corrected without much enthusiasm.

Regina scowled.

"I think they just announced your plane."

Regina made that smirk—raised eyebrow and pursed lips which, Deb had learned, was best translated as "whatever"—and stood up. She slung a ratty denim bag over her shoulder, cut from the same ratty denim as her jeans and jacket.

"We'll walk you to the gate," Helen said, reaching for the cigarettes to return to her purse.

"No, forget it. It's just right there."

There was a moment of silence.

Regina glanced at Deb.

"Bye, ol' buddy ol' chum," she said softly, and suddenly gave her sister a powerful bear hug ambiguous between expressing affection and attempting suffocation.

Deb was crying, from the hug, from the gesture, all of it.

"Bye, Mummy," Regina said quickly too, and leaned over to give Helen an awkward hug as well, what with the shoulder bag and Helen's still being seated and Regina's having stashed her cigarette back in her front teeth.

"Goodbye, sweetheart," Helen said quietly, also ambiguous

between correcting her daughter's speech and just saying goodbye.

Without another word Regina turned and began marching toward the door of the lounge. But then just as suddenly, by the door, she stopped and turned around.

"FUCK HIM!" she exclaimed loudly to the lounge, then turned around and disappeared out the door.

"Come," Helen said to Deb, "shall we go watch?"

Mother and daughter walked toward the gate, stopping at the large window nearby. Regina's plane loaded and pulled away a short time later. They watched it move toward the runway and get in line behind several other planes. Helen and Deb, standing next to each other, subconsciously moved a little closer and their bodies were almost touching as Regina's plane began its acceleration. As the aircraft's wheels lifted from the ground they were almost holding hands.

"I guess it is just the two of us now," Helen said softly.

Deb was still crying.

"We have to make this work, Debra," Helen said.

She gazed out the window at the empty tarmac as Deb stood beside her crying.

CHAPTER EIGHT
RETURN OF EDDIE LOVE

1

Deb, just past her sixteenth birthday, turned to the business of making it through high school while her mother, just shy of her forty-eighth, returned to the business of being a single woman. It was hard to decide whose business was less enviable.

Let's see. Deb had all the usual miseries of high school such as the social anxiety, the social anxiety, and the social anxiety. But then she also had some added advantages. She was not a naturally good student, not because she wasn't bright—she would eventually earn a Ph.D.—but because she was prone to distraction, which meant that when schoolwork loomed she could always find something more compelling to do. She also had an older sister who had been as fastidious in her schoolwork as in her chores, and who thus had breezed through school two grades ahead of Deb setting academic precedents Deb had no hope of following.

"What a pleasure to have another Gale in my class!" the teachers would say to Deb at the start of the school year, roughly five or six weeks before they would stop speaking to her altogether.

And then of course Deb had the advantage of coming from a home so badly broken that it made Dresden, Germany, circa Feb. 15, 1945, look spanking brand new. *You* try studying when your sister is playing awful music and grunting unintelligibly in the room next door, your father is having affairs so brazenly you can practically hear *him* grunting down the hall, and your mother is sobbing around the clock, pausing only to light up yet another cigarette.

Deb did have two friends, though. These would alternate being her best friends and being her sworn enemies, especially whenever boys were involved. She referred to them as her bosom buddies, referring, naturally, to her enormous bosoms. What teenaged boy, in his hormone-driven fantasies, doesn't imagine a girl with tremendous breasts to be the luckiest girl in the world? A girl who dictates the rules, who runs the show, who has all that *sex* in her hands any time she wants?

But teenaged boys are not exactly known for their insight, maturity, or wisdom.

Deb despised her breasts.

A girl whose natural gregariousness had long been suppressed by the irrepressible forces of her sister and her mother does not need the world's attention on her, which was what her mammaries brought about. A girl whose main male role model was Theodore Gale does not need the males of the world staring at her chest, whistling or muttering, or simply turning bright red when she enters the room. A girl who wants nothing more than for her sister not to hate her does not need her sibling's ongoing sarcastic commentary on her endowment. And a girl who was now left alone with an emotionally battered and abandoned mother does not need any more weight to lug around on her chest.

So Deb despised her breasts. But then again, she would sometimes admit, she was also rather attached to them, so to speak. After all she and they had much in common: they stood out, didn't fit in, were always uncomfortable, and were very much alone in the world.

The night after Regina's departure Helen and Deb fell asleep on Helen's bed, surrounded by the deathly quiet of their empty apartment. But before falling asleep they spoke for a while. More precisely Deb spoke for a while to her mother, who listened. It wasn't a lot but it was a little, which *was* a lot. She talked about school, about her upcoming junior year, about her resolve to do better now that Theodore was out of the picture and Regina—not that she would say anything bad about Regina to Helen, just yet—was not around to distract her.

It was very simple.

They spent the whole next day together, a Saturday, back-to-school clothes shopping for Deb. This consisted of Deb trying on outfits with Helen commenting, aiming to find something which met both their standards. This task was complicated by the fact that neither realized the other was using different criteria: Helen was looking to accentuate her daughter's beautiful curves and full bosom while Deb was looking for the opposite. The shopping ended up about as successfully as you would imagine.

Much easier was the search for shoes.

Their shared love of shoes, Deb would later say wistfully to Dr. J., was perhaps the only thing that kept her relationship with her mother alive during the, oh, ten or twelve years before Deb's junior year of high school.

"An exaggeration, surely, Debra," the good doctor would observe, aware, and in fact quite fond, of his charge's attraction to emotional drama. "It only felt that way to you, sometimes."

"Exactly, doc."

"That it was an exaggeration?"

"No," she replied evenly, "that it felt that way."

The second night after Regina's departure, Deb and her mother, in bed, spoke about shoes. They spoke about Deb's shoes mostly, about shoes past (scattered over the floor, on the stairs, or blocking the front door), about shoes present (the two new pairs they had acquired that day along with one new pair for Helen), and about shoes future—for there were always, always shoes in their future.

They fell asleep holding hands.

But in the middle of the night they were both awake.

"You," Helen said groggily, poking her, "are hard to sleep with."

Deb barely stirred, emitting a gentle deep snore. After about twenty minutes of flopping around, twisting diagonally, lifting her head and plopping it back down on the pillow, she was now settling into a more settled phase.

"Move over," Helen said more urgently, poking her again. Deb was lying half across her mother's delicate body, her ample bosom hogging more than its share of the mattress.

Deb did move over, but the wrong way. She was now almost fully on top of Helen, and snoring.

"Wake up this instant!" Helen said not loudly but in *that* tone of voice.

"Sorry," Deb muttered and rolled off Helen.

There was a moment of silence. Helen, who had turned away from Deb and was now lying back-to-back to her, watched the digital clock mark off two minutes.

"Are you awake?" she whispered.

"No."

"Very amusing."

"Amusing is being screamed at by your mother at two in the

morning."

Helen rolled over to speak to Deb's back. "That was hardly a scream."

"I was talking about my dream. About this afternoon. We were back in Wickenden's and I was trying on that muumuu I really liked. And you screamed that it was very unflattering and how could I possibly think about wearing that."

"*That* was hardly a scream."

There was another moment of silence. Helen could see the silhouette of her daughter's body since Deb had earlier kicked off the blanket on her side.

"You know it *was* unflattering," Helen added softly. "How *could* you think about wearing it?"

Deb didn't say anything.

Then Helen said something she had never said before.

"Dub?" she whispered, and touched her daughter's shoulder.

And her daughter was crying again, and Helen reached out and hugged her, from behind, and her daughter rolled into her arms and she was holding her crying baby like she used to hold that little crying baby long ago, before it had all fallen apart, and then after a minute or two Helen asked her, so gently, why exactly she was crying, and they started to talk, to really talk. They didn't talk about Theodore, the main subject of the preceding year-and-a-half. Instead Deb talked about her social anxiety, her problems with school, even said a few truthful things about Regina; and finally she talked about the untalkable, who could talk about such things with their mothers, with *Helen*, cold, repressed, angry Helen—but talk she did, about boys and her body and her breasts.

And Helen, cold, repressed, angry Helen—listened.

"But you," Helen said at one point when the tears at last had ended, "have such a beautiful womanly body, Deb."

"Yeah, but you also think that pink winklepickers are beautiful shoes."

"I'll have you know, young lady, that Eddie Love just *loved* those winklepickers."

Eddie Love was always good for a mood-lifter. At some unguarded moment during the last years of the marriage Helen had told her daughters about her fling with Eddie Love way back in high school. Eddie Love soon attained epic significance in the minds of all three female Gales. Even grouchy Regina shared with her younger sister the occasional fantasy of how things might have gone had the Eddie Love story gone differently. For Eddie Love was glorious, handsome, and cool, the real deal, not the bloated fraudulent pig that was Theodore Gale. Eddie Love was decent and dashing and a delicious dancer; Theodore Gale was an overweight oaf who danced only around the truth or in the direction of delicious desserts. Eddie Love, simply, was good and Theodore Gale was bad. In all three females' minds Eddie Love had become Helen's great lost love, lost opportunity, lost life. The annoying fact that Eddie Love had abruptly disappeared from Helen's life back then was easy to overlook.

"In that case I take it back," Deb said, not missing a beat. "I guess I *do* have a beautiful womanly body."

Helen smiled. "Perhaps we should go shopping again tomorrow."

"Yeah, do you know any stores that sell burlap sacks?"

"Maybe not burlap."

"How about a fabric store that does custom orders?"

"I do, but I forbid you to even think about burlap."

"Okay, I'll give in on the fabric if you give in on the shape of the thing. I mean shapelessness."

"You," Helen said suddenly, "are very funny."

There was a silence.

"Funny ha-ha," Deb asked, "or funny strange?"

"Ha-ha," Helen said very seriously.

There was another silence.

"You can be too, Mummy," Deb said.

And another silence.

Helen slowly reached out her hand toward Deb. "My name is Helen Gale," she said. "I'm pleased to meet you."

"The pleasure," Deb replied even more so, taking it, "is all mine."

2

They didn't hear much from Regina over the next couple of years. And what they did hear *wasn't* much. She never picked up the phone when Helen or Deb called and when she did call herself it was usually to ask for money—of which Helen had little, given all the contested funds still tied up in escrow along with the finalization of the divorce itself—and to promise that she'd come back to visit soon. But she didn't. She found a job waitressing out there far away for the first summer, and was too busy then and during her sophomore year to make the trek back. Deb became convinced that Regina not only had had a boyfriend but had been impregnated by him, had an abortion, and then been dumped.

"What on earth makes you think that?" Helen asked over supper.

Deb had gradually been taking over the cooking. The cooking lessons that Helen had halted when the marriage began seriously to decline they had renewed upon their move into Teagarden Towers, and by this point Deb was more than competent in the kitchen—though not yet ready, Helen reminded her with a smile, to learn the secret recipe banana cream pie.

"It's the way she refuses to speak to me. It's different from the way she used to refuse to speak to me."

"You, my dear Debra, are inheriting your grandmother Dottie's paranoia."

"I call it intuition."

"Well, can you be more specific?"

"No. She just sounds like a girl who's been dumped by a boy whose baby she's aborted."

"You are overcooking that cavatelli," Helen interrupted.

Regina *was* to make it back home for Deb's high school graduation, however. "I want to see this miracle for myself," she had said, just after asking for the airfare money. She spent most of the week at home visiting with her high school friends, then sat through the graduation ceremony barely saying a word but with a vaguely uncomfortable expression on her face, which Deb preferred to interpret as "Congratulations, sis, I'm really proud of you!" Then a few weeks after returning to far away she let them know, by a postcard, of a change of location. She was going to spend her junior year doing mathematics at an even more impressive college located even further away, and would let them know once she had her new address and phone number.

Deb's graduation was indeed a miracle.

The girl was bright, after all, despite being the "emotional" and "distracted" one. Not bright enough to avoid a low overall GPA for high school perhaps; that was mathematically impossible, given her first two years' performance. But she did well in her final two years once she was free of her sister and the collapsing marriage, and subject only to the distractions of boys, her breasts, and shoe-shopping trips with her mother.

And there *were* a few boys.

More precisely there were many boys who ogled her breasts and a subset of these who ogled *all* of her, for as Deb emerged from her early teens she was blossoming into an attractive young lady. Of that subset most could be ruled out as too silly or immature. After going on a few dates Deb found she could winnow the set further by simply ruling out every male under the age of eighteen. She was, it turned out, mature for her years, not merely physically but emotionally and culturally and even, for an "emotional" person, intellectually. You couldn't grow up under Helen Gale without absorbing some of the woman's refinement and class, after all, and Deb got her share.

And what was Helen doing during this period?

Well there weren't any boys around, that's for sure. The era of long marriages had begun crumbling the decade before, and this was now the era when everyone was divorcing. This had two implications for Helen. It meant, first, that her story wasn't interesting. Oh, another philandering husband? How banal. But it meant, second, that there was a glut of middle-aged single women, since the ex-husbands were all philandering themselves into the arms of much younger women.

Nor was Helen at the top of her game, as she was fully aware. The smoking had not exactly benefited her face and teeth and skin and fingernails. The hair dye, still chemically primitive in those days, had not exactly benefited the condition of her hair. And Theodore certainly hadn't benefited the condition of her psyche. So here she was in the months before Deb's miraculous graduation, halfway through the year to her fiftieth birthday, feeling herself with not much to offer to any man under about seventy.

Theodore had not only left her but his lawyer had left her, too, with more or less nothing. The divorce proceedings were still stalled: Theodore's attempt to grab the island from Helen had left everything in limbo, including the Riverbend proceeds. All Helen had was the modest income of her modest job. And even that job had become less satisfying since her boss himself had divorced and then married a much younger woman who promptly became the company's primary Buyer. Helen tried hard to like this woman who usurped the position she had once coveted, and tried even harder because the woman really was a decent person.

"All the more reason to dislike her," Deb commented one night in bed.

"She means well."

"I don't think she does. I don't like her."

"*I* think she does. And I do like her."

"Well, she must not think too highly of you. I mean, that disaster." Deb was referring to the first—and only—date that Helen had gone on since The Very Busy Day. Helen's boss's wife had set it up right before departing with the boss on a two-month buying trip across Europe.

"To the contrary, she thinks highly of her father. And that is another reason to like her." The man turned out to be an old fogey in his late sixties.

"Yeah, but seriously, like how rude was he to bring his oxygen tank right to the table."

"Not everyone," Helen smiled, "has your exquisite etiquette."

"Eddie Love would never bring his oxygen tank to the dinner table."

"Eddie Love would never need an oxygen tank in the first place."

"Yeah, he's probably still going strong on the air he breathed in high school."

They were laughing now. It was much easier now for them to crack each other up. It was so pleasant in fact that Helen almost didn't mind when they were up half the night laughing, even if she was exhausted for work the next day.

"What if ..." Deb said gently.

"Yes, what if ..."

There was a silence.

"Maybe we should try to find him," Deb said.

"You *are* funny, Dub. Funny strange, I mean."

"No, I mean it. He's got to be out there somewhere."

"Perhaps you are forgetting that *he* disappeared on *me*."

"Only in *reality*. But this is, like, make believe, Mummy. And we can make believe whatever we want. Like, what if there was a good reason he disappeared. What if he was totally in love with you but had to disappear anyway."

"What if he is dead."

"Eddie Love is not dead. Eddie Love is unkillable. Eddie Love can kill death itself. Eddie Love eats death for breakfast. And that's why Eddie Love can make everything okay."

"Again you are forgetting, Debra, that he disappeared on me. Thirty, um," Helen calculated, math being as much a strength of hers as of Deb's, "three years ago. Or so."

"Perhaps *you* are forgetting that he was in love with you when he disappeared."

There was a silence.

"You only think that because I told you as much," Helen said. "You don't have anyone else's perspective. And maybe I was wrong. Maybe I misunderstood."

"And maybe you didn't."

There was another silence.

Finally Helen said, "I am not very attractive anymore."

When, exactly, had Deb slid over to her mother? When had she put her arms around that lonely little body?

"Mummy, if Regina, with her nose-ring—"

"You do not know she has a nose-ring."

"You can hear it in her voice!"

"She has always had a nasal voice."

"Snotty, you mean."

"Excuse me. That *is* my daughter we are talking about."

"Right, and as I was saying, if *she* can get some guy to knock her up, then you should have the men lining up around the block."

"You, my other daughter," Helen said, "are either very sweet, or very snotty yourself. Or just naïve."

"I am going to find him."

"You will do no such thing."

The best way to motivate a teenager, of course, is to forbid her from something.

3

Deb graduated from high school.

Regina popped back in for that quick visit only to prove that Deb had been wrong about her having a nose-ring: she had *two*. She was also irritated when her sister and mother, on meeting her at the airport gate, had looked at her and simultaneously burst out laughing.

"Fuck you, too," she muttered, her left nostril flaring despite the piercing's pinch.

Her mood didn't improve when her little sister retorted, "Love the nose jobs, sis." Next thing you know, Regina thought angrily, uppity Ugly would be giving *her* dead-arms.

An eyeblink later the week was over and Regina had departed further away. Meanwhile the miracles continued: not only did Deb finish high school but she was accepted at a college. Or two, to be precise: the local college, and the university.

It was Helen who had insisted Deb apply to the latter. "The local college is not exactly—impressive, Debra," she'd said. "You can do better."

"It isn't so bad. At least now that they've gotten rid of *your* school." A few years before they had finally done away with the embarrassing School of Administrative Assistance from which Helen herself had graduated three decades before.

Helen smiled. "Just humor me, please, and apply? To keep your options open?"

So Debra had yielded, figuring she would be rejected from the university in any case. Her expectations unexpectedly foiled, she was now attempting to close that option.

"But—*he* is there," she objected, referring to the man who was now enjoying his life, as a tenured professor, after having wrecked theirs.

"It is a big school," Helen answered. "You will never see him."

"But what if I do?"

"You shall cross that bridge when you come to it."

"Jump off it, you mean."

"If you decide that is necessary, then yes."

"But it won't be pretty, Mummy. I'll be miserable to live with."

"That will be your roommate's problem."

"You're my roommate."

"You," Helen replied, "will live in the dorm, of course."

Deb gazed at her mother. "The dorm?"

"The place where young women live when they grow up and begin their own lives."

"But—you didn't live in a dorm," Deb said.

"Yes, and see what became of me."

There was a silence.

"And with what money, exactly?" Deb said.

"We will make it work," Helen said firmly.

There was a brief pause, and then they both laughed. Each

could recite a dozen times when *that man* had promised to make something work and then hadn't.

"It's not the money," Deb continued softly.

"Then what is it?"

"I need you to take care of me."

"You *are* funny," Helen said.

Deb was at this point doing most of the shopping and cooking. More impressively she was even keeping up with the tidying and cleaning. The one sore spot—speaking of impossibilities—were her shoes. She was incapable of not leaving them all over the Teagarden apartment.

"I'm serious, Mummy. Without you around I'd probably run off and get myself knocked up, and then after the abortion get my nose double pierced."

"You, Dub," Helen answered, "have enough sense to stop with the first piercing."

They reached a compromise: Deb would attend the university, but she would live at home. So off she went to her first day of college. Helen, who went in late to work that day so she could see her off, watched her drive away and tried to remember Deb's first day of school as a child. She recalled Regina's first day vividly, but for Deb's she drew a blank. And why, she wondered as she found herself crying, was she so emotional about it? The university was only twenty minutes away; her daughter would be back for supper. Helen pulled herself together and then headed to the bus stop to go to work.

There were some changes.

Deb became busy in the months ahead, dedicating herself to her schoolwork, to her part-time job in the university's social science library, to making some new friends, to dating some, well, men. She was often out in the evenings now, working or socializing or, well, dating. Helen spent evenings watching television, reading fashion magazines, and smoking, and slowly getting (she observed in the mirror) less and less attractive. Once in a while she'd find herself thinking about Eddie Love, wondering if Deb had just let that go, thinking her chances of attracting him—if he were still alive, still available, still interested—were evaporating with each passing day.

A few nights Deb didn't come home at all.

She always called beforehand.

"Mummy," she would say, "I don't have to stay out."

"But you do, Debra," Helen would reply with the smallest quiver in her voice.

"Say the word and I'll come home immediately."

"You come home and you will hear a word or two from me, you can be sure."

"Well let me give you the phone number to reach me."

"Debra," Helen would ignore her, "I will see you tomorrow."

Deb always hung up in tears apologizing, and then obeyed her mother and did not come home. Helen's bed on those nights felt as empty and quiet as the rest of the Teagarden apartment.

4

Speaking of *that man*, well he surely was enjoying his life with tenure. For now when he said things like, "Nah, I didn't work on my book this summer, I was too busy *living*," he could then add, "but hey, I've got tenure!" His lack of guilt about not working was not itself new, but now he didn't even feel like he *ought* to feel guilty. And yet even here he could not resist the thrill of lying. For, oddly, now that he no longer felt obliged to work he found himself often, on the sly, actually working. When the initial flurry of divorce activities settled down he found himself searching for his abandoned manuscript on Ignoratio P. Elenchi; and then found himself rereading it; and then found himself rewriting the entire thing from scratch. Before too long his book—*Coleworts and Caterpillars: The Evolution of Ignoratio P. Elenchi's Erucarium Ortus*—would be under contract at a leading academic press.

Things with Jane were going swimmingly as well. Even with Benny's bequest on hold they were living as large as he was growing, especially since Jane and Maxey had started some absurdly profitable venture about which they assured him it was best for him to remain in the dark. Along the way he and Jane had also moved into a larger condominium downtown, acquired a larger summer home on the peninsula, and furnished both with much larger beds.

Only one thing *wasn't* going swimmingly: Theodore's sperm.

Jane wanted a baby, you'll recall, and normally what Jane wanted she got, immediately. But it wasn't happening. Theodore fended her off for a while, but you'll also recall her manners of persuasion and before long—maybe ninety seconds after she threatened to *stop* persuading—he had relented. But even once both his spirit and his flesh were willing, the little buggers inside were not. Maybe it was the living large, maybe it was the *being* large, but his little swimmers were mostly floating belly up. Where once Theodore had been King of the Beasts he soon became just Prince, and then more like the Jester. Or as Jane liked to put it: with respect to their reproductive project he was not pulling his weight, only gaining it. For two people with a taste for instant gratification the roughly three-and-a-half years between Theodore's relenting and Jane's becoming pregnant were extremely challenging.

"You finally did it, big man," Jane said to her big man one night, adding, before he could lumber to his feet and start pounding his graying hairy chest, "Now I think we should get married."

"Married?" Theodore exclaimed, aborting the lumbering process and sitting back down. "But that means I have to deal with getting unmarried again."

"Yes," Jane said. "You do."

So once more Theodore retained Bilker—energized from having just dismantled the local Public Television affiliate—who for a stunning fee dashed off another of those wonderful letters to the female Gales.

5

Thus came the news to Helen and Debra, in early November, that Theodore wanted to remarry on New Year's Day.

The unpleasant letter also contained a proposal to restart negotiations on the property settlement; and announced that barring a successful property settlement· they would obtain a divorce decree without the settlement. Helen consulted with Melvin and consulted with Deb and at one point tried the new phone number for Regina as well. Her older daughter's voice muttered the answering machine message—"You called, you must want something, so state your piece"—but Regina never called back.

"Nothing has changed, substantively," Melvin observed in one of the meetings he, Helen, and Deb had had on the subject, on the evenings his wife Michelle would let him get away. "In terms of the proposed division of assets, that is. They're proposing exactly the same hard-line division we left off with three-and-a-half years ago."

"Can they really just get the divorce without settling the property?" Deb asked.

"Pursuant to the local laws, yes."

"Do we gain any bargaining leverage," Helen asked, "by not consenting to the divorce?"

"Not really. They can get the divorce without your consent, so withholding it doesn't help us."

"So what do you recommend, Melvin?" Deb asked.

"It's not for me to recommend, exactly. But if you can live with the assets continuing in escrow this way, then I would let them have their divorce for now. Then wait till the situation changes in some way, and fight for the property again when you're ready."

And so that's what they did. After Melvin drafted their response Helen and Deb went out to the trendy new wine bar near the apartment to smoke some cigarettes, drink some glasses, and celebrate both that the divorce would soon be final and that that man's impending nuptials to that bimbo of his barely bothered them.

Deb was indeed busy that fall. But no, she hadn't forgotten about Eddie Love, and Theodore's remarriage seemed to make The Search all the more imperative. The main reason she'd chosen the library job in fact was to facilitate The Search. This was before the internet, mind you, and tracking down old acquaintances required more than just some clicks on a keyboard. The library had resources to this end. Deb scoured old newspapers from that distant summer, looking for any clue as to why Eddie Love had disappeared or where he might have gone. Over some weeks she managed to track down some of his former bandmates and their phone numbers; but all dead ends, as none had any idea what had happened much less where he might be now. She was able to access local and more remote police records, the public sorts anyway, looking for his name in the criminal domain. She remembered everything her mother had told her about him, his love of music and dancing, his being a smoker, and tried to imagine where a musical smoking dancer might end up—in the theater, maybe?—and followed many a red herring through old theater listings.

Then there were the phone books. Again.

Deb managed to obtain phone books from nearby cities, increasing her geographic range over time. The Search was complicated by the fact that, though Eddie Love was not a common name, it was also not unique; she was turning up several hits a week at one point. She would have loved to call them all to save time, but that required long-distance telephoning, and the money—not to mention the odds of success—was too short to warrant those calls. So she prepared a form letter, made copies on the library's Xerox machine, used her salary to buy stamps, and off they went.

No replies.

One evening during the phone book phase she was at the Xerox machine when she glanced up at the main entrance to the library, an ornate glass door easily visible from behind the circulation desk where she worked. Just then walking through that door she saw the instantly recognizable figure.

It was *that man*.

Her heart immediately in her throat she ducked behind the reshelving bookcase, trying not to breathe too loudly as she peered out through the cracks above the books waiting to be returned to their proper locations. She watched as Theodore disappeared up the stairs to the stacks, and she remained hidden, her heart now descended back into her chest where it was thumping wildly, until he had himself descended ten minutes later and come to the circulation desk to check out his book.

"Hallo?" he called out to the deserted desk. "Hallo?"

Shit, Debra thought, remembering that her job description was "circulation manager."

She took a deep breath and stepped out from the behind the bookcase, grabbing a couple of books as she did so to make it look like she was doing something.

"Oh," Theodore said when he saw her.

"Your library card, please," Debra said without looking at him.

There was a moment of silence.

"You work here," he said.

She hesitated. "Your card, please."

He fumbled in his pocket and pulled out a wallet.

"Listen, Dubs—" he began as she took the card.

"It's due in May," she said, stamping the book and returning it.

She glanced up briefly.

Her father's bright blue eyes looked sad and swollen. "Dubs, listen—"

"Have a nice night," she said quickly (or was it "have a nice life"?) as she dropped her eyes and disappeared into the women's restroom located around the corner from the circulation desk. There she knelt over a toilet and attempted, unsuccessfully, to vomit. When she finally came out, fifteen minutes later—again remembering her job description—he was gone. By the time she returned home that night she was calm enough not to mention the episode to her mother.

One other thing she didn't mention was this: that while her head was over that toilet she had also suddenly remembered Helen once mentioning Eddie Love's fascination with Asia, and that he'd always wanted to visit there. Since her local search had so far been fruitless, the next evening at the library Deb began using Inter-Library Loan to order phone books from major Asian cities, at least where English versions were available. This was a low-probability strategy but nothing else was working. Anyway it only took a few minutes to place the orders and would take but a few seconds to look up the name and then drop the books onto the return shelf.

And then one afternoon at the start of December it was there.

He was in Hong Kong. Or at least *someone* named Eddie Love was in Hong Kong, at an address and with a phone number right there before Deb's eyes. She had a feeling ... but she also had no money and no long-distance telephone. So she made a copy of her form letter, got some airmail postage and sent it on its way. Since the end of the semester was approaching she turned her attention to studying for her exams and forgot, for the moment, about Eddie Love.

6

"I thought you were going to a party."

"I *was* going to a party."

"That is what girls your age do on New Year's Eve."

"That is what most girls my age *are* doing tonight."

"I don't understand," Helen said.

They were just finishing the early supper Deb had prepared, early because Deb was going to a couple of parties with her, well, boyfriend, an earlier party to welcome in a later one and the later one to welcome in the new year. Nothing remained on their plates of the Chicken Relleno with the amazing Sweet Pickle Relish

Stuffing.

"I don't feel like going out."

"You are eighteen years old on New Year's Eve. Of course you feel like going out."

"We can go get some ice cream, if you're so keen on going out."

"Of course you feel like going out with your boyfriend."

"He is not my boyfriend."

"Boy space friend, then. And please stop pointing at me with your fork."

"Sorry." Deb put down her fork. "But man space friend, actually." Mark was a senior, at twenty-one; Deb didn't date "boys."

"Whatever." That awful word was infiltrating Helen's speech just often enough that it was transitioning from mocking her daughter's speech to being part of Helen's own. "I want you to go out."

"I have a headache."

"You do not have a headache."

"I'm on the rag."

"Then I definitely want you to go out." Deb's periods were notoriously awful, for the people around her.

"This morning's crossword puzzle," Deb ignored her, "is demanding to be done. And I can't do it without my crossword buddy."

"We can just do tomorrow's crossword puzzle. Tomorrow."

"All right then. What if Eddie Love calls tonight? I want to be here."

"It's more likely that I will win the lottery tonight than that Eddie Love will call. And I have not even bought a ticket." There was a major lottery drawing scheduled for a minute before midnight. More or less everyone had bought tickets except for Helen, who was opposed to gambling in all its forms, including marriage.

At least for herself, anyway. If that man wanted to get married again, tomorrow, to that person—well let them have it.

"Mummy," Deb said. She had carried some dirty dishes to the sink and turned back to look at Helen. "I am not leaving you alone on New Year's Eve."

And especially not with *him* getting married tomorrow, she did not add.

"Debra." Helen came up to the sink and caressed her daughter's cheek. "You will go out tonight and you will have a wonderful time. I forbid you from coming home before 3:00 AM. And I would prefer that you not come home at all."

Kids these days! They just don't respect their parents anymore.

Mother and daughter picked up a couple of half-gallons of ice cream and a couple of Rob Lowe and Emilio Estevez movies for the video player, finished the first half-gallon and first movie and moved on to homemade popcorn when Dick Clark came on, checked Deb's lottery ticket when the winning numbers were drawn (she matched none), and then shared a quick smooch as the Times Square ball hit the ground of the new year. "Yecch" both said simultaneously and cracked up, so boisterously that they almost didn't hear the phone ringing.

"Oh my God," Deb said. "It's Eddie Love."

"It is not Eddie Love."

"It's totally Eddie Love. Pick it up, quick!"

"Let the answering machine get it."

"Mummy!" Deb exclaimed, too late. On the kitchen counter the box which Theodore had brought home years ago clicked on. They heard Helen's serious voice reading from the user's manual script—an outgoing message was a formal affair for her—and then the beep.

"Deb, this is Mark calling. You know, your *man*friend." There were party sounds in the background, loud music, some shouting, whooping it up. "I'd just like to, uh, introduce you to, um ..." There was a muffled sound, something like Mark saying "what's your name again?" ... "Here, here's Gwen." The phone was handed over and a young, drunken woman's voice came on. "Uh, like hi? I'm Gwen? Who is that?" The phone was apparently yanked from her hand and Mark's voice returned. "Just wanted to, uh, you know, wish you a happy new year and to, um, let you know I'm having a great time here." Mark's voice disappeared but he evidently didn't hang up properly because the party sounds continued and they could hear, muffled, the young lady saying something like "Hey, like, where are you going?" and maybe Mark's voice saying, "Get away from me ..."

Deb clicked the machine off. "He's such a boy."

"I'm sorry, my angel."

"It's all right. He'll be crawling back tomorrow."

"No, I'm sorry that it wasn't Eddie Love."

"Hilarious. Speaking of Eddie Love, should we watch the next movie? Looks like a greaser thing. Right up your alley!"

"I think I would rather go to bed."

"But it's only midnight. The night is young."

"Yes, but I am not."

"Come on, Mummy, you're as young as you feel."

"That is precisely my point." Helen stood up and started down the hallway.

"Okay, then. I'll come in a few minutes."

"All right. Happy new year, my angel."

Deb smiled, looking up at her mother. When, exactly, did Debra become such a beautiful young woman? "Happy new year, Mummy."

At 2:30 AM the phone rang again.

7

Deb was a deep and restless sleeper. She had been known to flop out of the bed and roll halfway across her room without waking up. Once the house across the street on Riverbend had nearly burned to the ground overnight and Deb had slept through three fire engines, two ambulances, and all the town's police personnel.

Helen, to the contrary, was a light sleeper. Not that that mattered since she was wide awake anyway next to Deb's gently snoring body, ruminating on just how okay she was that that man was remarrying in less than nine hours and—let's see—twenty-nine minutes. Thus it was no surprise that Helen got to the phone on the bedside table first; only a surprise just how instantly Deb woke up once her mother began speaking.

"Yes … Yes … Who? … Oh my goodness … I'm divorced … I don't know, two, two … daughters, both girls … grown … divorced I said …"

"Who is it, who is it?" Deb tugged at Helen, whose face was ashen.

"*Him*," Helen breathed wide-eyed. "No, sorry, I was talking to my daughter … Yes she is right here … Yes in bed with me … Long story …"

"What's he saying, what's he saying?"

"Shhh!" Helen waved her away. "No I was talking to my

daughter …"

"Oh my God oh my God," Deb was now pacing the room.

"Get out!" Helen hissed at Deb, covering the mouthpiece of the phone.

"Aaargh!" Deb groaned but complied, casting her mother a look making clear that she was going to be right outside the closed bedroom door listening. The conversation did not last long. After maybe ten minutes Deb could hear that her mother was no longer speaking and she opened the door.

"Mummy?"

Helen was lying on the bed, her back to the door, sobbing.

"Mummy." Deb climbed into bed and put her arms around her and started crying too.

"What happened," she asked after a few minutes.

Helen shook her head.

A few minutes later the crying began to subside.

"What happened," Deb asked again softly.

"A cigarette," Helen said. Deb reached for the pack on the bedside table, lit one for her mother and one for herself. After a few drags Helen said, in a near whisper, "Is it too late, do you think, to buy a lottery ticket?"

"Tell me what he said!"

It wasn't so much the content of what he said but the fact that after thirty-three years, the last thirty-two of which he'd spent primarily as a make-believe fantasy object, Eddie Love was once again a concrete commodity. He was living in Hong Kong, almost three decades now. He was recently divorced too, for the second time, from the same Chinese woman he had mistakenly reconciled with after their first divorce. No children as far as he knew; a sense of humor, apparently. He'd gotten the letter from Deb that afternoon and called immediately.

"I cannot believe that you disobeyed me, incidentally," Helen added sharply. "I told you that I didn't want you to look for him."

"Yeah, right."

"Damn right, more like it."

"But wait," Deb said. "What happened? When he disappeared?"

"We didn't get to that."

"You didn't get to that?"

"He's going to call again tomorrow." Helen glanced at the clock: just before 3:00 AM. "I mean today. At noon."

"He's going to call again at noon?"

"I believe that's what he said."

"You *believe* that's what he said?"

"Would you stop repeating everything I say!"

"Sorry. But that's quite a coincidence, isn't it? I mean noon."

Helen shook her head a little too vigorously.

"Well I think it's, like, pretty symbolic," Deb said.

"It's *like* pretty symbolic or it *is* pretty symbolic?"

"Fine, forget it. What else did he say, then?"

"You will not believe this."

"I will believe *anything* at this point."

"He sells shoes."

"What, like he's a clerk or something?"

"Debra, for a college girl you are awfully dense sometimes."

"Just tell me!"

"He has his own import-export business. I think he said something about owning factories in Asia. And are you paying attention?"

"TELL ME!"

"*He specializes in women's shoes.*"

"Oh … my … God!" Deb exclaimed as both women broke into laughter, hearty, soul-wrenching laughter, laughter that would take forty-five minutes and the second half-gallon of ice cream in the freezer to finally control.

8

"Out of the apartment," Helen commanded.

"There is no way I am leaving this apartment," Deb replied the next morning. It was ten minutes before noon. They had been up all night. The last hour had been mostly spent arguing about whether Deb could remain on the premises.

"I will harm you physically if you do not leave within the next two minutes."

"Mother! It's freezing outside."

"Go somewhere. Sit in the lobby. You may return at one. Not one second earlier."

"Fine. But when I come back I want to hear that he has proposed to you, minimum."

"That's a minimum?"

"A lifetime supply of imported shoes would be nice too."

"Get out!" Helen was pushing Deb out the door as the phone rang precisely at noon.

That, Helen thought running into the kitchen to answer it, was a propitious sign.

Equally punctual were the handful of guests at the wedding of Theodore Gale and Jane Nepean. These were at this moment assembled at the Office of the City Clerk downtown, just beginning what would turn out to be an impressive wait for Theodore, and his best man Maxey, to arrive. Jane felt some queasiness but attributed it to the three-month-old fetus still rather hidden in her almost forty-year-old womb. She was thankfully not aware that that fetus was just beginning the early stages of what would in fact be its final stages.

At 12:59 PM and 59 seconds Deb walked back in the door. She had spent fifty-nine minutes and fifty-nine seconds in the Teagarden Tower One lobby downstairs, listening to the Walkman her probably ex-manfriend Mark was probably in the process of abandoning to her, and stepping out twice into the freezing air to smoke.

Helen was just hanging up. She glanced at the clock.

"You're early." Her face was as ashen as the night before.

"Every word." Deb sat at the table and took her mother's hands. "Every pause, every hiccup. Now."

"I will do my best," Helen said weakly.

"Yes you will. But first, when are our shoes coming?"

"No, first, my angel, a cigarette. Then shoes."

Shoes, indeed. Hong Kong. Extremely successful; shoe empire might be a good expression to use. Been there a long time, but travels a lot, mostly in Asia, visiting factories, some of which are his, and buying shoes from other factories before shipping them around the world, making a ton of money in the process. Did Helen have any particular interest in shoes? Most women did, he obviously knew, that's why he was so successful, but did she have any *particular* interest in shoes? Did she have an interest in shoes! That was great news, he would be happy to provide her with a generous supply of top-of-the-line designs.

"Oh my God," Deb whispered. "Is this reality we're talking about, or have we slipped back into make-believe?"

"It gets better. Or maybe worse."

Divorced twice, same woman, no children, covered that already;

his heart was never really in it either time. Just got married because successful businessmen had wives, he hadn't found Mrs. Right but the woman was good enough to be Mrs. Right Now, he thought, chuckling at his joke, and really she was Mrs. All Right. But she wanted more, she wasn't satisfied with the nice home, the nice things, she wanted children, children with a man whose heart belonged to her; and he, he had had to admit, was not that man.

"Is this going where I think it's going?" Deb asked hoarsely.

Helen nodded slowly.

Thirty-three years ago, he said, he was in love with another woman. A woman who was different from every other woman he had known since then. Elegant, refined, classy, beautiful. He was sure they were going to be together. And then two things happened.

"Spit it out!" Deb exclaimed.

Her mother, Edna, came to him one afternoon at the end of that summer. Just showed up at his apartment door. He had never met her before, had no idea she even knew about him, she just showed up. She proceeded to lecture him about how poorly suited he was for her daughter, he wasn't good enough for her, and so on. He listened politely, amused, he was really cocky back then and wasn't going to be intimidated by this snooty old lady in her stuffy clothes, overdressed for the hot August day, but he also wasn't going to be rude to her.

The old bat was, after all, the mother of the woman he loved.

"For Chrissake, why are you pausing?" Deb moaned.

He told me, Helen said, what he said to her, thirty-three years ago. He told her that he appreciated her visit but that he loved her daughter, that he would always love her daughter, and that nothing could make him stop loving her daughter.

Oh my God, Deb said.

And he said that thirty-three years later he still loves her daughter.

Oh my God, again.

And that not a week has gone by in the last three decades that he hasn't thought about that woman.

"Jesus Christ!" Deb exclaimed. "So why'd he disappear on you?"

"He got in some trouble," Helen said.

He was young, he was cocky, he was going to be a rock star and was already living the rock star life. He owed some people some money, people he shouldn't have been dealing with, this one really crazy guy, a kid really, scared the bejeezus out of him with this weird unblinking eye thing, so much so that he then did a couple of things he shouldn't have done in order to get the money he owed, so he had both bad guys and good guys coming after him. Then out of the blue some guy he knew got an offer to play a gig across the ocean and he thought, why not? Skip out for a while, let things cool off, he'll come back in a few weeks and reclaim the woman of his dreams. Then one thing led to another, thirty years disappeared, and he became a twice-divorced childless shoe emperor living in exile while his heart remained back home.

Or wherever it was, exactly, that one beautiful, perfect Helen Faire had ended up.

"Mummy," Deb said as Helen finished, "is that the most wonderful story I've ever heard or the most horrible?"

"Such a fine line," Helen said.

"And Edna did that? That little old lady in the pictures?"

"She wasn't always so old, you know. And I would do the same for you."

"Wait—for me or *to* me?"

"Such a fine line," Helen repeated softly.

There was a silence.

The two women continued smoking.

"So," Deb said after a while.

"Sew your buttons."

"Cut it out! You know what I'm asking."

"I don't know. He's going to call again in a few days."

"Oh my God. What are we going to do?"

"We shall wait and see, is what we are going to do."

"Mummy," Deb said, as if she'd just thought of something.

"Yes, my angel."

"Have I just been dreaming, seriously, or did Eddie Love recently call this house?"

Helen smiled. "It is a beautiful dream, my darling daughter, and I am glad that we are dreaming it together."

"Tell me the part about the shoes again?"

Theodore was by this point about twenty-five minutes into his second marriage. Assuming, that is, that one may count as having consented to marriage when one is too inebriated to count, period.

9

The female Gales had often wondered how things might have been had Mummy landed Eddie Love instead of Theodore Gale. Well, talk about having a second chance to find out!

That's what Helen and Deb did.

What if Eddie Love wants to come here? What if he wants you to go there? What if he wants *us* to go there? What if he rescues us from the money problems, the love problems, the life problems, not to mention from the past and the future as well?

What if a game of "what if" were actually to come true?

For a tired and lonely woman just north of her fiftieth birthday?

Helen mentioned none of these conversations to Eddie Love when he called three days later. In fact she put as positive a spin as she could on her life of the past three decades, but you'd have had to be either really dense or extremely insensitive not to pick up on the underlying currents.

"You know," Eddie Love said after listening for a while, "it sounds like you've had it pretty rough, Nellie."

"I would not say that," Helen objected.

"No, really. You've had your share of problems. I mean it. But now I want to give you another problem."

"Another problem?"

"I have a business trip scheduled in a few weeks. To visit some factories in Thailand, meet with some importers who haven't been cooperating lately. I'll be working part of that time. But I'll have some free time too."

"That sounds wonderful for you."

"It is. Thailand is a beautiful country. Fantastic scenery, restaurants, beaches, stores, shopping galore. The works. Whatever turns you on, they got it. Been there a dozen times."

"So what is the problem?"

"I want you to meet me there."

There was a silence.

"Nellie, are you there?"

"I assume you are joking."

"Eddie Love does not joke about such things."

"I am flattered, Eddie, really I—"

"Meet me there. For ten days."

"There are so many reasons that—"

"Meet me there. Just do it."

"I—I have no money."

"I'm paying. I'm loaded. Meet me there."

"I have a job. I've already committed my vacation time. In May I'm going to the—promised land with my daughter. Finally. We've wanted to do this since—"

"I'll buy your company. Give you more vacation time."

"I don't even know you. It has been thirty years."

"Ten days to get reacquainted. That's the whole point."

"I would have to ask for my own hotel room."

"I'll get you two. One for you, one for all the shoes I'll buy you!" He laughed loudly.

"Eddie—"

"Listen, Nellie," Eddie Love interrupted. "I told you I wanted to give you another problem. You've been Eddie Love's problem for a long time. So Eddie Love is now *your* problem. Meet me there, Nellie. Think about it. Or maybe don't think about it, you know. I'll call back in a few days."

"Of course you're going," Deb said approximately seven seconds later. The delay was for lighting cigarettes.

"Of course I am not going."

"How could you not go?"

"All the reasons I said. The money, the vacation time. Our trip."

"Mummy, we can postpone our trip. We'll do it next year."

"We say that every year."

"True, but this time we will *really* do it next year."

"We say that every year as well."

"Mummy, really, there's no rush. The promised land isn't going anywhere."

"Debra, it has taken us this long to book that trip. I cannot even tell you how many years we have maintained the long journey box. I do not want to wait any longer."

"But you must, Mummy. This is Super Eddie we're talking about. Super Eddie comes before all things. Even the promised land. Super Eddie can probably even *buy* you the promised land."

Helen hesitated.

"What have you got to lose, Mummy? There's nothing going on here, right now."

"There is you. And my job, which I do like, despite my

disappointments. And there is the principle."

"What principle?"

Helen took a deep breath. "Flying around the world to meet a man feels very—cheap—to me."

"Well then don't think about it as flying to meet a man. You are flying to travel, as you have always wanted to. To take a long journey. You are flying to obtain a boatload of new shoes. The man is just a bonus."

"What if," Helen said softly, "it doesn't work out, Dub?"

"And what if it does, Mummy? You're fifty years old. When are you going to do this, if not now?"

"Some other year?"

"Live a little, Mummy. It's Super Eddie. I told you he was unkillable. He's, like, a total zombie. Except he's come back from the dead to rescue you."

Helen was on the verge of a decision.

"Promise me one thing," she said.

"Anything."

"You will not get your nose pierced while I am gone."

Deb laughed. "I'll do even better. I won't even get knocked up."

10

After several more long-distance conversations it was finally settled in late January that Helen would depart on March 12 for Bangkok, with two transfers along the way, and arrive back home on March 24. Super Eddie took care of everything, and it was an exciting day when the envelope arrived at Teagarden bearing both the plane ticket and a generous stack of traveler's checks for incidentals.

The night before Helen's life was to change forever—or rather, as Deb put it, revert back to what it should have been all along—the two women went out to dinner at their favorite Chinese restaurant. This was the closest to Thai food they could come up with since other Asian cuisines, in those days, were not easy to come by. As they settled into their booth next to each other, big fu-fu drinks with colorful umbrellas before them, Deb withdrew from her bag a small gift-wrapped package.

"And this is?" Helen asked, a little tipsy from the fu-fu.

"Going away gift, long journey gift, happy new life gift, fuck the old life gift. Open it, open it, before I explode!"

Helen tore open the ribbon and unwrapped it.

It was a bright pink transparent negligée.

"Oh my," Helen whispered.

"Think how great that'll look with your winklepickers!"

Helen quickly buried the thing in her purse. "Who, but who, raised you to be so vulgar, I ask you?"

"The beautiful little sexpot formerly known as Helen Faire, is who. Soon to be known as Helen *Love*, appropriately enough, at least if that thing works its magic. I want to see that in tatters when you get home, Mummy."

"Oh my," Helen whispered again, digging in her purse. "I need a cigarette."

Late the next afternoon they found themselves having one last drink in the airport lounge—the one in International Departures on the opposite side of the airport from the lounge from which Regina had departed two-and-a-half years earlier. They didn't talk much, having spent most of the night before doing some last-minute what-iffing about this incredible turn of events. When Helen's flight was called they embraced quickly, happily, sadly, smiling, crying, and with about every other emotion in between.

"Tatters, Mummy," Deb whispered in Helen's ear.

Helen pulled away with a last ambiguous teary-eyed smile, turned around to have her ticket inspected and then left her daughter behind as she entered the jetway.

CHAPTER NINE
TATTERS

1

Helen had never been on an airplane before.

She had no reason to think she would be apprehensive about the flight. In the weeks of worrying about every detail it had not even crossed her mind to worry about the airplane itself. Well Helen Gale had her share of fears—mostly of dust, dirt, and disorder—but now it turned out she was also afraid of flying. A perfect thing to discover when you're five minutes into what would feel like days of air travel.

White as a sheet, gripping her armrests, staring straight ahead, Helen did what she usually did when she was anxious: she smoked, and that continuously for each of the eternal legs of her journey. She tried sleeping for a while but it's hard to sleep while you are puffing, and when forced to choose between the two the decision was clear. By the time she arrived in Bangkok a lifetime later she was exhausted, agitated, and sore in places she didn't even know existed in her body. Most noticeably of all she had an awful throbbing pain in her left thigh. As she hobbled down the jetway toward the gate, on the final approach to Eddie Love himself, she wasn't even what-iffing about the momentous meeting. She was what-iffing about what to do should the hotel not have hot water bottles to apply to her leg.

And then there he was.

At the gate, with an enormous bouquet of pink carnations.

"Oh my," Helen exclaimed under her breath, instantly recalling all the reasons she was, well, in love with him all those years ago.

For it was Super Eddie, the handsome rock star with the gorgeous smile who played the electric guitar; who wore his sunglasses indoors; who went shirtless pretty much all the time; who had the thick gelled hair; who made cigarette smoking so unbelievably cool; whose favorite hobby, for all these reasons, was collecting virginities. Of course three decades later he no longer possessed any of these qualities, thanks, respectively, to the arthritis in his wrists, the slight cataracts in his eyes, his now lacking a build inviting shirtlessness, his sporting a mostly bald pate, a mild case of emphysema, and the joint combination of all of the above. What was left, though, was that gorgeous smile, now rapidly approaching her along with those beautiful flowers.

"Somebody call heaven," that smile was saying as its owner neared her with his arms opened wide, after dropping the carnations on the floor, "They must be missing an angel!"

Well, okay, one other point in his favor: he still had a thing for Helen. And if she wasn't exactly feeling overjoyed in this very first moment of their embrace there was definitely some hope once she'd had a little sleep, a long shower, and replaced the nicotine in her system with some actual oxygen.

Oh and it turned out, too, he still drove a revved-up red convertible, or more precisely two of them back home in Hong Kong and a rental one whenever he traveled. It was into one such a vehicle that he deposited Helen and the flowers after carrying her bags from the baggage claim. She tried to suppress the thought that the two of them looked pretty ridiculous in this car. But at least the convertible part was a bonus. After the days on the plane the stifling muggy Bangkok air was almost a relief.

She could use a cigarette.

"Never touch 'em myself," Eddie Love said as she lit up. "They're killers, baby."

She looked at him in the driver's seat beside her and remembered her first smoke all those years ago, in Eddie Love's red convertible, in this same position.

And so began the fulfillment of the fantasy stretching over years in the minds of the three female Gales.

2

It got off to a bit of a rough start.

On the ride to the hotel Eddie Love told her some more about his success in the women's footwear business. "Some more" here meant repeating verbatim what he had already said on the telephone, and "repeating" here meant something like "regaling," an annoying word that kept popping into Helen's mind as she listened. She was just tired, that's all, she kept reminding herself; anyway the world probably *did* revolve around Hong Kong in general and around his incredibly successful business in particular.

"Would you mind lowering the radio a bit?" Helen asked as they drove.

"What was that?" The rushing wind from the open roof combined with the loud radio, along with his electric-guitar-damaged ears, made it a little hard for Eddie Love to hear.

"The radio," Helen said more forcefully.

"She's great, isn't she?" Eddie Love said, complying.

"Who?"

"You don't know who's singing?"

"I do not."

"You're serious?"

"I am."

"Sheesh, where have you been, baby? It's Whitney."

Helen stared at him blankly.

"Only the greatest singer ever," he added, then shook his head. "Nellie, Nellie, Nellie."

"What?"

"I thought you were a little more, you know—classy."

"I'm sorry?"

Eddie Love guffawed. "Just teasing! But seriously, you obviously need to get out more, get around. You shouldn't have just stayed back home all these years."

She was just tired, that's all, she repeated to herself, suppressing her irritation.

"So what musicians *do* you like?" Eddie Love was saying.

She hesitated a moment before answering. "Are you familiar with Tartini, by any chance?"

"What is that? Like a little Pop-Tart?"

He laughed. She grimaced.

"Only," she answered quietly, "the greatest composer ever."

"Oh, you *gotta* listen to this!" he interrupted, turning the radio up as "Whitney" commenced to caterwaul.

Their "discussion" of music continued later in the hotel.

"You don't know who this is either?" Eddie Love scoffed when she didn't respond to some other pop singer booming on the cassette player in his hotel room. When she shook her head, he shook his. "Seriously, Nellie. Where *have* you been?"

Nowhere, she thought to herself.

"You got to keep up with things, baby, it keeps you young," Eddie Love continued, not having waited for her to answer. "I'll catch you up quick. Just one word, Nellie. It's really the only word you need to know: 'Michael.' Can you repeat after me? *'Mi-chael.'*"

That last claim notwithstanding, Helen found herself, over the next couple of days, in need of several other words. "Pompous," "shallow," "uncultured," and "coarse" were among them, and these were the more flattering ones. The man was also slow to pick up on her subtle cues that she did not care for being teased, including her stiff body language, her unfriendly glares, and her repeatedly saying "I do not care for being teased." And when he wasn't teasing her he was grappling, unsuccessfully, with the concept of her perfume: "Tea perfume?" he repeated throughout the visit, blinking rapidly, not even attempting the "green" part. And yet his success in the shoe business had convinced him that he was a genius, which, in a way, he was—for only a genius could discover so many ways to offend the very woman he was trying to impress. One afternoon when he wasn't out browbeating some factory owner, Helen suggested they visit a museum of antiquities described in her guidebook.

"A museum?" he snorted. "That's just great. And should we go out after for a bite of Tartini?"

Another time she mentioned how proud she was of her daughters for going to college, in particular Regina, who was training to be a mathematician.

"And what is that?" Eddie Love asked. They were in a greasy street joint where he had muttered a few native words and obtained at their table some meat dish, a local delicacy he'd assured her.

"Why, it—" Helen began, feeling irritated at him yet again before she realized that, in fact, she had no idea either. "Well, it does not matter. What matters is that she is obtaining an education."

"Why is that such a big deal?"

"You don't think that education is a good thing, especially for women these days?" Helen replied, looking at her plate apprehensively.

"I didn't need to go to college. My seven years in high school did me fine. Ha!"

"No, but seriously, Eddie. You are successful, sure, but for most people education is a matter of getting the right start. Especially for women, no?"

"Nah," Eddie Love chewed vigorously.

"What do you mean, 'nah'?"

"I mean, nah. Most girls just go to college to get husbands. And that's fine. I mean, that's a good place to meet guys, I've got nothing against that."

"Are you aware what year this is now?"

"Yeah." He peered at the paper mat under his plate. "Year of the Dog."

"Yes," Helen said, unable to refrain from correcting his speech.

"Huh?"

"Nothing. If you do not mind, I am just going to have a cigarette."

"Not a problem, baby. Hey, speaking of dogs," he said, eyeing her plate, "are you gonna eat that?"

Worst of all was the shoes.

Helen loved shoes; of course. Eddie Love dealt in womens' shoes and they were there in Thailand for him to pursue those dealings. And so naturally they spent plenty of time perusing shoe stores, a nice mixture, he would say, of his business and her pleasure.

Except for the part about her pleasure.

"Women!" he snorted more than once as she examined some designs in one of the high-end malls to which he brought her. "You just can't keep 'em away from the shoes!"

"Well," Helen said the first time he said this, "I do appreciate shoes. But that isn't necessarily true of all women."

"Trust me, it's all women. Give a woman a hundred bucks in a shoe store and she'll find a way to spend two hundred."

"When I have a hundred—*bucks*—in a shoe store, I am likely to spend only half of it."

"Yeah, when it's your money maybe. But when it's your husband's, I bet, watch out!"

Helen bit her lip. "You do realize, of course, that that is a very offensive thing to say?"

"Hey, I'm just teasing, Nellie! Take it easy."

"Believe me, I *am* taking it easy when I say that I find your remark condescending."

Eddie Love wasn't sure what "condescending" meant but he did get that it wasn't a good thing. "Sorry, baby," he muttered, "let me make it up to you." He pulled out his wallet and withdrew two bills. "Here's two hundred bucks. Find yourself something nice, you know what I'm saying? They've got the Italian Batas in the back aisle over there. The new stacked heels. The ladies love 'em."

The most amazing part was that he made exactly the same comment—give a woman a hundred bucks and she'll spend two—the next day in another store despite the fact that Helen had walked out on him when he'd pulled the money from his wallet. For a woman with a left thigh still sore from her flights she had strutted surprisingly quickly through the crowded mall. For a man as out of shape as the real-life Eddie Love was, too, it was surprising just how quickly he had caught up to her and begged, begged, her forgiveness.

And then there it was again: "Women! Give 'em a hundred bucks …"

Wow, Helen thought, staring at him. This man who made his living selling women's shoes sure didn't have much respect for women who liked shoes.

It isn't clear how the last few days went because Helen would not discuss them no matter how hard Deb tried to pry it from her. But she didn't try that prying till rather later, for other things were more pressing upon Helen's return. For one thing, she needed rehydrating after all the weeping on the long flights home. For another, there was still that strange pain in her left thigh. It had almost gone away by the last day in Thailand but after the grueling flights it had returned with a vengeance, as Helen put it, embracing Deb in the airport back home—rather like the way Eddie Love had returned into her life. They requested a wheelchair from the ticket desk, which at least helped them collect Helen's luggage and get back to the car. As soon as they got back to Teagarden Towers Deb wanted to call the doctor but Helen resisted.

"A hot water bottle will be fine. I just need to relax the muscles."

Then, with what energy remained to her after the long journey, Helen filled Deb in on those unhappy details she was willing to divulge. Or she did so after allowing Deb, first, to open the duffel bag filled with shoes, *almost* all of them for Deb.

"Oh Mummy," Deb said as she looked, lovingly, at each pair. "These are so beautiful. And these. And these …"

And then after the initial shoe examination was complete—for there would be further, more thorough examinations in the days to follow—Deb said, "And now tell me, please, about The Jerk. I want every event, every word, every thought that crossed your mind. I want to be as appalled by him, please, as you are."

"My darling Dub," Helen began, so weary, so disappointed now that the anger was fading. But she did tell at least the initial version—for there would be further, more thorough versions in the days to follow—and she told enough to get Deb well on the way toward disliking The Jerk as much as she did, after thirty-three years of loving him.

Later that evening—it was only 7:30 PM but with jet lag and exhaustion it was definitely Helen's bedtime—Helen went to her suitcase and pulled out the transparent pink negligée that Deb had given her.

"I completely forgot!" Deb exclaimed with a disappointed face. "I guess it's not in tatters."

"Not yet, anyway. I was thinking I should give it to you. You will have more use for it than I."

Deb half-smiled. "I got myself one when I got that one for you."

"In that case," Helen said, "would you care to join me?"

Helen held the garment out to Deb, who took the other end.

"It's too bad," Deb said softly as they prepared to pull, "that you didn't have sex with him."

"Who said anything about not having sex with him?"

"What?"

"I may have despised him, but I waited thirty-three years to get him in the sack. And at my age you take what you can get. Now," Helen added, tugging on the strap, "make a wish!"

They laughed.

They pulled.

The flimsy garment ripped easily.

3

Prophetically Helen did not have much—okay, any—use for the now destroyed nightie in the post-Eddie Love months ahead. Then again neither did her extremely mature almost nineteen-year-old daughter. Deb broke up with Mark, who cried like a baby when she returned his Walkman even though he had threatened repeatedly to break up with her for ditching him New Year's Eve. She devoted herself to her studies, having decided to pursue psychology: with her screwed-up family and her own inner demons she would have an inside edge, she figured, and maybe even save some money on therapy bills. As her second year at the university got underway she even began thinking about graduate school, maybe even getting her own Ph.D. Who knew—Deb, the distracted one, was dedicating herself to academics just like her smarty-pants sister, wherever exactly she was.

The whole world was out of joint.

She continued working at the social science library, even though on two separate occasions she had discovered her father waiting for her at the library's main entrance. The first time, luckily, she saw him before he saw her, and despite her sudden shortness of breath she managed to skirt around to the side entrance undetected. The second time, a week or so later, she was less lucky, and forced herself to walk past him through the front entrance. It was all she could do to ignore him, his strangely plaintive "please, Dubs, can't we just talk?" tugging at her emotionally almost in the way she found herself half-wishing his hand physically would.

Maybe it was hearing that word, "Dubs." That hurt almost as much as the time one of her co-workers at the library, on learning that Deb's last name was Gale, had asked if Deb was related to the fantastic Professor Gale whose class she was currently taking.

Not anymore, Deb thought to herself, hesitating a moment before shaking her head.

She did not mention any of this to her mother, her mother who was encouraging Deb's pursuit of her academics but also encouraging her to go out a little and have some fun.

"But I find studying fun," Deb replied, not sure whether she was more astonished to hear herself say this or to hear her mother endorsing "fun."

"Yes, but a girl your age needs friends, girlfriends, maybe a—manfriend—too."

"You," Deb poked her, "are all the girlfriend I need."

"I am flattered, of course. But aren't you lonely? Just staying home every night, with your books and your elderly mother?"

"What elderly mother?"

"Seriously."

"Seriously, then, where would a boyfriend sleep? You already hog the bed."

"Coming from someone who flops all night across the bed that is some nerve, young lady. Now would you please stop poking me?"

The fall went quickly.

Deb spent a lot of time at school and the rest of her time at their apartment.

Most days Helen would come home from work and find Deb cooking supper. The cooking lessons were officially over: Deb was now a good cook on her own, and Helen was happy to yield the kitchen once Deb agreed to stop joking about Eddie Love's apparent taste, literally, for dog food. Only on the first Sunday morning of the month did the kitchen belong exclusively to Helen, for she remained adamant that she would teach her daughter the banana cream pie recipe only on her twenty-first birthday and not a day sooner. Most evenings, in any case, their suppers were a little rushed since Deb wanted to return to the library, but the food was lovely and the chance to converse was lovelier. When Deb left Helen would retire to the sofa for a crossword puzzle or two and a cigarette or three. Lonely, but not unhappy, she retired to bed by 10:00 PM. Deb would come home later and slip into bed without waking Helen, or at least not until she began her nightly bed-flopping. Helen poked her daughter through the night, to get her to slide over; and while she was annoyed at the sleep interruption she was so happy to have her daughter near her that she almost didn't mind.

Every once in a while The Jerk left a message on the answering machine. Turned out, Helen and Deb concluded after further analysis, that he was the kind of Jerk who has no idea what a Jerk he is. The man seemed to think that Helen's visit had gone well and was mystified about why she wasn't returning his calls.

Helen and Deb would listen to these messages once or twice, then erase them. This contrasted with Deb's treatment of the notes which occasionally arrived for her at the library, from her father. Though she wouldn't deny she felt tempted, these little missives she dropped directly into the trash, unread.

Even more undeniable that fall, however, was the recurring pain in Helen's thigh. When it got really bad Helen would sleep with the hot water bottle, which helped; except that Deb couldn't stand the heat, and so on nights when they retired together Helen would have to make do with aspirin, which did almost nothing, and on other nights she would invariably be awakened when Deb got home and removed the bottle from underneath her leg. By late October, when the weather became chilly, Deb demanded that she see a doctor.

Helen resisted. "I do not need to see a doctor. Big Red here is all the medicine I need." 'Big Red' was Deb's nickname for the water bottle.

"Look, it's either him or me. I can't stand that thing anymore."

"That is a tough decision."

"Hilarious. I'm calling Dr. Kanata this minute. Unless you can think of someone a little more, like, contemporary?"

"Deb, I do not need a doctor."

"I also can't stand," Deb added, "hearing you complain all the time. You're obviously in pain, Mummy."

"I am just an old hypochondriac."

"True, but that doesn't mean there isn't something wrong with your leg. Now be quiet—I'm on the phone."

Dr. Kanata confirmed that Helen's muscles were too tense, perhaps due to her sitting all day at work, and so he prescribed both muscle relaxants and that she try to stand up more during the day. For the latter she started taking short walks outside during her cigarette breaks, to get the blood flowing. As for the former, well, this was a particularly nice period in the Teagarden apartment since Helen's muscles were so relaxed all the time. Of course the pain didn't go away, just her need to complain about it so much. Deb was fooled for a while but within a few weeks became suspicious when she noticed that the bed had been warm several times when she'd come home late from the library.

After the third time she confronted her mother over breakfast.

"Big Red," Helen confessed.

"Why didn't you tell me your leg was still hurting?"

"I was too relaxed. Anyway I did not want you to criticize Dr. Kanata."

"Why not?"

"He is such a nice man."

"I knew it." Deb shook her head, upset with herself for not having found a better doctor. "The man needs to retire. Last time I saw him for a cold he was, like, considering bloodletting."

"Maybe, but he *is* a very nice man."

"He's practicing medicine so out of date that—"

"I should advise you that I am feeling far too relaxed to get worked up about this."

"Fine! I'll do it."

So Deb found another doctor whose medical degree was earned within the current century and took Helen for the appointment, not trusting her mother to go unchaperoned. At first she was pleased simply with his name: "Dr. Providence, it's very symbolic, don't you think?" Then she was even more pleased when, after joking that the reason Dr. Kanata was good at anatomy was that he'd been trained back when Latin was a living language, the doctor had concluded that her mother's condition was nothing serious: just a ligament strain that could be fixed with physical therapy and then Helen would be good as new again.

"How new?" Helen asked.

"Now let me see," he said, peering at Helen's chart. "Well, now!"

"What?" Helen and Deb both said.

"Your chart tells me that you are almost fifty-one years old. But the muscle tone in your legs is that of a woman in her early or mid-forties, maximum."

"He was *so* flirting with you," Deb said excitedly to Helen as they drove back through the early cool darkness of the late fall afternoon.

"That was not flirting. He was just expressing an objective clinical opinion."

"Yeah, right. I noticed he wanted to see you again."

"Of course he did. It's called a follow-up. And that is called professional competence."

"Yeah, right. I would call it very *un*professional to hit on your patients. But hey, I'm not objecting." Deb poked her mother across the car seat. "You still got it, Mummy."

"What I got is a pain in my rear end to go along with the one in my thigh."

"Fine. Just let me know when you want to borrow my nightie."

Their interest in Dr. Providence was soon extinguished, however, when it became clear that physical therapy was doing nothing for Helen's thigh. In fact if anything it made things worse, as the pain began to spread down her leg.

Helen was now often walking with a small limp.

Deb began research to locate another, more specialized, doctor, or maybe a clinic of some sort. Meanwhile the weather turned into early December cold. Helen stopped the physical therapy since it was too difficult to get there and too unpleasant to battle the cold on the way to and from. Deb's pending final exams had her studying every night at the library, and even skipping suppers lately. Helen realized one evening, heating up for herself some leftover Beef Ribs with Mustard Sauce, that she was, lately, feeling *really* lonely. She was glad when her birthday came; despite her having aged yet another year it meant that Deb would take a break and they'd spend the evening together at their favorite neighborhood café for pastry and tea and maybe also a glass of wine.

They were at the table starting in on their third glass when Tartini's "Devil's Trill Sonata" began playing over the sound system.

"They say," Helen said, feeling good considering the circumstances (her life, as she put it), "that he had six fingers on his left hand."

"Who?" Deb asked.

"Tartini. That's how he could play those trills so easily."

"Mummy," Deb rolled her eyes playfully, "listen. It's your birthday. You're only fifty-one once. I command you to let loose."

"And what do you call going out on a work night, young lady?"

"Unwind, I mean. Unravel. Go *crazy*."

"All right, then," Helen said after a moment, "I shall." The combination of birthday, pastry, Debra, and three glasses of wine were curbing, just slightly, her attention to table manners. "Are you ready?"

"Bombs away."

Helen placed a *very* large piece of buttery pastry into her mouth.

"You're out of control!" Deb exclaimed.

"How about this?"

"What?"

"You didn't notice?"

"Oh my God. You spoke with your mouth full!"

"'I shall now eat my fill of this delicious pastry,'" Helen said in a perfect imitation of that strange but all-too-familiar British accent despite—or maybe because of—the mouth full of whipped cream.

"Who *are* you?"

"Just," Helen replied, "a woman scorned, seated before a very dangerous piece of frangipane. And now," she was reaching into her purse, "for the post-pastry cigarette."

"Hey," Deb said, now sipping her tea. "I found another doctor. At the Montebello Clinic."

"So?"

"Sew your buttons. I got you an appointment for next Tuesday morning."

"Don't you have an exam that afternoon?"

"That's not a problem."

"I can go myself."

"You cannot go yourself."

"I am a grown woman."

"You won't go."

"Yes, but my point is that I *can* go myself."

"Seriously, the appointment's at 10:30 AM. I'll pick you up, but I will let you find your way back to work afterward. Will that satisfy you?"

"You are talking to a woman who has just finished some exquisite pastry and a cigarette, celebrating her birthday with her wonderful daughter. I need no further satisfaction."

And yet further satisfaction was to come her way—when the new doctor asserted that Helen's sore leg would best be treated by an aggressive use of the hot water bottle.

"Big Red is back," Helen gloated as they left the clinic together.

"Shit. Maybe I should get myself a manfriend."

"You might consider giving Red a go. He is more dependable on these cold winter nights than any male human being you are likely to find."

Deb looked back at her mother while doing her own impression of Regina's arching-eyebrow and flaring-nostril.

There was much laughter.

4

New Year's Eve rolled around again. Once more Deb claimed she didn't feel like going out, once more Helen protested uselessly, and once more they picked up ice cream and videos, shared a smooch when the ball dropped, cracked up, and then allowed the answering machine to pick up when the phone rang at 12:30 AM. The only difference from the year before was that this year their mutual date, Big Red, was squeezed onto the sofa with them.

It was, once more, The Jerk.

"Nellie," that voice came through on the machine, "how are ya? My accountant tells me I had another great year so I can afford the long-distance calls, ha! ... Just wanted to wish you a happy new year ... Um, listen, I'm still wondering why you never call me back, the past few months. Maybe it's the money for the phone call, I'll send you some cash if that's why. Just, uh, send me your address again. Anyway I keep thinking about your visit—you looked so great, you know, after all these years—and what a blast we had ..."

Deb and Helen looked at each other and shook their heads.

"Still, um, trying to figure out why you still wouldn't sleep with me. Back then, all right. But I paid for you to come all the way out here, after all those years, you know, I treated you so nice, all the shoes, the fancy restaurants—and we had that great, you know, connection—what was up with all that, you know what I'm saying?"

Deb was staring at Helen, who had dropped her eyes.

"Anyway, I also just, uh, wanted to tell you, I met someone else, in case you were wondering why I haven't called lately. She's a great girl, she was working in one of my stores in Korea, we just hit it off, you know how it is. We're gonna tie the knot in a couple weeks, guess I haven't learned my lesson about the ball and chain, ha! But she's a sweet kid, and I like, you know, having someone to treat nice."

Deb too had dropped her eyes.

"Anyhow—that's it. I probably won't call again, now that I'm getting hitched again. Unless she ends up being a piece of work too, ha! But, anyway, I thought I, uh, should just let you know. Okay, um. Call me back if you want. Okay? And, uh, happy new year. Nellie."

Then the click.

They didn't discuss it. Instead they just snuggled into bed, the three of them, Helen, Deb, and Big Red, and stayed toasty warm through the coldest night of the year.

5

In late February Helen developed a mottling of the skin all up and down her left leg. The pain was also now in most of her leg. Deb did some more research to find the best dermatologist in town—a Dr. Davol, who was also the only female professor at the university medical school—and insisted over her mother's objections on getting an appointment.

Dr. Davol was different from the previous quacks. She gave Helen a complete physical examination before even turning to the leg, asked questions about Helen's life and diet and smoking and drinking, and then spent a good twenty minutes inspecting every inch of her leg. This was nerve-wracking for the two female Gales, since of course there was nothing *seriously* wrong with Helen's leg so why was the doctor spending so much time on it?

At last the doctor spoke.

"Well," she said, "I believe there's nothing *seriously* wrong with your leg."

That was a relief.

"But what's with the rash?" Deb asked.

"Tell me," the doctor looked at Helen, who had quickly dressed. "Do you apply a lot of heat to this leg?"

"What is a lot?"

"I'm guessing nightly hot water bottles?"

"More like twice-nightly," Deb interrupted. Helen often got up in the night to refill the bottle. "Would that cause the rash?"

"It isn't a rash. What happens is that either high or continuous heat can damage the blood vessels in the skin. So blood starts to leak just beneath the skin's surface. That's what causes the mottling."

"So much for Big Red," Deb teased her mother.

Helen remained silent, standing.

Dr. Davol looked at Deb inquisitively.

"The hot water bottle," Deb explained. "Anyway, would that also explain why the pain has been moving down her leg?"

"Well, it *is* possible that the blood vessel damage might have painful consequences for the tissues or muscles lower in the leg."

"You sound skeptical."

"That's just one possibility. I'm going to send you for more tests. I'll get you in to see one of my colleagues in rheumatology here at the medical school."

"More tests?" Helen said weakly.

"The mottling is definitely due to the heat, but we need to determine just what has been causing the pain in the first place."

"So the next step is the rheumatologist?" Deb said.

"No, the next step is to get rid of Big Red." The doctor smiled. "Speak to the nurse on the way out, she'll arrange the appointment with my colleague."

"Well at least there was *some* good news," Deb said in the car, driving Helen back to work.

"He'll be back," Helen said evenly.

But that was all they said during the ride.

6

Deb took Helen in for several tests including an MRI of the leg, and about three weeks later they were seated in Dr. Scold's office.

"I can go to my own doctor's appointments," Helen said,

continuing their argument from the car.

"It is not a problem, Mummy."

"I do not like you missing your classes."

"I do not like you missing your work. But it has to be done."

The nurse called them in. Whereas Dr. Davol's manner had been warm and delightful Dr. Scold's, in a word, was not. He stood before them holding Helen's test results but not saying anything about them. He began by asking about the history of Helen's thigh pain. Deb began with the flights to Thailand but he had already cut her off before she was even halfway through the offensive episode in the shoe store.

"Forget the question," Dr. Scold said, pulling out the grainy MRI. "Listen. Right there, there is a small mass in your thigh."

"Oh my God," Helen whispered.

"What does that mean?" Deb asked.

"It means that something is growing there. We'll need to operate."

"Oh my God," Helen said again.

"What something?" Deb asked. "What kind of operation?"

"We'll go in and cut it out, do a biopsy."

"Oh my God," Helen moaned. "A biopsy."

Deb yelled at her mother. "You don't even know what a biopsy is. Stop panicking." She turned to the doctor. "Please. What does all that mean?"

"Hard to be clearer," he answered as he slipped Helen's MRI back into the folder. "We'll cut it out and see what it is. Could be anything."

"I'm dying," Helen moaned in the car as Deb drove her back to her office.

"You are not dying," Deb said angrily.

"I've got that disease. It's obviously that disease."

"You do not know that. It could be anything, he said."

"What else could it be? I'm a smoker. I've been smoking my whole life. Don't you read the newspapers lately? It's obviously that disease."

"Smoking affects your lungs. This is in your leg."

"That would be just my luck. To get that—lung disease in my leg."

"You," Deb said firmly, pulling up in front of Helen's office, "do not have 'that disease.' You get out now and go back to work. I will take care of everything."

"Yes, start with the undertaker. Get some recommendations."

"You stop now. I am about to slap you."

Helen, slowly, calmed down. "You do not expect me to go to work right now."

"You will go to work. I will go to my class. What's left of it." Deb reached over and touched Helen's arm. "This was just a doctor's appointment. This is just a regular day. There is nothing dramatic going on here."

"That's easy for you to say."

No it wasn't, Deb thought. "I'll pick you up after work. Maybe we'll get some pastry for dessert. And if you're really good—"

"What?"

"You can have Big Red tonight."

"You are too generous."

"Yeah right. I'll sleep on the sofa."

7

Dr. Scold was a busy man.

The procedure could not be scheduled before early May. It was not an operation, Deb noted to Helen, it was just a procedure. A week before the procedure they would go in for a "pre-op," a few more tests before the operation—procedure—itself. This was an inconvenient time for Deb as once again her exams were rolling around, but that was the first available appointment and she would not let Helen delay it any further. Helen meanwhile had made some peace with the situation, mostly by denying it existed altogether. She began referring to the appointment as her dentist's appointment and said she was looking forward to the new toothbrush.

It went without saying that the postponed trip to the promised land would be postponed once more. Over the winter they had been talking about going in late May again, immediately after Deb's finals, but that talk ceased once the skin mottling began and certainly there would be no further discussion until after the dentist's appointment.

Helen was so calm these days—Deb suspected the muscle relaxants on the sly—that she barely expressed disappointment when a few days before the pre-op, in late April, they were informed there would be another delay. Dr. Scold had been called out of the country and would not be available for several more weeks. Helen was relieved since the delay would enable Deb to prepare for her exams, but Deb had the opposite reaction: more weeks to worry and be distracted from her exams. She would rather have the resolution—the good news—sooner rather than later.

And so it was not until early June that they finally went in for the pre-op. Fortunately they didn't have to see the uncharming doctor himself and instead were treated by a technician and a medical school resident. Wonderful people they were, calm and supportive, so Helen felt about as comfortable as even she could be as they poked and prodded her naked body under the johnny gown. Whether it was their personal manner or just the extra muscle relaxants, Helen didn't even resist when they did the routine chest X-Ray which was a routine part of the routine pre-op—or rather pre-procedure procedure.

"We'll call you next week with the details for the procedure itself," the technician said, smiling, "once the doctor has looked over today's tests. You enjoy the weekend, now, honeys."

8

Armies were withdrawing in defeat, surgeons general were confirming what everyone already knew, and the weather was warming as Deb's twentieth birthday approached.

Since Regina had moved away almost four years before, Helen and Deb had begun celebrating the younger daughter's now solo birthday by making a day-trip out to the small family island. Sure the family had been there often enough over the years, though their visits had decreased once Theodore started complaining about the mosquitoes. But still the fact that Helen and Deb were going on their own and spending an entire day together, and enjoying it—which would have seemed impossible even a few years earlier—is what now made it so special.

It was a two-hour car ride through fields, then rolling hills, and then seriously rolling hills. Then passing over a crest you could see from a distance the wide sprawling river which wound its way through those parts. Then you arrived at the small fishing town of Galilee on the eastern bank and caught the chartered ferry for the twenty-five-minute ride to your destination. It was a beautiful early summer morning when the two remaining female Gales disembarked onto their small pier and headed up the hill toward the island's cabin.

And so they had the most splendid of days, this Wednesday, June

8, on the family island, celebrating the two decades of Deb's existence. The remainder of the morning was spent cleaning the cabin—to make Helen happy, which subsequently made Deb happy. Then there was the picnic on the rocky promontory side of the island overlooking the river, a delectable spread (featuring a divine Salmon Salad) that Deb had prepared the evening before and that Helen had space-efficiently packed into the picnic basket. Then there was the lazy afternoon gazing out over the water, enjoying the sun and the warm breeze and the birds overhead and the leafy green trees, lying down for a while, smoking a cigarette or two. And then as their wonderful new annual tradition approached its close it was time to space-efficiently pack everything up, reassemble their cleaning supplies, and wait for the return ferry.

On the boat ride back to Galilee the sun was just descending in the perfect western sky when Deb settled her head against her mother's shoulder.

"Mummy," Deb said.

"Yes, my birthday girl?"

"When would you say, exactly, that we became close?"

"I don't know, Dub."

"How could you not know?"

"My attention," Helen answered quietly, "was elsewhere."

It was such a lovely moment that they asked one of the other passengers to take their photo, with Deb's head nestled onto her mother's shoulder as the sun sank behind them. There was something about their gentle expressions in this photograph that he just loved, Dr. J. would observe to Debra later: the two women looked almost like sisters.

When they got back to their Teagarden apartment that evening the red light was blinking on the answering machine. Deb was in the bathroom (having run there upon walking in) when Helen, not really thinking, pressed the button.

"Yes, this is Dr. Scold," the flat monotone said. "I'm looking over the pre-op tests. It seems that—"

Helen instantly shut off the machine.

She took a deep breath, her heart pounding, and walked unsteadily to the end of the hallway. Deb was just coming out of the bathroom and standing at the doorway.

"Message for you," Helen said softly.

CHAPTER TEN
IT *WAS*

1

"Damn! Damn! Damn!" Helen was howling, lying flat, pounding her fist on the sofa.

"Mummy, stop, please," Deb pleaded, kneeling beside her.

"Damn! Damn!"

"Mummy!"

The message on the answering machine was not good. The routine chest X-ray during the pre-leg-biopsy procedure had revealed a "significant" mass in her left lung. Dr. Scold wanted her to come in immediately to discuss the next steps.

"It's over," Helen was sobbing. "I'm finished."

"You are not finished."

"Promised land. Never."

"Promised land next year, Mummy."

"I'm done."

"You're not done. We don't even know what that means."

"It means that my leg—my leg disease is in my lung."

"He didn't say that. He said a mass."

"He said next steps. He said referrals. Oh my God."

"You stop," Deb said sharply. "Listen to me. Whatever this is I am going to fix it."

"You cannot fix this," Helen said weakly.

"It will be fixed. By me. You will see."

Helen was crying and not listening.

Fortunately it was summer so Deb did not have to worry about schoolwork as she shuttled her mother between work and appointments and tests over the next two months. This was made more complicated by the fact that for someone who had spent her adult life mostly lamenting that life, Helen was suddenly showing a lot of attachment to it, making it clear that she was not going down without a fight. Unfortunately most of that fight was directed

217

toward Deb, who was largely running the show and was thus the closest target. Helen resisted making every appointment and undergoing every procedure, and when she did inevitably relent she equally inevitably complained the entire way about every little ache and pain.

"I'm dying," Helen would moan repeatedly on the way to and from wherever they were going.

"Yeah right," Deb would retort with maximum patience but only a fraction of the normal sarcasm. "You're just a big old hypochondriac."

"Even hypochondriacs die," Helen moaned.

In need of a break from her mother Deb left her at home with Big Red when she met with the specialist, a Dr. Oppenheim, at the end of the summer to get the completed diagnosis and prognosis.

The news was awful.

"Two months?" Deb gasped, the blood drained from her face.

"Maybe three. Maybe four. But maybe one," Dr. Oppenheim said gently.

"Oh my God."

"We've found it in several places. The leg, the liver, the bones. Just since that first X-Ray in June it has spread. It's aggressive."

"Oh my God."

She was seated across from his desk. She closed her eyes and leaned back in the chair.

"Can I get you a glass of water or something?" the good doctor asked.

"No. Thank you." Deb forced herself to sit up. "What—how—the treatment? What's the next step?"

"I'm afraid I would recommend palliative care."

"What's that?"

"You aim to manage the symptoms, the pain, the quality of life."

"But of course you would do that, no?"

"In contrast to curing the disease. Or even slowing it. I don't think that is feasible here."

There was a long silence.

"I don't accept that," Deb said.

"Please, absolutely." The doctor had come around his desk and was kneeling beside Deb's chair. "Get some other opinions. That's completely standard. But I must tell you that I'm confident you will hear the same prescription. Your mother's case is unfortunately clear."

"I appreciate that. I just don't accept it. I want to fight it."

"And I appreciate *that*. But perhaps we should speak to your mother?"

"*We* want to fight it."

He contemplated a moment. "All right. There are some things we can try. Surgery would not be a realistic option, but we can attempt certain therapies. There are also some alternative approaches you can try. I can refer you to a remarkable pharmacist who can guide you there. But I have to advise you: none of this will be pleasant, and the odds are strongly against success."

"We want to fight it."

"I must also advise you that your insurance is unlikely to cover any of it, given the diagnosis. It will be expensive."

"We'll find the money."

"All right, then," Dr. Oppenheim said, slowly, as he got to his feet. "In that case I'll need you both in my office tomorrow. We'll work out a plan of action. On the positive side I can tell you that medicine is not a perfect science, and anything is possible. But then again, Ms. Gale—"

"Yes?" Deb said weakly.

"I also have to tell you that the odds are poor."

Deb nodded, tears in her eyes, and left the office.

2

"He says the odds are good," Deb recounted to Helen on returning to the apartment.

Helen didn't say anything.

She was sitting on the sofa in the late afternoon shadows, an untouched cup of tea on the tea table before her, staring at the darkened television set.

"We're going to do some therapy," Deb continued, joining her on the sofa. "But we also have a few other options."

"Mm-hmm."

"I spent the day at the library. I've learned about some really great treatments. Alternative things, but really promising. Mummy, are you listening?"

"Mm-hmm."

"Tomorrow's going to be busy. I've got an appointment in the morning with a pharmacist who specializes in the alternatives. Then we've got an appointment with Dr. Oppenheim to discuss the—the therapy details. And then there's a women's support group meeting at the—"

"I am not going."

"You *are* going. *We* are going."

"I will go to the appointments. I will not go to the support group."

"But Mummy—"

"I will not share my woes with a horde of sick women."

"They'll share *their* woes. Maybe we'll learn something. Some strategies—"

"I am not interested in their woes. Or in sharing mine."

Deb sighed. "All right, fine. We'll ease into this."

There was a brief silence.

"Mummy. We're going to beat this. I won't let it go."

Helen was gazing at her.

Deb sighed again. "All right. I picked up some lamb chops for supper tonight. Something to mark the beginning of our victorious battle. Are you up for cooking or would you like me to do it?"

"I am not really hungry," Helen said quietly.

"Of course you're hungry. I said *lamb chops*. I'll cook."

"No, that's all right. I'll do it," Helen answered. "You've got to keep your strength up too."

Helen did cook that night, and even nibbled a bite or two. But the next night Deb cooked, and the night after that, and so on, at least whenever Helen had anything of an appetite.

3

Regina said she would come home.

Deb was astonished that she said anything at all. They hadn't heard from her in almost two years despite leaving many messages on her various answering machines, wherever precisely they were located far away. Deb left one last message after the news from Dr. Oppenheim and then gave up. Helen was so distracted herself by the awful news that she seemed not to notice that her firstborn child had apparently abandoned the family for good.

But then late one night in the early fall Regina called.

"Hey Ugly," she muttered.

Deb had answered the phone in hushed tones so as not to

disturb her mother sleeping beside her. By this point their sleeping patterns had reversed: Helen slept all the time while Deb could barely close her eyes. "Regina where the fuck have you been?"

"Out, about. Taking care of business."

"Yeah right, that's informative."

"Fuck you too. I'm calling, alright?"

After Deb switched phones into the kitchen Regina asked a question or two about their mother's condition, about the therapy. But she was not interested in the medical details, and certainly didn't step up when Deb mentioned the need for funds for their mother's care.

Regina snorted. "If you want money you're barking up the wrong tree, Ugs."

"It's for Mummy, it's not for me."

"Well I don't have any. In fact I was hoping *you'd* have some."

"Yeah, well that's just great."

"Well, do you?"

"Are you fucking kidding me?"

"Fine! Forget it. You don't have to get so bitchy about it."

"Yes I do, *sis*. I'm trying to deal with this all by myself, you know. Would it kill you to think about somebody other than you for a change?"

"Fuck you too," Regina muttered slightly less aggressively, which may have been her version of an apology. "I'm pretty busy here, you know."

"Yeah, with what?"

"You don't want to know."

"Try me."

"Trust me, you don't want to know."

"Trust *me*, I do."

"All right," Regina sighed. "I'm studying norm inequalities for composition operators on weighted Bergman spaces, if you must know."

"Fine," Deb answered after a moment, "so you were right."

"I've started the master's program at—"

"I *said* you were right."

Regina snorted in a possibly non-hostile way. "And you? How's the university treating you?"

"I'm taking the semester off. To help Mummy."

"Oh," Regina said.

There was a silence.

"Regina," Deb said softly, "do you think you could come home?"

There was a longer silence. One of those silences that could go either way.

"I don't know," Regina finally answered. "I'm sure you two lovebirds will be fine without me."

"What?"

"You heard me."

"What are you talking about?"

"You know perfectly well what I'm talking about."

"Trust me," Deb said impatiently, "I don't."

"That last time I came home you two were totally vomitacious with your little inside jokes and holding hands and sleeping in the same bed. I couldn't get out of there fast enough."

"What?"

"What, now something's wrong with your hearing?"

"I don't understand. You and she were always—"

"No, it was *you* and she," Regina interjected sharply, "with your shoes, and your animals, and all your little special things. She always liked you better and now you've got her all to yourself, *Dubs*, like you've always wanted. So pardon me if I don't feel like crashing your little party."

"Regina," Deb was barely able to breathe, "did we grow up in the same house?"

"Unfortunately," Regina grunted.

"Regina," Deb said, breaking into tears. "Please come home. *Please*. You're needed," she added, crying, "*here*."

There was a silence.

"*I* need you," Deb said, crying.

There was a long moment of silence. One of those that could go either way.

"All right," Regina finally said. There was yet another moment. "I'm sorry," she may have whispered as she hung up.

Deb stayed on the dead line, listening to the emptiness and sobbing.

4

The therapy was brutal.

The only advantage of the devastating side effects was that

222

Helen was too worn out to maintain her resistance to everything Deb inflicted upon her. And thank goodness for the pharmacist to whom the doctor had referred them! An older man by the name of L. Alan Hemp, he was also the founder of the recently formed local chapter of The Hemlock Society. Thoroughly trained in traditional pharmacology and nutrition as well as in all the alternatives, committed to the highest quality of life and then to the highest quality end of life when the former was no longer attainable, he possessed the right balance of knowledge, wisdom, and compassion to keep their otherwise unbearable situation within the ballpark of bearable. With his wide-ranging expertise, Al (as he liked to be called) managed to keep Helen relatively free of pain and relatively resistant to nausea, so that she could at least sometimes appreciate Deb's now mostly therapeutic cooking.

"I am only sorry, young Debra," Al said daily with regret, stroking his white beard, "that I cannot manage the expenses for you here."

Alternative medicine was not alternatively priced from traditional medicine, it turned out, and as Dr. Oppenheim had predicted neither was covered by insurance. The most exorbitant item was the shark cartilage, which was then seen as a promising new treatment. But shark cartilage was not easy to come by, nor to store and maintain: it cost several hundred dollars for a week's supply, and even then it sometimes spoiled before it could be used. The other alternatives also added up quickly. The lamb's thyroid gland was thought to boost the immune system and so might help Helen's body both fight the disease and resist the therapy's side effects: that cost several hundred dollars for a two-week's supply. And then there was the personal cocktail of vitamins and minerals that Al blended for them, ultimately, by the final recipe, involving seventeen different ingredients and several hundred dollars per one-month supply.

So Helen was busy those first few months after the diagnosis. She had regular therapy, was constantly swallowing vile vials of liquid cartilage, and would spend fifteen minutes two times a day downing the pills of Al's cocktail. You could say that her spirits were good if you could say that she displayed any spirit at all. More accurately she simply did what Deb told her to do and swallowed whatever Deb handed her throughout the day.

The one-month mark came and went.

And then the two-month mark.

And then the three-month mark.

It was now early December.

Helen was, somehow, not dying.

"It's remarkable," Dr. Oppenheim said to Deb across the desk in his office. "I've never seen the disease regress in this manner. Much less this quickly."

"What does that mean? Is she—cured?"

"No, no. We couldn't say that. Cured would mean that it won't come back, and we can't say that now."

"But it's—gone?"

He shrugged. "I don't want to say that either. But there's no clear trace of it at the moment. I can't honestly say what happened. I'm not comfortable using the word 'remission' either, yet. This is fairly unprecedented."

Deb's heart was pounding. "So what do we do?"

"Keep doing what we have been doing. We'll break from the therapy, for now, but we'll keep going with the alternatives. A promising study on cartilage just came out in fact—I'm sure Al will have the details—and clearly something is working here. And obviously, we'll keep a close eye on her along the way."

Deb nodded, with tears in her eyes.

The good doctor had once more come around from his desk and was kneeling beside her again. "Ms. Gale, I am not an optimistic person by nature, and I cannot say to you that your mother is out of the woods here. But this is heartening news, and we'll enjoy it while we have it. Have her back in two weeks, all right?"

The doctor told his wife that evening about how he loved the good days when he had good news for his patients, when the tears shed in his office were of relief rather than grief and pain.

With respect to Deb, however, he was only partly right.

5

They were out of money.

Helen's wonderful boss had arranged for a medical leave at most of her salary. But that money only covered their basic living expenses, even in their modest Teagarden apartment. Deb had worked part-time at the social science library through her first two years of school of course, but that money barely covered her own daily luxuries—cigarettes and tea, though lately more often coffee—much less contributed to the household budget. And when she'd stopped school to care for her mother she had quit that job.

Their savings were gone now. Even the long journey box was depleted.

Over the past couple of months Deb had also been sneaking over to the Dedham Road storage facility and begun selling off, through classified ads, those things of her grandparents' which had any value. It broke her heart to do this, and to do it behind her mother's back. But there was no choice. She was going to defeat the disease and to defeat the disease she needed the treatments, and to get those she needed the money. The past might be meaningful to them but the future was more so. Better to have her mother outraged at her and alive, than neither.

But now the cash was gone. Maybe three weeks' supply of the meds remained. And no money for any more.

Jesus Christ, Deb thought, trying not to panic.

But first, she impressed upon herself, there was something to celebrate: the apparent retreat of the disease. Helen's fifty-second birthday was also approaching and so it was decided—by Deb, against Helen's resistance, which had (for better or worse) also returned—to have a party.

Deb and Jacqueline, Helen's oldest friend, set to work. Jacqueline had plenty of time on her hands these days, for when her three daughters had grown up and left the house her husband had wised up and done the same. Deb and Jacqueline spent several days on the phone, rounding up everybody they could find. They managed to pull together many of the dispersed family members, the aunts and uncles who were still alive, the cousins still in or around town, one of Helen's brothers *not* still in prison; many of these people had not seen each other since Theodore's doctoral ice cream party now sixteen years before and felt that a family reunion every decade-and-a-half or so was just about right.

Deb, grateful for all of Melvin's *pro bono*, if unsuccessful, legal work, allowed the man the honor of paying for the party. "Believe me, the privilege is all mine," he said tearfully over the phone when they made this secret arrangement. Deb was longing to ask him for the money to continue Helen's treatment but just couldn't go that far. She knew her mother would kill her if she did that; but then again Deb was as afraid that stopping the medications would kill *her* if she didn't.

Well, she had a little time to think about it. There were still over two weeks of meds left. And maybe, just maybe, there would be other options.

Deb left a message for Regina, who had still not yet come home, with an invitation to the party as well. Regina didn't respond until several days after the party, leaving a return message saying that now that Mummy was better she was going to keep her focus on her graduate work for now. "If you have any more questions about weighted Bergman spaces," she'd concluded her message with a snort or grunt, "feel free to give a call."

It was a beautiful night for the celebration.

Early winter, the air crisp and clear, a million stars speckling the sky above the gorgeous house that Jacqueline's husband had left behind. Helen, despite her initial resistance, had found herself caught up in the excitement of the planning and actually wandered into the Teagarden kitchen for the first time in months to whip up three banana cream pies for the party, banishing Deb from the apartment while she did so. Toward the end of the evening, as things were winding down, Melvin, sweet Melvin, having managed to leave poor spouse Michelle at home, clinked a fork to his wine glass and demanded everybody's attention.

"Tonight we celebrate," he began, "the next stage of the life of the beautiful Helen Gale. I have loved her ever since she first taught me the subtle tricks of matching nail polish and lip gloss ..."

This got a good laugh, even from Helen. "Melvin, you've been drinking!" She looked almost healthy in that pink dress and head scarf, having regained some of the weight, most of her creamy skin color, and almost all of the hazelness in her eyes.

"And thank God for that!" he retorted. "But seriously, for class and culture, and impeccable taste, there is and could be no one to match *her.*"

"Melvin you need to drink some more!" Deb shouted out.

"And I shall! But let me conclude by saying what an honor it is to be able to celebrate this beautiful occasion, on this beautiful night. I look forward to the next fifty-two years in the impeccable life of the ever lovely Ms. Helen Gale."

"Hear, hear!"

Helen hugged Melvin warmly, a hug he returned as well as he

could despite his buckling knees. Another couple of hours went by, the remaining guests had gone, Melvin was home in bed explaining to Michelle why he had stayed so late, and Helen and Deb were back home at Teagarden drinking tea on the sofa where they had spent so much time in the past several months. Peaceful cello music was playing on the new CD player that Melvin had given Helen the week before, in celebration of Dr. Oppenheim's amazing news.

They were not smoking.

"Dub," Helen said quietly.

"Mum."

"I'm really sorry."

"What about?"

"So many things."

"You're just tired."

"I am. Really tired and really sorry."

"Let's go to bed, then."

"My angel," Helen said softly.

"What?"

"Dub."

"*What?*"

"I just want to thank you for a really special evening."

"Mummy, stop now."

"And for being my—daughter."

She snuggled in closer and embraced her daughter, and held her, while Deb began to sob.

Thirteen days of meds left.

6

The semester was nearly over. If *he* were at all inclined to fulfill his professional obligations then this would be a good time to find him in his office, what with students wanting to consult on papers, prepare for exams, and so on.

As she trudged up to the fourth floor Deb found herself partly hoping that he wouldn't be in. She couldn't stomach the thought of seeing him. But then again she could stomach even less the idea of stopping her mother's medications when there was a pot of money just sitting here, tied up in escrow nearly six years now, but tied up right here on the fourth floor. Sick as it made her feel, she had no choice.

His door was open.

She stood just outside the doorway.

There was some girl in there, asking questions about the final exam in whatever course she was taking with him. What Deb could hear had all the stereotypical trappings of such conversations: the flirty sing-song tone of voice, the question marks after every sentence, the nervous "um"s and "like"s, and then the self-important bloviations of a man just soaking in the attention and respect that his office, if not his person, commanded.

Deb leaned in to listen. "I didn't, like, fully get that stuff about, um, that guy Elenchus? And the, um, headless—cabbage?" the girl said, or sang, sort of. "Will that be on the final exam?"

"That was Elenchi, young lady," Prof. Gale's voice sighed. "And colewort. And are you referring to my lecture on his work," he had clearly stood up now and begun pacing the room, "or to my lectures explaining my book on his work?"

"Um, like, I guess all of it?" Deb couldn't see but she knew the girl was playing with her hair.

And off Theodore went, with the "I argue that"s and the "I prove indisputably that"s and the "changes the entire direction of scholarship"s and so on, his pleasure at performing in front of this captive audience far outweighing the irritation any normal person would feel at a student expecting you to summarize in one sitting several weeks' worth of class material.

Why, Deb wondered, listening, should hearing his voice make her heart pound so? She'd heard it several times over the past year after all, most recently maybe five months before when she'd been on line to buy cigarettes at the university convenience store and heard that voice behind her. "Dubs, is that you?" it had said with unexpected urgency. "Please won't you talk to me?" She had simply paid for her smokes and walked out without turning around.

That was at the end of the previous semester. Right before her birthday.

Right before the diagnosis.

As the voice in the office commenced what would clearly be an extended monologue Deb exploited the reprieve to go back downstairs for some coffee. When she came back up twenty minutes later the girl was just leaving the office. There was a twisted curl on the left side of her head where she'd been playing with her hair.

Deb took a deep breath and stood in the doorway.

Theodore, enormous Theodore, was seated at his desk, clicking buttons on his computer. This was before the world wide web was so world wide, so this clicking merely constituted, as far as Deb could tell, some sort of computer game. On one of the shelves in the crowded bookcase behind him was a snapshot of her and Regina taken back when they might still reasonably be referred to as his daughters. Next to it was a faded snapshot of Theodore and Debra sitting on the bench outside Iced Cream some afternoon, enjoying some illicit frozen treat after having spent the morning playing with the animals at a nearby pet store.

She remembered her grandfather fumbling with the Instamatic that day to take that picture, and felt her stomach tighten.

She took another deep breath and knocked.

Theodore glanced up at her. "Well, well," he said, arching his bushy brows. "Look what the cat dragged in."

"Yeah right," she said.

There was a long silence.

"Well if the cat dragged you this far he might as well drag you all the way in."

Deb entered and took the seat opposite his desk. Behind and all around him were bookcases stuffed with disorderly piles of books and papers. There was an old cot folded up in the corner. You'd have thought he'd have dispensed with that by now.

"Don't tell me the cat's got your tongue, too?"

He was breathing heavily and sweating in the overheated office. On his desk was a half-eaten Danish next to a half-eaten box of Danishes. In his beard, now mostly gray, were remnants of everything he'd eaten since that morning.

She fought down the urge to scream at him.

"You've gained some weight," she said calmly.

"I call it living large, my friend."

"Yeah right," she said again.

There was another silence.

"This is a busy time," Theodore said. "What with final exams and all that sort. So may I inquire, to what do I owe the pleasure of this visit?"

Deb cleared her throat. "I thought that after—all this time, it might be time to talk about the settlement again."

"You did, did you?"

"Yeah. But, you know, without the lawyers. Just person to person. Human being to human being. That sort of thing."

"*Mano-a-mano*, eh?"

"Yeah, if that means person to person."

"All right, so talk. Oh hey," he said, suddenly remembering his manners as he gestured ambiguously toward the half-eaten box and the half-eaten Danish, "you want a bite?"

"No. Thank you."

"All right, then, I'm all ears."

Deb cleared her throat again. "You know, Mummy has been sick over the past year."

"The grapevine hath spoken."

"But she's better now. Really pretty miraculous."

Theodore was just looking at her.

"But, um," and here Deb entered into the part she had been rehearsing for several days, "the experience got her thinking, as is only natural, about, you know, the bigger picture. She wants to get her affairs in order, basically. She's ready to settle, find something more than fair."

"Is she, now?"

"Yeah, she is."

"Well, like I said, I'm all ears." He was more than that, actually; he was also substantially stomach, a growling stomach for that matter, so while Deb continued he grabbed a fresh Danish from the box, leaving the half-eaten one on his desk.

"Okay, then." Deb squirmed in her chair. It was awfully warm in here, how could he stand it? "You keep all of Grandpa's money, you keep three-quarters of your pension, you keep half the value of the Riverbend house even after your second mortgage—and you keep your hands off the island."

And no charge for all the goddamn oxygen he'd consumed in their house, Deb added in her mind.

"Hm," Theodore said, lazily chewing.

"That's pretty much everything you wanted. You win."

"So what do you get?"

"We get this business behind us, our affairs in order, and the money from the house finally released from escrow."

"Yes, but why the sudden rush?"

There are moments in life when you wish you could have a do-over. The female Gales had spent years playing what-if with those moments, spending almost as much time fantasizing about what might have happened as they did living through what actually did happen. Later—a microsecond later—Deb found herself longing for a do-over of her reply to Theodore's question.

"The meds are running out," she found herself saying stupidly, stupidly, stupidly.

"I see," Theodore said, experiencing either the sudden hit of sugar to his diabetic body or the realization that he'd just obtained some important information, or both.

There was a silence.

"Well?" Deb could barely breathe in the stifling office.

"Come here," Theodore said, gesturing toward himself. For a frightening moment Deb thought he was going to give her a hug. But he was gesturing toward the window behind and to the right of his desk. "Come take a look."

She got up and looked out the window into the parking lot below.

"Look there," he said, standing nearer to her than he had been in years. She could feel the heat from his body, suffocating her. He was pointing at a sharp-looking little sports car parked in front of the building. "Sweet, isn't it?"

"Isn't that a No Parking spot? Fire zone?"

"Yeah," he laughed. "You like it?"

"Why are you showing that to me?"

"I'm not showing it to you. I'm showing it to *everybody*. Got it last week to go with my new jacket." He gestured toward the coat rack in the corner of his office. On the floor beneath it was a crumpled brown leather bomber jacket, the kind of jacket you generally saw on fit young bomber pilots rather than overweight middle-aged academics.

"You got a car to go with a jacket?"

"Yeah," he laughed again.

She was silent.

"All right, all right, have a seat. Let's talk. 'Person to person,' as you so eloquently put it. Damn lawyers cause half the world's problems. Other damn lawyers cause the other half. Ha!"

She returned to her seat and looked at him.

"I just want to let you know," he began, "that I forgive you. And maybe even that sourpuss of a sister of yours. Although less so."

Deb was too astonished to reply.

"You treated me badly, young lady, when all I ever wanted was to show you a good time. Help you out when your mother was too hard on you. All that sort. But you were young, you were a kid, you were under *their* thumbs. You can't really be held fully responsible. So I forgive you."

"Amazing," Deb said.

Theodore took this to be referring to his generous act of forgiveness. "I know. I have a big heart. To go with my stomach. Ha!"

"Anyway."

"Anyway," he continued, a bit irritated at her non-reaction to both his clemency and his humor. "So, all right, you want to talk."

Deb gazed at him.

"I've tried talking to you, of course," Theodore said calmly. "Many times. As you know. Did you even read any of the notes I sent you?"

Her eyes swelling, she pursed her lips and shook her head.

"And why, may I ask, not? Why you couldn't have given me that smallest of courtesies?"

"Because I couldn't," Deb trembled, holding back the tears.

"But why not?"

How badly she had wanted to, Deb thought, glancing at the photo from Iced Cream again. "Because I couldn't do that—to Mummy."

"What? Just talk to me?"

Deb hesitated, then nodded.

"But what does that have to do with her?"

"Everything," Deb whispered.

"So you just tossed me aside. After—everything *we've* done together. You and me."

"But you," she answered, "left *us*."

"I left your mother."

"You left *us*."

"She drove me away," Theodore said quickly. "She left me no choice."

"You left *me*," Deb added softly.

"No, Dubs. It didn't happen that way."

"But it did," she said, now firmly, no longer feeling that need to cry. "And you can't just make it not have happened."

232

Theodore looked at her for the longest time.

"All right," he finally said, those blue eyes of his burning through his glasses. "I appreciate your offer. The settlement, I mean. And I promise you this, I will think about it carefully."

Deb had almost forgotten about the original reason for the conversation. "What do you mean," she shifted gears, "think about it? What's to think about?"

"I need a little time."

"What for?"

"To mull it over."

"What?"

"Work it through. Do the math. All that sort."

"But it's clear. You win. Release the money."

"Haste makes waste, my dear. I'm just protecting my interests, that's all.

"What the fuck? What interests?"

"Well, we haven't gone public with this yet, but—Jane and I are expecting. And these things require money. I have to make sure my—family is taken care of." Theodore said this while scratching the bushy white chest hair sticking out at the top of his shirt. He was still feeling greatly relieved that the aggressive fertility treatments he and Jane had been undergoing—financed with that wonderful cash from Jane's ongoing secret enterprise with Maxey—had finally borne fruit.

"You're bringing more children into the world?"

"Yes. Isn't it grand? Life goes on?"

Deb could hardly breathe. "I told you we were running out of meds."

"Yes." He peered at her through those now slightly fogged glasses. "You did."

"You fucker! *You fucking pig!*"

Theodore removed his glasses and wiped them on his shirt after wiping away some Danish crumbs. "I'll have you know, young lady, that that kind of language can get me so upset that I might need some extra days to settle down before making my decision. And besides, that is no way to speak to your father. Where I come from—" He returned his glasses to his nose and peered through them, once again, toward Deb.

She was already gone.

Outside in the parking lot, fighting back tears, not quite fighting back rage, Deb scratched her apartment key along the entire driver's side of that little sporty car on her way to the bus stop. I will get him, she thought to herself as she added an extra scratch along the front of the car. I will destroy him. I will bury him.

The first serious flakes in the first serious snow of the winter were just beginning to fall.

7

The meds were done.

So was their money.

No word from *him*.

But for the moment things were stable. Helen felt all right, with an uncharacteristic optimism about the months ahead despite the lack of meds. She was planning to return to A World Away in the new year and was excited about it.

"Strange," she observed as she and Deb awaited the dropping of the ball on another New Year's Eve together, a mostly empty bottle of wine on the tea table before them, "how for years I felt bitter about my job, and now here I am counting the days until I can resume my duties once again." She took a sip. "Four, to be precise."

"That took you a long time to count," Deb said.

"Unlike your sister I was never strong in mathematics."

"I'll say. It's actually three."

They both laughed.

"And you, my dear daughter, should return to school."

"I don't think so, Mummy. Not yet."

"But I am fine."

"I know. But I'm not ready. I'll get a job maybe. Start again in the fall."

"You should go back to school. You need to start focusing on your own life."

"Mummy," Deb said. "Maybe we should sell the island."

"Maybe you should think about another glass of wine," Helen raised the bottle toward Deb's glass.

"I'm serious."

"I'm not?"

"It's the only way to continue the meds."

"But I don't need them anymore."

"Of course you still need them. Look, I've been thinking about it. We only go there in the summer, pretty much, maybe two or three times a year. We barely use the place. And if we can get anywhere near what Melvin estimated for it we'll have more than enough money for your meds. *And* to get ourselves to the promised land for a good long time. We'll go for six months, maybe a year. Maybe we'll just move there. Isn't that what you've always wanted?"

Helen *was* serious now. "We go there for your birthday, Deb."

"We'll go somewhere else for my birthday."

"It's too risky."

"How is it risky?"

"We move to the promised land, and then what? The money might get us started, but then what?"

"We get jobs."

"No one will hire me. I'm—an old secretary. I don't even know how to turn on a computer."

"I'll get a job. I'll support you."

"Dub," Helen said softly. "What happens when it comes back?"

"We'll have the meds. It won't come back."

"For a while. Not forever. It's too risky, Deb."

"Mummy," Deb insisted, "you have wanted this your whole life. It's a possibility now. Forget the risk. Life is risky. There will be no better time."

"What I have always wanted no longer matters. What matters now is you. And Regina. But mostly—obviously—you."

"Well," Deb said softly, "selling it is what *I* want."

"But you only want that for me. For my life."

"So?"

"Sew your buttons."

"Stop that."

"Debra," Helen said, gazing at her daughter. "That house, that island, is your security. Your future. I would not prolong my own life a few miserable months at the cost of your future. Much less satisfy my frivolous desire to go to the promised land."

"But it's not frivolous. It's been your whole lifelong desire."

"My frivolous lifelong desire, Dub. It's just a picture in my head. Put there, maybe, by—my father—when I was a girl. But it's not real. It's not important." Helen paused, then added quietly, "It's frivolous."

"So then what about the meds?"

"All I ever really wanted, Dub, was to have a long meaningful journey *somewhere*. And it turns out I had one, right here, with you. I don't need anything more."

"Please, Mummy," Deb pleaded.

"I'm sorry, my angel," Helen said, touching her daughter's arm. "Now let's drink this wine and see if The Jerk graces us with another call this year."

He didn't.

8

Three weeks into the new year Helen was sick of and bitter about her job again, Deb was starting to get sick of and bitter about hearing Helen complain again, and an aggressive envelope with the all-too-familiar return address arrived in the mail.

So much for "person to person."

"Should we call Melvin?" Helen asked.

"Just give it to me, Mummy." Deb was relieved to finally have heard something as well as outraged that the pig had taken over five weeks to respond.

The first thing that slipped out was a $600 repair bill from an auto body shop for "extensive scratching."

That wasn't good, Deb thought miserably.

It got worse. Stephen Bilker, Esq., fresh off his successful campaign to remove the local tax-deductible status of charitable donations, was pumped up. Getting right to the point the letter announced its expectation that a deal was at hand, that consisting of Theodore keeping all of the inheritance, all of his pension, and half the proceeds from the Riverbend house, in exchange for which he would agree to yield on their damn island. This generous offer to forgo the marital island was, however, further conditional on their receipt of a notarized waiver, to be signed by both Regina and Debra Gale, forgoing in return any claims on Theodore Gale as a father, that is, any rights or claims to his current or future estate, not to mention rights to bug or nudge or taunt him in any way including the calling of certain derogatory names such as "*Theee*-o" and "Doctor Crock." Upon receipt of this waiver—in addition to the $600 for the paint job—they would also generously agree not to press charges on the vandalization of the little sports car.

"Debra?" Helen said.

"I'm sorry. I couldn't help myself. I scratched up his stupid car."

"I approve of the scratching. But—did you go to see him?"

Deb nodded.

"When?"

"Last month."

"Why didn't you tell me?"

"Yeah right. You would have just forbidden me to go."

"Yeah right I would have." Helen paused. "Please do not tell me you asked that man for money."

"Just for our money, Mummy. To settle, so we could get out of escrow."

"And now this."

"And now this."

There was a silence.

"Can they do that?" Helen asked. "Demand a waiver like that?"

"Last year Bilker sued a homeless, mentally ill, seventy-five-year-old decorated war veteran for offering politely to wash people's windshields for a dollar," Deb answered, "and won. I think he can do this."

"They cannot do this," Melvin disagreed strongly, having left his family in the middle of supper to rush over and study the letter. "It's blackmail, pure and simple."

"How so?" Helen asked.

Melvin's face was red with anger, which was not something Helen could recall having seen before. "Look, it's one thing to negotiate—in horribly bad faith, to be sure, but at least it's negotiating—about the assets in question. The claim on the island was disgusting but at least it's within the realm of negotiation, from the legal perspective. But to demand a waiver from the girls, who aren't even a party to the marital assets—not to mention the implicit threat to press charges for the damage to the car—well, that is out of bounds. Pure blackmail."

"But how can he do that?" Helen said. "He's a lawyer."

"They're bluffing," Melvin said, calming down. "He knows they can't win in court. It would be thrown out immediately. They want to intimidate you. Accept the terms without a fight. So we fight."

"Meaning?"

"We go to court. We sue. We win. We get a much better deal imposed on them by the court."

"All right. Let's do that."

"We don't do that," Deb said firmly.

"But it's a no-brainer," Melvin said. "They have crossed the line here. I am sure we will win."

"How long will that take?" Deb asked.

"Well, we'll need to file some paperwork. Get a court date for a hearing. Prepare some briefs, assemble some documents. Then wait for a decision."

"And how long will that take?"

"And then," Melvin continued, less fight in his voice, "they will almost surely appeal. So there would be another hearing, and so on."

"And how long will that take, Melvin?" Deb insisted.

"What difference does it make?" Helen asked.

"All the fucking difference in the world."

"Debra!"

"We need to get back on the meds, Mummy."

"But I'm fine. There's no rush."

"You've been complaining about being tired this past week."

"I just like to complain."

"I'm not taking a chance. We need to settle, get the money from the house, and get you back on the meds. As soon as possible."

"You are not being rational, Deb," Helen said. "Melvin says we'll get a much better deal if we're only a little patient."

"Melvin," Deb asked again, *how long will that fucking take?*"

"Months," Melvin said nearly inaudibly. "Maybe a year."

"Then we take the shitty deal," Deb said.

"Debra," Helen said.

"Will you put the island on the market instead, Mummy?"

Helen shook her head slowly.

"Then we deal."

"Let me pay for the meds," Melvin interjected. "Helen, I *beg* you."

This offer was not as sudden as the declaration itself was. Since The Very Busy Day, just over six years before, Melvin had asked to help out financially several times. Each request had been met with firm rebuffs by Helen, constituting ever new setbacks in his now decades-long quest for her heart. For the past three months he had been bursting with the desire to pay for the meds, it had almost bubbled out of him multiple times, but he had managed to restrain himself, fearing Helen's fearsome wrath. Listening to this debate now he could no longer remain silent.

Both women stared at him.

Then responded simultaneously.

"Melvin thank you—" Deb exclaimed.

"You will do no such thing!" Helen exclaimed.

"Mummy—"

"Debra, this does not concern you."

"Of course it concerns me." Deb felt her stomach begin to churn. "We get the meds, we can be patient for the courts. Just let him do this."

"Helen—"

"Melvin, no thank you," Helen said firmly.

"Mummy, please—"

"Enough," Helen said in *that* tone of voice. "I've had enough."

"Well, I haven't—"

"*Enough!*"

There was a long silence.

"Mummy, you are so goddamn stubborn," Deb said softly.

"I am," Helen said softly too, "my angel."

There was another long silence.

"Then I guess it's settled," Deb said. "We settle."

9

Serial killers were being executed, religious leaders were seeking sacrilegious heads, and February, brutal February, seemed interminable. The cold weather was relentless. The snows of January had never receded, instead providing the foundation for the multi-foot drifts of February.

The process was underway.

Regina had responded to their answering machine message surprisingly promptly. After a blistering tirade against The Fucking Pig in a return message she had signed and returned the waiver that Melvin drafted which essentially legally severed the parental relationship between Theodore and his offspring. The materials were now working their way through the court system. Deb called one office or another nearly every day to check on the status of this, or that, and to find out when, oh when, the money from the house would finally be released from escrow incarceration. Melvin had overcome his fear to offer at least to advance the funds for the meds, to be repaid when the house money was released, but stubborn Helen stubbornly refused.

Everything about February seemed interminable. Or everything except for Helen, at least once her remission went into remission in that month's final miserable week.

They acted quickly; Melvin and Deb, that is.

Dr. Oppenheim did not have a good day, that day, his heart breaking as he informed Deb over the phone of the most recent test results. Deb, her stomach in her throat, finally goddamn directly overrode her mother for the first time in her life and phoned Melvin, who immediately arranged their resupply of liquids and pills from pharmacist Al and the next round of aggressive therapy. With the awful news and the awful therapy Helen once again stopped resisting and simply did whatever they all said, the good doctor, the good pharmacist, and especially the good Debra and Melvin. The stubbornness with which she had resisted Melvin's advances over the years, both romantic and financial, was now nowhere evident in her dealings with her returned disease. She seemed, you might almost think, *at ease* with the process, if Helen Gale could ever be said to be at ease with anything.

Melvin and Deb did act quickly; but so did the disease.

One day Helen Gale was a miraculous survivor. Then poof! in one instant it was a dark and endless night.

The weight, partially regained, was re-lost and then some. The hair disappeared more quickly than it had returned. The money from the house came through in late April and Helen briefly gathered enough strength to insist on reimbursing Melvin immediately. Deb was running the home, obviously, shopping and cooking and cleaning and somehow getting the bills paid—again with help from Melvin, a secret kept from Helen—all while keeping her mother's meds stocked and consumed and getting her to appointments and holding her hand through the renewed therapy. She interrupted her mother's care only to wash down handfuls of TUMS with capfuls of Pepto-Bismol to battle her own always upset stomach, or else to sleep a few hours a night, now back in her own bedroom on Helen's insistence, since Helen's ability to sleep had gone the way of the weight and hair. Regina at one point left a tearful message that may have ended with a declaration that she was going to come back home soon, except that Deb, flustered by hearing the "smart" sister's suddenly displaying emotions, inadvertently erased the message before hearing it to the end.

Melvin came by the apartment every evening bearing magazines and crossword puzzles and, twice a week, fresh purple pansies to replace the previous ones in the vase in Helen's bedroom. And what were flowers without a little imported chocolate to go with them? Chocolate which, toward the end, was about the only thing that Helen was able to keep down.

One evening in mid-May, Helen, so pale and so thin, said to Deb over a simple chicken broth supper—Deb's stomach was none too keen on eating these days either—"You know, I almost think this is worth it."

"What is?"

"All of it," Helen answered with almost a smile. "For all the attention."

"Yeah right," Deb said. "Mummy?"

"Yes?"

"Did you just lick your fingers?"

Helen broke into a half-smile, half-smiles being the most of which she was now capable. "If not now, my angel, then when?"

10

Who knows what might have been, Helen sometimes thought during those weeks, if they had only settled earlier, if she hadn't been so stubborn about Melvin, if there had been no break in her meds. Or if there hadn't been all those misdiagnoses of her leg pain, if she hadn't gone on that trip to Thailand for the future which never was. Or if she hadn't put up with *that man* as long as she had, or hadn't endured that marriage. If she hadn't lingered the extra minutes in Cozzen's Café, if she hadn't made that phone call long ago at the corner of Seventeenth and Waterhouse. If her family hadn't disintegrated, if her father hadn't died on her. If she hadn't finally relented to dating Eddie Love in the first place.

If she had never picked up that first cigarette.

But then again, had all those things never happened she would never have had Debra either. And when in the course of the irresistible what-iffing of those days this thought occurred to her then her response was immediate. Indeed it *was*, Helen thought to herself, feeling a momentary sense of lightness, all worth it. All of it.

And now she had just one last thing to accomplish, or rather two: to put the finishing touches on her gift for Debra's approaching twenty-first birthday, and then to make it to that date in order to give it to her.

On the first Friday evening of June, six days before her daughter's birthday, Helen, feeling a burst of strength, insisted on cooking supper for the first time in a long time. "Just ravioli," she conceded to her daughter's objections. "Nothing difficult. Maybe Four Cheese, with the Debra Special sauce." During that quiet supper with her daughter she suddenly developed a high fever and began to cough, a deep spasming cough accompanied with sharp abdominal pain. Deb, trying to keep herself together, ignored her protests and packed her into the car and headed directly for the overcrowded Emergency Room.

CHAPTER ELEVEN
'MORNING, MORNING

1

"Dub," Helen whispered.

"Mummy," Deb whispered back.

There were noises all around. The hallway was crowded, intense, and very alive for a place where many people were busy dying. Someone clattered by pushing a heavy piece of equipment. Doors opened and slammed shut, punctuating the monotonous hum of the air conditioning. They heard everything but could see nothing from under their sheet, on the gurney they were sharing. They'd have felt almost like sisters, like *real* sisters, camping in a little tent, holding hands, but for the mostly ominous sounds surrounding them.

And for the fact that Helen's face was flush from the fever and her eyes barely open.

"I'm so sorry," Helen whispered again.

"For what?"

"Your childhood. For a start."

"Jesus, Mummy, stop."

Machines were beeping, an elevator was arriving somewhere; another gurney jostled them as it was pushed past. People were talking all around them. Deb could have listened to the doctor instructing his medical student, to every detail of the nurse's complaint about the ornery patient in 117, to every curse muttered by the technician repairing the broken vending machine down the hall. Instead she heard only her mother's slow, labored breathing. Under that sheet together, the two of them, their private space in this most public of places.

Helen opened her eyes. Those deep hazel eyes had somehow maintained at least some of their vitality despite the events of the past few years, the past few decades, despite *him*.

"How is your tummy?" Helen asked, gazing at her daughter.

"Please stop worrying about my tummy already!" Deb objected. Two hours earlier, at the apartment, Deb had mentioned the usual nausea. Helen had been inquiring after it every twenty minutes since.

"But I'm your Mummy. It's my job."

"It's not your job. Getting better is your job."

"Well it was my cooking."

"I've had stomach problems since I was a kid. It wasn't your ravioli."

"I don't mean tonight. I mean when you were a child." Helen's face scrunched up in pain again. "I told you I was sorry."

Deb ignored her. "I'm going to go ask again. This is outrageous."

"No, don't. I'm fine. Right here."

Under the sheet they heard someone else come by, pushing another machine on its way to save someone else's life. Yet another jostle to their little gurney. There were a lot of emergencies tonight, and not a single room was available. But the nurse had said something would open up soon.

Helen coughed. Then coughed again, more violently.

"That's it," Deb said. "I'm getting you into a room. And for once in your life, Mummy, please don't argue with me."

"Dub."

"Mummy, enough."

"Don't leave me."

Don't leave *me*, Deb thought, her stomach fluttering. Fighting back tears she gazed at her mother in the shadow under the sheet, then kissed her warm forehead. "I'll be right back."

She slipped out from under the sheet and got up off the gurney. The bright light of the hallway was jarring; the activity all around, unsettling. There were other people on other gurneys spaced along the corridor.

"I'm cold," her mother whispered, turning away and pulling the sheet back over her head. Her unnaturally thin form remained visible under the sheet.

Deb stared at it a moment.

Then she went in search of a doctor, a nurse, a staff member, anybody who might allow her mother to die with a little more dignity than that afforded by a thin cotton sheet. Her mother would not die in a hospital hallway; in this hallway; she would *not*.

The nurses' station was just a few steps away. Four women and one man in scrubs were milling about around the desks, which were arranged in what struck Deb as a defensive circular way. They were chattering in an indeterminate murmur. From under the sheet their conversations were separable and distinct yet when Deb was in their presence they were barely discernible.

"May I help you?" The head triage nurse wore scrubs patterned with some lovely daisies but a facial expression more suggestive of herbicide.

"Helen Gale. In the hallway there. Still waiting for a room?"

"That's right. We'll get you when one is available."

"You said that it would be just a few minutes."

"And how long has it been?"

"Forty-four minutes."

"That *is* just a few minutes."

"Excuse me," Deb exclaimed, "but my mother is in a fucking hallway!"

"Excuse *me*, ma'am, but it's a Friday night."

"So?"

"It's like this every weekend. We're underfinanced and understaffed. There's nothing I can do for you right now."

"But she's *dying*."

"That doesn't make a room appear." The nurse's expression softened. "I'm sorry. We will come get you when something opens up." She returned to her clipboard. The other nurses had disappeared.

Deb glared at her. And then felt bad for the nurse. It wasn't exactly her fault that there were more sick people than resources to accommodate them. Though perhaps her attitude could use some adjustment. But then again the nurse had to deal with this situation day in and day out, the same problem, the same complaints. This was Deb's one and only mother, of course, but then again it was *everyone's* one and only mother.

"I'm sorry," Deb said with somewhat less vigor. "Is there at least a cafeteria somewhere?" Her mother might appreciate some hot tea; her own troubled tummy as well.

The nurse glanced up. "In the main building, ma'am." She pointed down the corridor opposite them and returned to her paperwork.

"I'm *very* sorry, but I also need a payphone."

"Next to the cafeteria." This time the nurse didn't look up.

Deb set off in the direction indicated. She passed room after room, each filled to and beyond capacity. Every bed was occupied. Next to the beds were occupied gurneys, and then there were the gurneys in the hallways.

There was a sign for the cafeteria pointing through a set of double doors. Deb would have gone straight through them except for the fact that they turned out to be locked. Instead she crashed into them, banging her shoulder badly. She turned back around and looked down the corridor.

Suddenly the hospital felt empty. Here she was, alone at the end of a long corridor, stuck behind locked doors. She couldn't go forward and she did not want to go back.

Where the fuck was Regina?

And goddamn *him*.

She started to cry.

Not just for this or for that; for the long wait, the gurney in the hallway, the rude nurse; the locked doors.

For all of it.

"Ah, let me get that for you," a deep velvet voice suddenly said.

A doctor had appeared. A beautiful man in a long white coat. Perhaps not beautiful for his actual features: his eyes were bleary, he was many hours away from his last shave, and his otherwise white coat had numerous stains Deb preferred not to identify. He was beautiful simply for being there. Around his neck he wore a long chain with an ID card on it, which he was now clumsily attempting to slide through a magnetic reader next to the locked doors.

"They lock these at 9:00 PM," he explained. "But I can't get the hang of this new technology."

He was struggling to find the right orientation for the card. On his coat Deb could see the name *Jeffrey* sewn in red thread. Finally the doors clicked loudly and he pushed one open, holding it for her.

"Always the last one you try," he said. "Obviously." He peered at her. "Hey, are you all right?"

Deb quickly collected herself. "The cafeteria's down there?"

"To the left."

She nodded, and started walking.

"One more thing," he said, stopping her.

"What's that?"

"You'll want to avoid the chili."

"Oh?"

"Yeah. It could put you in the hospital."

Deb gazed at him uncomprehendingly.

"Sorry," he said, grimacing. "A little levity. Probably inappropriate."

Deb half-heartedly smiled and made her way through the doors and down the corridor. She found the payphone and called Melvin, who, whispering, promised he'd be there as soon as he could. She then thought a moment, called information, and connected through for another call. The cafeteria was nearly empty, devoid at this hour not merely of people but also nearly entirely of food. The only options were cold drinks from a cooler, chips and cookies in little bags on a rack, and fortunately coffee and hot water for tea. Deb prepared teas for herself and her mother, adding a spot of milk to each. After paying for them she made her way back through the corridor and was relieved to find that the double doors were not locked on this side. The beautiful Dr. Jeffrey was nowhere to be seen. She retraced her steps past the crowded rooms, through the noisy corridors, back past the nurses' station which was now abandoned.

The sheet covering her mother's gurney was still.

All these gurneys along the walls, all these people streaming up and down, back and forth, everybody, everything, everywhere. But nobody noticing that the sheet covering her one and only mother wasn't moving.

She approached the gurney. She put the hot cups down on the floor next to the wall, held her breath, and lifted the sheet.

Helen was lying on her side, holding the remains of a chocolate bar which she was clearly savoring. Next to her on the gurney was a large red hot water bottle.

"Got you these," Helen whispered.

"Mummy you scared the hell out of me! I thought you were dead!"

"I more or less was before this arrived. Good for a second wind. Slight breeze, anyway. Now climb back in before this thing gets cold."

Deb obeyed, and they were back under the sheet.

"For your tummy," Helen explained hoarsely, passing over the hot water bottle. "Also for your tummy," she added, passing over the remaining morsel of chocolate. "Sorry there's not much left."

"I got you a tea. For *your* tummy."

"Thank you, my angel. But I'm all right now."

"And how did you get yourself a candy bar and a water bottle?"

"Not a candy bar. A Neuchâtel."

"A Neuchâtel, then."

"Connections, my darling Debra."

"But you don't know anybody."

"I do now. Some nice doctor stopped by and asked if we needed anything."

Deb groaned. "Let me guess. You also asked him for a manfriend for your daughter."

"I did not," she objected hoarsely. "I asked him for a hot water bottle for my daughter. The manfriend was for me." She laughed with some difficulty. Any exercise of her chest muscles was painful.

Then she coughed again, for a long minute.

"Mummy," Deb said.

"Dub," she said so softly her daughter could barely hear her, even under the sheet. Then she said, "I don't think I'm leaving this place."

"Of course you're leaving this place. I just made a reservation next week at Twenty-One. For my birthday. For us."

"Dub," she whispered.

They didn't speak any further.

A few minutes later the triage nurse showed up with a burly assistant. Deb got off the gurney, pulled the sheet down to her mother's shoulders, and walked alongside it as the assistant pushed it down the corridor. They turned left at the end of the corridor, then went down another long corridor, and then another, before finally entering an empty room.

2

It was a long weekend.

It was all too brief a weekend.

Helen's fever proved difficult to control. Shortly after midnight she slipped into a coma. Deb was watching when it happened, when her mother's body slackened and her eyes became unfocused and then seemed to roll upward. She screamed for the doctors, people came running, tubes were inserted, somebody steered Deb out of the way while the team was at work. They neatly deposited Deb in the uncomfortable chair in the corner of the room.

Melvin had come and gone by that point, having dropped off some magazines before returning to his family for the night. He had called Regina too, leaving a message with the phone number of the hospital, but so far the phone in Helen's room had not rung. He departed with a promise to come back in the morning.

Deb spent much of the first night talking to her mother, pausing only when medical personnel wandered in to do medical things and immediately resuming once they were alone again. She reminded her of their plans for next Thursday, Deb's twenty-first birthday, they were going to skip the island this year and make a picnic at Moswanicut Park on the lawn near the central fountain and maybe drink some wine from a paper bag. Then, assuming Helen were up for it, they would let their hair down—a little joke, in light of the recent therapy—for a night out at Twenty-One. Deb then recalled for her mother how they had spent each of the previous dozen or so of Deb's birthdays, for Deb could remember not just the past few years when their relationship was blossoming but all the way back during the years when they barely had a relationship at all, when her mother—here Deb stopped herself, feeling that knot in her stomach, and switched gears—and instead began recalling all the birthdays of her mother's they had celebrated, going all the way back years, able to remember every single thing they had done together and every single gift that she had ever made or acquired for her mother.

You cannot die, Mummy, Deb was saying as morning finally crashed into the room, you will not die. I *forbid* you from dying. He got to have you and Regina got to have you but I just got you, I've only had you a little while, I will not let you go, you cannot abandon me now.

More medical people came in, tubes were checked and reinserted, a breathing machine set up. Melvin arrived with pastries and pansies and a new book of crossword puzzles, not realizing that Helen was now in a coma. He tried to convince Deb to go home and rest a bit while he took over the vigil, but his enthusiasm for his argument was tempered by the obvious fact that it had no chance of succeeding. They sat together much of the morning, not speaking. Deb dozed off periodically in that uncomfortable chair.

It was such a strange contrast from the night before, when they had arrived at the Emergency Room. Already that seemed like a million years ago but the thing she would most remember from it was the noise, the nonstop noise, the hospital noises, the slamming and buzzing and crinkling and talking and shouting and loudspeaker announcements. What she was most to remember from the days spent in her mother's room now would be the silence, the occasional hum or beep maybe, but mostly the overwhelming and oppressive absence of sound.

Melvin left, came back later, left again. Some relatives wandered in, stayed a while, left, some returned. Someone during the day had left a chocolate bar, like the one from the night before. Everyone urged Deb to go home and get some rest. As if she would trust her mother's care—this vigil—to anyone else. I'm fine here, she thought. This shitty chair already feels like home.

3

There were stirrings, awakenings, movements. Deb would jolt to attention, press buttons, medical people would come in. But then they would pass.

At some point a woman came in and asked to empty the trash and clear away the meal trays which Deb had left untouched and the candy bar wrapper which Deb must have dropped on the floor.

The phone in the room never rang. Twice Deb walked to the nurses' station to ask if anyone had called or tried to reach her, left a message, anything.

4

Melvin returned with fresh flowers and another crossword book. "Hope springs eternal," he explained softly. He sat for a while in the other chair. He left.

Another relative or two arrived, left. Someone left another chocolate bar. Once or twice Deb gave her mother a light spritz with the green tea perfume she'd asked Melvin to retrieve from the apartment.

The phone didn't ring.

5

The door to the room was kept open during the day. Felt less claustrophobic that way. And she was feeling no need for privacy anyway. There is little more anonymous than being a dying person hooked up to beeping tubes in a crowded hospital.

A couple of times she sensed a presence at the door. She sat up and turned toward the door but there was no one there.

Perhaps she had fallen asleep.

6

She must have fallen asleep.

She had this elaborate dream in which she was a little girl and her mother was not Helen but her grandmother, Edna, whom she didn't directly remember because she'd died when Deb was so young but with whose photographs Deb was very familiar, not to mention with whose furniture she was even more familiar, having grown up with it. There was cooking going on—maybe Edna was teaching Deb how to cook—or maybe bake—and then there was a fire in the oven, someone was screaming, and Alden came in, her grandfather who died before she was born, the one whom everybody loved, the one who had kept the whole family together, but it wasn't him it was Theodore, and instead of putting out the fire he was aggravating it. But then within the dream Deb once again sensed someone was present, right there, watching her, and suddenly there she was again sitting in that shitty chair apparently wide awake.

Her mother was staring at her.

The clock on the shelf behind the bed read 11:17 but Deb had no idea if that was morning or evening.

"Mummy?" she said.

7

Helen had enjoyed that all too brief respite from the disease some months earlier, and maybe she was now enjoying an all too brief respite from the coma in which she had spent the previous forty-seven hours or so.

"Where are we?" Helen asked weakly.

"We're in the hospital, Mummy." Deb pulled the chair over to the bed and gingerly took her mother's hand, not wanting to disturb the tubes.

So much silence around them.

"Mummy," Deb began crying.

"Don't cry, my angel."

"Don't leave me, Mummy. Please don't leave."

"I'm here, my angel."

"I just got you. I can't let you go. I can't."

"Listen to me, my angel." Helen's voice strengthened slightly, and she moved her other hand over to clasp Deb's. "Three things happened in my life that I—I never talked about with a soul. One I did, one was done to me, and one just—happened. They happened, I put them away, and I never looked back. Or so I believed." She looked at her daughter. "I'm so awfully sorry, my angel."

"I don't understand."

"Listen to me. The shoes on the floor don't matter. The closets don't matter. It just doesn't matter."

"Mummy—"

"Listen to me. I didn't understand. It wasn't clear. To me. But it was obvious. Just not to me."

"Mummy, I—"

"*Listen to me*, Debra."

"What?"

"I should have hugged you."

"What?"

"I should have hugged you."

"We hug all the time."

"Not now. Then."

"What?"

"When you were a child."

"Oh my God. Mummy," Deb sobbed.

"Dub," Helen whispered.

"Mummy," Deb whispered.

"I am so tired."

"Mummy."

"You'll let it go, won't you?"

"Don't leave me all alone, Mummy."

"All of it. Let it go."

"Don't leave me, Mummy."

"It eats you up. From the inside. Promise me."

"Mummy, please."

"Every last piece. Promise me."

Deb bit her lip, nodding, through her tears.

"Even *him*."

Deb's eyes were locked with her mother's.

"I'm very tired," Helen said softly.

"All right," Deb said.

"I'll sleep now. For a little while."

"All right."

"I'm so awfully sorry, my sweet angel."

"It's all right, Mummy."

"My sweet angel," Helen repeated softly.

There was a small silence. Helen squeezed Deb's hand.

"'Night, night," Helen whispered.

The two women smiled at each other.

The mother closed her eyes.

8

Some time later, in the early hours of the next morning, Deb was jarred awake by a penetrating noise.

It was her mother's breathing.

Long, slow, lingering breaths.

Inhale. Mornings, wake up, babies, diapers.

Exhale. Noons, lunches, toddlers, toys.

Inhale. Afternoons, naps, childhood, snacks.

Exhale. Dinners, school, youth, bicycles.

Inhale. Homework, adolescence, attitudes.

Exhale. Evenings, television, teenagers, trouble.

Inhale.

A long slow intake of breath that kept on going, all the way in, and then just stopped.

That bit of air was never to be let go.

Barely able to breathe herself, Deb was frantically pressing the button.

It was 3:06 AM on the morning of June 5, 1989.

CHAPTER TWELVE
WOMAN WITH A PARASOL

When everyone had gone, when the apartment floor was littered with flowers that Deb didn't have enough vases for, she sat down with Melvin at the kitchen table to take care of the most immediately pressing loose ends. The window was open. The warm early summer breeze was coming in. It would almost be time to turn on the air conditioner again.

"Next month's rent is taken care of," Melvin was saying. "The mail is on hold. The next month's bills will be directly debited from your mother's—your—checking account. Everything's taken care of on the other end. The pick up, the—interment, a service. Oh, and you leave tomorrow."

He removed an airplane ticket from his briefcase and pushed it across the table to her. He had also retrieved her passport from the safe deposit box.

"Melvin," Deb said, not touching the ticket. "I—"

He ignored her. "I'm going to have this place painted, too, while you're gone. It could use a little sprucing up. What do you say to purple for the bedrooms? Or maybe pink?"

She almost allowed herself to smile.

"Melvin, you didn't have to do this," she said, touching his arm. "You don't have to do this. Any of this."

His eyes filled up. She noticed that he really had beautiful eyes, a soft gray, with such a tender look.

"Deb," he said.

She looked at him, her hand resting on his arm.

"She wouldn't let me love her when she was alive," he said, the slightest quiver in his lip. "But now she can't stop me."

"Melvin—"

"That's all right, Deb." He quickly cleared his throat. "It's an 8:00 AM flight. I'll have the car service here at six. I'm sorry it's so early but—"

"It's a long flight. I know." She gave his arm a gentle squeeze. "You, um, definitely can't come. I suppose."

He smiled sadly. "I don't think Michelle would understand. And she has been remarkably understanding. For a long time."

Deb nodded.

"You'll call me when you get back. All right?"

Deb nodded, beginning to cry.

"And say goodbye for me, all right?" Melvin's momentary victory over his emotions was quickly crumbling.

"Melvin I can't thank—"

He lifted his hand to shush her and then just walked out to go find someplace to experience his heartbreak all by himself.

Deb was alone in the apartment.

The sun streaming in the window really did not match the mood.

It was the morning, she suddenly realized, of her twenty-first birthday.

Regina's twenty-third, too, then. Hmm. She remembered that period of time, during their childhood, when she wanted so desperately to share her birthday celebrations with her sister. But those feelings were now gone. Regina apparently chose not to show up.

So much for having a sister.

"I guess," she said aloud, as alone in the world as you could be while two-thirds of your nuclear family is still alive, "it's just me now."

She got up from the table and walked around the now enormous apartment.

The vast abandoned rooms. The gapingly lifeless bedroom she had shared with her mother almost to the end, on the bedside table of which still stood the unfinished book of crossword puzzles with the pencil slipped in to keep the place. The photo of herself and her mother on the ferry taken exactly one year earlier, on their return from the island.

She really, really wanted a cigarette.

It had been months now since they had smoked. But there had to be some cigarettes somewhere in the apartment. Only ten minutes of looking through cabinets, closets, and finally the drawers of her mother's dresser and she found them. A carton-and-a-half in a crumpled plastic bag, along with a receipt dated just a few weeks before.

She felt a lump in her throat when she saw the date.

Just then she noticed another package underneath the plastic bag. It was wrapped in purple gift paper and had an envelope on the outside. Deb sat on the bed and opened the envelope slowly, the lump growing in her throat. The cover of the card was one of their favorite paintings, Monet's *Woman with a Parasol in the Garden at Argenteuil.* Inside, in her mother's perfect handwriting, was a brief message. "For my darling Debra, on her twenty-first birthday: The way to a mother's heart is through her tummy, and you, my everything, are now in full possession of both. Your adoring captive, Mummy."

She didn't need to open it to know that it was her grandmother's lilac-covered notebook, the handwritten recipes adorned with her grandmother's commentary; nor to know that it would also include her mother's own handwritten commentary, both improving on the quaint old recipes and sarcastically commenting on her grandmother's commentary; nor to know that its final pages would contain the famous Faire family secret recipe banana cream pie.

Ohhh, she moaned to herself, barely able to breathe.

She allowed herself to linger awhile in that awful moment.

Then with a deep breath the second daughter grasped the still-wrapped book and stood up, and began getting her things together for tomorrow's long journey to the promised land.

The End

INCONCLUSIVE UNSCIENTIFIC POSTSCRIPT
BY THE AUTHOR

Maybe this book will do the trick.

Not any time soon, I know. I'll probably have to wait until a few people die before I try to publish it. Or maybe I can disguise the characters enough and make up enough stuff to obscure the identities. What do I know? I'm not a writer. I don't even know what I was thinking, in starting this. I definitely wasn't thinking about how to end it.

What I am is a doctor, and a damn good one if I do say so myself. That's why I was there that night in the hospital. I was a second-year resident, I had been working maybe sixty hours straight by that point—the system is pretty outrageous—when I wandered downstairs in search of better coffee, or at least stronger, than the dishwater they inflicted on us up in the residents' lounge. I was so tired, I must have zoned out, I think I was just standing in the hallway connecting the Main Hospital and the Emergency Room when there she was. Beautiful, beautiful woman, thick wavy dark hair, the most adorable nose, breathtaking really, she was just standing there sobbing, locked out by the double doors looking for the cafeteria. I'm a sucker for beautiful breathtaking sobbing women, I guess, but then again who isn't? I opened the doors for her and heard myself making a stupid joke about the cafeteria food. I could have just kicked myself. I mean, I may not have known much about medicine as a resident but I should have known that you don't try to flirt with women sobbing in the middle of the night in the Emergency Room. Or at least not with such a mediocre joke. But there it was, and there she was, disappearing down the corridor but not from my mind.

I went on into the Emergency Room. It was completely swamped there, crazy. But I managed to talk to the triage nurse—friendly gal named Cheryl, had met her once or twice—and got the low-down on my mystery woman's situation. Poor mom had stage four, presenting with high fever and acute pain. Being a resident I thought maybe there's something I can do, maybe make things a little more pleasant for them, at least while they're trying to find a room for her.

It was pretty creepy, she was lying on a gurney in the hall, under a sheet. I cleared my throat, introduced myself, asked if I could come in—another stupid joke, I just couldn't help myself—but she seemed to laugh, a deep raspy noise which I took to be a laugh anyway—and pulled the sheet down. I could see it was bad news. Really ravaged, thin, eyes glistening from the fever. But even so you could see how she must have once been really beautiful herself, before the cigarettes did their thing on her outside, before the disease did its thing on her insides. She asked me for something sweet, and a hot water bottle for her daughter. Talk about a lucky coincidence, at least for me. I happened to have a Neuchâtel candy bar in my coat pocket. I became addicted to them toward the end of medical school, my Mom used to send me a case every couple of months. I probably would not have survived the residency without them. She apparently knew her sweets since she made a comment reproaching me for calling it a candy bar, there apparently being some distinction between candy and chocolate. But I could tell that, as sick as she was, she was joking—not about the distinction but about offering it as a reproach. I liked her for that. It's too bad, to meet someone you might like when it's too late to get to know them. The doctor's lot, I guess. Anyway I told her I'd check in on her again, then got Cheryl to get on the hot water bottle, and I headed back up to my duties on the fourth floor of the Main Hospital, hoping nobody had checked out on me while I was gone.

My interminable shift finally did terminate the next morning. I went home, slept, showered, shaved, and came right back to the hospital even though I was off for the weekend. I wasn't going to try to hit on her, I just wanted, you know, just to see her again. Anyway I had promised her mother I would look in on her so by that point I felt obliged to go. The whole integrity thing, you know?

I found the room easily enough and was glad to see the door was open. I peeked in. The mom was not conscious. It was clearly bad news. My mystery woman—I knew her name by this point, thanks to Cheryl, but it was more exciting to think of her as my mystery woman—was sitting in that awful chair they have in the rooms, which she'd pulled up right next to the bed. She was just staring at her mother, her lips pursed, her eyes swollen from crying. I could see there the really striking resemblance between them, the one a younger healthy version of the other.

I stepped away from the door. I had seen her again, and that was all I had come for. And I had, I suppose, looked in on her mother too. So it was time to go. I left another Neuchâtel with one of the nurses to drop off whenever it was convenient.

I was back the next day too.

I had some files to pick up from my locker and I had completely forgotten to send out my allegedly white coat to the laundry services, so I had to go back. And who was I kidding. I grabbed another Neuchâtel from my locker and stopped by their room on the way out. Just peeked in. The mom was still out, my mystery woman was asleep in the chair. I just looked at her for a minute, realized I was getting a little creepy even to myself, and slipped away. I asked another nurse to drop off the candy—the chocolate—when she had a moment.

That was that, for the time being anyway. I was back on duty the next morning, Monday morning, and by the time I had a chance to wander over to their room it had been cleared out. I knew what that meant. My heart ached for my mystery woman, for her loss, and for me, for my loss—for I knew that there was no remotely acceptable way for me to track her down again. How would I explain how I'd found her? That I'd fallen in love with her while her mother was passing away? That I'd snooped around through their medical records to get her name and address?

So that was that.

Until it wasn't.

A year-and-a-half later, in December, approaching the holidays, I saw her again.

I was now in the first year of my fellowship. I was in the cafeteria looking for lunch when time, and my heart, both stopped. She was by the coffee machine filling the second of two tall cups. She looked a little thinner, a little tired, but she was not one ounce less breathtaking than I remembered her from our previous encounter. She was looking around for the creamers, maybe. I would say that I took a deep breath before I approached her except that my lungs had pretty much stopped functioning too.

I said, "I wouldn't drink that if I were you. At least that's what the toxicology department recommends."

She glanced up at me startled, shaking the cups on her tray, causing them both to spill.

"Jesus," she said, "do you always sneak up on people this way?"

"Only when it's absolutely, totally, completely necessary."

She looked up at me. She looked down at my tray.

"Chili," she said.

"I figure I'm already in the hospital anyway."

She was doing a senior honors' thesis at the university, in clinical health psychology, studying how women deal psychologically with health matters. Her focus was on terminal illness and depression. That's why she was at the hospital. She was working on a study her advisor was doing with some inpatients. She'd been coming in twice a week to conduct interviews, that sort of thing. Both cups of coffee were for her.

"Three cups a day, minimum," she explained across from me at the cafeteria table, "ever since I quit smoking. Dr.—" she peered at the name sewn onto my white coat, "Jeffrey."

"Just call me Jeffrey," I said.

She looked confused.

"That's my first name too."

"Your name is Jeffrey Jeffrey?"

"My parents have a sense of humor."

"Apparently not." The smallest hint of a smile appeared across her beautiful lips.

"In that case just do me one favor, please," I added.

"Yes?"

"Don't ask what my middle name is."

We met for coffee again a few days later, at that little place right in the crook of the aptly named Elbow Street. And again, the next day. Not three more days went by before I told her that not three days had gone by since we'd met that night in the Emergency Room without my thinking about her. When that seemed to be not unfavorably received I took a chance and told her that I'd peeked in on her a couple of times while they were in the hospital. That went all right, too; and when she didn't splash her coffee on me after I confessed that I had snooped into her mother's medical records in order to find out who she was, I decided to take a chance.

"Busy as I am with all my important things," I said, slapping my forehead with my palm, "I *completely* forgot to make any plans for tomorrow night. I know it's late, but any chance you might be free to get together?"

Tomorrow night being New Year's Eve, of course, I was essentially admitting that I was a complete loser for not having a date this late in the game. If there was one thing my father had tried to drill into me, without success, it's that the thing that most attracts women to you is their realizing that other women are attracted to you. "Then how do you explain why I'm still with *you*?" my mother would say when she'd hear him dispensing this romantic advice. "Once you married me," my father would reply without missing a beat, "you were legally stuck with me." They were cute this way.

Anyway, there I was making the world's worst tactical error. If my father had heard me he would promptly have died of a stroke and then turned over in his grave.

But Debra didn't say no. At least not right away.

She pondered it for a moment and said softly, "I don't actually have any plans. Or at least not with anyone else. If it's all right with you, I prefer to spend New Year's by myself."

The way she said this—so soft, so gentle, so sad, yet so firm—I knew it was over. I was crushed, defeated, destroyed. I was officially powerless to resist her.

"All right," I said, love for her welling up in my throat. "What would you say to breakfast then, the morning of the first? At Cozzens Café, maybe, downtown? It's a little run-down but the omelettes are to die for."

"Do they serve breakfast after noon?" she said, I swear with a tear in her eye.

"Any time."

"And how's the coffee?"

"The best," I said, reaching out to touch her hand, "you will ever have."

That was two years ago.

The coffee must have been good.

I'm still in training. I think I'm an Attending Physician now, or maybe a Fellow, or maybe an Attending Fellow; I can't keep track of the titles. Every year I learn new things which contradict whatever I believed to be the case the year before. It's pretty demoralizing sometimes, and I occasionally wonder whether I should have chosen a different career. Like maybe a writer, for example.

Ha! I still got it.

Debra's in the Ph.D. program at the university now, developing a dissertation proposal in women's health psychology. Fortunately her department is on the opposite side of campus from her father's, so she rarely crosses paths with him. When she does, she tells me, he averts his eyes and slinks away. A lot of the fight has gone out of him apparently, since that woman he was with ended up popping out twins and leaving him for his lawyer, who then sued him for child support. Makes you hope there could maybe be a little justice in the world. (Or maybe I'm just keen on the whole vindictiveness thing, who knows.) Unfortunately I think Debra may be on the verge of forgiving him, with that big heart of hers, despite my protests: loyalty to her mother, I insist, forbids it, whatever her mother may or may not have whispered to her at the end.

Not that Debra ever listens much to me.

My main occupation these days, of course, is trying to convince her to move in with me. She's a tough nut to crack, as they say. She doesn't exactly have a good model of a happy couple to work with, she tells me. I point to my parents, and she loves them, but she does think that what I call their bantering is often actually bickering and isn't always that cute. And, looking ahead, we do have a small difference of opinion over the issue of children. I'd be satisfied with maybe just one or two, I think. I was myself an only child and I came out all right, I tell her, if you overlook my pathological need for attention and my homicidal inability to share. She insists that if she ever has kids she has to have at least three. One is too lonely, my case notwithstanding. And two is too risky. If they don't get along then they're essentially on their own.

She hasn't heard from her sister since their mom died.

There is so much gorgeous love inside that woman, however, that I will not give up.

"I will actually *let* you love me, Debra," I say in my always generous way, "as much as you want, whenever you want, however you want. I will be your vessel, and you can fill me."

She smiles and says, "You don't really want me to move in, Dr. J. You don't even really know me. There are no other witnesses to my past. You have only my own testimony on who I am."

"But I do know you, Debra," I say, "because I listen carefully to your stories, and because I see so clearly that you are the truth through and through. *I* will be your witness."

She says, "You don't want me, Jeffrey. I'm like the box that arrives all crumpled and broken, bounced around en route."

"Debra," I say, "for your information I prefer the bruised fruits and vegetables at the supermarket. I yearn to give them a good home."

She says, "But I'm all twisted *inside*, Jeffrey. Distorted and swollen. I'm a gargoyle of a person."

"Debra," I say, "I spent my junior year in Europe studying art history. I love gargoyles."

"You studied art history?"

"I never told you that?"

"I would remember if you had. I assumed you were pre-med."

"I was. Pre-med and art history major." I pause. "You think I went the wrong direction?"

She says sadly, "Jeffrey, I don't want you to go the wrong direction now. But the wrong direction is pretty much the only one I've ever known."

"Debra," I say, taking her hand, "any journey with you is by definition in the right direction."

She just looks hard at me, studying me. "So you say, Doctor. But how can anyone know—I mean really *know*?"

"*You* can know," I say immediately, still holding her hand. "Because I am not *him*."

Her gaze lingers, and then at last something like a smile reappears. "And you're sure, doc, that's not just the pie talking?"

It's a Sunday night. We're enjoying a piece of the incredible banana cream pie she makes on the first Sunday of every month. I'm in charge of the coffee, of course.

"It's me, Debra Gale," I answer, squeezing her hand and not letting go, "all the way down."

And so it is—although I must admit that I would probably do almost anything to make that pie a more permanent feature of my life.

Maybe even write a book.

ABOUT THE AUTHOR

J. Jeffrey stands about six foot three, weighs two hundred pounds, and likes poetry. He has been known to climb the occasional mountain and tame the occasional lion. He sings opera as an amateur but is a trained masseur, and he is extremely partial to his wife's green tea perfume. He admires pottery and those who make it. He sees bad movies on a whim. He likes to drink coffee, travel spontaneously, and get as lost as possible. Two words: Florence, Italy. Pastry for breakfast, over the crossword puzzle, preferably after noon. Soup for lunch, preferably late afternoon, over another puzzle (the first having been solved). His favorite drink (after coffee) is red wine. He knows a word or two but will *not* play scrabble. Regrettably, he believes he might be happy if only you would think him as funny as he thinks he is. But most importantly, he is not to be trusted. He writes biographies full of lies, or are they novels full of truths? Such a fine line.

For more information, visit www.theseconddaughter.com.